Night Warriors
Beasts, Book 2

Brenna
Lyons

Veriel's Tales II: Losing Regana

FIREBORN
PUBLISHING

Fireborn Publishing Copyright Statement

Veriel's Tales II: Losing Regana
Copyright © 2004/2005/2009/2015 by Brenna Lyons
Print ISBN: 978-1-943528-17-2
First Fireborn Publication: October 2015

Cover Artist: Brenna Lyons
Photo Credit: 123rf
Editor: Kathryn Lively
Logo copyright © 2014 by Fireborn Publishing and Allison Cassatta
Licensed material is being used for illustrative purposes only. Any person depicted in the licensed material is a model.

This book is written in US English.

PUBLISHER

FIREBORN
PUBLISHING

PO Box 5216
Haverhill, MA 01835

Dedicated to...

My brothers and sisters, for teaching me that there is more than one side to any story.

John Malkovich's performance of Jekyll and Hyde in *Mary Rielly*, for confirming my belief that a man can be both villain and hero, driven to madness and torn to be what he can never be in either state.

My inability to believe that *anyone* can be all bad— or all good, even the Warriors.

My husband, my one and only soulmate, for introducing me to a love I would do almost anything to protect. No one ever said that soulmates were easy. They are simply worth the effort they require.

The Warrior spirit and the urge to protect a lady with your life and *all my SCA friends* who possess it.

My characters, for insisting that I listen to every point of view, even the most unusual ones.

Lisa, for making me see every story as important, even those I never dreamed of telling.

Glossary of Warrior Terms

Beast- Beasts are what humans erroneously refer to as vampires. The stories humans tell are obviously not correct, but you can't expect a human to get everything right.

Blutjagd- The "blood hunt." Warriors crave battle with the beasts, as the beasts crave blood. Warriors are tied to beasts in that they sense many of the beasts' special powers. A Warrior can feel the use of coercion, feeding, and other controls of humans. They also feel other Warriors engaged in *Blutjagd*, the death of beasts and Warriors in their range, and the presence of nearby beasts that are not fully ghosted. Rigorous battle training will quell the *Blutjagd* for short periods of time.

Elder- One of the original beasts, the Stone stealers who were damned for their crimes against the Stone and the Warriors. The elders are gifted with powers turned beasts are not, including the ability to reproduce with a *Blutjagdfrau*, the ability to turn other beasts, and the inability to be killed by anyone but a Warrior.

Endspiel- The point in printing when a Warrior must either seal printing or go insane. A Warrior who feels printing may not progress should break printing long before this point. Note that they are rarely smart enough to do so.

Fluch- The Warrior's curse, passed from father to son or daughter. The *Fluch* may be removed from a daughter but never a son. If the *Fluch* is not removed in the *Zeremonie der Freiheit* by the time the menses begin or the *Zeremonie des Schutzes* is performed before freeing, the daughter is cursed to become *Blutjagdfrau*, a female Warrior. Because elders target *Blutjagdfrau* as mates, Warrior fathers will go to any lengths to free a daughter not marked by the Stone.

Ghosting- A talent that both beasts and Cursed Warriors learn to harness. Ghosting can hide the physical form of Cursed Warriors or beasts and all they hold or carry from each other and humans. In a lesser strength, it can "blur" the image of the user so that humans do not note the passage in particular but still see a person there, which avoids accidental collisions. Even a ghosted beast cannot hide uses of power that a Warrior can track. Warriors sometimes ghost in tandem to remain visible to each other but not other Warriors or beasts.

Krankheit- The "sealing sickness." In the final stage of the transformation between human and Cursed Warrior, at or about the sixteenth birthday in males and a year after the start of menses in females, the sickness strikes. The young Warrior will suffer nausea, vomiting, a high fever, disorientation, dizziness and may become incoherent. It is usually the only time in a Warrior's life that he or she becomes ill, save morning sickness in a *Blutjagdfrau*.

Printing- Like imprinting, a Warrior becomes tied to his mate for life. He cannot choose another if she's lost, cannot be unfaithful while she lives, and cannot ever divorce or otherwise dissolve the union. A printed Warrior is the most stable of men, unless his mate or children are endangered or lost. Then he will suffer the printing madness and may have to be killed by his house. Likewise, a Warrior who breaks printing, even early printing, will suffer for it. A Warrior who breaks printing too close to *Endspiel* will face the madness.

Veriel- The Mad Elder. The Destroyer of Lives. The Mad Deceiver, who led the traitors and freed the elders from the Stone. The most hated and hunted of all the beasts. Fixated on one woman, he would destroy the world to own her. Or... At least, that's what the stories say of him.

Warriors- Also called Cursed Warriors, *Krieger der Nacht*, *Soldat der Nacht* or Sons of the Stone. The Warriors were an ancient race of protectors who spawned the beasts and now are driven to hunt their former brothers to extinction.

Section One
Fierce Ilona

Chapter One

Early Winter, 1107

Jörg stood in the midst of the Christian hell. He'd thought nothing could touch his cold heart save Regana's soul reborn, but this chilled even that organ.

The small village had been attacked like the others had, savaged nearly beyond recognition, the structures burning...and the crops, the populace decimated. The dead included not only able men and boys, but also women, the elderly, and babes. No one had been spared...knowingly.

The boy was small, even for his age, and Jörg guessed him to be about eight. He was shivering in Evul's arms, though he was wrapped in a fur and seated as close as possible to the fire. Jörg suspected he shivered more from fear than from the night air that heralded the coming winter.

"These men," he began in a soothing voice he'd thought he'd lost a century or more before. "Did they make demands of the people of your village?"

The child's voice was tremulous and ragged, most likely from crying, though he was certain not to admit such a thing. "No demands, master." He'd already learned that Jörg's men called him master; he was an intelligent boy.

"Did they ask anything?" An attack like this was meant to do something. While Jörg rarely concerned himself with human wars, this one had his attention. It defied all reason.

The hair rose at the back of his neck, a warning that Jörg was missing something basic, something dangerous.

"Nothing. They simply came into the marketplace and started cutting down anyone they saw." He bit back a sob, and Evul held him closer to his big chest.

Jörg's man had once had a son. Perhaps the boy would be as good for Evul as the former farmer would be for the orphaned child.

"Did they say anything?" he demanded, certain that the child had been spared to give some clue. What gave him that certainty when nothing else in life was sure, he could not say.

"They were looking for someone," the boy offered.

That was more like it. "Who?"

"I know not. A woman, they said."

"What description did they give? Did you hear it?" His heart sped, and again he could not state why it did.

"I was close. They gave no description."

"Then how did they hope to find her?" he asked, exasperated.

"They said..." He paused, looking to Evul as if seeking counsel.

"Answer the master, boy," he was instructed, though kindly so.

The child nodded. "They said this woman would find them, if they encountered her...lair."

Jörg's heart stuttered. "Regana," he breathed. Surely, no woman but Regana would seek out confrontation with such men.

"Master Jörg?" Evul asked.

"We follow, Evul. As fast as we can."

"And the child?" his man asked.

"If he slows your pace, leave him in the care of a few who will protect him well. They can travel at their own pace." If it was Regana, he owed this child more than he could name. He considered what would likely come next. "That might be wise, Evul. And the men should dress for battle at all times."

Jörg left the fire, waiting to dematerialize until he was well away. No one asked what he intended, though no one knew why he would follow immediately in brigands' wake.

* * * *

Ilona stared down the length of her sword, hating the man she faced with every muscle and tendon, every bone and organ she possessed. It wasn't enough to single out hating him with all of her heart. This went deeper, taking all of her.

Cessius had killed her family, everyone from her warm old grandmother to her sister's youngest, a babe no more than a few weeks into this life. He'd done it while she was far afield, and it had been over before she'd had time to respond to the fires he'd set to destroy the rest. The men had been slaughtered in the outlying buildings, probably before the beast had descended upon the few women and children, though he might have taken them in unison, splitting his troops to accomplish the task.

No. That was unlikely. Cessius was a man who seemed to enjoy his slaughter a little too much for that. He would have wanted to see every life stolen personally.

His smile widened. "You cannot be serious, girl."

She noted the rough men closing slowly in nothing more than the same cold detachment. "You need your men to fight one armed woman?" she challenged.

"I have need of no one."

Ilona would have said the same until that day. She did need others, but now her others had been destroyed. Even the crops would be gone, if an unexpected rain showed no kindness to her.

She almost snorted in disbelief at that thought. When had anything or anyone but her family showed her kindness? Never that she could recall.

Cessius spoke again, perhaps believing that she had no intentions of speaking now that her challenge had been issued. "You and I, then," he decided.

She nodded slowly, retaining her calm.

He drew his sword, gazing down its length with a fondness that was unseemly and unsettling. Then he came at her.

Ilona was no babe with a sword, but she found that even she was pressed to match him. Not that she intended to fail in that regard. Though his men would surely kill her for it, she would make sure Cessius preceded her to death.

Beads of sweat ran down her back beneath the fur tunic that shielded her from the wind that spoke of coming winter. In moments, her muscles burned and her lungs labored.

Then she saw it...the opening she needed. Cessius saw the blow coming, but not early enough to avoid it completely. Blood coursed down his face from the cut she'd drawn from the bridge of his nose to the line of his jaw. Even if he survived, he'd be scarred, marked for life.

Cessius reeled in surprise and she vaulted toward him, her sword coming up for the tender flesh of his stomach.

She never connected. Hands and bodies swarmed over her, pulling her back and down. Ilona fought them, screaming out her fury. Of course, he'd broken his word. Cessius was nothing short of a scheming carrion eater, and she'd known that at the outset of their battle.

Her sword hand was pummeled, her sword wrenched from her weakened grip. Her knees and elbows bit into one body part after another, prompting grunts and shouts of complaint. A fist found a solid shot at her stomach, and Ilona half-curled against the hold on her, swallowing down a scream of pain.

It was all the opening they needed. The moment of her incapacitation ended with her pulling her legs against restraining hands. Then she was spread out on the ground, her extremities pinned down beneath the formidable bulk of Cessius's fighters.

She looked to their leader, taking pride in her mark, the blood shimmering in the fires' glow in the dying light. Though it was unlikely his men would dare tell others how he came by such a wound, there would be tales, speculations that it had been she. Every time they came to Cessius, he would remember how close he came to death at her hands.

Ilona shook in a sudden chill, her body aching. The time passed slowly, and the death blow didn't come. She supposed that Cessius meant to take it himself.

He turned, and the slow perusal and knowing smile made his true intention more than clear. Ilona set her jaw, determined not to give him the satisfaction of a reaction. She'd lain with men before, so there would be no terrible pain a maiden suffered. Anything else, she could bear in silence.

At Cessius's nod, the men at her legs reached for the ties on the trews she wore beneath the tunic. Ilona threw her hips up, trying to evade them though she knew it was hopeless.

"I believe she is anxious for you, Cessius," one of his men taunted. He laughed and others followed, a mocking sound that called her a fool for moving against them.

Fury burned in her. She laid there, her muscles coiled in preparation for an attack she knew she'd never gain the opening for. Her trews were unlaced and eased away, baring her to the frigid air around her.

In a moment of clarity, she knew it was going to hurt. Though her barrier was no more, neither was she aroused. Her body was dry and would remain so, and Cessius would delight in forcing himself into her in that manner. Ilona fisted her hands, willing herself to be silent, no matter the cost to her.

Cessius unlaced his trews, baring himself. As she'd expected, the miserable excuse for a man was aroused, ready to best her in the only way he felt mattered now that she'd bested him at sword.

She spat at him, the only weapon left that accurately reflected her disdain.

His eyes hardened, and he dropped to one knee beside her, reaching for her hair.

It was a move he never finished. One moment he was leaning over her. The next, he was screaming in pain, four blades protruding from his chest, unbelievably where she knew his ribs to be.

Blood soaked his tunic, and Ilona stared at it, struck by giddy disbelief. Had the gods answered her prayers? They'd never done so before, but she supposed it was possible that they had.

Cessius's men moved. Some scrambled from her, only to be cut down by soldiers dressed in strange black clothing that blended into the shadows of buildings backlit by the roaring fires. Others rushed toward the unseen force behind Cessius.

In an instant, Cessius had been tossed far from sight and the true carnage begun. Whatever it was, man or beast, it moved faster than any man should, a veritable blur to her eyes. One by one, they were cut down. Blood sprayed her uncovered body, cooling fast in the night air.

One last man stayed his place, still holding to her arm. Ilona didn't note his presence until she tried to move. Her surprise seemed matched by his own. He grabbed for her, no doubt hoping to use her as a shield or kill her before he died himself. She struck him across the face with the bottom edge of her fisted hand, trying for a kick before he could right his senses, but her legs were still tangled in the trews they'd half-removed.

His face swung back toward her, and his dagger was unsheathed before she'd recovered from her misstep. He never had a chance to use the weapon; his head swiveled half the distance around his body with a sickening snap. Ilona recoiled from the slap of his unwashed hair, half-swallowing a cry of alarm.

His body jerked to the side, and she was left staring at a fitted pair of boots unlike any she'd seen before. The ankles parted, the legs pivoting out as the man in those boots crouched. She looked up past hide trews, then a dark tunic to the harsh lines of a man's angry face.

Her breathing went ragged at the sight of red eyes. Ilona grasped at the hope that it was simply the firelight reflecting off, but what man had eyes the color that would cause such an eerie glow?

The certainty that he was a demon sent her heart skittering in her chest. Realization that she lay out before him, uncovered as if a sacrifice, coated in blood a demon would find an invitation, did strange things to her, things it had no right doing. She'd heard it said that demons had insatiable hungers for flesh...both of appetite and sexual longing. Still, the idea of him slaking them on her was wildly appealing. She blushed in the knowledge that she was dampening in invitation, scenting for him.

He leaned over her, and reached for her trews. Ilona gasped, closing her eyes, anticipating his touch.

* * * *

Jörg could hardly control his emotions. Fury that they'd dared try to rape her warred with the ache of needing her. She was laid out, open to him, her sex preparing for him, even now. He could send his men away and end this madness.

She is my descendent! How foul a creature am I?

9

She is of Regana's line.

I don't know that for certain...which means, she may not be of my blood, at all. How would I trace it after so many years?

Even if she were, she was dozens of generations removed from him. If any of Jörg's blood still ran in her veins, it was so diluted as to be hardly worth notice. She wasn't a sister or even a close cousin. People much more closely related married every day.

Her soul is Regana's soul. She is already mine, my mate!

But not in this time and place. Not in this incarnation. She had to choose him again to be his.

The look of invitation in her pale blue eyes told him she would choose him if he asked, but it would be dishonorable to take a choice given in these circumstances.

Instead, he grasped the trews, watching her eyes close on a gasp, and eased them up her legs. She tipped her hips up, at the surface a move that helped him dress her, but her open mind spoke the truth of it. His hands were close to her center, and she wanted his touch. She wanted—

Jörg closed his mind to her abruptly, aware that his fangs had descended and his eyes were glowing a hot red. His cock throbbed, a maddening insistence on fulfilling the scenes in her mind.

The trews at her waist again, he grasped at the ties. Her head rocked back in a look of ecstasy. Her hips rose to him again, as if she were unaware that he'd covered the straw-colored curls dotted in blood and the fragrant slit beneath.

He couldn't do it. Jörg couldn't tie them shut with his hands shaking as they were.

"Master Jörg?" Evul intoned, doubtless confused by his indecision.

Jörg motioned him for silence, leaning over the woman until he was nearly nose to nose with her. He cupped the base of her skull in his hand, raising her head from behind. "Look at me, woman."

Her eyes opened, pleading...and he knew very well for what without opening himself to her mind again.

"What is your name?" He had to know. He had to know everything about her. It was his madness, his curse, his damnation.

"Ilona," she breathed.

He nodded. "Your protection is my only concern, Ilona," he lied. He wanted much more than her protection, but that was the only choice he would ask her to make this night. "Do you believe that?"

"Yes." Her breath was sweet with arousal, hot and fast against his face.

"Ask for my protection, and you will have it." He hadn't asked that question in all the years he'd been a beast, but he was asking it now. Enough Warrior remained in him to want to protect his mate. Though he could not give her an amulet and dared not speak the entire ceremony aloud, he knew what he was promising.

She seemed confused by that.

What will I do, if she refuses me? He knew he couldn't trust himself to accept it gracefully.

"I want you," she whispered.

"You want my protection?" he qualified. *I will ask no more than that tonight.*

"Yes. Only you."

Jörg nodded in understanding. Something of Regana remained in this woman, something that knew him on sight.

He let his hand relax beneath her head, and she dropped it back again, baring her throat to him. The voices within—the ones telling him that he was wrong to consider this—were drowned out by the pounding of her pulse.

Her skin was hot against his lips. Salt and musk played on his tongue. Jörg bit down, masking her pain in pleasure, his head spinning at the taste of her.

He drank slowly but long, seeking out the information he needed to protect her well. Her family was dead, killed only this day by the one who'd thought to rape her. This band was part of a larger, headed by Cessius's brother. When it was learned they were dead, there would be retaliation.

Ilona rose against him. Her hands fisted in his tunic, her scent sublime. Her panting breaths became moans, then a sharp cry of climax. She pleaded with him to give her more.

Information he sought about her family came next, faces and names, none of them a husband, thank the gods, though she'd known men before. Fury rose up at that piece of knowledge. That was one thing he could not allow her; he would be insane in jealousy if another touched her.

Jörg sent an order for her to sleep, then closed his feeding site, lingering over her, cleaning the small amount of spilled blood from her pale skin. Gods, but he would taste all of her.

"Master Jörg?" Evul called. "Are you well?"

Well? He could fly in this form, if called upon. Jörg brushed the tangled hair from around her face, fisting it to imprint its feel on hands starved for her.

"Master?"

"We travel to my home, Evul," he managed. "No man touches Lady Ilona but myself, save for her protection."

There was shocked silence.

"Am I understood, Evul?" he inquired in a warning tone.

"Of course, Master. But if I may be so blunt... Who is this woman?"

His fangs extended, and his fury burned. "She is *mine*. She has my full and uncompromising protection. That is all you need know."

"Should I—?"

"No." Jörg grasped at Evul's wrist, halting his reach toward Ilona. "I will take her as far as I can." The less another man handled her, the safer they all would be.

His man eased his hand away, looking at it in confusion. "As you wish."

Jörg stood, cradling Ilona to his chest, waiting only long enough for his men to mount their horses before he sped off, keeping pace with them toward his home.

Chapter Two

Ilona found it hard to catch her breath. He was over her, in her, tasting her, touching her, thrusting hard and fast, and driving her to climax. She cried out harshly, arching up...against a blanket.

She forced her eyes open, staring at the strange room, her heart pounding hard. Where was she? What was that dream? The vision she'd just had? It was so real that her body had responded and continued to do so.

"Are you well, Lady Ilona?" a deep, masculine voice asked.

Ilona searched him out, noting the dark clothing with a niggling of unease. She'd seen that clothing before, the fighters who'd slain Cessius and his men. But who were they? Why had they dared engage Cessius? And who...or what was their leader? Where had they taken her? And why had they?

"Lady—"

"Where am I?" she managed, moving her hand to her waist beneath the cover of the blanket. Her sword was missing, but her dagger was sheathed as she'd left it. They were sloppy.

"A small village along our route."

"Our route to where? Where are you taking me? And for what reason?"

"Our master's home. Surely, you remember asking his protection."

Yes. Only you. What had he done to her? Had she been bewitched?

"Mi'lady? Do you recall it?"

14

"Yes, I recall it." Would it do any good to plead that she'd been exhausted or confused? A peek at his hard expression convinced her that it wouldn't. But there were still questions to be answered. "Who are you?"

"Evul, mi'lady."

"No. I meant... Who are you? Your band of men. Who are you to engage Cessius and invite Domias's wrath in doing so?"

"We serve Master Jörg."

The name sent shivers of delight up her spine. "The demon," she breathed.

"He is nothing of the sort," Evul replied hotly.

His anger put her off balance. Would questioning him about his master make him even angrier? "Where is your master?"

Evul shrugged. "Close, I imagine."

"You *imagine*?"

"It is always wise to believe Master Jörg is close, and since he vowed his full and uncompromising protection to you, he would not be far."

"Why would he do such a thing? What am I to him?" Why would a soldier with an army the likes of this care whether she lived or died? Why would he make any vow to her, let alone one his men believed he would keep?

Evul shifted as if discomfited. "That would be the master's concern and none of my own."

"You did not ask him?"

"One does not question the master. One obeys him."

Ilona pushed the blanket back to her waist, making certain it caught on the hilt of her dagger to hide it a little longer. She sat up and eased her legs over the side, sliding into her boots and stomping them down. Whoever this Master Jörg was, he was undoubtedly not a man she wanted to find herself indebted to...or at the mercy of. That meant she had to take her leave before he returned to her.

"Mi'lady—?" Evul intoned.

"I have troubled you enough," she interrupted him.

"You have accepted the master's protection."

"Which he gave for as long as I needed it. I am grateful, but I have—"

"You cannot mean to leave. There is nothing left of your village."

Her heart ached at that. "I know it, but I am a woman of skills who can—"

"The master has not released you from his care," he protested.

Her hand itched to draw the blade. "He made no mention that I was to be in his service. I am free to—"

"He will track you."

Ilona considered that. She would have to move with stealth to—

"Wherever you go... Whatever you *think* to do, it will fail. Master Jörg can track those under his protection, and considering his vow to you, he will."

She stood, unsheathing her dagger. "Then he will have to." It was unlikely that she could fight her way free of Jörg's men, but she would play as if she knew she could, if it would be to her advantage to do so.

Evul stared at the blade, nodding silently and clearing the way to the door. Ilona stayed outside his range, watching him warily, but the big man made no sign that he would stop her.

Others waited in the main room. At the sight of her blade, several made as if to subdue and disarm her. Ilona pulled the blade back, ready to attack the first to reach her.

"Halt and draw back," Evul ordered.

She glanced at him in confusion, but a scan around at the retreating soldiers proclaimed it wasn't a trick. "Why would you give that order?" she whispered.

"Master Jörg gave orders that no man was to lay hands on you."

"And...if I would have rushed you with my blade?"

He didn't reply to that, leaving her to wonder if he would have broken with his orders or not. Most likely, he would have. No leader held that much power over his men.

Ilona headed for the door, watching Jörg's men pull back, clearing a path for her, then closing in around her as if they meant to follow her, perhaps to follow in her wake wherever she led.

A body-length from the door, it swung toward her, and Ilona brought her blade around toward...

His eyes were hard in seeming fury that made her heart race. Jörg ducked through the doorway, rising to his full height within range of her weapon, but she found herself lowering it instead of attacking.

Jörg's eyes were a startling silver, not unlike a polished blade. Ilona wondered if the firelight might simply have been reflecting as she'd first supposed. She'd never seen eyes that color, never known such a thing existed.

Or did they? Was this another color that only one like himself could possess?

He stepped toward her, his hand circling the wrist of her blade hand. "Release it." His breath combed through her hair, warming all of her.

Her blade thudded against the packed soil floor, and Jörg took her empty hand in his own, raising it between them to kiss her knuckles. "You do not need your weapons with my men," he assured her.

Ilona started to nod her understanding.

"And they would have died rather than lift a hand to stop you."

She tried unsuccessfully not to shudder at the thought that he wielded such power over these men. Would he expect to order her in such a way? What was this power he had over her?

Jörg pressed her hand to his chest, letting her feel the heart racing beneath. He said nothing, confusing her further. The moments slipped away in silence. Even his men were unmoving, barely breathing.

He spoke abruptly though kindly. "Evul was correct. I would have tracked you, had you run."

"Why? What am I to you?" she asked. There had to be some reason for his actions. No one extended such interest with no plan of gain.

Jörg paused as if uncertain of what answer to give. "One who would see you safe from harm. You accepted my protection. Do you intend to demand freed to a life of danger from Domias?"

"Then I am not free?"

"You are...as free as you wish to be." His jaw tightened as if it pained him to make such a statement.

Ilona raised her hand, stroking the line of his jaw, fascinated by something she had no name for.

"Do you accept my protection?" he asked again.

"Yes." Though she could not say why she did.

* * * *

The tension in Jörg's chest eased, though other tensions ate at him. Her hand still lay against his throat, her thumb stroking at his chin and jaw, nearly brushing his lips. He took a step closer to her, crowding her body, reveling in the warmth of her.

She'd always been warm, save the night she'd died as Regana. It seemed Jörg was never as warm without her as he was when their bodies touched...or nearly did.

His men backed away, conversing quietly. Though he could clearly hear them, Jörg chose not to listen. He concentrated on Ilona's steady breathing, the beat of her heart speeding as she explored his face.

"Master," Evul interrupted their moment. "The Warriors..."

He didn't need to be more specific in his concern. Evul believed Jörg was exerting coercion over Ilona. That would draw the Warriors to them, and even Jörg had tired of battling Warriors long ago.

"It is time," Jörg agreed. It wouldn't be wise to let anyone know this fascination was not some trickery of his own. If they knew what he felt for Ilona and what she felt for him, it could only go badly for them both.

"Time?" Ilona repeated, her body responding to his comment as if she perceived it to mean it was time for him to claim her properly.

"We must reach my home before Domias learns his brother is dead. Would you like to eat before we leave?" he offered.

She shook her head slowly, her gaze locked on his lips. Every muscle in his body tightened at that.

Jörg forced his mind to function, well aware that he could not protect her appropriately if he was shackled by his own base urges this way, distracted from everything around them. "Her sword, Evul," he ordered. "And a horse for her. A strong one that will not fail. Stay prepared."

Stepping away from her and turning to the door was the single most difficult thing he'd done since he'd stood over Syrith's grave and forced himself to move on. Still, he managed it somehow.

"Master Jörg," Ilona called after him, slightly breathless.

He didn't look back, and he fought the urge to glare at her for using the title as if she were one of his men. "Yes?"

"Will you ride with me?"

"I cannot," he admitted. In truth, the horses would not tolerate his kind as a rider, but she did not need to know that much about him. "My duty is to your protection. I must...ride in a position to defend. You must ride in the center of the group. I will have your word on this, Ilona."

It couldn't hurt to issue the warning in advance of any antics she might consider. Regana's souls had never embraced the better part of valor, living to fight another day.

There was a moment of silence. "If you wish it." But, she was angry at giving such a vow. Yes, she was Regana's soul in all ways.

Jörg nodded curtly and headed into the night, dissolving to mist to watch over them from the skies.

The gods alone have mercy on any who would attack her.

* * * *

"Your name is Evul," Ilona ventured, peeking at the big man who rode at her right.

He bowed his head slightly. "I am, Lady Ilona."

That nonsense had to stop. "I am no lady." She'd never found nobility of much use, and it rankled her to be counted among them.

A smile curved his lips up, but he didn't laugh. "My apologies, Lady Ilona. The master claims that is your name. You should...perhaps, take up the matter with him?"

"Be reasonable, Evul. Do I look a lady?"

"I cannot say. I imagine not all nobility looks it, in the throes of battle."

"Do I act like a noble?" She'd never been accused of it. The usual description of her was akin to a barbarian.

"I would not know. Master Jörg is the only noble I am acquainted with, and you do not act much different than he does," he reasoned.

"Who is Master Jörg?" She turned to look at him more directly, controlling the urge to moan at the change in how the horse beneath her rubbed at her still-aroused body.

There was a moment of silence. Even the other soldiers in the column around them stopped speaking in their hushed tones and seemed to wait for the answer. Or perhaps they were shocked or appalled that she'd asked it so directly.

Evul met her eyes. "What are you asking, Lady Ilona? What do you seek by asking it?"

"Where does he hail from?" she qualified. "His...words are strange and his inflection as well."

"Very far away. South...and west. I do not know the precise place. He has been here for some many years, though. That place is no longer considered his homeland."

"If he possesses such an army, why have I never heard of him? Is his home very far from my village?"

"Only a few days more travel," he offered. "And Master Jörg does not use his army to... He is not of the same ilk as Domias and Cessius."

She steeled herself for his displeasure. "What is Master Jörg?"

Evul's jaw tightened, and he offered no answer.

"You claim he is no demon," she continued.

"He is not." It was said simply, without embellishment of any sort.

"Then what—?"

"This is something you need to discuss with Master Jörg, Lady Ilona. It is not my place to explain the whole of the master to you. It is his." He paused, seemingly considering something. "But—on the gods and my life, here and after—I can tell you that he is a good man."

He turned his attention back to the track they followed, making it clear that the discussion was over.

* * * *

Jörg took form outside the stable they'd bartered use of for the night. He wished he had better for Ilona, but short of coercing the owners of the house to his will, that was unlikely. Doing that would bring the Warriors down on Ilona—most likely drawing Pauwel's soul with them—and intensify Ilona's feelings of unease with his methods. Neither was acceptable.

He strode around the corner and into view, nodding to several of his men as he pushed through the doors into the structure. It was a simple thing he planned. He would check on her well being and walk away.

He'd had all the time in the world to think while he'd watched over her. Regana's soul or not, it wasn't right to pursue Ilona. If she was, as Marie had been, of Regana's line, that meant she was of his line as well. Though she was dozens of generations removed from him, there was something distinctly uncomfortable in the thought that she was his descendent.

She was there...alone, the heavy fur tunic set aside in favor of the light woven one beneath. Her eyes were closed, and she rubbed away the dirt from her face with a piece of cloth dipped in a bowl of water. Droplets of water beaded on her skin, sliding slowly down her throat and wetting the edges of the tunic.

That simply, his thinking mind left him. His mouth went dry, and some dark corner of his consciousness urged him to stride to her and drink the water from her body. It would be tangy with her sweat and musk, a feast for his starved senses.

Her eyes opened, and she looked up at him, startling. Her fur tunic was pressed to her chest a moment later, shocking Jörg back to his senses.

Then their gazes locked. The fur eased down, revealing nipples beaded against the woven, a blatant invitation.

The prickling awareness of the coming dawn made the decision his lust-drowned brain seemed incapable of making. This was definitely the wrong time and place. Even if they did... His cock came fully erect that quickly. Jörg panted back his arousal through clenched teeth.

It cannot be now. "Are you well and fed?" he asked, as if that was the only concern he had for her.

Ilona nodded. "Your men care for me well."

A spark of jealousy lit in him. For their continued health, they should not *care* for her too closely. Jörg conceded that he should warn Evul, before it became at issue. "Good. Sleep well, Ilona." He turned to go.

"You will not be sleeping here?" she asked.

He couldn't decipher if she was upset by that or confused. Jörg didn't turn back to check it; if she was upset, he might do something stupid in response. *Like take her now...or try to sleep with her in the coming day.* "No. I must—"

"Be in a position to defend," she finished for him.

"Yes. I must."

"With so many soldiers?" she questioned. "I thought lords let others work for them."

"Some lords do. I do not." He let his voice go brusque in order.

"And when we reach your home?" she continued in what sounded like a challenge.

"It is very defensible."

"And will—?"

"The sun is rising, Ilona. I must take my place. Until nightfall?"

There was a moment of silence, followed by a sigh. "Of course."

24

Chapter Three

"Is there a problem, Lady Ilona?" Evul asked from the back of his horse.

Ilona grimaced. She'd forgotten to ask Jörg to have his men cease using that ridiculous title for her, yet again. It had been three days, but it seemed every time she looked at Jörg, she forgot the more mundane concerns that lay between them.

"Lady—"

"Pardon?" she asked.

"You sighed. I asked if there was a problem. If you need to stop or—"

"No, Evul. I have no need of it."

He nodded and turned his gaze back to the track. He and the other men had been much more reserved toward her since the second night of travel. Ilona didn't understand why that was, but she assumed it was another of Master Jörg's strange orders at work.

There were so many things Jörg ordered that seemed to make no sense. One very glaring one was the child seated behind Evul. What soldier takes his child into battle?

In all honesty, it seemed they hadn't taken the child into battle, since he'd been nowhere in the company for two full nights. They had retrieved the boy along the way, but still, Jörg acted as if attack was expected at any moment. Why bring the boy out from the safety of their stronghold, at all?

And then there was their method of travel...

"Evul?" she asked.

"Yes, Lady Ilona?" He answered promptly and with patience. He'd never told her there was a question she couldn't ask, though he'd told her several times that there were questions he couldn't answer for her.

"Why do we travel at night? Do we not lay ourselves open to attack?"

He seemed to consider that for a moment. "Most armies sleep the night," he suggested.

"With good reason. You cannot see attack coming in the night."

"We can," he stated with a certainty that confused her.

"I do not see how you could."

Again, he paused to plan his next statement. "You have very light eyes, Lady Ilona...blue in blue, and ice at that."

She nodded. "They are unique. In all my village, no one had eyes like mine."

"When the sun is bright, do you seek to shade your eyes? Are they sensitive to it?"

Ilona stared at him for a moment. "How could you know it?"

A weak smile curved his lips. "You have asked several times about Master Jörg's eyes. They are also...unique. Like yours, they are sensitive to the high sun, but at night, he sees like a cat."

"I wish I did, at times," she admitted. It would almost be worth the pain of direct sun, if she could see so well at night.

No wonder Jörg was so far to the fore that Ilona never saw him as they traveled. He was literally the eyes for the entire company.

"Perhaps not," Evul mused. "The world is not kind to those who are different."

"How well I know it," she grumbled.

* * * *

Ilona followed Jörg past the inner gate, gawking at the stone walls that seemed built to repel several armies at once. Behind them, members of his band led horses inside or dispersed to whatever lay beyond the great doors of the main structure. It was order embedded in seeming chaos.

Each man knew what Jörg expected of him and performed his task. The men smiled and joked, but there was no unruly show.

The doors shut, and crossbeams were lowered into place. Ilona stopped to watch them with eyes that had become acclimatized to the darkness. This place was a fortress.

As if Jörg overheard that thought, he confirmed it. "There is nowhere you will be safer than with me."

She met his eyes, her breath catching. That sounded of a promise.

He hesitated, staring at her. "It is my most sacred vow, Ilona."

That was what made him so successful in battle: his wonderful eyesight, his speed, his strength, and his ability to walk the minds of others.

Jörg's backward move startled her, and Ilona stumbled away from him in response. His hands circled her waist, steadying her, drawing Ilona toward him.

"Master Jörg!"

He stilled at the sound of his man. His expression hardened, and Jörg turned away from her, placing Ilona at his back, as he often did around other men. "Yes? What is it, Mavid?"

"The scouts have sighted the enemy."

Ilona tensed.

Jörg didn't do the same. "How far?"

"Three days."

"Their direction?"

There was a moment of silence. Ilona fisted her hand in the back of Jörg's tunic.

"South. Along one of the fake trails."

Jörg hesitated and then nodded. "Evul!" he called out. "Show Lady Ilona to the rooms prepared for her."

"Yes, Master," Evul intoned. "If you would, Lady Ilona?"

She forced her hand to release, then followed the man's slowly-retreating back. She peeked at Jörg, hoping to see him watching her leave. Ilona stopped short, scanning the courtyard in shock.

He was gone. Jörg was nowhere in sight. In a hand of steps, he'd completely disappeared. The one named Mavid was where he'd been moments before, still staring at the spot Jörg had occupied.

As if the thought summoned him, Mavid turned and stared at her. He cocked an eyebrow up and turned away.

"Lady Ilona?" Evul asked.

"Where is he?"

The soldier appeared beside her. "Mavid? There." He pointed to the retreating back.

"Jörg... Where did he go?"

"There."

28

She followed his gesturing hand, but all she saw was a shadow-cloaked doorway. "Where?"

"There... Well...probably out of sight now."

Ilona turned to him, trying to gauge his expressions. Evul gave her little to work at and little time to do so. He gave Ilona his back and led the way into well-kept corridors.

The rooms prepared for her were high in the walls but on the sunward southern reaches. There was a wide bed with a gown laid across it.

She stared at it, certain Jörg meant for her to wash and dress in that fine gown. That he meant to share the bed with her. Her body responded to the thought.

Obviously misunderstanding her silence, Evul spoke. "If the gown is not to your liking, there are others, mi'lady. In the trunk."

Ilona ambled to it and lifted the lid. It was a large trunk, large enough to hold two of her. Yet it was full of gowns, undergowns, and cloaks. "How could Jörg have all of this prepared in so little time?"

Evul didn't answer. She swiveled her head, watching him in unease. The soldier wouldn't meet her eyes, and he shifted nervously.

"He's had women like me before." Her heart ached at the thought of it.

"Never in my memory, Lady Ilona, and I have been in the master's service for many years."

She stared at him, her head spinning. "Then...how could he—?"

"That is a question for Master Jörg, mi'lady. There will be a meal in two hours. If it pleases you, I could have it delivered to you here."

"No. I would like to explore."

His jaw tightened, but he offered a curt nod. "Ask any of the servants. They will guide you to the hall."

Before Ilona had a chance to answer, he was gone, striding down the corridor with a child she'd assume was his son in his wake. Little more than a hand of heartbeats later, other servants were scurrying about, filling a bath for her.

* * * *

"Jörg?"

He look up at her from across the table, smiling in welcome. His cock ached at the sight of her in the blue gown with beige. It fit her as if sewn to her body. Though he never knew what else to expect, Regana was always of a size he could anticipate.

Belatedly, he remembered she'd addressed him. "You have need of me, Ilona?" *Gods, if she answers 'yes,' with that heated look, she will not eat this night.*

She settled onto the chair provided for her. "What am I to you? Why did you...take me into your protection?"

It was a question she hadn't asked since their first days together, and he was no more certain how to answer it now than he'd been then. Jörg drained the goblet, cleansing it and himself before it left his lips, so Ilona would have no hint to what it had contained.

"Jörg?"

"Why do you ask?" If she had memories of him, as he'd dreamed so many times she would, he would provide a bit of their past to calm her.

"The servants say..."

He tensed at that. Were they telling tales about him? What tales? He feigned indifference. "What do they say?"

"They say you have owned these garments for many years, yet they fit me as if made for me alone. They say you have had no woman here, save servants, in all the time they have known you, and many have known you for years."

Jörg's mouth pulled up at the corners. "You are very perceptive, Ilona."

She waited for him to explain it.

He stared into his goblet, searching for the words that would not cause her further unease. "Have you ever met an oracle? A teller of futures?"

"No, but I have heard of them. Have you?"

"Many times."

Ilona bit at her lower lip. "And you...trust in such people?"

Jörg shook his head. "Not all, but several have told me the same tale, the tale of a woman in danger who would need my aid."

"What leads you to believe I am this woman?" She was direct. Regana had never been one to be circumspect.

"You are the Warrior they foretold you to be." *The Warrior you have always been.* At least, she hadn't stuck a blade in him this lifetime. *Yet.*

"And...that is all?" It was clear she didn't believe it.

"The clothing fits. You know, there is a folk tale about the clothing...or perhaps it was shoes—"

"You are joking!"

Jörg laughed, despite his better judgment. Ilona glared at him. Gods, but it was good to tease her again.

She crossed her arms under her breasts, and he stared at the nipples pressing out against the fabric, hard and inviting. Her voice broke him from visions of laying her across the table and feasting.

"That is all. Your reasons are so inconsequential as—"

Her challenge sent him into motion. Without a thought, he vaulted the table and landed like a cat beside her.

Ilona gaped at him, her eyes wide but not frightened. Jörg leaned over her, planting one hand next to her head. Their gazes locked, and his heart skipped in excitement. It had been too long since he'd sampled her lush body, and her scent invited him to do so.

"You feel it," he breathed. "You hunger for me. I know you do."

"Yes. I do."

The sounds of the servants bringing food shocked him back to his feet. If there was one thing Regana had taught him, it was not to let those who might use her against him know her value to him. He was back in his seat before they breached the doors, his heart aching at her look of hurt and confusion.

The servants started setting platters of food before Ilona.

She watched them, her brow furrowed. "They serve me before you?"

"You are my guest, Ilona."

"But you will share the meal with me, will you not?"

The lie he'd planned stuck in his throat. Jörg tipped his head in acceptance. It had been far too long since he'd done something as simple as sharing a meal with her.

Mavid's wife stared at him for a long moment, then rushed away to collect another place setting.

* * * *

Ilona woke from a restless slumber to the sunlit chamber, her body hot and heavy. The dreams of Jörg were maddening in their specificity and intensity. She'd had them since their first meeting, dreams of him unleashing the lust she could see in his eyes and his tensed muscles, every time they drew close to each other.

In the two days she'd been in his keep, they'd come close to the edge of a violent joining a hand of times. Every time, someone or something had interrupted them before they could do more than steal a touch.

Even now, Ilona could feel the press of Jörg's fingers against the engorged nipple begging for him. A wild urge to feel his sucking mouth against it, his teeth scraping flesh, had her arching up to empty space.

She had to end this. Somehow, Ilona had to draw Jörg from his people and into her bed...or his. If she knew where he slept, she'd go to him now and impale herself on his cock, if it meant an end to this madness.

Her fevered body opined that it would only be the beginning of her madness. A taste of Jörg would never be enough.

Where does he sleep?

Jörg's home was huge. Though the servants allowed her to explore to her heart's content, she'd yet to find more than the hall and a library that held the distinct feel for her that they were places Jörg frequented.

There and the upper courtyard he loves so well.

Chapter Four

"Jörg?"

He turned toward her voice, sucking in his breath at the sight of her. Ilona stood in the doorway to the upper courtyard, clothed in one layer of gown, the laces removed so that it gapped to the lower line of her breasts, baring the creamy swell to his hungry gaze.

She stepped toward him, gliding, her hips swaying in an age-old dance he'd learned well with Regana. In an instant, he was as hard as a man could get and aching for her.

Jörg let her come to him, his mouth watering in anticipation of her flavor on his tongue. He could scent her already. She was wet for him, wanting him.

Ilona's hands flattened against his thighs, then slid upward, taking his measure and arousing him further. This was a woman who knew her way around a man's body, a woman he wouldn't have to slow for, to worry about hurting in his need.

He cupped her chin and raised her face to his, teasing at her lips. She opened to him, as ravenous for the sensation as he was. Ilona went to work on his trews, baring him to her hand.

Reason intruded. She would chill here. He broke off the kiss. "Inside," he managed.

She nodded, letting him guide her hands to his chest. Jörg lifted her, fitting Ilona against his body, striding for the corridor that led to her rooms. She didn't waste the time; her hands stroked through his hair, and she buried her face against his shoulder, unconsciously seeking out the blood mark through his clothing.

That was nearly the end for him. Jörg pressed her to the wall only an arm's length from her door, capturing her mouth again when she rolled her head back in passionate display. He rode into her through the insubstantial barrier of her clothing, a demonstration of what was to come. He could extend a single claw, razor sharp, rip away a hole large enough to...

Ilona whimpered into his mouth, her hands fisting in his hair. She would welcome his cock this moment. She would scream for him, shatter around his length.

That shocked Jörg into motion. He would not ravage her in the corridor when there was a perfectly serviceable bed a few scant body lengths away. More than serviceable. She'd been given the finest he had to offer...the finest anyone had in this time and place.

He held her to him with one hand while he fumbled the door open. Once they were through, he kicked it closed and strode to the bed.

Jörg hesitated, his mouth locked with hers, considering how to get her dress off quickest but without showing her precisely what he was.

Her mouth left his. "What is it?" she gasped out. "What is wrong?"

A smile pulled up at his lips. "I am considering tearing this dress off you, so we had best divest—"

"Tear it then."

Gods, but she was going to drive him mad.

As if I am not mad, already.

She will surely finish the job.

He set her on her feet, then fisted the edges of material over her breasts and yanked, weakening the weave with one sharpened nail-point that he knew she couldn't see. It shredded in a line, baring her from throat to navel.

Ilona moaned at that, wiggling against him, as if to push the material off of her body in the process. Jörg lifted her to the center of the bed, following her down. He yanked the tattered edges of the dress back, trapping her upper arms at her sides and baring her breasts to him, suckling hard at them in turn. She screamed, arching her back to force herself deeper into his mouth.

He allowed her thoughts to wash over him, her musings about what manner of man or beast he really was. The fact that she didn't care what the answer to it was and only wanted his hunger, no matter what caused it, herded him on. Ilona wanted him to rip and take. She wanted him to possess her like a demon would, impatient and insatiable.

That was not going to be difficult to grant her, since it aptly described the need searing him.

He grasped the dress again, ripping the remaining length in two tugs. Her breaths came in gulps and gasps, and her hands pulled at his tunic, trying to rip it away as well.

Jörg captured her hands, pinning both wrists to the mattress shackled within one of his fists. She pleaded with him to take her, fevered in arousal. He wanted to taste it, but he wanted to drive her to climax first, so the cream would be sweet and plentiful.

Her slit was wet and heated, and it quivered against his probing fingers. Ilona forced herself downward as far as his grip on her wrists allowed, trying to capture him inside. Unable to restrain himself any longer, Jörg thrust two inside her, and her breathing hitched, her head rocking back.

For a moment, neither of them moved. Then Ilona started tipping her hips back and forth, forcing him in and out slightly, becoming more adamant and more vocal. She squeezed her inner muscles around him, and Jörg could stand no more.

He thrust and twisted his fingers, feeling her blood pumping fast and hard in her veins. She panted out pleas for more...for all of him...and quickly.

Then she stiffened, her nude form arching off the bed with a scream of pleasure, her sheath rippling around his fingers, her honey coating his hand. She collapsed to the mattress beneath him, trembling, her breathing ragged, her hair disheveled.

"Jörg," she begged him.

He released her wrists and pushed back on the bed, leaving her warmth and jerking her legs wide around his body. Her honey was warm and pungent, and he bathed her slit with his tongue, greedily sampling her.

Ilona grasped handfuls of his hair, tugging as if to guide him over her. "Please," she whispered. "Oh, Jörg, pl—"

He thrust his tongue deep inside her, closing his eyes as she shattered a second time, her hands tightening in his hair. That scream was muted, choked off by her riotous breathing.

Her hands pulled at his tunic again, and Jörg clawed the fabric away, baring himself to her exploring hands. In moments, her hands were back in his hair, demanding that he abandon his feasting and sate them both.

His trews took no more time to dispose of than his tunic had. Jörg came up over her with a curse in the ancient language of the Stone, burying his cock deep inside her still-spasming sheath. She cried out harshly into his blood mark, her arms and legs wrapping around him, her hips rising to him, seeking the last of him restlessly, until he rammed inside to the root.

Her contractions and pleas went on and on, while he thrust hard and fast, claiming what was his. Her short nails scraped at his skin, raising welts that would disappear by morning. He sent up a silent plea that she wouldn't shed his blood. Surely, the stench of it would steal her arousal and convince her that he truly was a demon.

His climax roared through him like the winds that ripped up trees in some areas of the world. Ilona's breathing went harsh, and her hips pressed hard to his.

Though his heart pounded hard against his ribs, Jörg reveled in the peace in his soul. She was back. Regana was in his arms and bed, and no one would dare take her from him.

* * * *

Ilona moaned at Jörg's retreat. He couldn't mean to stop now. Not when he'd proven that a man could make her feel all the things the other women had proclaimed their men made them feel. She'd thought it was wishful thinking and teasing until now, but it was possible.

She pushed up on the palms of her hands and pads of her feet, rising as he did, seeking his lips with hers. Jörg hesitated only a moment, then parted her lips again, ravenous, a conquering soldier on a different field of battle.

He went to his back, pulling her over him. Ilona left the kiss, lowering herself around his still-straining cock. Jörg didn't move. His silver eyes assessed her, seemingly waiting for something she couldn't name.

At a loss, she moved her hips as she had when he'd used his fingers to pleasure her. His hiss, the hands grasping at her hips, and his hungry expression told her she'd pleased him with the move. Ilona did it again, her breathing going ragged at the feeling of his cock lodged deep inside her.

"Don't stop," he pleaded. "As before..."

She had no concept what before Jörg could mean, unless he was referring to something she'd done in the last few moments. Her hips moved as if of their own accord, first in the swiveling he seemed to enjoy so much, then up and down his shaft, seeking the sensation of him stroking and in and out of her heat.

Jörg growled, his hips rising and falling, forcing his cock deeper, meeting her hard. "Don't stop," he ordered.

Affecting him so was an aphrodisiac. Her body ceased to be her own and became Jörg's for the taking. They came together as animals might, unrestrained, without the cares and the veneer of niceties humans indulged in.

Her body sizzled in pleasure...then burned. His cock answered, pouring his fluids in. But they didn't douse the flames. Instead, they stoked them.

As if Jörg could sense it, he rolled her beneath him again, forging on with a cock that seemed never to go limp and a body that never tired.

Ilona groaned in indescribable pleasure. "How long can you...continue?" she gasped.

Jörg didn't laugh, as she'd suspected he might. His expression was starkly serious. "All night. Every night you'll agree to share your bed with me. I love you, Ilona."

Her mind and body rioted at that. How could he come to love her so quickly? How could she do the same? But her body attested that his words had been sincere.

Jörg herded her toward another climax, wiping away such frivolous concerns.

Chapter Five

Ilona stretched in bed, her smile turning to a scowl at the emptiness beside her. Jörg had left her again. Why? Had he no feelings for her?

The previous night, she would have sworn he had, but waking to an empty bed belied it. Was he ashamed of her? He was a lord, after all, and despite his insistence on it, she was no lady.

Perhaps Jörg simply had a lord's cares to tend to. Whatever the case, she would ask Evul or one of the others to point her to Jörg and ask him. Troubled, she rose from the bed and donned one of the many dresses he'd given her.

In the corridor, she paused, listening. The keep was still...too still. A shiver worked its way down Ilona's body at that. Though she'd been here only a few days, it seemed there should be more activity at what, by the sun's position, she would assume to be late afternoon.

Panic assaulted her, and she forced it back. The keep would repel armies, and a battle of that sort would have risen the dead from sleep. No matter how much of the night she'd spent in hearty activity, Ilona would have woken to it.

Step by step, she moved toward the great hall she'd shared meals with Jörg in, listening all the time for sounds of movement, for any indication that she wasn't the lone occupant of the keep. None came, and her heart beat echoed in her throat.

A flash of motion sent her back two steps, and she swallowed a scream of fear. Evul's young charge came into focus, and Ilona smiled at the child.

It was short-lived. The boy grabbed her by the hand and dragged on her arm. When she resisted, he motioned for silence and then waved her with him.

Ilona glanced around, her nerves jumping, and followed him down a dim corridor. Turn after turn, the boy moved further into the dark recesses of the keep. Finally, he stopped and started working a wooden grating from low on the wall.

"Where is Evul?" she whispered.

He hesitated, swallowed hard, then went back to work. "Dead, mi'lady. They are all dead. All but the traitor."

She closed her eyes, her stomach churning. That it explained it all. There had been little battle, all at the far corners of the keep no doubt, because they'd been betrayed.

Ilona forced herself to ask the question her heart ached to hear the answer to. "Master Jörg? Is he dead, as well?" Her mind said it was impossible, but if they attacked in the day, his great vision would work against him.

"I have not seen him, mi'lady."

The wood worked free with an ominous scrape, and Ilona turned, searching the shadows for signs of movement. There were none, and she let out her breath in a long stream of air.

"What is your name, boy?"

"Niko, mi'lady." He pulled the grate away and ducked down, waving her toward him.

Ilona nodded, going to hands and knees to follow the child into the darkness. Whether Jörg lived or not, she had to escape the enemies within the keep. She wished now that she had brought her weapons along, but she hadn't foreseen the need for them in such a secure location. Berating herself for the lapse, she maneuvered her head and shoulders into the cramped space.

Niko moved with stealth for one so young, leading Ilona to wonder if he had stolen to survive. She'd heard rumors that the boy had been the lone survivor of his village's destruction. Perhaps his skill at hiding had been the reason for it.

The scrape of leather behind her sent her heart skittering. She surged into the tunnel, trusting that a man would be too large to follow her, but a hand closed around her ankle before she was safely away.

Ilona kicked with her other foot, hoping to win herself a moment, just enough time to escape his reach. Instead, another hand closed on that ankle, and a cruel laugh echoed around her. Before she could reason her way to an attack, they both pulled, prompting a grunt of frustration from her.

Niko turned back to her, wild-eyed, his hand extended toward her. Ilona waved him away, hoping that he'd obey. Chances were better than even that the men behind her didn't know the child was there. If they didn't know, they wouldn't look for him, and he might escape yet again.

They yanked back, dragging her across a hand's length of rough stone. She grasped at it. There was no purchase, though her hands screamed at the skin being stripped away in patches. She cried out, setting off laughter from the men pulling at her.

Why hadn't she brought weapons with her? Why had she trusted that she'd be safe here?

There was no time to obsess over such concerns. In the next instant, she was on her knees, surrounded by dirty soldiers who smelled of a week on trail. Ilona surged to her feet, trying to strike out at them, but the skirts hampered her efforts, and she was soon held to sweat-soaked leather plate, her arms immobilized in the hands of at least three.

She scrunched her nose up, turning her face away.

"I don't think she likes us," the one holding her stated in faux hurt.

"You smell like a waste trench," she replied, putting as much disdain and acid into her tone as she could muster.

"She thinks she's too good for us," another noted.

The first laughed harshly. "When Domias is done with her, she'll be ours. After sampling his tastes, she'll be happy enough to service anyone else."

Ilona struggled for freedom, though it was no use. In the end, the three half-dragged, half-carried her through the corridors to the great hall. As they neared it, other soldiers took notice, joining the procession. Their wagers and plans of debauchery made her skin crawl and her stomach lurch.

There was no questioning who was seated in Jörg's chair. Domias had the look of his brother, had the latter left whatever remaining sanity he'd possessed behind. His expression was one of manic pleasure, and his eyes were crazed.

It took a moment for the cloaked figure kneeling by the man's side to draw her attention. His head was lowered to Domias's forearm. At first, Ilona believed he was praying or kissing the leader's arm.

The sounds of suckling reached her in the silence, and her stomach threatened to empty its acids onto the floor. Whatever or whoever the cloaked figure was, he was drinking Domias's blood. She tried to escape the restraining hands again, letting loose a weak cry of alarm, as the figured pulled his head back.

Ilona stared at the forearm, shaking her head at the line of healed cuts. Perhaps he hadn't been eating, after all.

The figure unfolded, coming to his feet, and turned to her. His smile pushed her toward unconsciousness. His teeth were jagged, capped by sharp fangs as a predator might possess...dripping blood.

All the soldiers save the three restraining her went to their knees. A low chant of "Domias" rose around them, and the man approached her.

It took a moment for Ilona to realize the low whine of alarm was her own. She backed further into the mass of male bodies, no longer aware of their stench, let alone caring.

The chant got louder, and the surety that Ilona had been mistaken made her ill. The one on the chair—the one who resembled Cessius so much—wasn't Domias. Both brothers had been servants of the creature approaching her.

"Well done, Ilona," he purred, his fangs easing back. He pushed his golden hair away from eyes as red as hot coals. "And their...assistance has borne fruit of the sweetest bush."

He stroked a hand over her throat, and she swiveled her head in an attempt to bite him. Domias was faster, and her teeth closed on empty space.

"You don't want to do that," he chided her. "My blood would do things to you that are written in nightmares."

Ilona forced an even breath, wincing as he fisted her hair and pulled back on her head, baring her throat. The certainty that he meant to rip her throat out caused tears to well in her eyes.

"No," he breathed against her skin. "Not that. Whoever owns you owns all. I swore it centuries ago. You will be mine."

His tongue slid against her throat, and she fought the soldier's hold avidly enough to raise bruises.

"Yes," Domias whispered. "You have fight. I believe I would like to taste the fight of a strong woman like you. Release her."

The three backed away, leaving Ilona free to engage her enemy. Again, she wished she'd carried her weapons.

The lack of them wouldn't stop her from fighting for her life. She brought her fist back and—

His grip on her wrist was crushing. The bones snapped, and Ilona screamed. She weaved on her feet, lightheaded in pain. Before she could recover, he released her arm and dragged her to his chest. His breath was hot and fast in excitement, and his cock rose between them.

He's excited by hurting me. The realization brought her back to fighting readiness.

Just in time for Domias to sink his teeth into her throat. The pain was excruciating, and she screamed again.

His voice invaded her mind. *Your pain is so sweet. Your sex will be as well, Ilona.*

His hands fisted in her skirts, dragging up at them. She pushed at his chest, seeking escape, but his arms were immovable. Her head swam, and her hand slid away.

At first, the grip of a weapon in her hand made no sense. Some corner of her mind screamed at her to grasp it, to escape him, to kill him.

{Take it. It will protect you. Take it. Take it now!}

Her hand fisted, and she pulled back. Domias released her, reeling back at the sound of the blade against sheath.

His eyes widened in surprise. Then his smile spread. "And what do you intend to do with that, little one?" he taunted.

The blade seemed to glow blue-white in her hand. Ilona looked from it to the matching spot in the center of his chest.

{There. That is the place. Strike him. Kill him.}

Domias reached for the dagger, and she struck, her uninjured hand sure, intent on nothing less than his death. The blade cut through his tunic as if it was water, and there was a satisfying crunch of the tip piercing bone, the slide of slicing meat.

The beast's smile disappeared, and he stared at the dagger embedded in his chest in shock. His hand came halfway up, then dropped away from her. He crumpled, leaving her with the blade coated in foul, black blood in her hand.

Ilona chuckled. She laughed. She laughed until tears coursed down her cheeks, mixing with the blood making thick streams down her throat and chest.

The rising battle cry made little impression on her scattered senses. The swords piercing her body made little more. Darkness rushed up to take her.

* * * *

Jörg sat on the ground beside the newly-turned soil, fisting a handful...letting it drop. He'd failed her...again. Though he'd felt the attack on her, he'd been too far away to make the distance in time. By the time he'd reached Ilona, there'd been nothing for him to do but scream out his loss, dig her grave with his claws and hands, and light the fires that would destroy this place.

And avenge her, her reminded himself. If it took him months to do it, he would track down every soldier who'd touched her, who'd taken a blade to her, or threatened her.

The fire reached for the night sky, escaping the windows of the rooms he'd given Ilona, destroying everything but the memories that would haunt him forever.

It should destroy it. What good had all his planning done him? His defenses had fallen all too easily. He just wished he understood how they had.

A noise from the direction of the keep brought his head around. Jörg moved that direction, faster than any human man could travel, grasping up the marauding creature who dared defile his Ilona's home.

A high-pitched cry of fear stopped him with his claws halfway to the dark creature's midsection. The feel of woven cloth made it through the haze of his fury.

"I tried to save her, master." The voice was laced in panic. "I tried, but they caught her. She ordered me away. I swear it." Frightened little whimpers escaped the lips hidden by arms wrapped around a boy's head.

Jörg searched out the child's name in his unresponsive mind. *Niko.*

The claims of trying to save Ilona made it through just behind, using the trail forged by the name. Jörg started to ask what he meant, hesitated, then searched out Niko's thoughts. The sight of himself, threatening a child, stung him.

He forced his claws and fangs back. "How did you try to save her?" he breathed.

Niko stuttered out something that didn't make sense. The words didn't matter. The memories coursing through the front of the boy's mind were enough. Jörg closed his eyes, letting memories of Niko warning Ilona about the traitor race from the child to him.

Traitor! A traitor let them in. Whoever it was will die screaming and begging for death.

Visions of Ilona's panic as the rough soldiers dragged her from the air shaft made his heart stutter. *Niko reached for her.* Jörg ground his teeth at the sight of Ilona waving the boy away.

He didn't run. The realization shook him. He'd stayed, hidden in the dark recesses. Niko had snuck after the soldiers—

Jörg forced the memories away with a growl of frustration. The time to live the horrors would be later.

Niko's safety had to come first; the child was his only link to the faces he would need to exact justice.

He cradled the boy to his chest, his heart stuttering at what he was considering. Niko was a child. Revenge wasn't business for children. But he was the only link Jörg had to those he had to kill.

"Come. We have far to go tonight." West, the same direction the unruly band of rebels had taken.

There was one thing he had to know. Jörg argued it several times, then gave in. He opened himself to Niko's thoughts. "Who was the traitor?"

The memories of Evul falling to another's blade touched him deeply. Evul, at least, had been loyal to the end. It was another reason to protect the child his servant had taken such a liking to.

Niko's gaze slid from Evul to the soldier standing over him. Then the boy ran.

Jörg nodded grimly. "Mavid. He will be the first to die then." But not just Mavid. *A man with obligations should not make such choices.* He smiled. Perhaps he would let Mavid live a few months to regret that choice and learn his lesson well.

Section Two
Fair Caitrina

Zeremonie des Schutzes

By the gods who forged us all, I grant you the protection of the House Schwertträger. Any and all of our kind and kin shall lay down life to preserve yours from the evil that walks among us. Walk blessed among us now.

Chapter Six

October 1st, 1497

Regana

> As the mother of all, proudly she stands.
> The Stone knows her secrets as no man can.
> Happiness and love she holds in her hands.
> Heedless of laws that control every man,
> The flames of passion her loveliness fans,
> Drawing her lovers to deepest desire.
> Silken hair dark as night and heart of pure fire.

Caitrina de Leon stared at her reflection in the mirror as her lady's maid, Jacquine, fussed with her hair, arranging it in curls cascading from the clips high on the back of her head. Her hair was black as a moonless night in the deep wood, much darker than either her mother's or father's hair had ever been.

She sighed as the maid continued to pull and puff at her hair. "What does it matter, Jacquine?"

"It will not be so bad, mi'lady."

Her brows shot up over deep blue eyes and rosy cheeks. "Not so bad?" she replied testily, letting loose a bit of the temper her father always warned her to control. "Father has taken leave of his senses."

"Lord Schmeidt is a well-acquaintanced gentleman," Jacquine chided her gently. "Your father obviously felt his offer was a good one."

"Everything was arranged with Jacque. Why would Father end that agreement now?" *And accept a lord from a far-off estate in Southern Germany?*

"There are rumors of that," Jacquine whispered in a conspiratorial tone.

"Of what?"

"Lord Cambion's—tastes ran to things best bought in dockside taverns, I hear. It took quite a lot of money to cover up the mess when one of his male...friends was injured in their play."

Caitrina screwed up her face in disgust. Was there no decent, sane man left in the world? "Damn the man!"

"Mi'lady," she gasped. "If your father hears—"

"I care not, Jacquine. I am not a hound or horse to be passed hand to hand this way," she asserted.

"You've hardly been handled, mi'lady. To hear you tell it..."

Caitrina waved her hand in dismissal. "It matters not. I had an agreement with Jacque. He abused my trust."

"You cared not at all for him," Jacquine reasoned. "Perhaps it is providence that he will not be your husband."

"At least I knew him." *At least he was of my own country.* "Betrothed to a man I've never set eyes on," she fumed. "I thought Father thought better of me."

"He does. Your father dotes on you, mi'lady."

A brisk knock came at the door, and Caitrina stiffened her spine.

"It is time," Jacquine whispered.

"I am well aware of that."

Caitrina stood and strode to the door, her skirts rustling as if whipped by a strong wind. She didn't wait for her father's servant to lead her to her doom. Lord Jörg der Schmeidt would find that Caitrina de Leon was not a lamb to be bullied by dogs.

She entered her father's study with her head held high and her back straight. "You called for me, Father?"

Rober de Leon pushed the errant strands of white hair from the blue eyes that so closely matched her own. Were it not for her eyes, speculations about her parentage might have continued for Caitrina's entire life. She had been a late gift, conceived when her father was near forty-five with his new, young bride. His first two wives had presented Rober with no children, and even Caitrina's mother had borne him no others.

"Come in, Caitrina. Do not keep Lord Schmeidt waiting." It was spoken kindly, not so much a rebuke as an indulgent greeting.

Caitrina opened her mouth to protest that she was not a child...and near forgot to shut it again.

Lord Schmeidt stood. He was a giant of a man, a full head or more taller than her father was, and Rober de Leon towered over most men. His hair was a rich brown that fell like silk strands to his collar. It shone like a deep, polished amber.

He turned to her. Her intended was broad of shoulder, a man who could snap her in two if he were angered with her. Caitrina had never found muscular men intimidating before, but there was something more than Lord Schmeidt's size that added to the feeling of danger about him.

Caitrina moved her gaze from his chest, her eye level, to his face. His eyes held her, pinning her in his gaze. The color was unusual—molten silver mixed with gray pearl.

Her face heated. Caitrina pressed a hand to the stomacher laced over her houppelande, the smooth material a comfort to her shaking hand. A disconcerting trembling settled deep inside her. It made the trembling in her hand feel like a placid pond in comparison.

Lord Schmeidt smiled. He was young, very young to hold a title the likes of the one he did. He couldn't be much older than her own nineteen years. Lord Schmeidt was a lovely man, and that smile made her heart race.

"Caitrina?" her father asked, his voice laced in concern.

Lord Schmeidt crossed the room to her, his footsteps silent on the stone floor. He took her hand and kissed it gently. "Caitrina is well, Rober."

No. I am not, her mind protested. His voice was like silk brushed over her skin, sending shivers down her spine. *I am most definitely not well.*

His smile widened. "You are well. Are you not, *Geliebte?*"

Her heart stuttered. Caitrina pulled her hand from his embrace, a nameless panic scattering her thoughts. She shook her head and turned, running blindly from the room.

Caitrina came to a halt deep in the garden. She gulped the chill air into her aching lungs. Her entire body shook, and she found herself wishing that she could return to her carefree youth and climb a tree to escape whatever came for her.

What was wrong with her? Caitrina couldn't sort her thoughts or emotions. She didn't fear Lord Schmeidt precisely, though he unnerved her. What caused her panic? What was this feeling when she looked at him, and who was Lord Schmeidt to affect her this way?

"Jörg." His voice came from close behind her.

Caitrina whirled around to face him, the deep blue brocade of her dress snagging on the thorny vines beside her. Any other time, that might have upset her but not when he was so close to her. Lord Schmeidt steadied her, his hands on her shoulders.

His eyes narrowed as she shivered. He stripped off his cloak and pulled it around her shoulders. "You will chill." His grasp of the language was surprisingly good and his accent almost non-existent.

She glanced around him, hoping her father was nearby.

Lord Schmeidt shook his head, chafing his palms up and down Caitrina's arms to warm her. "Rober left it to me to calm you, Caitrina. It is nothing more than nerves, to be expected considering the circumstances."

"No." Her teeth chattered but not in the cold. "It is not. I am not a swooning female, Lord—"

"Jörg," he insisted. "My name is Jörg."

Caitrina took a calming breath. "Jörg."

He smiled. She backed away, suddenly wary. It wasn't natural, this feeling that assaulted her when he smiled. Caitrina looked at her body in dismay. It was a riot of sensation. Her womb ached. A dampness made her core sensitive to the brush of her underdress against her body.

Her nipples beaded against the bodice of her gown. Lord Schmeidt watched the faint outline of those nipples avidly. Caitrina gasped, draping her arm over them.

He guided her arm away slowly. "It is a natural reaction, Caitrina." His voice was rough. "It is a good sign that my proximity excites you."

She shook her head. "No. It is not. I have never—"

His hands closed on her waist. His eyes darkened as she tried to retreat again. The wall was at her back, blocking her escape.

"It is natural," he insisted. "You know." He lowered his face toward her. "You know I am the one you have waited for."

Good Lord! He means to kiss me. I don't even know him. Caitrina jerked her head aside, grimacing as a thorn scratched her throat.

He stilled and met her eyes. Caitrina shivered, longing for the kiss she'd denied him even as she argued the madness in wanting such a thing.

Lord Schmeidt laid his lips over the scrape, and Caitrina swallowed a moan of pure delight. This wasn't right. She wanted... Oh, she wanted Lord Schmeidt to make her entire body feel as good as that spot on her throat.

"Jörg," he reminded her, pressing another kiss to her skin.

Caitrina nodded, drinking in his scent. He smelled of rich earth and pungent spice—and something heady, a scent that was undeniably male.

His lips touched hers. Caitrina expected the copper of her own blood, but when he breached her lips; her senses swam in the taste of cinnamon and clove, warmed wine and candied fruit. Jörg's tongue caressed hers, and his groan vibrated down her body to that ache at the juncture of her thighs.

"Jörg," she pleaded. Caitrina touched his chest, tracing the contours of him through the fitted cyclas in the Italian style.

He tensed. "You do know. Don't you, Caitrina?"

She nodded. What did she know? That her marriage bed wouldn't be a chore with Jörg? Was she mad? If her father had seen that kiss—in plain sight in the garden with a man she had just met? She was surely mad.

Jörg pulled her to his body, his mouth seeking hers. "No. If anyone is mad, I am—for you."

Caitrina looked at him in shock. Jörg knew her mind as if he resided there. The thought was banished as her body exploded in sensation. Her eyes fluttered shut. Dizziness assaulted her, a sense that she was moving, though she had no sense of direction or speed. Her skirts rustled, though she felt no wind.

Jörg's hand cupped her breast, and she laid her head back, stunned at the feeling of grass beneath her cheek. Caitrina stared at the twinkling stars in confusion.

"Jörg?" she asked weakly. "What is happening to me?"

"You feel it," he whispered. "You remember." Jörg pulled the cloak back and moved his gaze over her body breathlessly.

Caitrina shifted, the touch of his eyes like a physical caress. She bit back a cry of pleasure at the sensation of phantom fingers skating down her stomach, disappearing, then inching up between her thighs. Caitrina spread for him, shamelessly offering herself.

A rational kernel of her mind rebelled. She was laid out for his pleasure in a garden, swallowing cries that would bring her father to witness her wanton display.

Her head spun. Where in the garden was she? The bushes beside her were nothing Caitrina remembered seeing. The gardens were quite large. It must be a corner she didn't typically see at night.

Caitrina gripped Jörg's arm, shuddering as his fingers breached her body. Her skirts were hiked up to her hips, folded gently under her body so that her buttocks rested on the wool of his cloak. A moment of unease stole over her. When had that happened?

Do you truly care? No. She didn't. Caitrina moved against his hand, crying out, then tensing in the realization of what she'd done. Panic welled in her.

"Gently," Jörg soothed her. "No one will hear you."

"But—"

Jörg's mouth was on hers, and his fingers massaged the sensitive flesh between her legs. He shifted his body over hers, his kiss more ardent. His fingers left her, and Caitrina growled a protest against his questing tongue. She no longer cared where she was. Her core was tender, needing, and Caitrina would have what she needed from him.

Jörg pushed back slowly. "You are pure," he commented. "Virginal."

If that reminder was meant for her, Caitrina couldn't find a care about the situation. Her urge to be his was too strong. It was more likely that the reminder was for himself, but he was her intended. She belonged to him.

"I can make it painless," he offered, "but I would prefer you to accept me without tricks. I don't have the restraint to make it painless without—"

She shied. "Pain?" Yes. There was pain in losing a maidenhead...burning, tearing pain. Jacquine had told her that. Caitrina shook her head. She didn't want pain, not when she was already so tender there.

Jörg nodded grimly. "No pain. You have my vow."

Caitrina bit her lip in confusion. "There is a way without pain?"

He nodded, smiling a predatory smile that made her ache for him increase.

"Why would a man hurt a woman if it is not necessary?"

Jörg sank over her, laying his lips on her throat again. "Not all men are as gifted as I," he teased.

Caitrina started to protest that sexual prowess in a man so young was nothing to pride oneself in. She gasped in shock as Jörg licked at the column of her neck, nudging her chin up and aside to love at her more fully.

His mouth did delicious things to her body and mind. His lips brushed over her flesh, soft and smooth, warm and welcome. Those lips parted, and Jörg tasted her with the sinful tongue hidden behind them. He sucked lightly at her, and Caitrina bowed up to him, seeking what he offered. His teeth nipped at her, scraping her skin.

"Please, Jörg," she whispered. "I'll die."

His hands held her head gently and his body pressed down into hers. The hard ridge of his cock teased at her thigh.

Caitrina's breath caught in her lungs as a sharp pain assaulted her. Her scream dissolved into a moan. What was Jorg doing to her? The feeling of his suckling echoed through her breasts and the depths of her sheath. It wasn't painful. Caitrina was sure that it had never been truly painful. The intensity of the sensation had merely surprised her. She wrapped her hands in his hair, drawing his mouth closer, reveling in the feeling of that insistent suckling.

Jorg eased his hips away, lifting her thighs open around him and pulling her ankles to the back of his hips. *"Hold me to you, Caitrina."* His hand brushed her thigh as he worked at his clothing. He gripped her hips, and his tongue skated over her throat. He straightened and settled the head of his cock at her entrance.

Caitrina pulled at his shoulders, desperate now to feel the fullness of that cock buried inside her. He thrust deep, his eyes closing and his muscles tensing beneath her fingers. Caitrina licked her lip, watching the ecstasy etched on Jörg's face hungrily.

"Now," he rasped. His body retreated, then lodged deeper still.

Caitrina cried out, her sheath gripping him, desperate to hold him forever. Jörg's eyes glowed like fine jewelry in firelight as he thrust again and again into the tightness she afforded him. Her body tensed, her legs pulling him deeper. She felt it coming for her, a rush of blood in her ears that made her body hot and hungry.

"Jörg," she whispered. Caitrina had no name for what stalked her, what waited just out of reach. She feared it even as she knew she had to experience it to be whole.

Jörg nodded in encouragement. "Let it take you," he urged her.

It did. Her sheath spasmed around him, and Jörg cried out harshly in response. Waves of warmth rode her veins, coursing through her body, making her feel weak and sensitized. Every brush of his body became a welcome agony of intense pleasure.

Jörg roared, wash after wash of his seed filling her. It felt wonderful. It felt right. Caitrina met his eyes, her body still on fire for him.

He nodded. "*Sleep, love. Tomorrow, our journey begins.*"

Caitrina furrowed her brow, her eyes heavy in exhaustion and confusion. Had Jörg spoken to her without moving his lips?

"*'Tis all a dream, Geliebte. Sleep. You will remember none of this—for now.*"

She tried to protest that such a thing was impossible. With his cock still buried deep inside her, how could Jörg say something so ridiculous? She wouldn't remember this—the most startling experience of her young life? Was he mad? Her mouth moved to tell him, but Caitrina couldn't seem to form the words. Her eyes slid shut, and her hands slid from his body. Warmth enfolded her.

Jörg left her body. Caitrina wanted to beg him to stay, but she was too comfortable to be vexed by anything for long.

Sleep took her, a deep sleep full of impossible dreams. What was Jörg doing to her? His tongue bathed her inner thighs and her core, tickling the depths of her until the burn bit into the haze in her mind. Caitrina screamed his name as bliss took her again. Then she felt nothing.

Chapter Seven

Caitrina opened her eyes, regarding Jacquine's concerned look with confusion.

"You are well, mi'lady?" she asked nervously.

Frustration welled in Caitrina. Why would any sane person be concerned that she was well? "Of course," she snapped, trying to ignore the nagging ache in her skull. "Why would I not be?"

Jacquine's eyes widened. "Do you have no memory of your collapse in the garden, mi'lady?"

Caitrina rubbed her forehead, trying to disperse the fog gathered in her mind. "I went to the garden." She recalled that much, nodding. Jörg unnerved her, though she wouldn't admit that to Jacquine or to anyone else. "Jörg—" She felt her face heat at using so familiar an address for her intended. "Lord Schmeidt came to speak to me and...gave me his cloak."

She remembered that he tried to kiss her—or did he kiss her? The half-memory of a mouth sweet in spice taunted her.

"Yes?" Jacquine prodded her.

She'd backed from him then. Caitrina ran her fingers over her throat, finding the small scab. "A thorn. A thorn pierced me, and— Oh, dear Lord." *His mouth was on my throat. Thank the merciful savior Father hadn't seen that.*

"Mi'lady?"

"Lord Schmeidt— His mouth was on my throat?" Hazy remembrances of heat in her blood and his mouth and hands on her body assaulted her. Caitrina denied that she enjoyed those things even as her nipples tightened against the thin shift and heavy quilt. Her womb ached. The feelings were maddening, exciting—familiar. Had she done this when he'd touched her?

Jacquine smiled in relief and brushed Caitrina's hair away from her throat. "Good. You remember."

Caitrina felt her face darken. "It is hardly something to be proud of," she grumbled. "A thorn—"

"A sting. You were stung. 'Twas not a thorn."

"What?" Caitrina rubbed at her head, trying to cut through the damnable fog obscuring her memory. "It was a thorn," she insisted.

Jacquine shook her head sadly. "No. A sting. We nearly lost you like your poor mother. Were it not for your young—"

"I have been stung in the past. Surely, you remember my father's panic. I have no such frailty."

"The surgeon says one may be stung many times and suddenly respond ill to it—or fall ill from a bee when a wasp offended not."

Caitrina placed her hand on the scab, rubbing it absently. Was it truly a poison? If it was an insect, why did she remember a thorn so clearly?

Had she thought it was a thorn and been wrong? That hardly seemed possible. Her mind had always been clear on such things. But, had her mind ever been clear in the company of Lord Schmeidt?

"Lord Schmeidt saved you. When he gleaned your distress, he removed the sting and sucked out much of the poison. It had not assaulted you full when he acted for you. When he carried you in— Oh, mi'lady. You were so pale and your heart so slow, your skin cool;

your father near went mad in worry. He waits to see you still. Shall I send for him?"

"Please, Jacquine. I do not want to worry him."

Her maid left with a nod.

Caitrina pressed a hand to the pulsing in her womb. *It is just the poison from the sting*, she assured herself. It could be nothing more. If Lord Schmeidt had taken advantage in some way, Jacquine would have seen some sign of it when she'd undressed Caitrina. The rest was simply her own imaginings.

* * * *

Jörg smiled, swallowing an outright laugh at Caitrina's attempts to explain away her arousal. He shifted against the windowpane, dressed again in the image of leather leggings and a training-style tunic. Jörg was always most comfortable in the clothing he wore in his earliest days, when he'd been a Cursed Warrior and not a damned beast.

The image was perfect, right down to the feeling of the fabric against his skin, recreated from those long lost days of freedom. They were so much more comfortable than the real clothes he'd worn to greet his mate, though in retrospect, Jörg was glad he wore those clothes.

The image of clothing would not have kept Caitrina warm when she ran from him. Even making her body disregard the cold would not have protected her from it, and the power outlay would have drawn Warriors to him.

Caitrina looked at the window curiously, looking through Jörg's ghosted form and into the dark night behind him. He hardened as he visited her thoughts. She remembered. Caitrina remembered much more than Jörg had anticipated, much more than her soul ever had in past lives.

She not only remembered her arousal, her body's response to his touch in the garden. Caitrina remembered her soul's past. She felt the ties that bound them, one to the other. Caitrina remembered his touch from past lives, fleeting sensations of rightness that her conscious mind didn't actively pursue. None of the others had felt it as strongly.

Jörg took it as a sign, something he thought he would never be able to do again. He would succeed this time. He'd lost Regana again and again, finding her only to lose her before a month was done. This time would be different.

This time Jörg had found the foul human who'd threatened her before he'd approached his mate. He wouldn't be clumsy enough to lose her that way again—not after Marie. Jörg had found the human beast and dispatched him in a manner appropriate to his crimes.

Jörg's stomach clenched at the thought of Jacque de Cambion ever laying hands on Regana—on Caitrina. The man was unclean in body and mind. His tastes ran to brutal treatment, humiliation, even blood in his love play.

He sobered at that. Jörg wasn't like that with Regana's soul. He tried to forget the rush of pleasure her blood gave him. After Regana, feeling pleasure from taking her blood should sicken him. It did sicken him, when Jörg wasn't lost in the ecstasy of feeding.

Jacque— It was better to think about Jacque. One of the other elders would think Jacque the perfect candidate to be culled as a turned, encouraging the human to indulge in his tastes as a human minion in service before setting him loose on society as a turned. Jacque would be mad in disease soon, perfect material for his damned brethren to use.

Jörg had set out to save Caitrina from Jacque, but on closer inspection, it would be better to kill the human beast. As a turned, he would be too much of a threat to Caitrina. When the sun set again and she was far from harm, Jörg would end Jacque de Cambion quickly and go to her.

Yes. He would go to her while she traveled and awake Caitrina's desires again. Jörg hadn't planned to claim Caitrina that night, but as he'd learned in his earliest days with Regana, he possessed little self-control when it came to his mate.

Jörg shivered, but not in the bitter cold of the night air. As a damned beast, things like weather, walls, and human eyes were inconsequential to him. He had ceased to worry about such things almost a thousand years earlier.

He shivered in the reminders of why he needed to maintain his self-control this time. Jörg had hurt Regana in countless, callous ways. He would not hurt her again, in any of her lives.

Already, Caitrina was different. Her first time had been without pain. Jörg had even held off his pinnacle until she'd reached her ultimate pleasure. He had been tempted to enhance her pleasure, but Jörg hadn't wanted tricks between them.

Jörg sobered again. There had been tricks. He had taken her blood to free Caitrina from the pain of taking her maidenhead. Her blood was sweet, the beauty and purity of her soul making it so. Jörg hadn't wanted to feed from her, but he was glad that her blood was so sweet.

Regana's blood had been bittersweet, tainted by her melancholy and the desperate request she'd made of him. Jörg shuddered. He'd owed Regana the release of her death, but he would never forgive himself for granting that request.

He turned his mind back to Caitrina. Jörg had taken only as much blood as he'd needed to make her first time pleasurable and to grant her freedom from the duty of facing her father with the memory of their lovemaking in her mind. It was a temporary block. When the knowledge would not cause her guilt, Jörg would return a version of the truth to her—a version without his feeding involved.

Jörg had hidden the proof of their lovemaking carefully. He'd cleaned the blood and their mixed fluids from her, inside and out; he'd even used his cleansing power to aid in the task.

Jörg had been forced to coerce the maid, Jacquine, a bit, even then. He prayed that small outlay of power within the Leon household would not be enough to bring the Warriors down upon them.

He bit back a groan, stroking the stirring length of his cock as he remembered how Caitrina had cried out to his ministrations in her half-aware state. Jörg would even thank the damned Stone that made him a beast if she made the same joyous sound fully awake.

The itching started in the back of his neck, the niggling awareness that dawn was approaching. Jörg cast one last look at Caitrina, wrapped in her father's arms. Yes. Rober would protect her until Jörg's men came for her.

The old man had done a fine job of raising Caitrina for Jörg, so much so that Jörg felt bad for using Rober's greatest fear against him to explain his daughter's slight pallor. Rober hadn't questioned Jörg's story, though Jörg could have easily handled it if he had, as easily as he'd handled the old man's qualms about letting Caitrina travel today.

Jörg dematerialized and floated away on a breeze. The human insect sniffing after Caitrina would soon be no more, but there were still grievous threats to her safety. There was a Cursed Warrior somewhere near. There was always a Cursed Warrior waiting to take Regana from him—and other beasts.

He lit on the ground behind the hapless Warrior, solid again but ghosted better than this barely trained pup could comprehend. Jörg scowled. This wasn't the Warrior he sought. This Warrior was young, no more than two or three years past first night.

Jörg followed the boy as he picked his way down the hillside Jörg had taken Caitrina to. A low burn of annoyed *Blutjagd* burned in the pup's skin. He had missed a kill, and he wasn't happy about it.

What should I do? Jörg could draw the other easily by killing the pup.

The young one with the smell of Haus Kaufmann about him—*it must be Franz*—was here for one reason. He knew a beast had fed. The Warrior hadn't locked onto Caitrina.

Franz obviously had no idea what beast he sought. If he did, the Warrior would have called in his lord to help him. No Warrior faced "The Mad Elder" alone and lived to tell the tale.

Jörg dematerialized and streamed away to the hilltop where he'd loved Caitrina to take his rest. He sank into the ground, drinking in the imagined smell of their union around him.

It was better to leave the Warrior—for now. If Jörg faced more than one now, he might be injured and unable to rejoin Caitrina for several days while the earth healed him. Now that he'd had her, such a thing was unacceptable.

Chapter Eight

Caitrina shivered, pulling her cloak close around her. She still didn't understand why they had to leave today, but her father and Lord Schmeidt had decided that it would be so.

Two small trunks had been loaded into the smaller carriage, and the rest of her belongings would follow later with other men. Ten of Lord Schmeidt's men would accompany Jacquine and herself. Two rode on each carriage, and six were mounted. All of the men were armed.

Lord Schmeidt was nowhere in view. Martin, the captain of his guard, had assured Caitrina that her lord had simply ridden ahead to see to some business while they made their way to his estate.

She slid her gaze over the lord's carriage. It was a strange design, one Caitrina had not encountered before. The carriage was fully enclosed, complete with heavy drapes over the interior of the flaps to cut down on the cold evening wind, dust, sound, and sunlight that could enter the interior when one did not wish it. It was monstrously huge with a wide, deep velvet seat and ample space to stretch out even the lord's long legs.

It was a most comfortable way to travel, almost decadent. The color was reminiscent of his eyes, a soft gray that was oddly pleasing to her senses.

Martin bowed to her smoothly, a fine figure of a gentleman, though he was a man of the Isles—most likely one of the conquered natives by his look. "G'day, mi'lady," he intoned pleasantly.

She offered him a strained smile and put her gloved hand in his as Martin reached to help her into the carriage.

The attack came without warning, a black-clad man of about her own age appearing from nowhere to grasp Caitrina by the upper arm. He whipped the hood from her head and forced her chin up with a fist wrapped around the hilt of a dagger the length of her forearm. His eyes narrowed.

Caitrina shuddered, looking to Schmeidt's guards in confusion. They made no move to help her, stilled by Martin's upraised hand, though all of them grasped their weapons in warning.

Martin nodded his assurances to her. "Release her," he ordered calmly.

The madman motioned to Caitrina with a tilt of his chin. "Your master should have hidden his work better than this."

Martin shook his head. "The lady was stung last night. There are witnesses."

"There are always witnesses." He sneered. His hand tightened on her arm. "What is Veriel's interest in her, minion?"

Caitrina swallowed a cry of pain as his fingers bit into her arm. "W-who?" she stammered.

"The one who did that," the young man exploded.

"A-an insect," she whispered.

He made a sound of disgust. "He took your memory, of course. Answer me, minion."

Martin settled his hand on the hilt of his sword. "You may kill me and every man who serves me, Warrior, but I know your code. The lady is an innocent in this battle."

The man ground his teeth, fixing a look of pure fury on Caitrina. "Ask for my protection," he growled.

She shook her head. "I don't want your protection." Caitrina didn't want anything from him.

"Release her, Franz," a new voice ordered. "She is an innocent. You know the laws."

Franz pushed her toward Martin, stalking to the older man with that same look of malice. The other was dressed much like the youth was, black boots and breeches, tunic and cloak. He had identical deep brown eyes and black curls.

He bowed his head. "Mi'lady," he greeted her.

Caitrina nodded shakily.

Without warning, he struck Franz across the face, knocking the young man to the ground. The older man reached his hand, stained in Franz's blood, toward Caitrina.

She shrank behind Martin, terrified by this barbaric display.

The man nodded grimly. "My nephew will not injure you again. If he does, I will present his corpse to you. You have my vow."

Caitrina flicked a shocked look at Franz. The young man bowed his head to her, looking much less threatening.

She turned her attention back to the older man as he started speaking again, wiping his nephew's blood on a length of cloth—black like everything else about him.

"I am Etienne of Kaufmann, mi'lady. And you?"

"Do not answer him," Martin growled.

Etienne smiled, a disarming smile that made him appear little more than a boy though he was surely near thirty years of age. "As you will, mi'lady. Where do you travel?"

"Get in the carriage, mi'lady," Martin ordered, only slightly less gruffly.

Caitrina hesitated, confused by this exchange— and by her reactions. Franz frightened her, but Caitrina trusted Etienne in some strange manner she couldn't comprehend. He was a barbarian, yet at the same time, he was genteel and possessing of a strict code of honor that dictated he would slay a boy of his own family rather than let the impetuous pup hurt her.

She furrowed her brow. *Pup? Now, why would I choose such a term for this dangerous young man?*

"Mi'lady," Martin reminded her.

She nodded and met Etienne's eyes. "I thank you for your assistance, sir." Caitrina turned into the carriage, using Martin's hand to steady herself.

"Caitrina?" her father called. "Is there a problem?"

She looked to where Etienne and Franz stood a moment before. They were gone, disappeared from view. Caitrina noted Martin's pained expression uneasily.

"Caitrina?" he called again.

"No, Father. I am well," she lied.

* * * *

Jörg materialized by the side of the road. He'd passed his men and their precious cargo more than a league back. They would be upon him soon.

He closed his eyes, concentrating on his link with Caitrina, picking the strand from the hundreds of active feed strings within him. Jörg had fed from all of his bought humans as a part of their pact. He could track Martin or any of the others, but he chose to track Caitrina, to experience the thrill of feeling her draw near.

Martin drew up beside him and motioned for the carriages to stop. He nodded to Jörg stiffly.

"There was a problem?" Jörg asked, keeping his distance from Martin's mount. Animals tolerated him only at a distance, and Jörg had no wish to upset the beast unnecessarily.

"Warriors...two of the animals. The young one handled your lady."

Jörg nodded, wishing for one mad moment that he had killed the pup where he stood the night before and ended this before they found their way to Caitrina.

Martin laughed a humorless laugh. "He tried to order your lady to take his protection. She refused him. His master struck him a single blow for his appalling lack of self-control."

"Caitrina?"

"Shaken and frightened." He scowled. "We outnumbered them ten to two."

His meaning was clear. Martin would have liked nothing more than to end the Warrior who'd touched Caitrina. Jörg sighed, recalling Martin's price.

Jörg had come upon Martin as he'd crouched over his slain family. Their bargain was a simple one. In exchange for Martin's service, Jörg had delivered the bandits to their hell personally and painfully...and delivered their heads to Martin. Jörg had fulfilled his side of the promise before the sun rose.

Martin had given his blood willingly and served faithfully ever since. Of all his bought, Martin was his most loyal—and the only human Jörg considered a friend.

"And they would have slain twice your number easily. I have seen it," Jörg reminded him calmly. *I have done it, and much more.*

Martin nodded, chastised by the reminder. There was a reason Jörg had told them not to fight the Warriors if they came for Caitrina. Jörg could handle the Warriors. He could handle the beasts. Martin's only job was to safeguard Caitrina from humans who might harm her. Anything else would likely cost Martin his life.

Jacquine opened the door to his carriage and stepped onto the runner. "Why have we stopped?" she demanded, sounding slightly annoyed.

Jörg approached her, giving the horses a wide berth. "Forgive me, Jacquine. I grew tired of riding and wished to join my lady." He made sure to add the illusion of trail dust to his clothing to complete the image of a long, hard ride before he reached a field of clear vision for her.

She nodded and turned back.

"Alone," he qualified.

Jacquine shot him a look of confusion and concern. Her thoughts were a riot. The servant had no wish to anger her new lord, but it was unseemly to leave her lady alone with him before they were properly wed.

Jörg drew in his power, exerting his coercion over her. "Caitrina will be safe with me," he whispered.

She met his eyes, nodding slowly. "As you wish, my lord."

He smiled as she climbed into the second carriage, using Matthew's hand to balance herself. Jörg shot a warning look at the young bought, and Matthew scurried away to his mount, reminded silently of his place. Jörg would have to arrange for a bit of entertainment for the men when they reached a stop.

Despite his warning that Jacquine was not to be molested, that she was under Jörg's protection, she was a luscious bit of female flesh, and the men were starved for female company. Perhaps Jörg would take a bit of blood from the whore before he turned her over to pleasure his men. It never hurt to check for disease to keep his men healthy before they indulged.

He sighed. Perhaps he should take a bit of Matthew's blood as well. It was unlikely that his bought had decided to turn on him, but a bit of blood should tell the tale.

Restless and unnerved, Jörg left the carriage, ordering Jacquine to sleep via coercion. He motioned to Martin to keep Caitrina busy if she decided to investigate the long delay.

Matthew paled when Jörg motioned to him, but he dismounted and came to the back of the second carriage as Jörg ordered. Matthew had never cared for giving his blood when it was called for, but Jörg had kept to his end of the bargain, keeping the young man's sister well-cared for in service to a kind lady who owed Jörg more than a few favors of her own.

"Be still, Matthew. You know our bargain," Jörg soothed him, exerting just a touch of calming coercion.

The young man extended his wrist for Jörg's use, sucking in his breath as the first pulse of pleasure washed over him. His eyes dilated as his arousal grew.

Jörg promised pleasure for the taking of blood, but there was only one type of pleasure he could give.

Matthew's mind opened wide to Jörg as the blood sated his raging hunger. Jörg exercised strict control, taking only two swallows from the man and sending him over into an orgasm as he closed the feeding site.

Matthew leaned heavily against Jörg's chest, gritting back the cry of release he wanted to vent. His heart thundered in his chest. He gasped, shivering as he gave in to his body's need to physically release.

Jörg's fangs extended further. It would be so easy to cross the line with his men as his brother elders had on so many occasions. The urge to sexually release with a willing partner while he fed was always hard to resist, but men were not to his tastes—or so he told himself, when one of his men climaxed in his arms and Jörg rose to the occasion. He hadn't crossed that line, not in the thousand years since Jörg became what he now was, and today was not the day he would start.

Matthew recovered slowly, not quite meeting Jörg's eyes. The fact that he couldn't stop himself from experiencing the natural reaction to Jörg's push of pleasure embarrassed him.

"You serve me faithfully," Jörg assured him. "When we stop tonight, the first woman is yours. You have my word."

Matthew managed a wolfish smile at that. He really had been too long without a woman. Jörg would have to be more mindful of that in the future. Even his most loyal would turn on him, if Jörg didn't see to their needs.

"Can you ride?" Jörg knew he could, but it couldn't hurt to show his concern for the man.

"Yes, master."

"Then do so."

Jörg returned to the carriage, forcing his fangs down along with his errant cock. He used his cleansing power on himself to be fresh and untainted for Caitrina.

No. He wouldn't cross the lines he'd set for himself. He wasn't fully a beast and never had been. Even if he was, Jörg had a willing partner, one he would much rather sate himself in.

Jörg smiled as he swung up into the carriage and motioned for Martin to start them moving again.

Chapter Nine

Caitrina looked at him with wide eyes, searching for some sign of Jacquine behind him. Her heart hammered in her chest. Jörg felt the blood rushing in Caitrina's veins in a mixture of fear and arousal. He closed the door, leaving only the bright moonlight that sifted around the drapes around them.

Jörg fell to his knees before her, kissing Caitrina's hand as the carriage started out. "Calm, *Geliebte*," he whispered hoarsely. "Are you well?"

"No," she gasped.

He kissed her wrist, feeling her pulse jump at the touch. Her musk teased his nose. "What ails you, love?"

She hesitated. "Men— As we left, two men accosted us. Martin seemed to know them. Who are they?"

"An old enemy that would steal all I possess," Jörg explained. That described the Warriors perfectly.

"Including me?"

Jörg nodded, kissing her racing pulse again. "If they knew you were mine," he confirmed. *They do know, but Kaufmann will not live long enough to take you from me.*

"You do not—" She faltered as he nipped at her wrist.

"Do not?" he prodded.

"Possess me."

Her body called her a liar. Jörg hardened painfully as her core flooded with her delicious honey.

Jörg placed his hands on either side of her thighs on the seat. "Do you remember?" He brushed his lips over her jaw, then her lips.

"Remember?" Caitrina asked in a voice thick in her arousal. She fisted her hands in her lap.

Jörg smiled as hazy half-remembrances filtered into her consciousness. He played his tongue along the seam of her lips slowly. "Open for me." He pressed his lips to hers, trusting that Caitrina's body would remember and respond.

She didn't disappoint him. Caitrina parted her lips dutifully, accepting his tongue. At the first taste of him, she groaned, her memories unraveling at a maddening, leisurely pace. Their kiss was fevered, each of them taking away more than they poured in with every passing second.

"Jörg," she groaned.

He nodded. "Yes. Do you remember what we were doing when you were stung?"

Caitrina licked her lip, shaking her head, dazed. "You kissed me?" she guessed.

"Do you remember that?" he asked, knowing that she did.

"Yes," she admitted.

Jörg palmed the softness of her breast, meeting Caitrina's eyes as she gasped. She reached a hand to his chest slowly, seeking his approval as she explored his body. Caitrina watched her hands, absorbed in her discoveries. Jörg pulled his tunic off for her, encouraging her to carry on.

After centuries without her touch, Jörg felt he might die if she didn't touch him. He sobered. If he could die any natural death, he would welcome it. Jörg pushed that thought away. While he had Regana in his arms, dark thoughts of his half-life and death were unwelcome.

Caitrina moved her gaze over him breathlessly. She touched the blood mark on his shoulder, the last vestige of his life as a Cursed Warrior. Caitrina leaned forward, kissing it as she always had. Jörg cradled her head as she loved at the mark.

"Regana," he crooned. "*Geliebte Mein.*"

"*Reg,*" she whispered.

"Yes," he hissed. "Remember me." His blood mark was the sign of Reg, the intensity at the base of the fire. Regana had always been drawn to the mark.

Her hands feathered over his stomach and traced the head of his cock. Jörg blocked her thoughts, at the edges of control. If he watched the progression of images in her mind, he would ravish her—again, and Jörg had promised himself he would never do that to another of Regana's souls.

"Do you remember what we were doing, Caitrina?" he rasped.

"Show me." Her mouth returned to the blood mark, her fingers playing at his rigid length. "Please, show me."

Jörg drew her skirts into her lap, stroking his fingers over her heated core, slick with her juices.

She shuddered. "You touched me inside." Caitrina's voice was a plea; for understanding, for clarity in the jumble of thoughts that assaulted her, for what she remembered.

He slid two fingers into her, smiling as her core clenched at them. "What else do you remember?"

Caitrina tipped her hips back and forth, rocking his fingers in and out. That wasn't something she had done the night before.

A vision of Ilona the night before she died forced its way into his mind. Yes. Ilona had moved like that on his hand. Jörg captured her mouth, massaging his fingers in her as Ilona liked, twisting and thrusting.

She laid her head back, watching him with slumberous eyes. "I remember something else you did, Jörg."

"Which is?" He resisted looking into her mind, afraid that his control would snap.

Caitrina ran her fingers over his lips. "Your tongue. You put your tongue where your fingers are."

Jörg closed his eyes, letting her fever for his mouth wash over him. "Take off your dress," he requested. "Take off your dress, and I will do as you wish."

She paused only a moment, then drew her clothing off slowly. He suckled at her nipples as they appeared, a need to taste all of her making him crazy.

"Please, Jörg."

He nodded, rolling his tongue around one peak. There would be time to indulge himself later. Caitrina wanted the sensations she remembered vividly, despite his coercion and mind games. This encounter was for her.

"I promised," he commented more to himself to her. Jörg pulled her knees over his shoulders, supporting Caitrina's weight as he sampled her juices.

She cried out softly, grasping at his hair. "Jörg," she rasped.

"Tell me when you remember more." Jörg prayed that moment would come soon.

He sucked at her nub until Caitrina cried out harshly. She bit her lip in the near darkness, holding in her pleasure.

"No," he chided her. "The horses are too loud for the men to hear. Do not hold back. Please." Jörg buried his tongue in her, groaning into her body as Caitrina cried out again.

I would even thank the Stone...

Jörg pushed that thought away. The damned Stone could wait for its thanks. He drove her body on ruthlessly, drinking in every quivering movement and whimper. Jörg was starved for it, starved for her.

The truth came to Caitrina in a moment of startling clarity that sent tongues of pleasure up Jörg's aching cock. He peeled his clothing back, preparing to claim her. She remembered the feeling of his complete mastery of her, of her body holding him in as she shattered in his arms, of his heat flooding her channel with seed that could never give her a child.

I will make that right. Whatever I have to do, I will.

{Anything?}

He pushed the thought away, aware that there were some things he would not do, even to assure Caitrina's happiness.

Caitrina didn't tell him. Her hands fisted in his hair, and she urged him closer. Jörg obliged her whim; heartened that Caitrina wanted him so desperately in any form, that she was comfortable enough to demand a specific pleasure from him.

Jörg pushed her on, drunk on her taste and driven to the brink of a brutal possession by her breathless cries. Her thighs tightened reflexively, and she bowed her back, screaming out his name. A wash of her personal flavor flooded his mouth.

Caitrina's mind demanded what her body was incapable of forming the words to request—his cock buried deep inside her, filling her. Jörg sat back, drawing her body down his until the head of his cock breached her. Caitrina's eyes widened, and she squirmed in his grip, seeking more of him.

"Slowly," he growled. "You will still be tender."

Despite his healing touch as he bathed her blood and their fluids from Caitrina, his invasion was new and physically traumatic. Jörg hadn't been as gentle as he should have been with her. His feeding could make her not feel the pain, but it could not stop the harm inherent in his fervor.

Jörg lowered her around him, fingerwidth by agonizing fingerwidth, allowing Caitrina's body time to adjust to his length and girth. She was so tight and warm; it was both a torture and a delight.

In the long centuries between Regana's incarnations, Jörg took many women. His body craved release. If Regana was not embodied for him, Jörg took release where he could, much as a Cursed Warrior would when he was widowed.

He thrust deep inside her, drinking in Caitrina's scream of pleasure. She was embodied now. Jörg was buried deep in the one woman who gave him peace. He wouldn't think about her leaving him. Not now. Not while her sheath gripped him tight.

Jörg moved restlessly, needing that peace again. Caitrina met his eyes, pushing down on his length. His control fled. Jörg gripped her waist, pushing back the madness as he captured her mouth. Caitrina wanted him. She was willing, coming to him as Jörg tried to convince himself that Regana had in the beginning.

He threw his head back, drinking in the stillness in his soul as he poured wave after wave of his semen into her. Caitrina's fingernails bit into his shoulders, her body rippling around him.

"Yes," he breathed.

Caitrina sank to his chest, shivering in the aftereffects of her pleasure. Jörg groaned as her lips traced the blood mark. Flashes of Regana on their last night together raced through his mind.

"I love you," he said, cringing that he hadn't said it the first time he took Caitrina, that he hadn't said it that last night with Regana.

Jörg couldn't be that bastard this time. He couldn't let Caitrina ever doubt what he felt for her. "I love you," he repeated, stroking a curl between his fingertips. "I will tell you a hundred times a day. I will prove it in a thousand ways. I have always loved you."

"*Stay with me,*" she replied in the ancient language he'd spoken with Regana, her voice thick in sleep. Caitrina had no idea what she was saying. Her dreams were talking, dreams of her life after he'd left her behind. "*Do not ever leave me. I couldn't stand it.*"

Jörg swallowed a sob. She remembered those dark days after he left. "I will not leave you." *Never again. I will never leave you without my love and protection again.*

* * * *

Caitrina woke, smiling at the tender aches of loving a man. She opened her eyes, taking in the strange room in confusion. Where was she?

"Ah, awake at last," Jacquine said brightly.

"Where are we?" *And, where is Jörg? He promised not to leave me.*

Caitrina sobered. She was being ridiculous. What would it look like if he shared her bed?

"A small inn. We reached it late in the night. Lord Schmeidt didn't want to disturb your sleep. He was very courteous. He carried you to this room and barely left your side to see to his men's comfort before returning to you." She blushed, her dark eyes glittering over a smile.

"What is it?" Caitrina asked, bracing herself for knowing comments about her intimate relationship with Jörg.

Jacquine dropped down on the edge of the bed, patting Caitrina's hand. "He loves you so dearly. You should have seen him, sitting on your bedside. He talks to you, even when you are not awake to hear his words of affection."

Caitrina felt her cheeks heat. What had Jörg said in the carriage? *A hundred times a day...a thousand different ways.*

"What things?" she whispered. "Oh please, Jacquine. You must tell me."

Her maid laughed heartily. "Lord Schmeidt talks of his love for you in terms of forever—forever before and forever more. 'Tis poetry to hear it." Jacquine sighed, pressing a hand to her heart.

Caitrina's heart fluttered at the thought. "I wish I could have heard it," she admitted wistfully.

"I am certain he will say it again."

"What else did he say?" she asked urgently.

Jacquine's face lit. "Promises, mi'lady. Lord Schmeidt made so many promises. He would do nearly anything for you."

Caitrina looked at her hand sadly. "I care little about such things, Jacquine. You know I do not. Jacque offered me as much."

She shook her head. "No, mi'lady. Not furs and jewels. He makes promises for your happiness."

"My happiness?" Caitrina asked uncertainly.

Jacquine nodded. "What would you have of him? He would do anything your heart desires if it would make you smile. What is your fondest wish? You have but to tell him, and it is yours."

Caitrina darkened, as her body made her desires known. *I must be depraved.* "I should like to eat and to see Jörg."

"We will dress you and join the men downstairs."

She nodded, her heart light at seeing Jörg again. Washed and dressed, Caitrina fairly ran to the common room. She nodded to Martin as he stood to greet her, standing on tiptoe to search for Jörg over the heads of the other men.

"You are well, mi'lady?" he asked.

"Yes, Martin. Very well. Where is my Lord Jörg?"

"Ridden on, mi'lady. He will meet us when we stop for the evening meal."

Her heart sank. "Why?" *He promised not to leave me. Are all his promises worth so little?*

"Your safety is most urgent to him. Lord Schmeidt chances nothing, even to me."

Caitrina nodded and took his arm, allowing Martin to lead her to a table. A girl set out a hearty meal for her before Caitrina could catch her breath to ask for what she brought. Caitrina ate a bit, reminding herself that it would be many long hours with little more than bread, cheese, and water in the carriage before they would stop for another meal.

She chided herself. Jörg promised not to leave her, but it was childish to expect him to coddle her. She couldn't expect that a man of his station would sit with her and hold her hand every moment of the day—to love her at every private moment.

Caitrina ran all the loving words Jörg said to her over and over in her mind. He'd talked about always loving her, loving her from forever past. *Do you remember?* Jörg had asked her that in the garden. What had there been for Caitrina to remember then?

A chill raced up her spine, and she turned, catching the barest flash of black at the edges of her vision. Then it was gone. Caitrina searched the room fearfully, sure that something had been close behind her moments before.

"Is there a problem, mi'lady?" Martin asked, setting down a warm tea for her.

"I thought— No, Martin. I am sure it was just my imagination."

Martin did not seem so convinced.

Chapter Ten

Jörg walked in the deep shadows beneath the trees. The sun was not fully set, and it hurt to look at it directly, but he was no first-turned fool. Jörg could walk about on darkly overcast days or in deep shadow with only a niggling unease that he was doing so. Few of his kind could stand sunlight of any kind, but Jörg had never truly been like another of his kind...except Pauwel.

He shook away the memories of Regana's second husband. Of all the mistakes and horrid choices Jörg had made over the years, turning Pauwel Lord Crossbearer had been one of his worst. Jörg's only salvation that night had been Pauwel's love for Regana. Pauwel had printed on her as Jörg had. The printing alone had allowed them to retain one thing no other beast did...their kind emotions.

At moments, like the time Jörg spent in Caitrina's arms or at her bedside, he praised the depth of the love he was capable of. At others, he saw it for what it was, the gods' harshest torture for him.

Even as a Cursed Warrior, printing and madness walked arm in arm. A Warrior who lost his mate too late in printing, who waited too long to claim his mate, whose mate was endangered, or who found himself widowed was apt to go mad and have to be killed by his brothers to protect Warriors and humans alike.

Jörg knew all the madness a Warrior could feel in that regard intimately. While a Cursed Warrior knew he would never love again and sought solace in that fact when he was widowed, Jörg was well and truly damned. He had no such assurances.

So far, Regana's incarnations had lain dead in his arms five times. Five times, his printing had sent him through the fires of his loss...four times, the madness of losing yet knowing her soul would call for him again.

Her death had been at Jörg's hands only in Regana's first incarnation. The next four had died because of his failure to protect them fully from humans, beasts, and Warriors alike. Still, Jörg felt the guilt of their loss as if he had stopped their hearts himself.

He'd loved them all—Regana, Marie, Andaswintha, Syrith, and Ilona. He loved them still. The loving was a form of madness. The losing was worse.

Her voice caught his attention, and Jörg moved toward Caitrina faster than any man or Warrior could travel. The sun was nearly gone, the last red rays a halo around her. Jörg strode toward Caitrina, ignoring the itching and burning of his sensitive eyes.

He also ignored the look of stunned disbelief Martin shot him for such folly. No one but Regana could entice Jörg to walk into even a weak sun.

Caitrina looked up at him, blushing prettily as she met his gaze. Jörg hardened at the unspoken invitation in the depths of her blue eyes, at the subtle change of her scent on the breeze between them.

He sank to the cloth beside her, laying a kiss on her jaw below her ear. "Good evening, *Geliebte*. You are well?"

She lifted a sliver of meat to his mouth, and Jörg took it with a look that promised feasting of another sort. He savored the offered treat with only the slightest pang that it could not sustain him as completely as it once had.

Jörg had taken blood that morning, a small amount from a whore two towns from where he'd left Caitrina and his men to supplement the mouthfuls he'd taken from Matthew and from the whores he'd given to his men. Jörg would not have to eat again for more than a day.

Caitrina laughed as he sucked at her fingers, taking the next bit of food from her hand. "I am well," she assured him.

He shook his head as she offered a bit of cheese. "You eat. You should keep up your strength."

She swallowed, turning slightly from Jacquine to hide the depth of her blush. "Will you join me in the carriage now?" she asked hopefully.

Jörg raised her hand to his lips and kissed Caitrina's knuckles gently, each in turn. "Would that please you, my love?"

"Yes," she admitted. "It would please me very much."

"Then no force beneath the stars could drag me from your side." *Beneath the stars.* Only the sun could drive him away from her, and so he could not make that promise to her.

Caitrina nodded, quiet though her mind was crowded with disconcerted thoughts tumbling one over the other.

He stood. "Come, dear one. If you are finished dining, we will depart."

She nodded, allowing Jörg to draw her up with him. Caitrina motioned her servant to the second carriage, then moved on without waiting for a response.

Jörg closed the flaps and curtains Jacquine had opened for the day, turning to Caitrina. He sank beside her, needing to understand what upset her, yet not being able to unravel the twist of emotions holding her fast.

Scattered images from this life and others assaulted her. Visions of Warriors, past and present, worried her.

He searched Caitrina's eyes and her mind. Had she seen a Warrior this day? No. Just something that reminded her of them. Jörg relaxed slightly.

Caitrina didn't give him a chance to question her. She turned to him, searching out Jörg's mouth urgently, pulling at his surcote and tunic. Jörg groaned, his cock responding frantically to a heated encounter he had not seen the likes of since Regana's first incarnation. She was willing in a way that she hadn't been since before he'd left her.

No. Not willing. Caitrina is panicked.

He eased back, meeting her eyes while the beast within him howled for completion. Jörg wasn't the heartless bastard who thought only of his own pleasure anymore. He touched her lips, shaking his head slowly.

"Tell me, Caitrina. What is troubling you?" he whispered.

Outside, Martin let out a piercing whistle. The carriage lurched forward and then started to rock gently.

"Please, tell me," he repeated.

Caitrina's eyes were full of pain and confusion. "How do I know you, Jörg? What is this trust? This..." She launched on, just as he opened his mouth to answer. "What are these memories you ask of me?"

Jörg took a calming breath and put his arms out to her in invitation. Caitrina hesitated, then crawled onto his lap and into his arms.

"We have... We have known each other for many lifetimes," he began.

"Blasphemy," Caitrina gasped.

"No. Search your heart. You know me. You have always known me, Caitrina."

She stared at him, looking lost and confused. Caitrina brushed her lips over his again, teasing and nipping at him.

"Caitrina," he groaned. "I want you to understand."

"I understand this," she insisted quietly. "This doesn't confuse me."

Jörg fought back a wave of nausea. "Not this time," he decided. "You won't believe this is all there is between us this time."

"How do you remember—? You do remember these past lives. Don't you?"

He nodded. Yes, Jörg remembered every detail, good and bad, in searing clarity. He couldn't drink it away, fuck it away, or die to find peace—not until his Stone-ordained murderer took him in battle.

"Tell me," she begged. "Please tell me about us."

Gods alive! How could he even begin to tell her all there was? "Your name in the first life we shared was Regana. We grew up together, only two seasons apart in age. Our lands lay aside one another. I was a Warrior, and you were strong and bold as one. You asked to be a Warrior, but women were not permitted to be Warriors."

Caitrina laid her head on his chest, playing her fingers in Jörg's surcote. Her mind stopped its insistent rioting to take in the tale of her life.

"We were lovers, secretly because we were not permitted to wed."

"Why?" Her voice was sad, as if she remembered the agony of waiting for the day they would be allowed to commit to each other openly.

"As a Warrior, it was against our laws for me to wed until our enemy was vanquished. I was mad with wanting you." *So mad that I was brutal in claiming you, and still you loved me.* "If we had been caught, I would have been executed by our laws for laying hands on you."

"Did we ever marry?"

"No. Some of my brother Warriors learned that I was your lover." He paused, at a loss to continue into his greatest shame, his most damning crimes.

Caitrina pushed back, tears pooling in her eyes, pale, shaking her head in disbelief. "They killed you." Her voice shook in anger. "They killed you because of me."

"No. Never because of you," he soothed her. "I pursued you. You agreed only because you knew I was nearly mad in needing you."

She fisted her hand in his clothing. "They killed you," she repeated.

"No. They did worse than that. They threatened to have you killed unless I stole something they wanted from our temple. They made me a traitor. I allowed it to save—

"Afterward, I was dead to our people." *And damned to this half-life.* "I had nothing to offer you. They would have killed you if you came to me. My home was destroyed and my lands taken. I was hunted—and hated." *I was feared. You feared me.*

"You left me." Caitrina didn't ask it. She remembered that much clearly. The pain and confusion of those days washed over her.

"Yes," he admitted. "I was a fool."

"And my other lifetimes?" she asked.

"I was clumsy. I would find you only to lose you, but I never left you again. Perhaps, I should have...some of the times we met. I am dangerous to you."

"No," she gasped. "You cannot leave me."

Jörg smiled weakly. "I cannot. I cannot stomach the thought of it." *I am printed to you. I cannot stomach hurting you in any way. I would die if you asked me—if it would make you happy. If I could.*

Caitrina nodded and sank into his arms, exhausted.

"Sleep," he whispered, sending the command to her battered mind. Jörg sighed as she relaxed in his arms. He stroked the hair from her cheek.

I did not lie. I told her the truth.

{Not the whole truth. You know you didn't tell her everything.}

I cannot. You know I cannot tell her everything.

{You have always been a beast.}

Yes. I have.

* * * *

Jörg stood over her, his face a study in fury. She backed from him, terrified, running her hands over the baby she carried—her son.

Andris. His name is Andris.

"You carry his child," Jörg spat, his hands fisted in fury.

Caitrina weaved in dizziness. Words passed between them that had no meaning, angry words in a strange language that she did yet did not understand...pleading, shouting.

The internal thoughts were easier to understand, more primal and urgent.

I have to hide the truth. He cannot know. He will destroy me if he knows the truth. Why will he not leave? He must know Pauwel comes. I have asked him to go, but Jörg will not.

"If I hadn't chosen damnation, would you have been mine for the choosing?" he demanded.

"I don't—"

Kethe. I cannot tell him the truth in front of Kethe, though I should tell him that small truth.

She met his eyes, her heart aching at the choice she had to make. *I cannot lie to Jörg about this.*

{You must. This beast is not the Jörg you loved. He is mad, and he will kill you.}

He will kill me either way for this. "No," she whispered. "I would not."

Jörg's face went cold as stone, his once-beautiful eyes frightening in their intensity. He threw a piece of clothing at her, and she recoiled as if the thing were a poisonous viper.

"I understand," he commented without inflection. There was no love in him, no tenderness. For some reason, that didn't surprise her.

You don't. Please, you don't understand. Why did I not tell him the truth?

{Because, he would kill both you and Pauwel for it.}

"I will leave your home, Lady Kreuzträger. There is nothing for me here. There never was. May you never live long enough to know what that is like."

He disappeared with dizzying speed. Caitrina sank to the stone floor, shaking and shedding bitter tears.

What have I done? It was only me he wanted. Now he will kill everything I love.

* * * *

Caitrina stiffened in Jörg's arms, pushing him away, sobs wracking her body. He cradled her, whispering calming words as she burrowed her face in his chest. Caitrina calmed, her sobs tapering off to hitching breaths.

"What is it?" Jörg asked. He prayed he was wrong. There were too many memories that would destroy their budding relationship.

"I betrayed you. I lied to you and made you think I didn't love you when I did."

"You didn't. I know you didn't." Jörg knew all of Regana's secrets from his fatal feeding. She had only done what he'd forced her to do, what she had to do to survive.

"I did," she insisted miserably. "I remember it."

Jörg took a calming breath. "Tell me what you remember."

"You were furious. You wanted to know that I had once loved you, and I lied to you. I watched you hurt, and I did nothing to stop it. I was— I betrayed you. I was pregnant to another man."

He shook his head. "No. You do not remember everything. It was a scene out of the context of your life."

"I took another man. I know I did."

Jörg nodded. "Lifetimes ago. That was your first lifetime."

A tear traced down her cheek. "I betrayed you."

"Never. I was dead to you, a traitor to our people. You married another man. You had no choice."

Her mind was muddled in confusion. She seemed to have problems forming the questions warring in her mind. "I was forced to marry? I didn't love the man?" she whispered hopefully.

Jörg grimaced. She knew she'd loved Pauwel. "In time, you grew to love him. Pauwel was a good man. He was kind and attentive, all the things I had not learned to be yet." He wiped away her tears, his heart aching. "Had I not left you, you would not have been forced to marry him."

"Why did I marry a man I did not love? Was it arranged by my father?"

"Your father and mother were both dead. Gawen— your brother and Pauwel sought to save your life."

"Why? What had I done?"

He hesitated. The truth would be difficult for her to hear—even more difficult for him to admit.

"Please, Jörg," she begged.

"The child was not your husband's. He was mine. You would have been killed for... I was a traitor," he reminded her.

"I lied to you. I didn't tell you. Did I?"

He shook his head. "I found out in time."

Not in time. I nearly killed Pauwel to learn the truth from him, in my fury and arrogance, believing I was best for you despite all evidence to the contrary. I turned him to give you back the one who was better.

Jörg couldn't bring himself to admit that much to her.

Caitrina paled. "I was selfish. Wasn't I?"

"It was the only way to save our son," he assured her.

"Andris," she whispered. "His name was Andris."

"Yes. He was a beautiful child—and a strong man."

He was gone too soon, killed by one of my damned brethren at the tender age of thirty-three. Andris never knew me. I never held him tenderly, mad enough to attempt feeding from him the night he became a Warrior lord to give him the truth of his parentage. Was I ever more than a beast?

Caitrina raised her hands, tangling them in the hair at the back of his neck. "And you loved me still," she noted.

"I have always loved you, even when you feared me."

Her eyes widened. "Why did I fear you?"

His heart stuttered. Caitrina remembered that she'd feared him, but she viewed it with only a burning curiosity. Regana's souls had always had an amazing capacity to forgive.

"You saw what a beast I could be," he admitted quietly. "I have not always made choices that were good ones where you are concerned. I have hurt you."

Caitrina shook her head. "You are not that man in this life. You are not a beast," she whispered. She drew Jörg's mouth down to hers, opening herself to his kiss.

Jörg fisted his hands in the back of her gown, fighting the urge to tear it from her body. Caitrina met his advances, lost in a firestorm of their shared need. Her hands skimmed down his chest and dragged up at his tunic and surcote. She freed his cock from the confines of his breeches, stroking his length as she continued to meet his mouth.

She pried one of his hands from the back of her dress and urged it to her mound. Jörg tossed her skirts into her lap, shuddering as she moaned into his mouth.

Her body was hot and wet, clenching tight on his probing fingers. Caitrina bowed up to him, forcing his hand deeper, her mouth leaving his.

"Now," she gasped. "Please, Jörg."

He growled, lifting her astride his lap facing away from him. Caitrina guided him into her core, crying out as his cock stretched her near-virgin sheath. Jörg stilled, reining in the urge to pound into her until he filled her with all his body had to give.

Caitrina shifted, planting her palms on his knees to lever her body up and down on his length. "Jörg, I want you. I want all of you."

Jörg leaned forward, cupping his hands over her breasts. He thrust deep, drinking in her breathless pleading for more. His body burned, and his control

105

melted away. Jörg thrust again and again, faster with every encouragement from Caitrina.

The hunger came on him hard and fast, his fangs lengthening as the beast demanded fulfillment. Jörg nuzzled her hair, taking the delicate lobe of her ear in his mouth and scraping his teeth over it. Caitrina tipped her head, granting him greater access to her, trusting him utterly with her body. If only she knew the restraint she asked of him.

"I want to remember," Caitrina whispered. "You've done—"

Jörg closed his eyes as hazy half-memories of his feeding on the hillside over her garden filtered into her mind. She remembered. How could she possibly remember these things?

"In the garden, what did you do, Jörg?" Her voice was dreamy, thick in passion.

He moaned as her arousal at those half-memories of his feeding filled his mind. Jörg kissed her throat, the need to taste her almost overpowering his common sense. "Why must you hurt yourself? Many of those memories are horrible things," he reminded her. "Let me build us new memories worth remembering."

"I am not whole without them," she reasoned. "I want to know them. I don't want to be haunted by dreams that I do not understand."

Jörg nodded. She would be. Her past lives would crowd in on her, no matter what he did to try and stem the flow.

He pulled her dress and underdress over her head and settled his mouth on the column of her neck, kissing at her skin, stroking her with his tongue. His teeth pierced her, and he wiped away her pain as she'd barely acknowledged it.

Jörg tasted her, her sweet arousal making his head spin. He forced his mind to his purpose. He couldn't drink too deeply. Feeding not only depleted her, but it drew Warriors to him. Jörg suckled weakly, taking only a trickle of her blood to keep the active link open.

He sent their earliest memories; their carefree days as children, some from his memory and some from hers. It was a montage of running and climbing trees, hunting and games, playing while the older Warriors trained, sleeping together in the dirt to the sound of weapons ringing out.

Caitrina gasped at the memory of their blood oath. "We will wed no one but each other," she repeated sadly.

"*You had no choice,*" he assured her.

"Show me the first time you loved me," she requested as he sped through images of Regana watching his training as a Cursed Warrior.

"*No. Please do not ask this of me.*"

"Please," she whispered.

He sent her images of his mounting madness to put his barbaric possession in context. Jörg had watched her, shivered at the sound of her voice, burned for her every waking moment, and dreamed of her every night.

Jörg groaned at the memory of their first kiss beneath their tree. That long-ago Jörg pressed her hard into the ground, stealing her breath and stilling her struggle.

He closed his eyes, unable to wash away the memory of pulling at her clothing, of muting her cry of pain as her barrier tore to his first thrust. She should have turned him over to Gawen that day. It would have been better for Regana and for everyone else if she had.

Why did she forgive me?

"*I am sorry.*" Jörg wanted to say much more, but there were no words to wash away the depth of his guilt. He rocked in Caitrina gently, all too aware of the brutal thrusts of the memory-Jörg in Regana for his own comfort.

The end came quickly, explosively. The memory-Jörg climaxed...then continued, taking her again while she lay stunned and trembling beneath him, issuing his weak excuses of printing and mad protestations of love.

Caitrina rippled around him, screaming his name. Jörg found himself drawn over with her, his cock pulsing as he poured himself into her.

"*I am a bastard,*" he berated himself. "*To find pleasure not once but twice in that.*"

"You needed me," Caitrina whispered. "This printing— You were going mad."

"*You could always forgive.*" Jörg cradled her to his chest. "*I can take away—*"

"No. Take nothing from me. Let there be no lies between us. Please, Jörg."

He closed the punctures, sick at the possibilities of leaving Caitrina with the memory of what he was.

{How had you expected to hide it from her? With more feeding? With other forays re-writing her memories to suit you?}

I do not know. I never considered how I would hide it.

Caitrina eased off of his lessening cock. Jörg let her go, his eyes averted and his heart pounding.

If she turned from him, he couldn't stand it. He'd let her go once. He'd given her to Pauwel and walked away. Jörg wasn't capable of such restraint a second time.

She turned toward him slowly. Jörg steadied her in the swaying carriage, though he didn't seek out her gaze. He cleaned her blood from his mouth with a thought, unwilling to let her see the evidence of what he was.

"You know what I am," he breathed, bracing himself for her damning words, for her anger and hurt at his deception.

Caitrina dropped to his lap again, her tiny hands on his shoulders. She tipped his chin up until their gazes locked. "You said that before, and I turned from you?"

He nodded. Why hadn't Caitrina turned from him yet? Any sane woman would. Even Regana had been smart enough to run from him.

No. She tried to accept me. I pushed her away and made a show of what I was to drive her from my side and to the perceived safety of her brother.

{One of the few smart things you ever did where she was concerned.}

Jörg nodded again at the truth of the matter.

"This is what they did to you? How they damned you? You have not lived lifetimes as I have, have you? For you, this is the same lifetime as the one you shared with her."

"Yes. I am a traitor to everything I once defended, and I will not die in the normal sense of the word."

"You are not a traitor to me. Promise me you will show me everything, good and bad."

"Caitrina, you do not know what you ask of me."

"Everything," she insisted.

"I cannot."

"It is the only way."

"I stole everything from you. I killed you," he pleaded. "Do not ask me to show you that."

She paled. "I want to know. Show me."

Jörg touched her face, stroking the baby-smooth skin of her cheek. "I will show you, and I will take back from you whatever you wish me to take back."

"Now?"

"No. It is too soon. Even when I take little from you, the loss weakens you."

"How often can you open new memories to me?"

"If I take as lightly as I did tonight, I can return your memories in short sessions...every five or six days."

"Then that is what we will do," she decided.

"As you wish, dear one."

Chapter Eleven

November 28th, 1497

Caitrina moved against his body, pulling Jörg's mouth tighter to her breast. Still, he taunted her, bathing the nipple in his mouth without piercing her skin.

She had requested that he use her breast today. It was her favorite means of experiencing the feeding.

Jörg hadn't used her throat since the first time he gave her back memories. She hadn't cared as much for the use of her shoulder, so he had only used it to feed once.

His favorite was using her inner thigh, pleasuring her to climax with his mouth, then stroking her core with his insistent fingers while he took her blood and returned her life to her. Caitrina liked that form best when she lay over him, giving Jörg pleasure while he took her, but he said that the distraction of climaxing in her mouth while he fed was too much a danger to do on a regular basis.

"Jörg," she reminded him. "You have put this off for a week. It is time."

"Let me love you," he begged.

"It is no different this time," she soothed him.

Jörg slid up her body. "It is different."

"Because I will see my death?"

"At my hands," he growled.

Caitrina traced the tense line of his jaw. "I have had lifetimes to dull the pain. I have the gift of knowing your suffering, of knowing how many times over you have paid for every mistake." She'd reminded Jörg of that over and over, but it never seemed to dispel his soul-deep fear that she would turn from him.

"Caitrina, you must understand how hard this will be for me—and for you."

She kissed him, her eyes fluttering closed as his passion grew. Caitrina encouraged his ardor. Jörg's resistance to showing Caitrina her life always seemed to crumble when his passions were inflamed.

Jörg managed to control his need to possess her without reason only until she made it clear that such a mating was what she wanted. When she did that, the man knew no reason or restraint. He was fevered need unleashed, tireless and intent on nothing short of complete servitude to her whims.

Caitrina stroked his length, hot and heavy in her hand. He jerked, hissing out his breath as he fought to rein in his desires. The tips of his fangs peeked from behind his upper lip, not fully extended but responding as they always did to her offer of allowing Jörg complete mastery of her body and blood.

"You want me," she whispered. "You want my mouth wrapped around your cock while you take my blood. Tell me."

Jörg's nostrils flared. His fangs extended minutely. "Yes," he admitted. "You know I do." He captured her mouth, teasing her lips and tongue with the scrape of his teeth.

"Mi'lady," Jacquine gasped.

Caitrina's eyes flew open. Jörg stilled. His teeth retreated as he forced them back. Jörg offered her a sad smile. They had always been careful. He had always encouraged Jacquine to sleep when he came to Caitrina at her rooms at an inn.

She looked to him in confusion. Had Jörg simply been distracted and forgotten, or was this a plan to avoid the memories he was to grant her?

Jörg grimaced, a sure sign that he was guilty of trying to evade her. He nodded once. "I will be gentle," he whispered as he brushed his lips over hers.

Caitrina turned as he rose from the bed. Jacquine's face paled, and she moved from foot to foot. Her eyes shifted from Caitrina to Jörg's cock and back.

"Look at me, Jacquine," Jörg ordered quietly.

Her maid met his eyes and stilled, color flooding her cheeks.

Jörg stepped to her silently, staring down into her face. "My order to keep her away is strong, but I can only reorder her memory of this in one way."

Caitrina stroked a nipple absently, her body heating at the prospect of watching Jörg feed. "Do what you must."

Jörg shuddered, pushing Jacquine's shift from her shoulder. Caitrina eased to one side, her breath hitching as his fangs extended. He lowered his head, finding the artery in Jacquine's shoulder. His cock bobbed in sexual excitement as Jacquine laid her head back on the wall with a sigh.

Caitrina bit her lip, her body responding fiercely to the sight of Jörg feeding, to the knowledge that he found such arousal in the act. She slid her hand down her stomach, fingering in the well of her body slowly. Scattered images of sexual fantasies danced in her mind.

"Hurry, Jörg," she invited. The sooner he came to her and released the tension building in his body, the better.

He pulled back, leaving the wound open, her blood making a lazy track down Jacquine's shoulder. Jörg ran his tongue through it. "What do you want?" he asked in a rough voice.

Caitrina shook her head in confusion. Her hand stilled. "I don't understand."

"You like to watch," he mused. Jörg licked the blood welling up again, closing his eyes and groaning his enjoyment of the act.

She gasped as his meaning became clear, yanking her hand away from her body angrily. "No. Send her away."

Jörg nodded, closing the wounds. Caitrina crossed her arms over her breasts, abruptly jealous of his handling of her maid. He sent Jacquine out of the room and returned to the bed, staring at the ceiling with a furrowed brow as if he was truly lost.

"I would offer you almost anything you desire," Jörg assured her.

"I do not desire you to—to be intimate with another woman," she stated in exasperation. "How could you think—?"

He raised her fingers to his mouth, rasping his tongue over the drying slick of her juices. "What were you thinking, Caitrina?"

She blushed. Caitrina had considered touching him while Jörg took Jacquine's blood. She had toyed with the idea of going to her knees and taking his cock in her mouth while he did. She groaned at some of the thoughts she'd had about the three of them.

Jörg nodded. "You wanted her to watch me take you, maybe to—"

Caitrina placed a shaking hand over his mouth. She knew what mad thoughts had wandered her mind those few moments.

He kissed her fingers and moved her hand away. "I could not be sure what you wanted," he continued miserably. "I would do almost anything you wish."

She felt her fury spike again. He shouldn't want such things. It wasn't right. Jörg was hers alone. "Would you have been so quick if it was another man I wanted?" she challenged. Unbidden, Etienne of Kaufmann's face loomed in her mind.

Jörg rose up over her on the bed, his eyes glowing red in anger. "No," he stated simply. "I would not." His muscles were tense, though he made no move against her.

Caitrina pulled Jörg over her, seeking his mouth. "I want you. I don't want another, and I don't want you to take another." She pulled at his buttocks, urging Jörg into her body.

He filled her in a single thrust, holding her hips to him. "Is this what you want?" Jörg breathed, his body setting a rhythm that made her ache for him all the more.

"You know what I want."

"This is not safe. If I feed again so soon, Warriors will converge on us."

"I must know."

"Then we must leave directly after," he decided.

"As you wish."

Jörg suckled at her breast. Caitrina squirmed beneath him, eager to feel his complete possession.

His teeth scraped over her skin. "You are sure you want this?" he asked.

"Yes. Show me."

His fangs sank deep, the burning dissolving into the intense pleasure that stole her breath. Jörg's mouth worked at her breast, his tongue playing at her nipple while he took all he needed from her at once.

"Show me, Jorg."

"*Your pleasure first. Give me this.*"

"Yes."

Jörg took her faster, his mouth insistent at her breast. When she shattered, he sent memories to her sex-muddled mind as his seed heated her aching body.

It came at her in a rush, the details he feared. Regana had begged him to kill her, all but killed him to force him to the act. Jörg had relented, killing her painlessly and with orgasmic pleasure. He'd held Regana until long after she was no more, though he'd been bleeding to death from the wounds she'd inflicted on him. His scream of loss as he was forced to ground by the beast within him was shattering, tortured.

As the blackness took the Jörg in her memories, it took her as well. "*Do not leave me,*" she begged. "*I couldn't bear to lose you.*"

"*Never.*"

* * * *

Jörg carried the bundle of his bride to the carriage, nodding to Martin. To his surprise, the human followed him in.

"There is a problem?" Jörg asked, settling Caitrina on the seat.

116

"Warriors. We have seen them skulking about. They seem to be waiting for something."

Jörg nodded. "They wait for Etienne Lord Kaufmann. They do not dare attack without him."

"You invite this confrontation?"

He hesitated, looking at Caitrina miserably. No. He did not invite this confrontation. Jörg would never willingly put Caitrina in the hands of the one who would be Pauwel.

"Jörg?"

"Of course not," he snapped. "But, it will come. No matter how I avoid it, it will come for us."

"Why do you invite it now? Why, when we cannot possibly defend our position?"

I have no choice. If Caitrina needs this to accept our life together, I will give it.

{You could refuse her until you reach safety.}

No. I cannot refuse her. I never could. Such is my madness.

"We move," Jörg ordered. He turned his face to the rain blowing in. "It will be more difficult for them to follow in this. Arrange for food. We stop for nothing but the ladies' comfort for at least two days."

"Feeding?" Martin asked solemnly.

Jörg shook his head. "I fed deeply tonight. I will not require it for several days."

"If you do..." Martin let the offer hang between them. Of all Jörg's bought humans, Martin would offer the last drop of his blood and beat of his heart to sustain Jörg if it came to that.

"Not from you," he promised. "Not from anywhere within twenty leagues of our course."

Martin nodded grimly. "I will guard her when the time comes."

"Only if my life depends on it. Otherwise, it is my battle. You know that."

He nodded. "I will live my vow, Jörg. You have certainly lived yours."

"I know you will, my brother. I know you will." *Though it will mean your death.*

Chapter Twelve

December 1st, 1497

Caitrina nestled her cheek to Jörg's chest, drinking in the scent of him. She looked around in confusion at the sunlight peeking at the edges of the heavy drapes over the window flaps.

She shook him frantically. "Jörg! You must wake up. You must go to ground. It is day."

"I will not leave you," he grumbled, unwilling to leave the depths of his day sleep.

"It is not overcast. The rain has gone, and the day is bright." Even on cloudy days, Jörg burrowed his exposed skin under a cloak or quilt when she opened the carriage door to take comfort.

"Your protection..." He yawned.

"You can do nothing about that. I have heard you speaking to Martin. You need the healing soil, but you have forsaken it for me. Please, take your proper rest— for me."

"Caitrina," he growled in warning. Jörg was always out of sorts when his day sleep was disturbed.

"You haven't had healing sleep in three days," she argued. He'd only left her the night before to feed when Martin pointed out his weakness to Jörg. "The Warriors are near, and you must be rested when they come for us."

Jörg's eyes opened wide as the carriage lurched to a halt. "Oh, no. They waited for the sun."

"Hold them," Martin thundered. The sounds of men shouting and blade on blade fighting snuck through the thick drapes.

Caitrina shook her head in disbelief. "You must go." But, how could he go when the sun was so bright? "You can fight them, but you cannot fight the sun."

He nodded miserably, listening to the clang of sword on sword. Jörg pulled her underdress over her head and drew his cloak around her shoulders as she poked her arms through the fitted sleeves. He laid a fierce kiss on her lips.

"Do not accept anything but sustenance from them," Jörg instructed. "Remember their laws. They may not injure you, molest you— Tell them, and they will keep their distance."

"And if they do not?" she asked nervously. Caitrina had no doubts that young Franz would not hesitate to break the laws of his people.

His eyes flashed an angry red. "The suffering I rain down on them will know no equal." Jörg stroked her cheek. "I do not leave you. You know I will come for you."

Caitrina nodded. "Go before it is too late."

She turned in dismay as the door swung wide, squinting against the glare. *Too late.* Caitrina braced herself for a scream of pain from Jörg, for his agony as the sun seared him.

The scream came, but it was one of fury from the figure silhouetted in the doorway.

Caitrina turned, laughing nervously. Jörg had gone, disappeared as the Warriors outside her home had done.

She sent her thanks to God, then sobered. Would her God approve of Jörg? Perhaps so. Jörg was more honorable than many Christian men she'd met were, and God loved all his creations, even the ones who lived off the meat of others.

She screamed in fright as the man grasped her arm and dragged Caitrina from the carriage. She stumbled into Jacquine's arms, gasping at the destruction around them. All their guards lay dead. Caitrina sobbed at the loss. Martin and Matthew—all of them had been good, decent men. Jörg didn't take men who were not morally sound into his employ. Now they were all gone, slaughtered by these misguided fools.

"Gone," the man holding her arm barked. "The damned beast escaped somehow."

Caitrina straightened her spine and glared at Franz. "I will thank you to take your filthy hands off me, Warrior. You do have laws," she reminded him coldly.

The boy recoiled as if she'd burned him. He wiped his hand on his black tunic, a look of disgust on his face. She met his eyes steadily; refusing to show the slightest discomfort though the near-frozen, wet ground made her feet burn in protest.

She gasped in surprise as Franz was nudged aside. Etienne took his place, his large body—almost as large as Jörg's—filling her field of vision. The lord's eyes were darkened with some emotion she couldn't name. Caitrina backed into Jacquine's arms.

Etienne nodded, tipping her chin up. "No more than twice," he mused.

Caitrina wrapped her arms over her chest as the big man ripped Jörg's cloak from her body and tossed it away. She shivered, her nipples making points against her arms, but not in arousal. She dodged his hands as he reached for her again, but Etienne was faster.

He dragged her underdress off of her left shoulder, then her right. Etienne touched the spot where Jörg had taken blood, finding the faint marks flawlessly. His eyes narrowed. He moved his gaze over her body, settling on her crossed arms. Etienne met her eyes, his jaw tight in fury.

Caitrina shook her head in understanding. "No," she pleaded. "Your laws—" She shivered in a cold wind, her breath coming in tiny cloud puffs between them, rushing from between half-numb lips that trembled in fear.

Etienne pulled the cloak from his shoulders and wrapped it around her.

"No," she protested, trying to push it off. *Nothing but sustenance.* Jörg had said to accept nothing more from them.

He grasped her wrists in one of his hands, yanking the cloak closed over her body again. "You will freeze," Etienne growled at her.

Caitrina glanced at Jörg's cloak, but it was half-sunk in a deep puddle of mud. She nodded, holding back tears. She had to stay alive until Jörg came for her.

Etienne swung her over his broad shoulder, mounted his horse, and settled Caitrina across his lap. "Bring the maid," he ordered Franz. He didn't wait for his nephew's answer before urging his horse on, cradling Caitrina into the shelter of his body.

* * * *

Etienne Lord Kaufmann watched as Caitrina sipped the warmed wine he'd offered her. He couldn't seem to stop watching her.

It was the most disconcerting thing he'd ever encountered. Etienne wanted her in a way he'd never wanted a woman, a deep, primal urge to have her. Never had anything caused his mind to wander from his duty as she did, and he had no idea why that would be.

Dealing with Caitrina was difficult in the extreme. She refused the amulet violently, leaving Etienne the choice of releasing her or allowing the blood tie to lead Veriel in.

The Mad Elder would come for her. There was no question about that. The beast was fixated in a way that beasts did not fixate. Etienne needed to know why Veriel did. If he took on The Mad Elder, Etienne would need any knowledge of weaknesses he could get.

She confused him. Caitrina de Leon held herself straight and proud. Though Etienne had seen the proof of the beast's foul use of her, she was unbroken of spirit, suffering no noticeable emotional stresses from prolonged humiliation as one might assume she would.

Veriel had doubtless taken her blood many times, but not enough to sustain himself. Caitrina was not blood weak from his use. She was barely pale despite his feeding. So, why did he continue to do it?

The beast had used her sexually. Caitrina had all but admitted it, though she would not permit Etienne to examine her for damage.

He fisted his hand in fury. He should have taken her that first morning when Caitrina was still confused, before she was enthralled by Veriel.

Etienne calmed himself. Veriel had used her sexually again and again, but Caitrina showed no signs of abuse or distress despite that use. It was not in a beast's nature to take release kindly. What was Veriel's game?

He glanced out the windowpanes. The sun would set soon. Etienne was running out of time to get the answers he needed.

Caitrina shrank from him as he strode to her. Etienne nodded to Franz, and the pup led the maid away. When they were gone, he turned to Caitrina.

"I only wish to protect you," he soothed her.

"And you kill my guards to accomplish that? They were good men, honest men."

Men who sold their souls into the service of a damned beast. Etienne crossed his arms over his chest.

Her eyes were full of pain at the memory of the men who'd died. "What did they do to injure you, Warrior?" she whispered.

"Etienne," he reminded her.

"I know who you are." Her eyes seemed guarded. What had the beast told her to make her mistrust him so?

Etienne squatted before her. "Who am I?"

"The one who would poison me to kill him. You are too late, Warrior. I know the truth this time."

"This time?"

She raised her chin in challenge.

"What truth?"

Caitrina met his eyes calmly. "You feel it. I know you do. You watch me. You will not win this time. I will not turn from him."

"Veriel—"

She stood, glaring at him. "Do not speak that foul name," she spat. "Your lies are wasted on me."

"What name should I use?" he asked curiously.

Caitrina threw her hands up in mute supplication to her God—or perhaps in frustration. "Would you use it?"

"Would it put you at ease if I did?" He didn't understand her upset. Etienne wished he did.

"Yes," she whispered. "Yes, it would."

"Then tell me the name."

"I have your vow?"

Etienne shifted nervously. He didn't want to give a vow for something he had no knowledge of, but he wanted to calm Caitrina more. "You have it."

"Jörg. His name is Jörg." She watched him for a reaction to that.

He rubbed a hand over the base of his skull. The beast was constrained from using that name. All the elders had been deemed unworthy of their human names. "He uses that name with you?"

"It is his name to use. The Stone never forbade him to use it, and so he does."

This conversation was getting Etienne no closer to the answers he needed, and arguing the point with her would only upset Caitrina. "What does he want with you?"

Caitrina paced the floor, her arms crossed over her breasts.

"He doesn't want you for a food source. He could have women sexually by the dozens."

She looked at him, trying to hide the pain in her eyes with an angry countenance. Her face flushed a vivid red that confirmed she wasn't blood weak.

"It is sex," he mused. *That makes no sense. Veriel takes what he wants. He has always taken what he wants.*

Caitrina stopped her pacing, looking at him in horror. "It is not," she insisted.

"Not—"

"How dare you! How dare you judge— Of course, I should have expected that, Warrior." Caitrina started pacing again, seeming more agitated.

"Ver—"

She glared at him, her blue eyes flashing over fury-dark cheeks, challenging him to say the forbidden name or to break his vow to use it.

"He is a beast, a killer."

"I *know* what Jörg is. It is you who does not."

"You know?" What did she know? What was this conviction?

Caitrina stopped, sending him a raised eyebrow.

Etienne put his hands up in a calming gesture. Upsetting her unnecessarily would be foolish. "All right. You know what he is, and I do not. You have certainly spent more time in his company," he groused. *Dear gods, she is enthralled with him.* "What does he want from you?"

"What does any man want?" she countered.

"You cannot carry his children," he informed her gently. Only a *Blutjagdfrau* could do that. If that beast had convinced Caitrina she would have a house full of babies—

Caitrina's eyes filled with pain. She bit back a grimace. She knew. Caitrina knew there would be no babies. Etienne felt for her, though her pain was misguided.

Her face hardened. "You believe that is the only worth a woman has?" she asked coldly.

"I never said that," he protested.

"You seem to feel that is what a man wants. Perhaps Jörg is simply a better man than you are. I should not have asked you to judge him by yourself."

Now, she was trying to provoke him. There could be no other reason for saying something so spiteful. Etienne took a calming breath and rose, crossing the room to her in three long strides. "Tell me what he wants with you."

"A wife. A companion. Love."

Etienne choked on his initial reply. "Ver— *It* has no kind emotions," he stormed. "Love means nothing to it. Marriage vows mean nothing. You—"

Caitrina slapped him, a jarring blow to his cheek. The resounding crack echoed off the walls. For a moment, they stared at each other, their breathing ragged.

"You mean nothing to him," Etienne continued gently. She had to hear that truth, even if Caitrina was too enthralled to believe him.

She drew her hand back to strike him again, and Etienne grasped her wrist gently but firmly. Caitrina tried to wrench her hand free, but he held his grip. Etienne stroked her wrist with the pad of his thumb, attempting to calm her while the connection was a gentle torture for him, scattering his intentions to the wind.

Caitrina watched his ministrations with wide eyes. She trembled, and her dark curls bounced as she shook her head. "No," she whispered. "Please."

Etienne released her, watching warily for another attack.

She rubbed her wrist with shaking fingers. "Your lies," she panted, "will get you killed. Give me a horse and set me free now, and I promise that Jörg will let you live. He will find me wherever you take me. You know he will."

Etienne nodded. Yes, the beast would find her, but he would take her back over Etienne's chilling corpse. "I am counting on it, mi'lady. Please, make yourself comfortable. Do not make me bind you."

Caitrina backed from him, sinking to the chair she'd fled earlier. She pulled his cloak around her body, looking uneasy for the first time.

Chapter Thirteen

Caitrina watched the coming night, trying to still her racing heart.

She knew who Etienne was. Jörg had confided that, in every lifetime, the principles returned to play their game again. Jacque had been the one known as Marclef in Regana's lifetime. She was Regana, and Etienne was Pauwel.

While she knew Etienne could not kill Jörg— She shivered, feeling the lord's eyes on her from his perch in the next room. Etienne could not kill Jörg, because he was of Haus Kaufmann, and the Warrior fated to kill Jörg was of Haus Jäger. She sighed.

There were still too many things that could go wrong, despite the fact that he could not best Jörg in battle. Etienne was a good man beneath the lies he was steeped in, but he was drawn to Caitrina. That made him a dangerous man. Etienne would never willingly let Jörg leave with her. If God was kind, Jörg would injure or kill Etienne. If He wasn't—Caitrina shuddered. Etienne would sooner kill her than let Caitrina choose Jörg. It had happened in a previous incarnation.

Caitrina's purpose here was simple. She was bait to draw Jörg into a trap, a slaughter. Jörg would not be so easy to trap. Of that, Caitrina was most heartily sure.

A swirling disturbance appeared in the room with her, and Caitrina launched toward it, knowing Jörg would hold her to his chest and take away this growing unease. Every moment in Etienne's company made her mind ache and her body itch with awareness of who he was. It was maddening to have memories of the souls of her two husbands.

She stopped abruptly, backing from the strange beast in shock. It was a beast. Caitrina was certain of that, but she was also certain that this beast meant her harm.

He had her by the arms before she could move out of his reach, or perhaps he moved faster than she could see as Jörg sometimes did. Caitrina screamed as he buried his face in her throat, drinking in her scent.

"Release her, Renald," Etienne barked.

Renald raised his head, smiling down at her, a cold smile that made Caitrina's heart skip in fear. She pulled at his grip ineffectually.

"Yes. You are the one," Renald purred. "He has waited centuries to find you."

Caitrina tried to wrench free again, desperate to escape his touch, but his hands were akin to iron manacles.

Etienne's voice came from just over her shoulder. "Release her or die, beast. You know that your assistance is the only reason I have let you live this long."

"Beasts are to her tastes," he taunted her. "Are we not, love?"

"No," Caitrina denied. Her breathing was strangled.

A dark blade passed between them and settled over Renald's heart. The beast released her, and Caitrina retreated to the chair.

Etienne nodded and backed toward her. "You could accept the amulet," he reminded her. "Renald could not touch you."

"Neither could Jörg," she snapped. "I want nothing from you."

"That is not true," he noted calmly. "You want my protection from this beast."

Caitrina's cheeks burned. She didn't bother to deny it. What was the point in lying when he could see the truth?

Etienne glanced at her and nodded in satisfaction. "What does the elder want with her? Tell me, Renald."

Caitrina rolled her eyes. Etienne still wouldn't call Jörg by name.

Renald smiled that same cold smile. "She is his wife."

"His intended," Etienne corrected, as if the distinction were leagues apart. "Why does he want to wed her?"

"No. Not his intended. His wife. How many lifetimes has it been, dear one? Does he still call you that? Dear one? *Geliebte*?"

Caitrina wiped away a tear. "Six," she whispered. "Six lifetimes, *you damned beast*." She slipped the curse out in the ancient language Regana had spoken in her lifetime, the language the Stone's texts were written in.

Etienne shot her a look of undisguised horror. "The Mad Deceiver had no wife," he argued weakly.

Renald laughed heartily. "He never told his brother Warriors that he had a wife, but he had one. He couldn't wait to sink his cock in her. Could he, dear one?"

"Who was his wife?"

The question was directed to Caitrina. She averted her gaze, uncomfortable with discussing her marriage

131

with the other man who would like to be her mate, who had been her mate in another time and place.

"Who was his wife?" Etienne demanded, his voice taking on an edge of warning.

"What does he call you?" Renald taunted her. "Do you know who you really are?"

She glared at him. "*If Jörg answers that question for me, you will not live to regret it.*"

"You do know," Renald mused. "Do you remember? I have heard that you actually remember your lives...Regana."

Etienne turned to her fully, his eyes wide in shock. "Have you the mark?" he asked in a hoarse voice.

Renald launched at him, taking advantage of Etienne's preoccupation with her.

"Etienne!" she screamed.

Caitrina blanched. Minutes ago, she'd hoped Jörg would kill Etienne, and now she was saving him. She shook her head, trying to reconcile her actions. She would be a fool to let Renald kill Etienne. Caitrina was safer with Etienne than she was with Renald. It was nothing more than that. It could not be.

She scrambled from the chair as Renald sliced Etienne's upper arm with a set of wicked-looking claws twice again the length of her fingers. The beast tore at the shoulder of her gown, as she grasped a sword sheathed in display on the wall. Caitrina turned back to him, ignoring the strange blade that was the same dark metal as Etienne's dagger. She also ignored the fact that the metal glowed an odd blue color in her hands.

Renald laughed. "You will be mine," he promised. "You know why I want you?"

She shook her head. Caitrina had never understood why beasts would pursue her. Regana had never understood it through any of her lives. She only knew that they did.

He reached for her, dodging her clumsy blow, and captured the sword between them. That trapped Caitrina between his body and the wall behind her. Renald was erect, his aroused member pressed painfully to her hip.

"You are the light we are all drawn to," he informed her. "Any of our kind would kill to possess you, Warrior or beast alike."

"Jörg is not like any of your kind," she noted defiantly.

Renald stilled, falling back from her. Caitrina took a hitching breath, her eyes locked on the dagger protruding from his back in relief.

Etienne rose, blood streaming down his arm. Caitrina stifled the urge to tend to his wound. The feeling was so elemental, it frightened her in its intensity.

He retrieved his weapon and closed on her, looking uncertain. She stiffened. He was even more dangerous now. If Etienne knew who she and Jörg were, he surely knew who he was, and he would be even more unwilling to release her.

"Caitrina, if you are Regana, you must let me protect you," he pleaded.

She shook her head. "No. I will not turn from him."

"I know what he wants from you now. He must keep you from your destiny. If you are Regana, you belong with the Warriors. You are a child of the Stone."

"Lies."

"You are in danger."

"From you," she accused. *Jörg will not harm me. He cannot harm me. I have seen it in his memories.* She backed away, shaking fiercely.

"From him. From—the one called Jörg. He will stop at nothing. He has—"

"Killed me?" Caitrina shook her head.

Etienne nodded, inching toward her again. "Yes. He has killed you."

"It was not that way. I asked to die. I was in melancholy."

"He told you that?" Etienne demanded.

"I remember. I—"

Caitrina swung the sword around as something lunged from behind her. She thrashed as a hand locked around her throat and another over the hilt of the sword.

"No, Franz. Release her," Etienne roared.

She fought for air, clawing at Franz. There was a blur of motion, and the young man backstepped, his eyes wide in surprise. Caitrina was dragged along with him by his grip. A tearing pain stole her breath. Caitrina crumpled to the floor as Franz recoiled.

Etienne screamed in frustration, cradling her head on his arm and applying pressure to her abdomen that caused dizzying pain. "Caitrina?" he sobbed. "Gods alive, what have I done? I didn't mean to. You know I didn't."

She faded into the black vortex calling for her, dreaming of Jörg meeting her in a halo of sunlight.

* * * *

Jörg streamed into the air from the spot in the shade of the carriage that he'd dematerialized to when he'd left the battle. He didn't waste a moment, not even for taking the time to say a final farewell to Martin. The human would understand his haste. Caitrina was most important now. There would be time for a proper burial when she was safe.

The healing Earth had returned Jörg to the strength he would need to combat the Warriors. He followed his link toward Caitrina, cursing the distance Etienne Lord Kaufmann had put between them. It would take him more than a quarter of an hour to reach her side.

Her soul called to him, in unhappiness and in upset. Caitrina hadn't turned from him, but the presence of the Lord Kaufmann confused her. She was in pain. It was always a strain when Regana's soul was presented with both of her husbands.

Jörg smiled. The fact that he felt her so clearly meant Caitrina had refused the amulet. He had felt her all day—her fear, sadness, strength, and fury. Even her struggles were heartening. Every moment she refused the amulet brought him closer to claiming her again with the full knowledge that she was his alone.

Caitrina passed from nervous preoccupation to happiness and then jolted into a fear and dread that made Jörg's fangs extend in the promise of violence. Her reactions confused him, mainly because of the fleeting moment of happiness. Jörg searched the close feed strands, looking for one near her, hoping all the while he was wrong in his assumption.

He growled at the knowledge that Renald was with her. Renald's presence could only mean one thing. Yet again, one of his turned had betrayed him. It was Resten incarnate. Resten was the only one of the principle players from the original encounter who did not reappear with every lifetime, but when he did appear, the end was always at its most painful.

Jörg whipped through the air, calling Renald to him. He was too far away to kill the turned outright. Even his call would take time to work at this distance.

He opened the link to Renald, letting the younger beast's experiences wash over him. Jörg smiled inwardly at Etienne's shock and confusion.

Yes. Now you know what you face—a mad elder in defense of his mate. Etienne wouldn't be intelligent enough to release Caitrina to Jörg's care. The Warriors never were.

Jörg cringed as Renald attacked the distracted lord. While it would save Jörg the trouble of killing the Warrior, Caitrina was safe in Etienne's care—much safer than she would be with Renald.

He was too far away to kill Renald, but Jörg could still affect his mind. The killing blow the beast should have dealt Etienne never fell; the turned suddenly forgot the threat existed, as Jörg commanded.

Etienne reacted much as Jörg had hoped he would, taking a killing blow on Renald. The dying beast's vision faded away, locked on Caitrina's pale, shaking form. A sword made in the style of a sacred weapon was clasped in her hands.

In her hands. Gods! Ilona held a sacred weapon, as well. She died with such a weapon in her hand.

Jörg screamed in fury as he felt Caitrina's pain and panic at an attack on her person. *They will die painfully for this,* he vowed. How dare the Cursed Warriors attack her!

He faltered as he felt the deathblow. *No! They've killed her.*

Jörg sped on, her pain searing him worse than even his transformation had. He felt empty, a burned husk left when the starfire destroyed the best of him, pitiful as that bit was.

Jörg stood over the dead form of Franz before his body had completely formed; striding into the room as his clothing took shape around his body.

Etienne made no move to defend himself. The Warrior knelt with Caitrina cradled on his arm, the opposite hand exerting useless pressure on her wound. The sacred weapon fouled with her blood lay next to her knee.

"I meant to hit him," he whispered hoarsely. "I meant to kill Franz for his lack of control. Ani, forgive me, I never meant to hurt you."

"How dare you touch her," Jörg roared. He sent Etienne skidding across the floor with a wound to match Caitrina's. *Let the beast die slowly, as slowly as the gods will grant him.*

She didn't hit the floor. Jörg gathered Caitrina to his chest, moving faster than the human eye could track. He scanned his gaze over the wound, heartsick. Jörg couldn't heal this much damage. He was too late.

No. I am not too late to save her...if I turn her. Jörg grimaced. He hadn't wanted this damned existence for her, but there were advantages. Caitrina wouldn't age and leave him. She was incapable of carrying his child either way. She already knew and accepted that fact.

Jörg kissed her brow, torn. He wouldn't turn her unless Caitrina wished it. Jörg would let her die now, if that was her wish.

"Caitrina," he crooned, touching her pale cheek.

She was cool to the touch. It would have to be soon. Her body was weak, the movement of blood in her veins sluggish.

"Regana, *Geliebte Mein*. Caitrina, look at me."

He coerced her, knowing he had to make the offer, even if she refused him. The outlay of power was immaterial now. Etienne's injury and the pup's death would bring the Warriors, whether or not he gave them added incentive to come.

She forced her eyes open, raising a bloodstained hand to his cheek. Caitrina shook her head, a single tear escaping her eye. "I...do not...leave you," she repeated his words of that morning in a series of gasps. "I will come...for you again."

"You do not have to leave me. If you feed from me—" Jörg couldn't continue. Could he do this to her? If she asked, he would. He could not lose her if there was any alternative to it.

"No," Etienne protested in a whisper, dragging himself toward them. "The Stone's curse. You know a woman will not survive with her sanity intact."

"Be still," Jörg growled at him. They hadn't attempted a female turned. There were dire warnings of what would happen if it was attempted.

She is printed to me. Printing saved my kind emotions. It will save Caitrina's sanity. It must.

Her eyes widened. Her fear seared him. She would leave him rather than stay with him in his form.

"We could be together always," he reminded her.

"Do not lie, foul beast," Etienne groaned.

"I am...no...hunter," she argued weakly. She wanted to be with him.

"No. You are not. I would provide for you. You could drink from me as I have taken from you." *Please. Please, accept this.* "Please, do not leave me," he begged of her. Jörg grimaced at his weakness. He had no right to ask this of her.

Caitrina nodded.

"No," Etienne rumbled, grasping for his discarded blade.

Jörg swept the blade away and tossed the Warrior to the far corner of the room without taking his eyes from Caitrina's.

"Do not fear me," he pleaded. "Do not fear what you will be."

Caitrina stroked his cheek. "I do not fear."

He willed away the illusion of his tunic. Jörg extended a single blade from his fingertip and sliced a cut in his chest, inches below the blood mark she loved. She watched the black blood well up in amazement.

Jörg brought her mouth to the spot, his heart pounding in anticipation of her touch. "Then drink," he urged her. *Quickly.* Without pressure on the wound, her lifeblood poured from her all the faster.

He swallowed a groan of pleasure as Caitrina collected the first drops on her tongue, tentatively, cautiously sampling his flavor. She pressed her lips to the thin line of the cut and suckled at him. Jörg hardened in the knowledge that she'd accepted him so fully that she would join him forever.

"No," Etienne sobbed.

"Do not seek to stop us," Jörg warned him, though Etienne was in no condition to do so.

He sent information to Caitrina through the blood link, as he had for all his turned, all the things she would need to know to be safe in her new life, all the powers and limitations she had.

Her suckling became more insistent, and Jörg groaned in response. He stroked her taut nipple, dreaming of the time when she could rise from the healing soil with him. He would make love to her as soon as she was able. Waiting would be a hardship, but it was well worth the trade of having her with him forever.

Etienne uttered a series of harsh curses, and Jörg snapped his eyes open, staring at his errant hand in dismay. Caitrina was injured. This was not the time to fondle her, especially in front of this dog. Still, there was a perverse pleasure in knowing his rival watched while Jörg touched her.

Jörg broke her hold on him before she could weaken him too much to complete his task. With Caitrina in his arms, he stood and left the house far behind. She would not be ready for the rigors of travel by flight for several hours.

He smiled as he felt the blood circulating through her begin to rebuild her system, stopping her bleeding and changing her body chemistry to that of a beast. Caitrina was calm, letting the changes happen without fighting them. That was good. It was only painful if you fought the changes...or touched the Stone directly. Jörg had once tried to tell Pauwel that.

"Sleep," he soothed her. "When you complete your transformation, I will fly you to our home and lay in the healing earth with you, our essences mixed in the rich soil. And when your healing is complete, you will feed from me again and become strong."

Jörg kissed her forehead tenderly. "You will live a life of bliss with me. We will travel where you wish— foreign lands, the finest entertainment, loving where and when we choose."

He laughed as her sleepy musings filtered into his mind.

"You wish to use our ghosting ability to make love in a crowded theater?" he teased. "Yes. That will be my second gift to you," Jörg promised.

"*Second?*" She experimented with the link between them.

"*First, I will make love to you in our bed.*"

"*While you feed me?*"

The longing in her voice made him painfully aware of the days it would take her to heal. He groaned in arousal that he could not sate for at least three days. "*Absolutely.*"

Chapter Fourteen

December 2nd, 1497

Caitrina tried to force her eyes open, but the blackness remained. She couldn't move. She couldn't feel her limbs. Caitrina tried to scream, but she could make no sound, feel no air in her lungs. Her mind rebelled.

"*Calm, Geliebte.*" Jörg's voice came from all around her, in her, a soothing touch of warmth when she felt nothing else.

She tried to speak again, but there was nothing.

"*Speak with the link,*" he instructed her calmly. "*Think to me.*"

"*Jörg?*" It was calming. She did exist. "*Where are we? Why can I not feel or see or move? Why can I not speak naturally?*"

A feeling like a sigh caressed her. "*We rest in the soil beneath our home. Do you remember your injuries?*"

Memories came to her, hazy memories of intense pain, fear, blood. Then there'd been a calm...the taste of rich spice and power. There was knowledge.

She was what Jörg was now. She could not feel or behave as a human, because she was disembodied and her essence was scattered through the soil with Jörg's, as he'd promised.

"*Yes. This is the healing sleep. You may not rise yet. Your injuries will require several more days to knit. Do you feel them?*"

It wasn't exactly a feeling of pain, but the realization that she was not whole. "*Yes.*"

"Good. You must sleep now. I will wake you when I have fed sufficiently, when it is safe for you to take a solid form and join me."

"Do not leave me," she begged. Though she could not feel his arms around her, the thought of lying alone in the soil frightened her.

"I do not leave you, dear one. I will always come for you, but I must feed deeply for the next few nights so that you may drink your fill when you wake and not weaken me."

"I understand." Caitrina didn't like the idea of being in the soil without him, but she would not compromise Jörg for her whims. He had to feed to be strong for her.

"Sleep."

Caitrina felt him slip from her mind as his push sent her from consciousness.

* * * *

December 5th, 1497

Jörg squatted on the ground above Caitrina, smiling. Her injuries were healed at last. She could join him. He sent the command, instructing her to solid form via the link between them.

She materialized, weaving on her feet and sinking into Jörg's arms. Caitrina held tight to him, trying to find her center while her urges warred within her. She was weak. The drive to feed was maddening to her. It all but buried her other urges.

He swept her to him, striding toward the rooms that were prepared for them. "Soon," he crooned. "I will sate all your hungers very soon."

Caitrina moved restlessly when he laid her on their bed. Her eyes glowed a hot red that showed her lack of control. Luckily, she was too weakened to escape him in the form of a mist.

Jörg took a calming breath. "You must feed," he instructed her. "If you feed, your beast will become more manageable. You will have to learn to feed. The three easiest sites for you to learn from are the large pulse point in the thigh, the one in the arm and—"

She stroked a hand over his neck, her fangs lengthening. Caitrina's hunger was fierce. She listened to the blood rushing under his skin intently. He shivered in the depth of her need for him.

"Yes. That is what you need," he confirmed for her. Jörg raised her in his arms, nestling her mouth to the column of his throat. "Feel the blood rush for you. Take what you need."

Jörg steeled himself for a brutal attack this first time. Caitrina had no experience reining in the beast that held her in its grasp, and the beast was strong in its urge to live while she was weak from her healing. Jörg would likely spend quite a bit of time controlling the beast for her until she learned the proper control, but he would let it have free rein this first time. She needed to know the danger of the beast intimately.

Caitrina licked at his throat in imitation of the times he'd taken her blood. She groaned as her fangs sank deep. Jörg stiffened at the pain. Caitrina took from him hungrily, and he hardened despite the discomfort involved. There was something inherently sensual in watching her feed from him. Was this what she felt when he fed from her?

"*Yes.*"

A spike of pleasure wiped the pain from Jörg's mind. He moaned as Caitrina stroked his length through the illusion of breeches he wore. Jörg removed them with a thought, allowing her free rein to touch. Her suckling slowed, as Caitrina brought her urges to take his blood under control. Her hunger was being sated. Her beast would demand that she sate other hungers.

"Take what you need," he offered. "I am yours." Jörg stroked his fingers into her depths, smiling as she bowed to him, her eyes opening wide in surprise. "Yes. It is always better when you feed. Is it better when you are being fed from?" he teased, knowing it was.

"*Now,*" she demanded, moving her body smoothly over his and forcing him back to their bed beneath her. She straddled him, seeking his cooperation.

Jörg teased her further, playing his cock only a few finger widths in her body.

"*Now!*"

He laughed aloud as Caitrina tried her fledgling coercion on him. It would not work, of course, even if she was stronger, but she was desperate for him. Jörg clamped his hands on her hips as she tried to force her body over him, offering a silent show of his strength in comparison to her own. Caitrina ripped her mouth from his throat, a warning flashing in her red-tinged eyes.

"Now," he assured her, filling her abruptly.

Caitrina's eyes closed in ecstasy. She drank in the feeling of his length as if it had been centuries for her instead of days.

Jörg urged her mouth back to his throat. "Feed," he whispered. "Take everything I have to give."

She licked the blood pooled on his chest and neck, then suckled at him again. "*Will you give me my memories as you gave me your knowledge?*" she requested. Her mind was clearing now that the beast's needs were being met.

"All of them. You have my vow." Jörg filled her with his body as he filled her mind with memories of all of her lives. He filled her with his seed as he gave her the memories of himself with her in the present life.

Caitrina closed the punctures at his throat, sated in every way she would require. Her fingers played at his chest. "Is true feeding like that?" she asked quietly.

"You will not feed from anyone but me," he decided.

She raised her head, biting her lower lip in confusion. Her fangs, not fully retracted, left adorable dimples in the deep red of her full lips. "Why?"

Jörg sighed, stroking her curls between his fingers. "You remember the moment when you had to have me inside you? You remember how you felt like you might go mad without it? You would have done anything to have it."

Caitrina nodded slowly, a blush covering her cheeks and rushing to her breasts.

"It will be like that every time you feed. You will want that completion, even when you deny yourself the pleasure of it. You are not strong enough to fight your beast. You may never be that strong."

"If I feed and come to you," she began, trying to reason a way out of his concern.

Jörg shook his head. "You will want it at the moment of feeding. You will want it with an intensity beyond what you felt when you fed from me. You will not care if you feed from a man or a woman. You will want the ecstasy of orgasm, no matter which you hold in your arms. You will not feed from anyone but me. Am I understood?"

"Do you feel that?" she whispered.

"Yes, but my beast and I came to an agreement long ago." He smiled warmly and teased her jaw with his teeth in a gentle warning. "When you have been on this Earth for a thousand years and have leashed the beast within you as well, we will discuss you feeding from another."

Caitrina laughed lightly and kissed him, remembering at the last moment to cleanse his blood from her mouth. She added the taste of berries and spice for him. "*I do not want to leash my beast. Feed me again. Feed me in every way you can feed my hungers.*"

Chapter Fifteen

March 10ᵗʰ, 1503

Veriel of Regana's soul

> Time and time again, I find you my love.
> I rush to your side when I hear your call.
> Your need flies to me on wings of a dove,
> And at your feet to serve, I gladly fall.
> To protect you, I always join the brawl,
> But, ne'er are you mine to hold in the end,
> Though to every whim of yours I would bend.

Jörg came to consciousness slowly. Something was wrong, but he couldn't place what it was. Caitrina's essence wasn't in the soil with him, but that wasn't unusual in itself. Caitrina required less sleep than Jörg did, and she typically rose before him and waited for him in the manor above.

He smiled. She was often clothed in some illusion to test his control—or nude in a place she wished him to take her— ready to sate her hungers again and again, and he loved every moment of it.

He streamed to their bedchamber and materialized, already hard in anticipation of her touch. They had been together for more than five years—five years of light, laughter, and love. There had always been intense love, physically and emotionally.

Jörg furrowed his brow in confusion. The manor was oddly still, bereft of the excitement of Caitrina's youth and energy. "Caitrina?" he called, though he

148

knew there would be no answer. Where would she go? It was understood that she was not to leave the circle of his protection. Caitrina balked at that order from time to time, but she had never disobeyed him.

What other possibility is there? No one could have taken her from within the walls without Jörg knowing her plight. No Warrior was that strong. No beast was. Even his brother elders were not capable of besting Jörg. The idea of humans besting Caitrina, let alone Jörg, was ludicrous. No, Caitrina had not been distressed. This was one of her child-like games.

He plucked at the link between them uneasily. It was unfocused. Caitrina wasn't blocking him. She would be incapable of such a thing even if she tried, but what could cloud the link?

Jörg knew that Caitrina needed a sense of her self-worth. She needed to know that he saw her as an equal, but this was a dangerous game, one he could not allow her to play at.

"*Caitrina,*" he ordered. "*Come to me. I will take you out later this night.*"

There was no response. Jörg paced the room. It wasn't like Caitrina to ignore him this way. Worse, even if she was far away, he should have a sense that she'd heard his call. There was nothing...complete silence that unnerved him.

"*Caitrina? Where are you? I will come to you.*"

He ran a hand through his hair. The link was strange, like nothing he had ever encountered with a turned or human. Drugs did not accomplish such a thing, nor did drink or injury. What was this attack on their bond?

Jörg tapped into her mind, something he'd promised not to do when Caitrina complained that it made her seem a child who was in need of leading strings. Though he connected, he couldn't hear her thoughts or see and feel the world around her. Only a vague sense of need assaulted his mind.

Jörg strode across the floor, launching skyward as a mist. He sped after the link, praying with every league that his connection to her would crystallize once more. It didn't. The change in distance made no difference in the clarity of the link.

He found her standing over a dead woman, her face stained in blood. Caitrina's breathing was quick and uneven. She looked at him without comprehension.

"Caitrina," he called in a soothing voice.

His mind supplied the answer numbly. Caitrina had gone feral, as his brothers' turned females had gone feral. They had tried little before giving up on the women. Jörg would not be so quick to discard any possibility. Resuming a sexual relationship did not turn them back to what they once were. If anything, they were worse.

Jörg locked on her bloodstained face in dismay. "Feeding," he mused. His brethren had not taken the care Jörg had with their mates. Their women had hunted almost immediately—and gone feral just as quickly. Jörg had always provided for Caitrina, though she'd wanted to prove she could do so for herself. It was feeding on humans that destroyed their minds. Why had he never seen it before?

"Caitrina," he called again, easing toward her so as not to startle her.

If feeding from humans destroyed them, perhaps feeding from him would reverse the damage. He had to restrain Caitrina until he found a cure for her. Jörg was unlike his damned brothers. He would not kill her simply because she had become troublesome. He would find a way to have her back.

She met his eyes, and Jörg allowed himself a moment of hope. If she remembered him, perhaps Caitrina was not completely gone.

Then she lashed out, digging her claws deep into his chest. Jörg fell back, cursing the pain as she fled the alley. He pushed to his feet, following the link again despite the blood loss that would drive him to ground.

Caitrina never saw the Warrior who took her life, lost in the madness her feeding had wrought. Jörg screamed in rage as he felt the sacred weapon take her heart. It was the only injury there was no way to heal. It was the single injury that she could not survive.

He beheaded the Warrior before the man turned to him—*Stephen of Schwertträger.*

Jörg caught her to his chest, weeping at the sight of her covered in her own blood and dying in his arms—for the sixth time in his life. He screamed again, a scream the likes of which he hadn't uttered since Regana was ripped from him as he went to ground.

She touched his face; her eyes clear again in her pain, in the "freeing" of her that the Warrior had accomplished. "*I am sorry. I did not know. Tell me in my next life. Do not let me make this mistake again,*" she pleaded. The light left her eyes before Jörg could offer his assurances.

Jörg howled in frustration to the cold, heartless stars. He was alone again.

He didn't think as he went about his routine. How could so monumental and shattering an event become routine? Jörg tried not to contemplate that as he buried Caitrina and burned their home.

It was like this with every incarnation of Regana. That first time, Gawen had buried her and the villagers burned his home. Jörg had left his life behind this way with each loss since then. There was nothing left here for him when her soul departed.

Departed, only to be born again when the pain is not so fresh! Jörg shook his head. He could not live with this—with losing her again. *The next time her soul calls, I will not go to her.*

Even as he decided it, Jörg resigned himself to the folly of that thought. He would go, because his soul was bound to hers. He would go, because she would be in danger from humans, beasts, and Warriors alike. He would go, because he was printed to her and could not live without her while Regana lived, in any lifetime she lived.

Jörg would go to every incarnation and suffer every loss, because the gods had set this as his unending punishment for turning traitor to them. They would torture him with mere moments in her arms and dreams of holding her in a midday sun to fill the long years between. As he had been for more than a millennia, Jörg was well and truly damned.

{Hunter born.}

The words seemed to float to him on the breeze, a taunt from the Stone to his ears alone. The vision of Regana as he knew her appeared in the flames. He would hold her in a midday sun and be pursued no more.

When? When the Warrior of *Haus* Jäger came for him? Would this be his reward in the afterlife? To be reunited with Regana in one of her many forms?

{Hunter born.}

"When?" he shouted back, but there was only silence, as there had been for the last fifty generations.

Excerpts from The Kaufmann

Histories

The lost page
As penned by Rober Lord Kaufmann in 1497

When my brother, Etienne, was struck down, I rushed to his aid. No beast had died by his hand that night. In the midst of a scene of fierce battle where Veriel left my brother to die in a growing pool of his own blood and my nephew cold and gone to the Warrior's rest, a wailing servant girl tried to keep Etienne alive, but it was not for the dying house lord that she wept.

Jacquine had been the lady's maid to Caitrina de Leon. The fair Caitrina had been betrothed to her lord Jörg der Schmeidt, a man of German descent but powerful, wealthy, and a noble gentleman who'd won her father's agreement to the match. Her tears were for Caitrina, mortally wounded in error by Etienne's blade as he sought to free her from the beast Veriel.

The Mad Deceiver, using his forbidden human name, had enchanted the beauteous maid to him so completely that she fought my lord with a sword in hand to remain the beast's alone. Never had Etienne seen such dogged determination for such a thing. It unnerved him to see such devotion to so foul a creature.

The young miss believed Veriel the perfect young lord, attentive and courteous, deep in his love and regard for her. He called his lady by German endearments—*Geliebte* and *Regana,* in his tender moments alone with her.

The maid knew not the import of such things, but we were chilled by the implications. Had this Caitrina been chosen and we lost our chance at an end yet again? She had not the look of a Stone-chosen, but Veriel had not the look of a true Warrior either, though he bore the mark. In fact, her deep brown hair and sparkling blue eyes might well be compared to the anomalous appearance of The Destroyer of Lives. The only truth was in the marking, and that was something beyond our power to check, as Veriel had stolen his lady away with him before my approach.

Etienne mourned the woman's loss, chosen or not, for his part in her exit from her human life, though I know it to have been honest error and not negligent loss. Worse, he cursed his inability to stop Veriel from feeding the lady on his foul blood and turning her from the light and goodness of her soul.

The Stone has long foretold the dangers of a female turned. In his final tortured cries to the gods, Etienne begged forgiveness for what his action and inaction hath wrought on the world.

I only pray, as I bury my brother and take my seal, that the name of Kaufmann is not forever synonymous with the heinous crimes the once virtuous Caitrina de Leon will surely commit in her altered state of being.

Having seen the foul deed and what her lady has become—and her lord always was, Jacquine has accepted my personal protection. Pray Veriel knows, if he ever dares come for her, he will find my blade ready to protect the girl with my life.

Section Three
Sweet Jacquine

Chapter Sixteen

December 2nd, 1497

Rober of Kaufmann looked around the cottage in disbelief. It was the type of scene that chilled the most jaded Warrior to the bone. His eldest nephew was dead; his Lord-brother lay dying. The smell of beast blood permeated the space, and he half-swallowed a cough in response, his eyes watering.

"Open the windows," he ordered his youngest brother, Marcus. Though it was bitterly cold outside, the fresh air would be a welcome reprieve from the foul stench of the dead beast two body lengths from Etienne. They wouldn't be staying there tonight, in any case...unless Etienne lived until first light.

Marcus obeyed without question, perhaps already thinking of Rober as lord though Etienne still breathed, and he'd not collected his seal.

Rober strode to his elder brother's side, fighting back *Blutjagd* at the idea that the beast who'd done this had escaped him. There would be payment for this. Any beast that killed a Warrior was marked for execution above all the rest.

He sank to one knee, meeting the gaze of the woman across Etienne's body from him. Her dark eyes were red from crying, her face streaked raw, and locks of her chestnut hair escaped the pins behind her head to curl against her cheeks, some plastered to the tracks of tears. She was in abject misery. His gaze settled at her bare neckline in surprise. No amulet graced the unblemished stretch of skin.

Why is she not protected?

She held her hands to the wound in a vain attempt to save Etienne. Rober lifted them gently, then more forcefully as she fought him.

"You cannot," she protested. "He will bleed to death if you—"

"Shhh. Nothing we do will stop that," he assured her. "It is kinder to let him die quickly." *Once I have the information I need to track his attacker.*

The lady looked to the downed Warrior, shaking her head, fresh tears beading on her lashes.

"Marcus," he called. "Take..." He waited for her to offer her name.

"J—Jacquine, mi'lord," she stammered, already shivering in the cold wind through the open shutters, her breath making thick mist before her mouth.

Rober nodded, offering her a strained smile. "I thank you for your kindness, Jacquine. Please, go with Marcus. He will protect you and show you to a place to clean your hands." He motioned to his brother to find her a cloak or blanket while he did it.

Marcus grasped her lightly by the waist with the intent of lifting her to her feet, and she startled, blushing deeply. Rober shot him a hard look for it. This was obviously not some rouged greensleeves to be handled in so familiar a manner.

He nodded, moving his hands to her elbows. "My apologies, Jacquine," the young man murmured. Marcus eased her to her feet and offered his arm to escort her properly, no doubt noting her shaking as Rober did.

Etienne's breathing was shallow and his color fading, but he still had life. Perhaps there was yet time to learn all he needed to know.

Rober smacked his cheek lightly in an effort to rouse him. "Etienne?" he called. "Etienne, speak to me."

The Lord's eyes opened, full of pain—*no, misery.*

"What is it?"

"I failed her," Etienne whispered. "The Fair Lady Caitrina. I failed her, Rober."

"Which beast?" Rober demanded. "Give me the name, and I will take a blood oath to your vengeance tonight."

"No time for that." He coughed, and blood dotted at the corner of his mouth. "I tried to stop him, but...he's turned her."

Rober shuddered. The texts warned of the horrors a turned female would commit. There was only one elder that was mad enough to attempt it. "The Destroyer of Lives," he managed. "Veriel... Why did you not wait for us? We were less than a day behind." Frustration welled in him. Veriel never lost in single combat, and Franz was little more than a first-night, hardly a match in battle for The Mad Deceiver.

"It was an opportunity that would not come again. He was with her always, even in the misty day. For that moment, the sun was our ally in taking the women from him."

"Until it fled and left you to battle alone," he exploded, then added several curses.

"Enough." Etienne coughed up more blood. "There is more that I must tell you. Lady Caitrina... She was..." He sighed heavily. "She was Regana, Rober. I fear the Stone's will has been corrupted, and I am to blame."

For a moment, Rober couldn't find his voice. What his brother believed simply wasn't possible, but was there a way to prove it and put him at ease? "Had she the mark?"

"The beast stole her away before I could check it, but he convinced her it was true and—"

"He is mad! Who knows what games will amuse him?"

"And she..." He grimaced.

"She what?" Rober asked, something in his brother's expression making him distinctly uneasy.

"She spoke the language of the ancients as if born to it. I know it sounds mad, but believe me when I tell you, it is true. I failed her, Rober. I failed us all."

"You did not." Etienne's doubts ate at Rober. If there was any way to give his brother peace to carry to the Warrior's Rest, he had to attempt it. "Veriel never loses in single combat. You could not have been expected to best him."

"It was my blade," he groaned. "The Mad Elder would only have taken her again and not turned her had I not misjudged. We could have taken her back. Now, she is lost in body and soul to him."

"An honest error," he surmised. "Etienne Lord Kaufmann is never sloppy in execution." There was no question in his mind that it was so.

The look of misery his brother shot him made his heart falter. "Only the gods know for certain."

Rober nodded. "Rest, now." It wouldn't take long for Etienne to die. Then the true work would begin.

* * * *

Jacquine looked up from the tabletop as the other Warrior entered the room after half the night at his lord's side. Marcus had told her that his brother's name was Rober, and he was the older of the two though younger than Etienne.

Rober didn't acknowledge her presence. He stood with one of their weapons in hand, his jaw tight and eyes hard. "I am Kaufmann now," he growled, meeting Marcus's gaze.

Without hesitation, the younger man turned toward him and dropped to one knee, his head bowed. "My blade is yours, my duty at your whim. You are my Lord Kaufmann."

She winced, the implications all to clear to her. Etienne was dead, and Marcus was swearing fealty to the new lord.

Rober relaxed, sheathing the blade. His gaze settled on Jacquine, and his expression softened. He waved his brother away. "Take what we must and dispose of the beast. Etienne will have his glory."

Marcus rose and left without a word. Near silence fell in his wake, and Rober took the moment to consider her carefully, his gaze settling on her breasts.

Jacquine pulled the cloak further around her chest, though Marcus hadn't laid this room open to the howling winds as he had the front rooms. "I am sorry for your loss," she managed. It was an inadequate statement; this man had lost a brother and a nephew, but she could construct no better in her exhaustion.

He sat across from her. "Have you refused protection?" he asked bluntly.

"I do not understand. You—you do not mean to protect me?" Marcus had led her to believe that she would be safe with the Warriors, that they would see to her safety.

His eyes widened. "No one has offered it? Etienne or Franz?"

"They took us into their custody. Was that not protection? I did not refuse it." Inspiration struck. Again and again, Lord Etienne had offered Lady Caitrina an amulet, and she'd refused it. *Have you refused protection?* "Do you mean the amulet?"

"Of course," he snapped, as if she should have known it.

"It—it was never offered to me."

His look was one of pure disbelief.

"I speak the truth," she defended herself. "Your Lor—Etienne offered the amulet to Lady Caitrina, but it was never offered to me." The fact that she would have likely refused it as her lady had was better left unsaid. Surely, they wouldn't hold her fear of the unknown against her now.

His gaze roamed over her body, and she felt her cheeks heat at his familiarity. She looked away, her heart pounding in a mixture of unease and interest. What was he looking for so intently?

"You know what the beast is?" he asked.

"I did not until I saw it," she admitted. "Franz tried to tell me, but..." She chanced a look at his eyes, expecting anger. Instead she found deep compassion.

"You did not believe him," he surmised.

"It was a mad story, but I do believe now," she hastened to add.

"I know. There is no offense in your disbelief. The beasts take the blood of others. You know this?"

Her stomach lurched at the memory of Lord Jörg der Schmidt feeding Lady Caitrina his foul blood. What spell had he cast to allow her to stomach it?

A cool hand touched the back of her neck. "Breathe slowly," he soothed her. "Deeply. In through the nose and out through the mouth."

Jacquine did so, her mind clearing though she emerged more drained than before. "My thanks," she whispered.

Rober knelt to her level. "Did the beast feed from you?" he asked earnestly.

"No." Franz had asked her the same.

He seemed confused by that. "Are you certain?"

"Of course. It is not the sort of thing one could forget, is it?"

His dark eyes narrowed. "Perhaps, I should examine—"

"You wouldn't," she gasped, horrified at the suggestion.

"Jacquine—"

"Unless he was angry, he had attention only for Caitrina." The words tripped out in her haste. He couldn't have fed from her, and she would not allow Rober to do something so intimate.

* * * *

Rober started to explain the need for certainty, but she pulled from under his hand, shaking like a snared rabbit.

"I will not," he vowed. *But, what if she is wrong and he has fed?* Like most victims left to feed from again, Caitrina had no memory of the Deceiver's feeding the first morning Etienne met her. Jacquine would not as well.

Whether she was fed on or not, Jacquine might need his protection. There was still her former mistress to consider. "The beast..."

"Lord Jörg?" she managed shakily.

Blutjagd burned fiercely in him. Something in his expression made Jacquine shy away. He nodded. "Never speak that name again. The beast's name is Veriel."

She nodded, clearly terrified by his reaction.

"Veriel...had a lover's name for your Lady Caitrina. Tell me what it was." Perhaps, she knew more than it seemed.

"There were three," she stammered.

"Go on."

"He called her 'Dear One' and '*Geliebte*'."

"And?" His muscles tensed involuntarily.

"Regana."

His blood ran cold. What foul game was this?

"Will..." She interrupted his thoughts in a meek voice. "Will Lady Caitrina be like the beast now?"

Rober swallowed a sour lump. "Worse," he admitted. He surveyed her again, a plan taking form. "You must let me protect you."

"Yes," Jacquine breathed, her shoulders sagging in seeming relief. "Thank you, Lord Rober."

He drew out one of the lord's amulets he'd taken from Etienne, settling it over her shoulders. First, he would say the blessing. Then he would explain why she must never remove it, especially for Lady Caitrina.

Chapter Seventeen

December 8th, 1497

Rober sat, his back against the barn wall, watching Jacquine sleep. The beasts hadn't come for her in the last six days, though by Etienne's account of the she-beast's injuries, it was unlikely they'd had much time to start the search for the missing lady's maid. Perhaps they would never come for her, but it was a chance he would not take.

He grimaced, cursing his printing solidly in a voice that would not disturb her slumber. The sensation was driving him mad. If Veriel did come for her, Rober would meet him, madman to madman.

Jacquine sighed in her sleep, and he bit back a groan, his fertile imagination supplying images of her sighing to his caresses, arching her back in the hay beneath her body as he thrust into her. His cock came to aching readiness, and he closed his eyes, praying for a reprieve that he reasoned would not come.

"Problem, Rober?" Marcus asked from beside him, appearing from outside swiftly and silently.

"I need a bit of time," he grumbled. Rober didn't wait for his brother's acknowledgement. He strode into the pink light of the coming dawn, seeking a place to sate his needs in peace. A secluded spot by the river beckoned. He pulled his breeches open and took the rather weighty matter in hand.

Even in his self-release, Rober couldn't escape thoughts of Jacquine. Visions of her danced behind his closed eyelids: Jacquine taking him in her hands, her mouth, her velvet sheath.

His breath came in gasps; his muscles went taut. Rober groaned, not in the relief of release but in the absence of any relief. Self-release had lost its effectiveness.

He closed his breeches over his still-aching cock, grimacing. "Gods, I am far gone." There was no option. He'd have to approach the matter directly and hope the lady accepted him.

* * * *

Jacquine rounded the barn, brushing another bit of straw from her hair in annoyance. As usual, the Warriors had risen before her and a fire was lit. The scent of meat and tea had drawn her from sleep.

Marcus sat at the fire, and a bolt of relief shot through her. At least she knew there was no chance of happening upon his—amusements this morning.

"Good day, Jacquine," he called out cheerily.

She settled on the ground, accepting the mug of tea he offered and drinking in its warmth with a muttered thanks to him and God. "Good day. Where is Lord Rober?" The elder brother was nowhere in sight, but he was never far.

Marcus chuckled. "He is...occupied." He raked his gaze over her body, a move he repeated often.

Her face burned in the realization that Rober was busy sating his needs sexually, as Marcus had done the morning before. "Oh. I see." She looked into the fire, trying to avoid his eyes, trying to avoid any chance that she might see Rober so engaged somewhere nearby, trying to avoid memories of—

Marcus settled beside her, his breath tickling her cheek. "I know you saw me," he stated.

Jacquine fought for a decent breath. "I did not intend to—to watch you. I did leave when I realized..."

"You did not have to leave," he informed her in a voice laced in amusement.

She snapped her eyes up to his, shocked at the thought of such a thing. "You would want me to watch you... To watch you..."

"Take self-release? It would not offend me to have you there. It would excite me quite a bit to have you watch." He shifted closer, his lips hairs away from her ear. "Or to have you join me."

Jacquine scrambled to her feet with a squawk, dropping the mug on his boots. She gasped as she collided with another wall of male body. Her eyes sought out Rober's, terror making her head spin.

His look of confusion disappeared, and fury took its place. Before she could flee, his hands closed around her arms, easing her toward him.

"Marcus has harmed you?" he asked gruffly.

"Of course not," the younger man protested.

"Silence!" His voice dropped to a whisper. "Did he hurt you?"

Jacquine shook her head, nearly groaning at the way his pungent scent made the dizziness more acute.

"You see," Marcus began.

"Silence," Rober roared. "You did something, frightened her somehow. She is trembling." His hands stroked her back, and Jacquine sank into his chest fully, letting him support her.

"Just an offer of my companionship," Marcus explained sweetly.

A growl rumbled from Rober's chest. "Apologize. Now."

"Rober?" The amusement left the other Warrior's voice.

"Jacquine is a protected woman, not a tavern whore. Your advances are unwelcome. You frightened her, and you will apologize or face me."

His tone made promises for her safety. Jacquine sighed, burying her face in the warmth of his chest. His fingers stroked her neck, then her scalp, under her tangled hair.

Marcus chuckled and then laughed outright.

Rober stiffened, his hands halting their soothing. "I warn you—"

"My most heartfelt apologies, Jacquine. It will never happen again. You have my solemn vow."

"My thanks," she whispered.

"Set food for us," Rober ordered sharply. "And, if you ever dare approach Jacquine again, I will leave scars."

"I trust you will," Marcus answered cryptically.

* * * *

Rober watched Jacquine eat, spellbound by every motion and expression. More often than not, he was broken from his trance by snorts or laughs from his errant brother. As if the thought conjured him, Marcus let loose a snicker, and Rober shot him a warning look. The sound stopped, but the knowing smirk still lit his youthful face in glee.

His *Blutjagd* spiked, and Rober forced it down, nearly losing his calm completely when Marcus let loose another snicker. It was bad enough that Rober was printing in these circumstances. The last thing he needed was his brother's taunting about it.

Of course, it was unlikely Marcus would accost Jacquine again. If his brother knew Rober was printing, he'd know the penalty for presuming so much with the woman Rober was fixated on.

Rober fisted his hand at the memory of Marcus sitting with Jacquine, cheek to cheek with her. He swallowed a growl at the memory of her flight into his arms and the stark fear in her eyes. By the gods, she probably thought Rober meant to force himself on her when he grabbed her, that they both did.

Marcus half swallowed another laugh, and Rober glared at him.

Jacquine's muttered complaint brought his head around in concern. She didn't seem to note his attention, and her difficulty became obvious in moments. Her hair was matted in places, and her clothing was in need of a washing. Jacquine's state had to be intolerable to her, but their situation and the weather limited their options for travel and comforts.

He stood and stepped behind her, working his fingers into her hair. She stilled, then lowered her hands, letting him groom her as well as he could. Her hair was smooth and warm as fresh cream against his palms once the knots were worked out.

"My thanks," she sighed, her eyes still shut.

"So beautiful," he replied, running his hands through the fall of hair set free for a few precious moments, half in a daze.

Jacquine wrinkled her nose. "I am a scandal."

Oh, how I would like to make a scandal of you. "Not at all."

"If only I could bathe..."

"In two days. You have my vow."

Her eyes opened, full of hope. "A bath?" she repeated wistfully.

Rober smiled, his heart skipping happily that he could wash away her upset so easily. "A bath with sage soap, clean clothing... I even guarantee a warm bed with as many quilts as you request of me."

A smile lit her face. "A bed? Clothing? It is a dream."

He massaged her scalp. "Not at all. My departed brother's wife has clothing stored at each of our homes, and—"

She paled, and the smile left her face.

"Jacquine? Are you ill?"

"Etienne," she whispered. "Oh, his poor... Will she be there when we—"

"No. You misunderstood. Etienne had no wife." Though Sabine would have to be told that her oldest son was dead, she'd faced the loss of Kev already, and she had two other sons to sustain her, neither of them old enough to first night.

Her eyes widened.

"Our eldest brother was lost two years ago."

"Oh. My apologies."

"There is no need." It was the lives they led, fighting beasts until the day one took them.

She moved away self-consciously, arranging her hair with shaking hands.

Rober ground his teeth in frustration. Marcus's expression didn't help. His brother's wince summed up the problem perfectly. If Jacquine couldn't accept the risks they took, she would refuse him. Rober was far gone already. If she refused him, the results would be extremely painful.

Chapter Eighteen

December 10th, 1497

"Did you find something suitable?" Rober asked, pouring the last pot of hot water into the tub in the center of the kitchen.

She blushed. "More than suitable. You are most kind, Lord Rober."

"Rober is adequate." He glanced at the dress she'd set on the table, controlling the urge to curse—barely. Without a word, he crossed the room, snatched it up, and headed up the back stairs.

She considers this ragged cleaning gown too kind? He seethed that she'd found something so *unsuitable* in his home. It took Rober only moments to find a dark green gown that would show off her beautiful eyes and hair. He coupled it with a pale yellow chemise of the finest silk. Satisfied with his choices, he returned to the kitchen.

Jacquine's eyes widened. "I cannot possibly. Rober, those things are far too—"

"They are yours. Sabine will be pleased to purchase new clothing." He stopped before her, locking his gaze with hers. "I expect you to wear nothing but the finest the trunks have to offer. Do not balk me in something so trivial."

"N—no. Of course not. If you wish it."

The thought of Jacquine in the gown he'd chosen had him uncomfortably hard. "Oh, I do wish it." And, he wished for the liberty to remove it.

She nodded, breaking eye contact.

Rober turned and started toward the inner door, stifling the urge to make his intentions clear to her. Now was not the time and place. Perhaps when she was clean and fed, he would find the moment he needed. "Very well. I will leave you to bathe then."

"As lord of the house—"

"It is my place to insist that you bathe first," he cut her protest off. Rober pushed through into the dining room and shut the door behind him.

There was a moment of silence. Then the sounds of her disrobing filtered out to him. Visions of her body appearing slowly made breathing difficult.

Gods, she has to let me claim her!

Rober forced himself to walk away. Listening to her splashes and sighs was likely to make his madness complete.

He went to his room, stripped off his shirt, boots, and weapons belt, and laid them aside for washing or inspection. Collecting clean clothing didn't take long enough. Rober found himself pacing nervously, trying to decide how to make his interest clear to Jacquine without spooking her as Marcus had.

Though she retreated to his side every time Marcus came too close for comfort, there was no denying that his brother made her uneasy. Eliminating that discomfort was the first thing he had to accomplish.

Marcus wasn't difficult to find. As the youngest Warrior in their party, caring for the horses—including Etienne's horse that Jacquine had been riding and Franz's that they had been leading along with them—and equipment had fallen to him. As Rober expected, he was oiling the straps on the saddles to protect them from the winter weather.

The smirk settled on his face the moment Rober stepped through the doorway. "I see you've prepared to convince her," he noted.

"Marcus," he warned. With comments like those, sending his brother away before he could embarrass Jacquine was essential.

"You cannot claim you do not want her. Every time you touch her, I see it. Every time you look at her—"

"Pack your things. You will be riding ahead to the manor, but... I will tell Sabine that Franz is lost."

Marcus was abruptly serious. "If The Mad Deceiver comes for her, and you are alone—"

"Stay close, then," he grumbled. Though he'd like to have Marcus far away while he attempted to win Jacquine, there was no denying that her protection had to come first, and Veriel would certainly win against Rober alone. "But far enough away that Jacquine does not know. I think the danger has passed. I intend to extend her the comfort of inns for the rest of the journey."

"And if she refuses you?" Marcus didn't meet his eyes when he asked. A Warrior's printing madness was not a subject widely discussed. Neither was a house lord incapacitated by any means, let alone his own curse.

"I will leave her at the manor in your care and fight my battle."

"The manor is ten days' ride. Though Jacquine sits a horse well—"

"I will survive it."

Marcus nodded. "Then I will collect a bag and take my leave. If you need me..."

"Thank you, but I can control my curse." *I hope I can.*

* * * *

Jacquine stretched her back, sighing that the water had gone cool. It had been a selfish indulgence she could not resist. Certainly, she would have to refill the tub for Rober and Marcus, but it would be well worth this soak.

She stood and reached for the drying cloth, gasping at the wicked feeling of the water coursing down her skin like the brush of fingers. The temptation was too much, and she touched herself. The slick of water and soap made the feeling of her hands on her breasts a sinful delight.

Jacquine closed her eyes, stroking her hands down her chest and stomach. Her mind supplied a lover for her; Rober's hands traced her wet flesh and he pulled her to his body. Phantoms, wisps of sensation from times he had touched her, played at her senses.

God, I do enjoy when he touches me!

How many stories had the older servants told her about what a man's body would feel like thrusting within hers? Listening had been a guilty pleasure, but she'd never dared do something as wanton as imagining a particular man. Until now.

Her fingers found the nub between her thighs, stroking slowly. She sank to her knees in the water. The cool liquid lapped at her, adding touches that were neither of her own hands nor phantoms, undeniably real and wonderfully exciting.

The memory of Marcus 'taking self-release' played at her arousal. His expression had been intense, compelling, his hand stroking his male flesh even more urgently than she was now stroking her own, his muscles tensed.

What would Rober look like when he was aroused? She shivered at the memory of his expression as he untangled her hair the morning Marcus had pursued her, stirring the water past her needing flesh. *Yes!* That was what he'd look like. She was certain it was.

Her fingers moved faster, and she licked her lips. Rober would kiss her, not the kiss on the forehead that he'd given her when he'd gifted her the amulet. He would kiss her as Mara had kissed the gardener in their stolen moments. She wished she knew more of what they did, but she knew only that it was a brazen meeting of two bodies. Just the thought of Rober—

"Jacquine?"

His voice shocked her into reality. Jacquine started to rise but slipped and landed on her backside instead. The water sloshed over the side of the tub and soaked her body again.

"Jacquine? Do you need my help?" His voice was sharp in anger or concern.

"No!" She struggled to her feet and grasped the cloth, wrapping it around her body. Fear that he would barge in on her warred with a sinful certainty that he would—and that he would make her fantasy come true. "I—I fell asleep. My apologies, Rober."

"Are you well?" His voice softened somewhat, making her sigh in relief.

"Yes. Very well, thank you. I will dress and freshen the bath for you."

"You will do no such thing."

Her heart pounded. He couldn't mean that she wasn't to dress, and she argued that fact, though a wild wish that he did mean it lodged in her mind. "Rober?"

"After you dress, you will rest in your room. If you feel equal to the task, you might prepare food when I finish my bath."

"Of course." Jacquine tried to keep the disappointment out of her voice, but it hardly seemed possible to do so. For the life of her, she couldn't name what it was about him that made her think such lustful thoughts, but she thought them all the same.

Jacquine wasted no time: drying her body and hair, pulling on the clothing Rober had provided, and heading for the door. She steeled her expression, acutely aware of the feeling of silk against her skin.

* * * *

Rober looked away from the window as the kitchen door opened, drinking in the sight of her as if it had been months instead of an hour since he'd seen her last.

The dress was the perfect cut to showcase her body. Though not as plump as Sabine, Jacquine had enough flesh to give a man ease and comfort in loving. Her breasts mounded neatly in the deep green bodice, partly covered by the layer of silk, his amulet nestled atop, almost as if it announced her as his. Her hard nipples drew his gaze, and his already-erect cock started throbbing in time with his hammering heart.

Her gasp broke the spell long enough that he looked to her face, trying to gauge her mood. What he saw shot the throbbing to an ache that rivaled the intensity of his *Blutjagd*.

Her wide eyes darted back and forth, surveying his body, pausing at his bare chest, then at the ready length straining his breeches.

A light blush colored her cheeks, but she didn't look away. Her eyes took on a dreamy quality, almost hungry, and the urge to stride to her and kiss her ate at him. Jacquine glanced at his face, then away, shifting uncomfortably, and the moment passed.

While her reaction to him gave him hope that she would accept him, her hesitancy told him clearly enough that it was not yet the time for such a move.

"Go rest," he suggested. "After I bathe—"

She turned back to him, her brow furrowed. "Marcus will not be bathing?"

Rober smiled. It was time to test her defenses. "Marcus will be riding ahead. I imagine he will bathe at an inn along the way." Since he wouldn't be traveling far from them, it was likely that he was staying at the Golden Stag and enjoying the many comforts of the widowed Jessimie.

A smile lit her eyes, a shy smile that made him want her all the more. He strode to her, scooped her hand to his mouth, and kissed her knuckles, his gaze locked with hers.

Jacquine stared up at him, her breathing coming in irregular bursts. "Until supper?" she asked.

"Rest well."

She nodded, easing her hand away and heading for the room he'd assigned her, her bare feet nearly as silent as his own on the smooth wood floors.

He fought back the urge to follow her, reminding himself that her interest wasn't a certain indicator that she was ready or willing to allow more. Her reserve kept him at arm's length.

If it weren't for her self-conscious reaction, he would have kissed her full on the lips. He would have taken her on the table had she proven willing, most likely unable to restrain himself long enough to reach a bed, truth be told. It hardly seemed possible not to touch her.

And her scent... By Ani, the tang of her arousal had him aching, even now that she'd left him.

Rober collected up his clean clothing and headed into the kitchen, determined to put Jacquine out of his mind long enough to make himself worthy of more than a pinched nose and a sour look from a lady.

Once he'd started the water heating, he deposited her foul clothing in the bag he'd burn. Though she'd scrubbed at the drops of beast blood until the scent had dissipated, the stains would remain on the gray wool forever, weakening, then eating holes in it over time.

He dropped his breeches beside the bag and went back to the tub, emptying half the water, bucket by bucket. He grasped the damp drying cloth Jacquine had used, intent on cleaning the spilled water with it.

A faint scent stopped him short. Rober raised it to his face, inhaling deeply. "Gods," he murmured as his body responded to her female musk. Jacquine had been aroused when she'd dried herself.

Her halting explanation echoed in his mind, bringing a wide smile to his face. A chuckle rumbled up. She'd been pleasuring herself when he called out to her. What a joy it would have been to walk in on that sight!

* * * *

Jacquine paced the room Rober had sent her to, looking to the darkness beyond the window panes in stark terror. She fingered the amulet, praying the bit of metal held the magic the Warriors claimed it did. If they lied, the beast Master Jörg—Veriel would surely kill her as he'd killed Etienne and Franz.

She'd been charged with protecting Lady Caitrina. The lady's father would likely die of grief when he learned his daughter was lost, but what of Veriel? Even when Jacquine had believed he was a caring master, she'd known he wouldn't hesitate to harm any who faltered in his or her service to his lady.

Jacquine had failed her most grievously—more than once.

How she'd missed the beast's foul uses of Lady Caitrina was a mystery that ate at her night and day. Rober had tried to explain the ways a beast could cloud her mind or control her actions, but such magic hardly seemed possible.

Worse—and likely the reason the beast would seek to kill her, she'd allowed Caitrina to be killed. Jacquine shuddered at the memory of standing in the doorway as the brash Warrior Franz attacked her lady, as Lord Etienne failed in his bid to save her from his nephew, killing her instead.

She'd failed, and now Caitrina reportedly lived in a damned half-life. Jacquine wrung her hands at the description Marcus had woven of the monster her gentle lady was now, a ravenous, soulless beast with no regard for friend or family.

If Veriel did not come for her, it was likely to be Caitrina. After all, the lady knew her failure better than any soul alive. Would she seek vengeance for it? Would she kill Jacquine for nothing more than the thrill of killing a former friend, as Marcus said she would? Rober had cautioned her not to be taken in by the beguiling lies of her former mistress turned beast.

She will say anything, use your fondest memories against you, all to get you to remove your amulet and fall prey. Do not let her take you, Jacquine. Never remove the amulet. Not even for me.

A knock at the door made Jacquine jump and turn. This was ridiculous! It was only the fact that Rober no longer slept a body length away that made her fear.

"Jacquine?"

She relaxed at the sound of Rober's voice, though she'd already reasoned that it must be he.

"I know you are awake," he informed her, his voice laced in amusement. "I can hear you pacing."

Her cheeks heated. "Come in," she whispered, knowing he would hear her. Jacquine managed a shaky smile for him. "I apologize for disturbing you."

He raised an eyebrow at that. "You have nothing to apologize for. I am typically awake at this hour."

"Of course." *How stupid of me.* Rober typically hunted the night as all his kind did. He would walk the halls of his home at night if he was not hunting. It only made sense.

"You are troubled," he noted.

She didn't bother to deny it. What else would explain her night roaming?

Rober sighed. "You still worry that the beasts will come for you." He didn't question it.

It was abruptly difficult to meet his eyes. "I do not doubt you," she blurted out. She could not doubt him. If Rober thought such a thing of her, what would become of her?

He strode to her, taking her shoulders in his hands gently. "I am glad to hear that," he drawled.

"Truly," she attested.

"Then you doubt the amulet." He rushed on before she could answer. "Or, perhaps you fear that I misspoke the blessing."

Her horror at that idea surely showed on her face. What if he had misspoken? Would the amulet still protect her?

"I see." Rober's voice was thick in some strong emotion. "I did not misspeak, but if it will put your mind at ease, perhaps I should repeat the ceremony."

The intensity in his eyes made her knees weak. "Yes." She cleared her throat, embarrassed by her rasping voice and the tightness in her ribcage. "Perhaps that is best."

* * * *

Rober nearly groaned at that. Her attention flicked to his mouth and back to his eyes, her nipples coming to hard nubs that brushed her dress with every breath much as he'd like to stroke them. By the sublime smell surrounding her, he knew her cleft was warm and wet for him.

He cupped his hands around her neck, letting the blessing roll off his lips in the language of the ancients. The choice to lay his lips over hers instead of over her cheek or forehead seemed a foregone conclusion.

Jacquine's eyes fluttered closed, and a light sound of longing escaped her lips.

His hunger took on a sharp edge at that. He'd dreamed of this moment since he'd seen her weeping over Etienne's body. Rober tilted his head, teasing the tip of his tongue through her slightly-parted lips, suggesting the further intimacies he desired as gently as he could.

She opened further for him, seemingly uncertain. Her hands grasped at his tunic as he thrust more purposefully into her mouth. Rober eased back his fervor as she stiffened, closing his eyes in pleasure at her muffled cry of protest to the change. He let his arousal lead him.

Her body trembled against his, and some measure of sense returned to him. Jacquine was not a lady to be tumbled lightly, and he wouldn't allow her to question his purpose for an instant.

Rober broke off the kiss, feathering his lips over hers several times. It was the telling moment. Either she accepted him or not. *Either she allows me to end this madness or I battle it, once she's safe in Marcus's hands.*

He had to fight the urge to fist his hand at that image. *Not Marcus.* He would leave Jacquine in the keeping of his last *mated* brother, Jean, with orders to keep Marcus at the furthest reaches of Kaufmann.

"My priest will join us tomorrow on your word," he vowed.

Her dark eyes opened slowly, drunk on his kiss. "Rober?" she breathed.

"Say you will marry me. Say it, and I will make you mine."

She looked to the door, no doubt noting for the first time that they were alone in the house, an innocent and a man twice her size, intent on having her. He'd sent Marcus ahead, knowing Jacquine would shy at the idea of consummating what she would deem an illicit interlude in the company of his younger brother. Perhaps, he'd acted in error.

"You have my vow that I mean to wed you. A Warrior always keeps to his word."

Her expression was abruptly uncertain. "Why? You could have any woman you wish."

"I wish for no woman but you." In the grips of printing, no woman could sate him *but* Jacquine.

Jacquine started to answer but faltered, shifting uncomfortably.

"Is it the thought of being my bride?" He forced his voice to remain gentle when the thought that she might refuse him tortured him.

"No," she gasped. "Any woman would be honored to have such a husband." Her cheeks went a stunning shade of pink. "I meant... Well, you are kind, a strong protector, fair and..."

"And?" His voice went rough at that, half in restraint and half in anticipation.

She flicked another glance to his lips, swallowing hard.

"Is it the thought of intimacy before the formalities then?"

She darkened to crimson. "I— Oh, dear Lord," she breathed.

Rober smiled, biting back a hearty laugh. "I can wait for you," he promised, though his heart ached. Other portions of his anatomy ached as well, but he forced himself not to think about them. "Will you be my bride, Jacquine?" His errant cock demanded release. If she agreed, he would be in agony until they were joined.

"Yes. I will."

He brushed another kiss over her lips and turned to leave, already calculating the earliest possible hour to demand this service of Pierre.

"Must you leave?" Jacquine asked hastily, panic edging her voice.

He stilled. His printing demanded that he soothe her, but it also demanded release she was not willing to grant him yet. Self-release would be useless, so fighting off the madness in solitude until morning would be the smartest move.

But she's frightened. "No. If you need me, I will stay."

Once Pierre joined them in matrimony, there would be no need for Jacquine to fear this way. Not even The Destroyer of Lives had ever been insane enough to attack a Warrior wife...since Regana. She would be safe soon, even if he had to leave her to hunt the night.

Her hands touched his arms, and her cheek pressed to his back through his tunic. His cock went from an uncomfortable fullness to a drumbeat that pounded painfully at both his body and soul. He had to touch her.

"I know a way to induce sleep," he found himself offering. *Gods, I will be mad by the time we consummate.*

Jacquine circled his body, her brow furrowed, biting her lip. "A tea? A glass of wine or milk, perhaps?"

He shook his head. "If I promise not to take your maidenhead tonight, will you let me bring you bliss?"

Her initial shock at the idea melted into a look of curiosity. "How would you do such a thing?"

Rober held himself in rigid control, his breathing labored. "May I?"

She nodded, her eyes hungry.

He groaned, swooping down on her lips and resuming his manic exploration.

* * * *

Jacquine gasped into his mouth as Rober lifted her at the waist and carried her. Some portion of her mind urged her to open her eyes and see where he was headed. Another argued that she knew where he meant to take her—and how he meant to take her, that by not looking she could pretend to be surprised when he pressed her into the bed.

The bed did meet her back, but Rober didn't press his body to hers. She opened her eyes, craving his weight over her. He stared at her, dropping to his knees before her. Jacquine shivered as he eased her skirts up, his eyes locked on the area beneath them.

Yes! He means to take me. He cannot help himself. She moaned at that as her skirts settled at her waist. She opened her eyes wide as his breath teased at her ready body, stiffening as his tongue flicked over the eye center of her need.

Rober kissed the spot tenderly, easing her legs over his shoulders when she moved away slightly. "Shhh," he soothed her. "Ride the sensations."

He didn't wait for her to fumble the words to question him. His tongue stroked at her, alternately tormenting her and driving her on.

Jacquine moved against him, begging him to continue, to explain what magic he held over her, screaming that she could take no more, screaming in ecstasy as the pleasure washed over her but did not abate. Rober groaned into her body, and the low rumble seemed to chase up her limbs, sensitizing every fingerwidth of her body, and still he lapped at her like a kitten with cream.

She arched her back, but he moved with her, thwarting her desperate attempt to escape the unending cascade of pleasure bordering on pain. She sobbed out a request for him to stop, pushing half-heartedly at his head and shoulders.

Realization that he might take her at her rash words and end the experience assaulted her, and Jacquine quickly begged him to continue. She screamed as he groaned into her again, adding a richer layer of feeling to those already blurring the edges of her consciousness.

Before long, her cries became moans of exhausted contentment. Her hands slid away from his shoulders to the quilt below her. She watched in detached comprehension as Rober kissed her mound slowly, his breath coming in sharp blasts that made the ache for him pulse in response. He lifted her onto the bed fully, sweeping the quilt over her with a smile.

He kissed her forehead sweetly. "Sleep well, my love. I will be standing guard over you."

Jacquine couldn't form an answer to that. Her eyes slid shut to dreams of Rober filling the aching void within her.

Chapter Nineteen

December 11th, 1497

"Do you swear by your Gods, Rober, and the God of Jacquine that you will live to these vows until the dark ones take you?"

Rober shot him a look of warning. Not only was Pierre asking completely useless questions of him, but he'd brought a reminder of his bride's greatest fear into what should be a happy moment for her.

"I do, indeed," Rober answered proudly. "In the way of my kind, my vow is unto death. It can be no other way." He slid the emerald band onto her middle finger, then raised her hand and kissed it solemnly. It had to be her hand. If he dared kiss her mouth, he would commit sacrilege, especially considering the fact that she'd spoken her vows promising forever, and his printing screamed to seal her to it.

She blushed, looking to Pierre shyly.

"Then by all the Gods assembled, I join you, man and bride. May they bless this union with a new generation of young Warriors."

Her blush deepened, but Jacquine nodded to the old priest.

Rober sucked in his breath painfully, repeating the reminder that she'd not given him leave to plant those babes by that movement over and over.

Pierre raised an eyebrow, making a show of laying a fond kiss on Jacquine's brow and saying a prayer of blessing for her health and safety. He clasped Rober's hand then hobbled away with parting words of luck and love.

Rober had no attention to spare him. The hope shining in his bride's eyes held him captive.

She'd given him such looks since she'd awakened that morning. Her willingness so acute, it had been all Rober could do to force himself to honor his vow to wed her before he bedded her.

But now, her ceremony was behind them, and the time to claim his bride in the way of the Warriors was upon them.

Without a sound, he wrapped an arm around her and led Jacquine to the carriage, lifting her to the seat effortlessly. It wasn't a fashionable affair; the last time it had been used was when Sabine's youngest son was a nursing babe, but it was functional and in good repair.

Rober took his seat beside her and urged the horses to a trot. She didn't question him, and she fairly radiated excitement as they neared the house. At the doors, he unhooked the horses and left them to graze on the few remaining green plants while he swung his bride into his arms and carried her to his bedroom.

He hesitated, holding her over his bed. "Tell me you are mine forever," he requested.

Her fingers pulled at the neck of his tunic, untying it. "Yes. You know I am."

The fierce need to possess her was even more powerful than it had been when she'd agreed to the vows Pierre spoke. He eased her to the bed, following her down until he lay full over her. She raised her head, seeking his kiss urgently. Rober obliged her, working the lacings on her dress until it could be pulled over her head.

He rolled away, freeing her from the press of his body long enough to remove it, then her shoes and stockings. His tunic and boots followed.

He returned to his play, sucking at her already-hard nipples through the chemise, unable to resist touching her though he intended to see her body— soon. Still, though she'd chosen a more modest gown to wear before Pierre, the chemise was not much of a barrier between them.

Jacquine cried out much as she had the night before, her fingers curling in his hair. He stared at the expression of bliss on her beautiful face, wishing he could see her eyes. Rober moved to her other breast, his gaze still locked on her expression.

Slowly, he cautioned himself. He'd asked Jacquine that morning if she were virginal or not, knowing he would claim her too roughly in his need if he didn't keep her state firmly in mind. While he knew he had to ask it, knowing he was her first had nearly driven him to take her then, using her eager looks as reason to break his vow to wed her first.

She arched her shoulders to force her breast further into his mouth. His hands trailed beneath the chemise, working it up her body slowly. Jacquine licked her lips, throwing her head back and forth, moving restlessly against his body, needy little sounds escaping her lips. The chemise slid off of her left shoulder...

Rober froze in a mixture of disbelief and the *Blutjagd* burning cheerily in him. *Marked!* The two pale ovals on her shoulder were a beast feeding site. It was undeniable.

But she swore she hadn't been fed on, he seethed.

He fought his rage back far enough to reason clearly. It was likely that Jacquine didn't know the beast had fed. If the elder reordered her memories as he did it, she could remember anything from seeing to her duties to a pleasant conversation with her Lady Caitrina to nothing at all in its place. Even if she saw the marks in a mirror, Jacquine might not recognize them for what they were—or even note the slight discoloration of her skin.

Questions with no answers filled his mind, taunting him with what he would never know. Had his sweet Jacquine come upon some proof of what the beast was? Had she questioned what the beast had not wanted questioned? Or, had she been simply a ready food source when the beast chose to partake?

Why did I never examine her? Because it would have frightened and embarrassed her? It seemed such a weak excuse now that he knew. Being in the beast's company as long as she had, it was nearly a given that he would have slaked his foul hungers with her. *Why did I never check?*

His stomach lurched uncomfortably. *Which hungers did Veriel slake? Just his lust for blood or his lust for female flesh as well?*

"Rober?" Jacquine asked, seemingly concerned.

He kissed her, possessing her mouth as he dragged the chemise up her body, releasing her to pull it over her head. She was exposed to him now, and yet he hardly dared notice all the little things he'd wanted to know about her.

Rober explored every fingerwidth, assuring himself that there was only one feeding site, so relieved to find site after site unmarked that he trailed hands and mouth over the unblemished skin. Jacquine moaned and writhed, mistaking his actions for lovemaking, and soon they were indistinguishable, even to him. And yet, what would he do if his final moves indicated that the beast had committed other atrocities?

Hunt! The primal urge to see the damned beast dead for such a heinous act burned in him, making his loveplay more fevered and desperate.

Jacquine gasped in delight, licking her lips. She pressed her mound to him in a mute plea to give her what they both burned for.

Rober pulled at his breeches, freeing his cock and settling over her. Blood would be spilled—her blood on his length or beast blood on his blade—before the sun rose again.

She is mine. His mind decreed that clearly. No beast would ever touch her again. Rober eased inside her body in one long glide.

He shivered as she screamed and then sobbed, her short nails biting into his hips, the unmistakable tang of blood scenting the air around them. He held himself still inside her, though the urge to thrust hard and fast beat at his entire body. He whispered prayers of thanks to Ani and Jee for watching over her, smoothing her hair and placing kisses on her forehead and cheeks.

Her trembling subsided slowly, and her hands unclenched. Rober kissed her lips solemnly, sliding back to the music of her whimper of delight. He thrust again, closing his eyes at her pleas for more. His intention of taking her slowly was forgotten amid kisses and cries, bodies moving against each other, seeking that one thing each of them needed beyond reason. Before he quite knew what was happening, he was thrusting madly, her sheath rippling around his length, his name a scream ripped from her lips.

Rober cried out harshly at that, his seed pumping into her and the gods-given ties between them solidifying. He groaned at the sense of peace it gave him, being grounded to a gentle, feminine soul. He laid kisses on her face, swearing a solemn vow that Veriel would pay for marking his woman, and that payment would be very dear indeed.

Chapter Twenty

February 25th, 1498

Caitrina stood outside the Kaufmann manor house, untouched by the elements, unseen by either human eyes or the senses of the Warriors in her ghosted state.

Jörg's arms circled her, and his lips teased at her throat. "If she is with the Warriors, you know she is safe," he stated again.

They are only a danger to me, she thought sadly.

"No more," he answered that concern, though she hadn't spoken it to his mind. "You are more powerful than they are."

She nodded. "I know. I must be certain, Jörg. I must know that she is happy here. If not..."

He sighed. "It is unlikely that she will accept your aid, even in offering her a better place."

"I know." But she had to know that Jacquine was content here.

It had taken them almost three months to find her former maid due to the blasted amulet that hid her feed string from them, and Caitrina could not walk away until she'd settled her uncertainties.

She approached the house, her acute hearing picking up the sounds of laughing women and children. The sounds of putting children to bed were unmistakable. Was Jacquine their nurse then? Her move to mist and enter the dwelling was stilled by someone coming down the stairs into the kitchen.

Her breath caught at the sight of Jacquine. The young woman fairly glowed in happiness, and her clothing rivaled those that Caitrina had owned as a human. In a fashionable wrap and with her chestnut hair loose around her shoulders, she hardly seemed the same woman they'd left behind.

A mixture of scents teased her hunter's senses, and Caitrina drew them in, starved for any knowledge of her former friend. Her anger that one of the damned Warriors was bedding her diminished with the additional scents. A whisper of new life lived in her, and if Jacquine carried a child, she was more than someone's plaything. She was mate to one of the men of this house.

As if they'd shared that thought, Jacquine suddenly smiled, reaching for a pitcher of water on the table.

Despite the amulet that stood between them and the mistrust Jacquine would harbor, Caitrina ached to hug her close and wish her well.

"No, Caitrina," Jörg spoke sharply.

She ignored him, unghosting.

* * * *

Jacquine looked up, confused at the sound of a male voice outside. Jean and Rober were upstairs with Sabine, Natalie, and the children. Marcus had only left on trail the night before. What would bring him back so quickly?

Her heart stuttered at the face in the window. *No!* It wasn't possible. It was a dark dream, and she was sleeping. Yes, that would be the answer. She'd fallen asleep while they put the children in their beds and was dreaming this.

Caitrina smiled, placing her hand on the glass between them, and Jacquine shook her head in disbelief, setting the pitcher on the edge of the table numbly.

"Jean," Rober called out sharply, no doubt sensing that Caitrina was near.

A second face appeared next to Caitrina's. Veriel's expression was one of fury, and Jacquine screamed, scrambling back to the wall. The pitcher overturned and shattered on the floor; water and broken pottery rained over her feet.

The thunder of footsteps matched the thudding beats of her heart. In the instant Jacquine blinked her eyes, the faces were gone as if they'd never existed. Then Rober had her in his arms, lifting her away from the scattered bits of pitcher. He placed her at his back, pulling her hands around his waist with a murmured command to stay at his back.

The cold blast of air let her know that Jean had reached the door. A series of curses left his lips, then the door slammed shut again. "Both of them," he stated. "It must have been the Deceiver and the she-beast."

Jacquine shuddered at the memory of Veriel's anger.

Rober sheathed his weapon and gathered her back into his arms. "He will never touch you," he breathed. His fingertips caressed her still-flat womb. "He knows the lengths I will go to now, and he will never dare."

She pressed her face into his chest. "I know." But, the sense of loss still plagued her. For just a moment, she'd believed the gentle look on Caitrina's face. Was this the deception Rober and Marcus had warned her would come? Or was there something even they didn't know? What was her former lady now?

Section Four

Remember Me

Note to the readers:

As I told you in 'Fair Caitrina,' Jörg is sometimes a hero and sometimes a villain. In 'Remember Me,' he's not easy to call. I want to insist he's still a tortured hero, but the mask comes off, and you get a stunning look at the cruelty inherent in the beast Veriel. Hope you enjoy this look into Jörg with the newest incarnation of Regana's soul, Yzabeau de Cambion. For those of you who've read 'Fair Caitrina,' you are not imagining a similarity in names.

Happy reading!
Brenna

Chapter Twenty-One

Introduction to the Stone

>From the dawn of human memory, I have stood: sentinel between the ancient gods of my kind and those who walked the Earth, source of power and knowledge to the servants of my gods, planner of destinies, and physical keeper of the beasts who threatened it all.

My weaknesses are few. I can only be defeated by one of my favored children—only by one who acts with good intentions in his heart. Jörg was such a son, acting only to save his mate.

He was the finest Cursed Warrior ever born, in this war or any war that came before, but power and madness walk hand in hand. Jörg was the epitome of the hand of our gods on the face of the world—as long as he was stable. When he lacked control, he was the face of the beast Veriel, the beast he'd accepted to save Regana.

Would that Jörg had chosen death for himself and his bride, all would have been well. Would that Jörg had asked any boon of the gods but his desire to protect Regana, this damned war would have ended more than a millennium ago.

A man committed to safeguarding love could only do so if he felt that love. And so he was damned to live his connection to Regana through her lifetime and every lifetime her soul lives. As a Cursed Warrior, Jörg rivaled the gods themselves.

As beast incarnate, intent on the goal of protecting his mate—of possessing that which was stolen from him, Jörg has proven my match. Until now.

My second failing is my own caring. I was created as mother to the Warriors. Endowed with feelings for those I protect, I cannot help but to see even those who turn against me as my children. Damned and Cursed alike are my sons, and I love them all.

Though I plan a destiny that ends the lives of those gone beast, it is not with malice to my sons that I plan. The death of their physical bodies means the freedom of their tortured souls and the imprisonment of the beasts who drive them. It is a kindness to free them.

For more than a millennium in the current war alone, I have stayed my hand. I have laid my plans, arranged the players and let my sons follow their hearts. I tire of war, of seeing my children suffer and die, fated always to sense the darkness of the other and battle to the death for it, never knowing peace while both exist.

Only in the extinction of the beasts are the Warriors freed, and only in death by a Cursed Warrior's hand are the beasts at rest. The time has come, for like any mother, I must enforce limits on the foolishness of my children.

Jörg has always had advantages in these encounters that the others do not. His beast powers and inherent abilities aside, Jörg retains full knowledge of his past and the rules of engagement that guide the players. While the others are only dimly aware of their course, Jörg plans for each encounter like a coming battle. He never rests, always searching for the next incarnation of Regana's soul I will lay in his path, though his foes are never forewarned. Such is the game the gods demand we play.

Once the favorite of my sons, Jörg has become my greatest adversary. He is as stubborn as he is talented. He is set in his ways, obsessed with a course that can never be. But, a mother has her limits. This is Jörg's final chance to be the man I know him to be without a mother's intervention.

May he learn to stay his own hand before it is too late.

Chapter Twenty-Two

March 15th, 1715

Yzabeau de Cambion cursed fluently as she rounded a corner and faced a dead end. The words she uttered would shock her sister Colette, but such concerns were the least of Yzabeau's worries now.

She'd run blindly, praying that God would show her mercy and lead her through the unfamiliar backstreets of Brest. Yzabeau searched for a means of escape, but there was no way out of the alley, not even a window she might shatter or a door she might somehow break in. She was through.

She swallowed a sob as the pounding feet drew near and pulled the small knife she carried from beneath her cloak. They would kill her either way. If she fought them, Yzabeau might die with her purity intact.

The three men rounded the corner, coming to a halt. Their leader smiled, a cold smile that sent chills down her spine. This was the only one of them she knew, an unsavory bit of scruff who'd come to collect a gambling debt from her brother Michel only days earlier.

Yzabeau had disliked Henri le Marinier immediately and intensely. The man stood too close, made himself too familiar, and his eyes followed Colette and Yzabeau too carefully for Yzabeau's tastes. If Michel noticed the man's rude behaviour, he gave no sign. With Michel, one could never tell.

The two men with him were not known to her, though Yzabeau had heard Henri call out to them as they chased her down: Marcel and Raoul. Yzabeau knew all she needed to know. The men kept poor company and took orders from a fool, a braggart, and a man who would not hesitate to murder anyone in his way. At the moment, Yzabeau might be considered 'in Henri's way.'

Henri's gaze roamed over her body, assessing her God-given attributes boldly.

She raised her chin in challenge, gleaning his intent. "My brother will kill you," she warned him, though it was most likely a waste of breath to try. That Godless dog Henri knew Michel too well for that bluff to prove effective.

He ambled toward her, heedless of her blade, which reflected the last rays of the setting sun. "You think I fear Michel?" he taunted.

No, she didn't think he did. That was the problem. It would be easier to escape this trap if he did, but it was no secret that their fortune had dwindled in the care of her intemperate brother.

Michel had sunk so low that it was likely her death or dishonor would only push him further into his dark humor. Even if he hoisted himself away from his bottle and other amusements long enough to try to avenge her, the best Yzabeau could hope for would be that Michel wouldn't get himself killed in the attempt. His enemies knew that, and so Yzabeau had become a target.

"You know I do not," Henri mused, "yet you came here at this late hour." He clucked his tongue and shook his head in censure, earning him hearty laughs from Marcel and Raoul.

Yzabeau swallowed a scream of frustration. She hadn't wanted to come to the marketplace this late, but Colette was ill and needed the herbs Yzabeau now carried in her pouch. She should have waited for the morning. Coming tonight had been foolhardy. Believing she could find everything she needed at a single stop had been a wager not even her brother would have taken.

"You cannot fight us all," Henri chided, reaching for the knife in her hand, as if Yzabeau would surrender it to his keeping.

She sliced at him, making a thin cut on his forearm as he fled the circle of her reach. "Perhaps the others will flee when you lay dead," she spat.

Henri looked at the blood staining his shirt in confusion. The man hadn't expected her to fight him.

The fool!

His face darkened in fury. "You will pay for that," he promised. He lunged at her.

Yzabeau drew more blood, but it was for naught. Her training was limited, and this man had doubtless been in countless fights with opponents more skilled than she. The stone wall was at her back and her knife lying out of reach in little more than the blink of an eye.

The smell of liquor was strong on Henri's breath. Yzabeau met his eyes steadily, though the sour taste of fear flooded her mouth. Her heart hammered in her chest.

"Blood for blood," he growled. "Though I need no knife to make your blood flow, do I?"

She shook her head, beating at him as he pulled up her skirts. Henri's body pressed hard to hers, driving the stays into Yzabeau's ribs until she could barely draw breath.

"Hold her," Henri ordered his men.

Yzabeau stilled as she looked over his shoulder. Marcel and Raoul were not coming to his aid. They lay on the ground, their heads at odd angles to their bodies.

A man stood between them, a mountain of a man with dark brown hair and silver eyes. His manner of dress unnerved her almost as much as his sudden appearance. He wore a fine pair of trousers and a shirt fit for a nobleman, but he was without any coat or cloak that would be fitting for a walk about the city.

She bit her lip, her heart racing at his appearance. Where had he come from? Why was he here? Sense intruded. He had killed Marcel and Raoul silently, easily. This man could be a strong ally.

"Help me," she whispered.

He nodded, his expression fierce.

"What are you..." Henri stopped in surprise as he spied the destruction over his shoulder. His gaze settled on the new arrival. He turned, dragging Yzabeau along by her arm.

She stumbled into him, then righted herself, loath to touch the foul man beside her.

"Who are you?" Henri demanded, though his eyes were wide and wild, belying his seeming calm.

The dark-haired man grinned. "The one who will teach you proper respect for a lady. Her *blood* is not yours to take."

"I am owed satisfaction. She is mine."

Yzabeau felt her cheeks burn in anger. He was not owed satisfaction. Henri was owed the few coins that Michel was short in his payment, and nothing more.

"No," her ally attested. "She is mine, and any man who touches her answers to me."

Yzabeau tried to hide her look of shock. She'd never seen the man before. He had no more claim on her than her attacker did. Still, her heart fluttered at the idea of being his.

His smile widened. "Dear one." His voice rumbled out, full of dark amusement. "Why did you not wait for me?" There was a hint of rebuke in that statement.

Henri tightened his grip on her arm, shooting her a look of confusion.

Yzabeau ground her teeth at the twinge of pain his grip caused. "I—did not want to disturb you," she lied, playing at the big man's game. *Jörg.* The name filtered into her mind. Even if it was not his name, she could use it.

She cast Henri a hard look. "You may not fear Michel, but I suggest you release me before Jörg is forced to teach you fear."

It was a bold move, a completely mad and presumptuous leap of faith. The dark-haired man—Jörg—raised an eyebrow at her bluff, something between amusement and exasperation etched on his disconcertingly beautiful face.

Henri looked from Yzabeau to Jörg. He released her and edged away, suddenly wary.

Yzabeau reached for her blade.

"Leave it," Jörg barked.

She looked at him in confusion. "But—"

"Leave it and come to me." His jaw tightened in warning.

Yzabeau nodded slowly, confused by her acceptance of his order. No man ordered Yzabeau de Cambion, not even her older brother. She strode to Jörg and placed a kiss on his cheek as if she greeted a lover.

Jörg's eyes burned in some fierce emotion she couldn't name. "Better," he complimented her. "Stay here."

It was another order, and Yzabeau didn't question that she would follow his command.

He crossed the space to Henri and grasped the smaller man's head between his large hands. "My bride is not yours to touch," Jörg whispered.

The resounding crunch of breaking bones echoed in the silence around them. Yzabeau shook her head in disbelief as Henri crumpled to the ground, his sightless eyes accusing her. She turned, intent on escaping the vision—and the man who could kill in so cold and calm a fashion.

Yzabeau squawked as she crashed into a broad chest. She looked up at Jörg without comprehension, then glanced back at the three dead men. *He was there,* she reasoned with herself, fighting back full-blown panic. *He stood over Henri just a moment ago.*

"Come," he growled, taking her arm.

Yzabeau pulled at his hold. "My knife," she reminded him.

"Leave it." He pulled her along down the alley.

She planted her feet, then stumbled along when he kept pulling. "No. I need to get my knife."

He turned on her, his face all harsh lines of fury in the shadows gathering around them. "So you can attempt something so foolish again? I think not. You are safer unarmed." He pulled her along more roughly. "You have never known when to turn from a fight," he accused.

Yzabeau felt her cheeks burn. Michel had said the same of her many times. Still, and despite her earlier musings, this man had no right to say it. "You are in no position to judge. I do not know you, *sir.*"

"You do not?" he taunted.

"I do not. Do you seek to anger me with this mad insistence that I know you when you know as well as I do that I do not?"

"You called me by name," he noted, not breaking stride as Yzabeau halted in shock. The man—Jörg—pulled her along, ignoring her stumbling, setting her on her feet without looking at her and without stopping for her, certain that she would follow along.

"A coincidence," she decided.

"You are claiming you have no memory of me?"

"Of course not. What memory could there be?" Yzabeau challenged.

Jörg turned to her, bringing his mouth down on hers, hard and insistent, his tongue forcing past her lips to brush over her own. The hand on her arm moved to her back, caressing her as it moved to the meat of her buttocks. The other joined it, and he lifted her to fit his body, molding Yzabeau to the hard lines of his chest and thighs.

Her body exploded in sensations that Yzabeau could almost name. Her skin burned.

The fires of hell. Nothing so sinfully wonderful could be Heaven's work.

An ache built inside her; not a pain but an emptiness, a wild, untamed need. Was this lust?

Jörg's mouth grew more urgent. His hands squeezed and stroked her body. Yzabeau met his kiss, delirious in the sensations drowning her mind's protests.

Yes. She knew this. She knew him. She experimented with half-remembered thoughts and wishes, learning from Jörg as he changed the movements and pace of his mouth again and again.

His member grew long and hard against her thigh. Yzabeau shifted in his arms, encouraging his arousal, inviting him to press the length to the ache gnawing at her. A certainty that he could light her ablaze and save her from the fire in a single touch drove her on.

He obliged her, pressing Yzabeau into the wall behind her. She moaned into his mouth as that delicious ridge nestled to her core, cursing the layers of fabric that separated them. If this was lust, God could ask any penance He wished of her—later.

Jörg tore his mouth from hers, his breathing ragged and his body trembling. "You remember me," he informed her.

Yzabeau nodded shakily, reaching for his mouth, desperate to feel his kiss again.

He shook his head. "Not here," he whispered.

She blushed. He was right, of course. They were in a dirty alley.

Jörg shifted as if to set her on her feet, and the fire in her blood flared, overpowering her sensibilities again.

Yzabeau touched his mouth. "I need you, Jörg."

Chapter Twenty-Three

Jörg shivered in anticipation. None of Regana's souls had come to him so readily. Even Caitrina had initially shied from his touch. He knew Yzabeau felt the connection between them, but kissing her had been an impulsive move, one born of frustration with her. Jörg hadn't expected her to accept him. He wasn't certain what he *had* expected of her, but he couldn't deny that her reaction was the finest gift he had been granted in over two centuries.

"Yes," he rasped, suddenly remembering that she had offered herself to him moments ago.

He didn't place Yzabeau on her feet immediately. Jörg fought down the mad urge to ghost them both and thrust into her here. He had been alone too long—more than two centuries without Regana, but he had coerced the human beasts into submission to take their lives in silence. The Cursed Warriors would arrive soon, and his counterpart was sure to be with them.

Jörg eased Yzabeau down his body, savoring the feeling of the curves he knew so well pressed to the hard planes of his chest again. He would claim her somewhere safe. His mouth watered at her look of invitation. *Somewhere close.* If Jörg had to smell her arousal, touch her skin, and see the pleading in her eyes without granting them both release soon, he would lose all remaining sanity.

He led her out to the boulevard, his hold gentler but his steps no slower. Anger still burned low in his gut. Regana's souls were endlessly taking chances that ultimately took them from him. This chance was the last Yzabeau would ever take.

Jörg steered her through the rear entrance to Blanche's establishment and up the stairs that the more social-conscious patrons took. Jörg took these steps on occasion, when he searched out a whore for blood and sex on a night that hunting didn't appeal to him.

He knew which room he wanted. It was a private room on the third floor. Jörg had used the room before, but not for its usual purpose. The room was typically used by lords and merchants with a taste for bondage and pain.

Jörg chose it for only two reasons. It was plush, decorated in silk and lace; overall, the only room in the establishment worthy of Yzabeau's presence. Better, it was secluded. It was unlikely that anyone would hear their passion. He owed Yzabeau that much, though he cringed that he had brought her to a brothel in his haste to have her.

Blanche appeared at the head of the stairs, her mouth curving in amusement as she eyed Yzabeau. "Any other man would be shown the door, Jörg," she purred.

Yzabeau stiffened. Her jealous fury was intense and immediate. Though she didn't note it, a flash of a fractured image lit in her mind and was gone again—Jacquine.

Jörg wrapped his arms around her before Yzabeau could launch at the older woman. "Leave us, Blanche. You will receive your usual fee for all the time we require."

Her smile was full of undisguised curiosity mixed with a large measure of avarice. "She is that special? Perhaps I should offer her a permanent position."

He allowed his beast free rein for a moment. His eyes glowed in the dim stairwell, and his fangs extended. "Only if your life has lost value," he growled. "I invite you."

She paled, moving aside to let Jörg pass with Yzabeau wrapped in his arms. "All the time you require," Blanche whispered. "No interruptions, Jörg."

"You serve me well."

Blanche touched the pale marks at her throat and shuddered. "Yes, Master." The door closed behind her, and her footsteps disappeared down the stairs.

Jörg released Yzabeau. She turned on him, pulling at the illusion of his clothing frantically. He forced her hands back.

"Jörg," she pleaded.

"Not yet." Until he handled the problem of her aging him as centuries of time could not, neither of them would discuss anything else. "You will learn a lesson first."

"Lesson?" she breathed, pulling against his grip. "What lesson?"

"You take too many chances. You try to kill me in fear for you. You will not again."

"You have my word," she begged. "I vow—"

"Not this time. You have a way of forgetting your promises when it suits you." He pulled her toward the bed.

Yzabeau licked her lip, her musk intensifying. Jörg hardened further in response, then shook his head to dislodge the urge to take her without making his point clear.

He sank to the bed and pulled her between his spread knees. "Undress."

Her movements were sensuous, a vision of Regana on their last night together. The layers of clothing disappeared one after another.

Too slow. He cursed this century, with the layers of clothing and lacing that made getting a woman naked in his arms both time-consuming and maddening. He longed for the days when he could have Regana unclothed for him in a few precious moments, even when she made a show of disrobing for him. Jörg tore at the last of Yzabeau's clothing, tossing it away. He dimly noted that he would have to provide her with new, but it was well worth seeing her body faster.

Yzabeau reached for the illusion of his clothing again, and he slapped her bottom soundly. She rocked forward onto her toes, her eyes wide in surprise.

"For going to the marketplace so late. You will not risk yourself again," he assured her.

Jörg smacked her again, studiously biting back a wince as she whimpered. "For attacking Henri with a blade that might have been turned against you." He stroked his fingers over the warmth he'd caused.

She licked her lips again, her eyes pleading with him to move on to what she craved.

"Close your eyes," he growled. She was undoing his resolve.

Yzabeau did so with a shiver. Her nipples stood out as points. Jörg pinched one, and she hissed out her breath. Yzabeau arched her back, offering her breasts to him.

Jörg smacked her bottom again, reining in his needs as she groaned and shifted against his palm. "For trusting a man who might have been worse than Henri without question." *For trusting me when you had no reason to.*

He dispelled the illusion of his clothing and lifted her across his thighs. His next smack was harder, his frustration with the chances she'd taken driving him. Had it been any other man she'd trusted and not Jörg—

He pushed away that thought, reminding himself that she had no idea what that smack had represented. "For challenging Henri with a man who might not have backed you—or who might have expected more than you were willing to give in return."

She needs to learn this lesson, and learn it well, he reminded himself. Jörg fingered one of the scars Pauwel had gifted him with early in his training. Pauwel had always been nearly his equal.

Lessons should be painful. His training taught him that. Jörg pushed away the other lessons he'd learned, the ones that said he should be killed for teaching a woman a lesson this way, especially a woman that was his to protect.

Yzabeau squirmed against him, her woman's curls taunting him with what they both really wanted of this bed.

Jörg smacked her again. "For not screaming and fighting when an unknown man killed in front of you and carried you away."

She bit her lip, her scent driving him near mad to taste her. Her fingers played at his hip, enticing him again to end his lesson.

"Be still," he ordered, striking her again. *For the Stone's amusement in giving you to Cambion's family.* Jörg touched the red print of his hand in a raging hunger.

"Please, Jörg," she begged. "I will not risk myself again."

"You submit to me?" he asked. The question was out before he had a chance to stop it. He'd never asked Regana's soul to submit to him before. He wasn't certain she was capable of being tamed willingly, though he had broken her to submission in the past.

"Yes. Anything."

* * * *

Yzabeau glanced up at Jörg as he smacked her bottom again, a gentler smack, as if symbolic of something she could not comprehend. She moaned in mixed pleasure and pain, the throbbing of her backside playing beautiful counterpoint to the throbbing inside her.

"Be still," he repeated.

His fingers nudged her thighs apart and slid inside her. Yzabeau fisted her hand in the comforter teasing her aching nipples, willing her body still as he stroked just inside her. Her body burned for him, for that length of him pressed to her curls.

She closed her eyes, remembering... *No, not remembering. Imagining...*

"Anything, Jörg," she begged, searching out his molten silver eyes. "I will submit."

A smile curved his lips. "Prove it."

She furrowed her brow. "How?" *Anything.* She would do anything he asked, if he sated the need clawing at her to know his body.

Jörg eased her off his lap and to her knees. His cock waved before her in invitation. A searing certainty stole her breath, the pleasure she could give him, the pleasure he would give her in return. Yzabeau kissed the damp head, tasting the pungent liquid coating him, licking at the proof of his arousal.

He groaned. Encouraged, she took more of him into her mouth, ravenous for him. Jörg's hands fisted in her hair, guiding Yzabeau in motions that held no hint of being foreign to her. She teased him, following a crystalline, inborn memory of what would please Jörg most.

Yzabeau drove him on, faster and harder, anticipating the coming moment. He would fill her mouth with his seed, a flood of his heat with the taste of wild, untamed need. The memory of that taste had the moisture from her core coating her thighs.

"Yes," Jörg hissed. "Remember me." He cried out harshly as he climaxed.

Yzabeau suckled at him, swallowing the taste she knew so well, greedily taking him deeper. She closed her eyes, determined to burn this moment into his memory for all time.

Jörg was far too well known to the woman on the stairs. He would never touch another. She would make him burn for her as she burned for him. He was hers alone.

Jörg collapsed to the bed, his hands loosening in her hair. He stroked at her mussed curls, shivering as she kissed at his inner thigh.

Yzabeau rose up over him, pleased with the results of her performance. "Have I proven my submission?" she asked, letting a smug note creep into her voice.

He forced his eyes open, a speculative look settling on his features. "Do you honestly think you have?" he challenged, his limp cock growing stiff again. He stood, towering over her.

Yzabeau felt her heart race at the power rippling through him as he stood. "No," she admitted. She wanted to own this man, body and soul. Submission had nothing to do with it. Yzabeau wanted to make her claim clear to him.

Her eyes locked on a strange deep red mark on his shoulder and she pressed her lips to it, tracing it slowly. Jörg's hands tangled in her hair again, and his breath was hot on the top of her head. Yzabeau licked at the mark, drunk on the feeling that she owned him, that this was somehow proof that she did.

"On the bed," he growled. "Now."

* * * *

Jörg watched the sway of her bottom, as Yzabeau crawled up on the wide bed. She lay on the silk comforter and waited for his next move, her body a riot of half-recognized memories of their lovemaking through Regana's lifetimes.

He raked his gaze over her body. Yzabeau shifted, bowing her back up to display herself more fully to him, moaning as the silk caressed her back and buttocks. The sensations—and memories of sensations—assaulted her.

Jörg reached into the cabinet beside the bed, uncertain for the first time. Dealing with Yzabeau posed several problems. Her mind and body were awash in the waves of these maddening phantoms, memories that were not truly memories, snips of sensation that taunted her with no coherent framework to set them into, tumbling over her in an unruly mob. Fractured memories of Regana's visits to his home melded with Ilona's memories and Caitrina's until it was a confused mass of disjointed images.

The effect made her reactions nearly uncontrollable. Her passion, love, and jealousy were volatile, and would continue to be until Yzabeau came to terms with the cascade of her past lives encroaching on her mind and body.

He paused with his hand on a stack of silk scarves. Yzabeau was lost in the minds of her past lives. Perhaps if the sensations of claiming her were different enough, she might form her own bond with him, apart from the others.

Jörg returned to the bed, arguing that idea with himself. He'd certainly never encountered anything like he just had with Yzabeau with any of her other incarnations.

A pang of guilt raced through him. He'd never struck Regana before, even in her first lifetime, when Jörg had treated her most shamefully.

The fact that Yzabeau enjoyed it could be attributed to the madness of her memories. Any touch would excite her. The fact that Jörg had enjoyed it was unforgivable. Asking her to pleasure him in this state was unforgivable.

Or so he told himself, as he bound Yzabeau's wrists to the bed. Jörg should hold her, explain what was happening to her, restrain her for nothing more than her own safety, not take her barrier until she was in her own mind again.

Her eyes closed in pleasure, and her scent called to him. Yzabeau pleaded with him silently for the touch she remembered, for every touch she remembered at once.

Jörg sank to the bed beside her, touching her cheek. "Yzabeau," he whispered. "We must not do this yet."

She shook her head, tears welling in her eyes. "You must love me," she pleaded. "You— I am yours, Jörg. Do not refuse me."

His heart ached. The temptation was strong, and Jörg had never excelled at refusing Regana's souls when they wanted something of him. "You are mine," he assured her. "I will love you, when you are yourself again, when you know yourself again."

Yzabeau pulled against her bound hands. "I am—" She faltered, her own name seeming foreign in her mind though no other name stepped forward to make itself known to her.

Jörg winced at the progression of her thoughts, at her battle to explain herself. "You are not certain. Are you?" He stretched out beside her, stroking her cheek in comfort.

"I am Yzabeau de Cambion," she insisted, though she was less than certain that the name was the correct one to use. It was the only clear choice to her, and so she grasped at it hopefully. "My older brother is

Michel, and my younger sister, Colette. I am twenty years of age."

"And?" he prodded gently.

"I am yours." Her eyes were full of pain and confusion. The whole of her existence had been reduced to only those few shaky facts and that one burning certainty, that she belonged to him.

"Why do you believe that? How do you know it? You yourself argued that you laid eyes on me for the first time this evening. Now you would give me any intimate pleasure I ask. You would surrender your purity to me."

Her expression was abruptly hopeful—and hungry.

Jörg grimaced. *Why did I suggest that?* "You are mine, Yzabeau. I love you. I dispute neither fact, but I want you to understand why you are mine."

Her brow furrowed. "Why?" She asked it as if there had never been a question of why she was his, that she simply was.

Why did I believe this would be easier? Knowing me out of the context of the actual memories of her lives? This intimate knowledge without the daily events to place it in perspective may drive us both mad.

{Ah. So, you do remember asking for this?}

Shut up. At moments like this, Jörg always tried to convince himself that he was mad and arguing with himself, but he knew the truth. *You are amusing yourself as usual, Stone.*

{I gave you what you asked for.}

As a good mother always does, he noted sarcastically.

{You prolong your pain...and hers. You know what you should do.}

Jörg looked at Yzabeau, his stomach twisting in something resembling fear. *No. She is mine.* He couldn't let her go, not when he had waited so long for her.

{You did it once. You walked away and left her to the better man.} Even in that simple statement, there was a hint of censure, a reminder of one of his greatest failures. Jörg had stolen everything from her, even then.

No. Jörg kissed her tenderly. "You are mine, because you were born to be mine. Do you believe that?"

Yzabeau nodded. She shifted her body against him, straining her neck to reach his mouth.

Jörg stroked her nipple, watching as it hardened for him. "Do you want to be mine?" *Only her choice matters.*

She arched her back until her nipple brushed his chin, offering herself to him. "Always," she gasped. "Forever."

He sucked in the offered nipple, closing his eyes as she moaned, feeling the burn of his printing again as if it were the first time he'd asked and she'd accepted him, the first time he'd bound his soul to hers.

Jörg started off slowly, but self-control had never been his strong area of battle with Regana's souls.

{Self-control has never been an attribute you could boast in any arena,} the Stone rebuked him.

As if proving the Stone correct, his fangs extended, and his hunger rose up, howling for the delights he'd so often shared with Caitrina. Jörg laid his cheek on her stomach, shivering as he reasoned his beast back.

Unless he planned to flee into the night with Yzabeau, he could not do anything the Warriors could track. Jörg couldn't reorder memories. He could not coerce her, even to entice Yzabeau to sleep if it were prudent to do so. Even if he truly wished to feed from her—and he didn't—that would bring the Warriors faster than anything else he could do would.

Yzabeau moved restlessly. "Jörg?" she asked, fear making her voice tremble.

She would like it if Jörg licked at her until she shattered in his arms, but Jörg pushed that idea away. Memories of Caitrina were suddenly fresh in his mind. Yzabeau's blood rushed in her veins, calling to him. The lure of the pulse point in her thigh would steal what little control he did possess.

Jörg settled over her, forcing his fangs back. "You want to be mine?" he asked again.

"Yes." She threw her legs around his hips, pressing her core to his aching cock. "Now. Please, Jörg."

It wouldn't be painless, as it had been for Caitrina. Jörg couldn't risk making it so. He would have to feed to erase her pain, and feeding would bring the Warriors.

He searched her face, considering his options. Yzabeau found every touch a joy, even when he'd pinched and struck at her. Perhaps it was fortuitous that she was half-crazed for him.

He nodded, grasped her hips, and worked inside her slowly. Jörg held her still when Yzabeau writhed beneath him, forcing him deeper. He thrust forward, taking her barrier smoothly.

Her eyes opened wide at the pain deep inside her. The scent of blood mixed with her arousal made Jörg's heart pound in anticipation, in longing—a feverent wish to share with her as he had shared with Caitrina.

He thrust deep, crying out as her body rippled around him, announcing her rising climax.

Jörg's control fled. He surged into her over and over. Yzabeau bowed up beneath him, yanking her bonds tight as she screamed his name. Jörg followed her over, roaring out his possession of Regana's newest incarnation.

She nestled her face to his shoulder, loving at his blood mark as she had in every incarnation. Regana's souls had always been drawn to the mark of Reg, to the intensity at the base of the fire.

{The intensity that always destroys her in the end.}

Quiet.

He released her hands, laying teasing kisses on her mouth and jaw.

Yzabeau barely caught her breath before her responses grew fevered again. Jörg groaned as he pulled her over him, allowing her to take what she sought from him.

{He will accept her. No matter what happens between you, Pauwel's soul will accept her. Your possession means nothing to him.}

Jörg ignored the Stone, taking Yzabeau frantically, holding to the hope that she would be his forever this time.

{Forever?} The Stone's voice taunted him with foreknowledge that he would never have his wish.

Jörg prayed that the damned Stone wouldn't remind him that a Warrior Jäger *geboren* waited to give him the only peace he deserved. *Shut up.*

Chapter Twenty-Four

Joseph Lord Armen crouched over the three dead men, while his nephew William held the lantern high for him. "A beast," Joseph mused. "An elder."

William didn't ask how Joseph could know for certain that the kill was the work of an elder. It was a gift of Joseph's, and not even the Stone seemed inclined to explain why he had such a gift.

As usual, the Stone was amusing itself with hidden plans, secrets, and puzzles. Joseph was just another puzzle designed to amuse the Stone, but the Stone's puzzles always had dire answers, games of life and death tied up in the depths of what was hidden from view. He shivered at that thought, at what game of life and death was being thrust upon the Warriors this time.

"Carstol was known to kill this way," William noted.

"In the early days. Yes," Joseph conceded, though Carstol typically stayed in sparsely populated areas. What would drive Carstol to a town as large as Brest? Lorian and Cerran preferred cities to farming communities...and The Mad Elder, of course.

"The blond one has other wounds."

"Not a claw." Joseph looked around, his eyes stopping on a glint of metal an arm's length away. He pulled it up into the light. "Blood. Human blood. It is a woman's blade. A noblewoman."

"Did she flee?" William asked in confusion.

"Unlikely. Why would she not report the attack?"

There was little chance that she had. The report of a noblewoman would have seen human soldiers swarming over this site long ago. The place was still as the deaths that polluted it. Were it not for the lantern Joseph had William light to allow him to track better—illumination that was not needed for any other reason—there would be no sign of life in any direction.

"The elder did not feed, so he could not have completely erased her memory of the events."

Joseph shook his head. "No. He did not feed," he agreed.

"And...he is not coercing her," William continued uneasily. Whatever was wrong, William felt it, as well.

"No. She went with him willingly—in some fashion."

"Or she was unconscious," William suggested hopefully.

Joseph grunted his agreement, though he was certain that wasn't the case. "Douse the light. I am through here."

He moved away, fingering the blade, his eyes adjusting effortlessly to the near total darkness around them. Something bothered him about this situation, an unusual sense of urgency. Joseph reached out to the Stone's mind, questioning the breach in his typical calm.

Joseph reveled in his connection to the Stone, blessing the comfort that came in speaking with the font of their knowledge. He often wondered how other Warriors, ones not chosen as Stone lord, lived with having to use Joseph as their go-between with the entity that guided them.

Instead of the usual calming flow of knowledge, the Stone added to his unease with the type of answer every Warrior dreads to hear. *{She will come to you.}*

His heart stuttered. It was a puzzle, the type of situation his father had prepared him for since Joseph first displayed his unusual gifts. *Who will come to me? How will I know her?*

{You will know her. You cannot help but know her. Let her come to you.}

An elder and a puzzle? This was a bad sign. *Which elder did this? Was it Carstol?* Joseph prayed it was Carstol, even as a sick certainty that it was not assaulted him.

{It is he that only you might survive.}

Veriel?

There was only one elder that Warriors feared to meet. Veriel had never left a Warrior alive when met in single battle. But what did the Stone mean? Joseph was named as the equal of The Destroyer of Lives? It was not possible, was it?

Silence met him, a stillness that made Joseph's blood run cold. It was Veriel, and the Stone had reached the limits of the help it could give him in their fight—for now.

Joseph uttered several harsh curses in three languages, tucking the blade in his pouch. "The damned Stone loves its games," he growled as he left the slain men far behind.

What do I do now? She will come to me. Who is she? Why is she important? Why will she seek me out?

That was the only question he could answer for himself. She would come for protection. The rest of his questions would go unanswered for now. If the Stone would not answer them, it was Joseph's puzzle to unravel.

"Joseph?"

He turned, smiling grimly at Jonrie.

Joseph didn't need more than the man's voice to recognize Monsignor Jonrie de Brae. Jonrie was a survivor, a protected human entrusted with the knowledge of the Warriors. The monsignor hid ragged scars beneath his robes, the remnants of a save Joseph's father had made before Joseph had first nighted and become a *Krieger der Nacht*, a Cursed Warrior.

Jonrie was a very useful protected, more useful than most. The Christian faith was the center of many lives. Jonrie could be most advantageous in gathering information and in giving his consent for the use of amulets...without Rome's knowledge, of course.

The gods of the Warriors demanded nothing of the protected. Since the Warriors' beliefs had spawned the beasts, it was a sacred duty to protect all who were threatened, no matter their religions. Still, many followers of the Christian faith felt accepting the protection of gods that could do what their own God could not was somehow akin to heresy. Jonrie was matchless in that regard, for his aid in convincing survivors of feeding to accept the protection they were due.

Jonrie was here for one reason. The kill was a beast kill. William's father, Martin, would have sent the monsignor to identify the dead. This was his parish, and these men were likely ones he knew. If this was an elder, or if there were some reason to the kills, perhaps Jonrie could shed light on it.

"What is it, Joseph?" Jonrie asked. "You are unusually pensive tonight."

Joseph nodded to William as the pup returned to their horses. "There is an elder in the city, Jonrie. The worst of the elders."

"The Mad Deceiver?" Jonrie gasped. "Here?"

"Yes." Joseph ran a hand over the stubble on his chin, passing an assessing eye over Jonrie. This was his parish. These were his people. If a woman was in danger in this area, she might find her way to Jonrie. "There is a woman. She will need my help. Watch for her."

"Who is this woman?"

Joseph fingered the bloodstained blade tucked in his pouch, the only link he had to the woman in question—or perhaps not. Puzzles were not always so easily deciphered. "A fighter, Jonrie." *Then how has he taken her without a fight?*

As usual when they needed it most, the Stone mocked them with its silence.

* * * *

Jörg feathered a kiss on Yzabeau's forehead, smiling as she moved against him in her sleep. It had been a long night, a night unlike any Jörg had experienced with Regana's souls. Yzabeau had turned to him over and over, with a hunger that seemed impossible to sate, a hunger that matched his own.

He sighed, the awareness of sunrise seeping into his conscious mind, crawling over his skin in warning. "I will return to you," he whispered next to her cheek. "I do not leave you, *Geliebte*."

The urge to take his day sleep with Yzabeau was tempting but unwise. If danger came for her, Jörg would be powerless to keep her safe, and his presence would increase the danger to her.

He needed the rejuvenation of rich soil. There was no denying that Jörg had depleted his stores between his outlay of power and his failure to feed. It was too late to feed now. If Jörg fed, it would be from Blanche or one of the other women of the house. That would draw Warriors directly to Yzabeau.

The alternative was taking his day sleep nearby and feeding deeply when he woke...before he returned to Yzabeau's arms.

Jörg would have to feed deeply. The attackers he'd killed were—none of them—the human he sought, the one who threatened Regana most. The soul of Marclef. That certainty chilled him. Beasts could not attack in daylight. Warriors lived by the rules of sanction. An unknown rogue human was the greatest threat to Yzabeau.

Jörg kissed her once more and clothed himself in the illusion of his beloved breeches and tunic. He dropped down the stairs to the kitchen, intent on a word with Blanche before he went to ground.

Blanche looked up in surprise at his continued presence. Jörg would typically dematerialize and leave when he tired of his diversions, taking pleasure and fading away before Warriors might arrive, seeking a kill.

She looked down the corridor at the bright morning sunlight streaming through the front windows, far from Jörg's position. Blanche paled. "Jörg, what will you do?"

"I take my rest here today, Blanche," he announced calmly, as if this was something she should fully expect for him to do. "My lady will likely rise before me." Jörg stretched out claws on the ends of his fingers in silent warning, scoring the wood tabletop and examining the cuts, feigning interest.

Blanche gulped, trying to still the shudder that ran through her. Jörg smiled, letting his fangs peek past his lips. His meaning wasn't lost on his bought human. Yzabeau would be treated with respect, or there would be a high price to pay. Still, it couldn't hurt to make himself clear.

"She will be treated with respect—as befits my bride. Anything Lady Yzabeau requires will be provided for her. No expense is to be spared. I will make certain that you are compensated fully for the outlay, of course. I will come for her again tonight." He straightened, retracting the claws and running his fingertips through the marks he'd left.

"Will you be staying long, Jörg?" she whispered fearfully. Like most of his bought humans, Blanche considered the best part of their deal the fact that Jörg rarely lingered long.

He flashed her a wide smile. "I believe we will travel before the sun rises again. This is not a place I wish to keep Lady Yzabeau on a permanent basis."

Jörg dematerialized and streamed to the cellar beneath the closed door as the sunlight crept down the hall. He chuckled to himself noiselessly, savoring the look of shock on Blanche's face as she sat rigid at the table. The idea of Jörg keeping a woman permanently was alien to her, but Yzabeau was the one woman he would keep for as long as she lived.

He sobered, praying that Yzabeau was granted a longer life than Regana's other lives had been. Jörg became one with the soil, sighing at the lonely hours left 'til nightfall.

Chapter Twenty-Five

Yzabeau smiled, drinking in the scent of Jörg surrounding her. She reached for him, but only cold sheets met her hands. Yzabeau forced her eyes open, searching for Jörg in the dim room.

Sobs wracked her. She was alone. Jörg had left her, and the sensation felt familiar, as familiar as his presence had felt, as familiar as his body claiming hers had.

"We have lived many lives together." Jörg had said that, one of the many assurances he'd given her as he'd claimed Yzabeau, assurances that she hadn't asked for. Those assurances had meant so much to her at the time.

He'd left her, abandoned her, and the aching emptiness felt familiar. It felt as if she'd cried these same tears a dozen times. "Have we spent so many lifetimes together, or has he left me every time?" she asked miserably, knowing there would be no answer.

Yzabeau left the bed, her entire body aching. She sank to the floor on shaking legs, pressing a hand to the pit of her stomach. Twinges of pain announcing her misdeeds were almost eclipsed by the need making her near mad for the absent Jörg. Yzabeau still wanted him, though she had no idea why she would.

She pulled her clothing to her chest, grimacing at the torn undergarments. She took stock of what was still usable. Her Pannier gown and stomacher were intact, hose and shoes wearable, but the lacing for her stays and chemise were destroyed.

Yzabeau looked at the destruction in confusion. Had Jörg taken a blade to them? She had no memory of it, but her memory of many of the little details of their night together seemed to have fled with the rising sun.

She examined the stays, laughing harshly as she tossed the garment atop the torn chemise. Even if she weren't so tender, what would be the point of lacing the monstrosity on when her gown was all that had survived? She pulled on her gown and shoes, managing to knot the stomacher awkwardly beneath her still-swollen breasts.

Her hands shook. How would she explain this to Michel? She sobbed. Would her brother care? The fact that he would not seared her.

Yzabeau looked around the room curiously. She hadn't taken the time the night before to question where Jörg had taken her.

She sobbed at that, covering her mouth with a hand to muffle the sound. Yzabeau hadn't questioned anything. She'd reveled in her lust, begged Jörg to make her a whore, enjoyed every sinful act, even scoffed at God's judgment.

The room was small and windowless, decorated in lush shades of red, green, and gold...brocade and silk. Yzabeau had never seen a room quite like it. She pushed to her feet, examining her surroundings more carefully.

The furnishings consisted of a large armed chair, a cabinet, and the wide bed. Yzabeau blushed at the sight of the silk scarves still attached at the head, then rubbed her bruised wrists. She turned to the cabinet, her hand stretching out to it automatically.

Why would I want to look inside?

Perhaps it holds some of Jörg's belongings, she reasoned. If she could learn more about him—

What? Will it bring him back to you?

Yzabeau yanked the cabinet open, furious with herself, furious with Jörg.

She looked at the contents in stunned dismay. She ran her fingers over a collection of small, leather horsewhips—some tipped in bits of what looked like the whalebone of her stays. There were carvings of polished wood and dark glass in the shape of a man's cock in various sizes, some as large as Jörg. There were jars of creams and powders, more silk scarves, and all manner of leather and metal devices, including what appeared to be heavy chains and shackles. Some of the devices Yzabeau had no name for, no understanding of what possible uses they might serve.

She sat on the bed, trying desperately to understand the meaning of what she saw. Yzabeau looked heavenward, seeking guidance she wasn't certain she was worthy of anymore.

She stilled, staring at the hooks and rings in the ceiling. Was she so lost the night before that she'd questioned nothing?

Yzabeau grasped her cloak and ran for the door. She didn't understand any of this, but there was one thing she was sure of. She was frightened by everything around her, and she was alone.

Home was the only thing she needed, a familiar place to hide. Yzabeau had never given Jörg her full name...she believed. Perhaps he wouldn't find her if she disappeared.

She bolted down the stairs, stopping in a well-lit kitchen, gasping for breath. A half dozen women stopped to stare at her. The room went still as a grave as the half-dressed women panned their gazes over her...some curious, some hostile, all intent on assessing Yzabeau. She took a step back, closing her cloak over her gown, conscious of her state of undress. Yzabeau edged toward the door, smoothing her tangled curls.

A woman rushed to her. Yzabeau vaguely recognized her from the stairs the night before. *Blanche—* Her name was Blanche.

She took Yzabeau's hand and urged her toward the table. "Lady Yzabeau," Blanche greeted her with a wavering smile. "You must eat."

"No. I should go," Yzabeau protested weakly. She didn't belong here.

"Jörg will be angry if I do not see to your needs," she whispered, tugging lightly to urge Yzabeau forward again.

Yzabeau glanced at the women at the table, then averted her gaze, nodding. She allowed Blanche to lead her to the chair the older woman had vacated. Yzabeau lowered herself into the offered seat, wincing at the tender tissues of her core and buttocks.

One of the women laughed. "You will grow accustomed to it," the blonde promised. "Jörg is very large, and it would seem you are not in the habit of—"

Blanche slapped her hard across the cheek. "Quiet, Marguerite," she ordered the younger woman who was now staring at her with wild eyes. "You will show the proper respect for Lady Yzabeau."

"Why is she any different?" Marguerite challenged, sneering at Yzabeau. "Why is she better than the rest of us?"

Yzabeau gasped, staring from one face to the next, taking in the rouge-stained lips and exposed flesh. She shook her head in disbelief, the realization of what this place was crashing over her.

Blanche leaned to Marguerite. Her expression brooked no argument. "She is different," she growled. "Lady Yzabeau is different, because Lord Jörg says she is, and you will remember that. Or do you wish to make an enemy of the Master?"

Marguerite blanched. "No. I do not wish to make an enemy of Jörg."

Hurt and jealousy knifed through Yzabeau. Jörg had taken her to a brothel full of his usual whores? "Perhaps we are not so different," she managed bitterly. *Perhaps a whore belongs in such a place.*

Blanche shook her head, taking Yzabeau's hand and shooting a look that promised retribution at Marguerite. "You must not say that. I have never seen such concern and caring from Jörg. I have never heard him speak of a woman as his own until you."

"Where is he?" Yzabeau croaked, biting back tears. *He left me. Where is the caring in that?*

"Away for the day, but not far."

Several of the other women looked around nervously, as if the idea of Jörg's proximity unnerved them. One of them, another blonde, went to the counters and started setting food before Yzabeau, her hands shaking slightly. She pressed a cup of tea into Yzabeau's hand with a nod of encouragement.

Yzabeau stared into the cup, fighting the spinning in her head. Nothing made sense.

The blonde pushed Yzabeau's hair from her shoulder. "Drink, mi'lady. Eat. You need to build your blood."

Yzabeau felt her cheeks heat. Surely a woman didn't lose all that much blood when she first knew a man. She furrowed her brow at the nods of commiseration the assembled women sent her.

"Isabelle, we will need rare meat, blood rich," Blanche instructed, pushing the blonde toward her seat.

Yzabeau put up a hand to still the confusing exchange, her stomach rolling at the idea of eating bloody meat. Michel preferred his meat in that fashion, but the sight of it had always made Yzabeau ill. "That is not necessary," she gasped, feeling her face drain of color.

Blanche placed a hand on Yzabeau's cheek. "Water, Isabelle," she ordered.

A redheaded woman launched to the pitcher set on the counter and returned with a cloth. Yzabeau groaned, as the cool cloth bathed her face and neck.

"You should return to bed," Blanche soothed her. "Jörg's...kiss is very potent. Is it not?"

"His kiss?" she asked weakly. Surely, a whore wasn't using petty euphemisms for the sex act.

Blanche touched her throat. Yzabeau focused on the pale circular marks she brushed her fingers over. A memory of Blanche touching those marks when Jörg threatened her settled in her mind. The image was fuzzy, and the whole scene seemed bathed in a strange red glow she couldn't account for.

Yzabeau searched the throats of the other women, her heart pounding as she located the same marks on each of them. Her gaze settled on Marguerite. The blonde wore a thick ribbon around her neck, decorated with a jewel. Yzabeau held her breath, certain of what that ribbon hid. Marguerite touched it nervously, confirming her belief.

Yzabeau pushed up from the table, forcing her breathing to smooth. "I need air," she managed.

Blanche led her to the door, throwing it wide and letting the too-bright sunshine pour in. "Now just take—"

Yzabeau shoved the older woman away, turning to bolt out the door. A cry of pure rage rattled her nerves, and Yzabeau stumbled, landing awkwardly on the stone stoop. She looked back, frantic, certain that Jörg would be on her, moving in whatever manner he'd used when she'd run from him the night before.

A black mist swirled in the half-lit recesses of the corridor that stretched the length of the building. Yzabeau stifled a scream of terror at sight of the strange apparition, at what she knew was Jörg in some form.

The other women were not so restrained. Marguerite screeched and vaulted to the far end of the kitchen. Isabelle babbled apologies for some vague offense, while the others stared at the black cloud and shook.

{Yzabeau.}

Jörg's voice was like a calming wave in her mind. She sighed, feeling drained.

{Come inside, Yzabeau. Blanche will take you somewhere safe.}

"Safe?" she slurred, her body so completely relaxed that she stumbled again as she made for her feet to obey him. Yzabeau sat on the stoop, staring into the hypnotic depths of the swirling mass, longing for Jörg to step out of his hiding place and hold her.

{You will not be safe here. Blanche will take you to my private home and bring you clothing.}

Visions of a manor with warm beds and a waiting bath filled her mind. It was lovely. *Home.*

{Prepared for you when I knew you were close. You will be safe there.}

"Why am I not safe?"

A face flitted in her mind and then disappeared, gone so quickly that only the vague impression of black curls and dark eyes, strength and trust settled in her mind. Yzabeau had not truly seen the man, but she had the overwhelming sense of—

"Beautiful," she whispered.

{No,} Jörg's voice roared in her mind.

Yzabeau's mind snapped into focus. She scrambled to her feet, shaking wildly. What had he done to her that she'd almost obeyed him?

She met Blanche's eyes and turned away, resolute. Yzabeau had no idea what Jörg was, but he was not a man. Had he bewitched her the night before?

She sobbed at that. No. She wouldn't lie to herself and lay blame with someone else. Yzabeau had felt nothing of that strange, draining power from Jörg the night before. The sin was her own. She stepped down off the stoop.

{Come back, Yzabeau. You are not safe away from me.} He pleaded with her, a lost sound that tugged at her heart.

Yzabeau faltered, staring at feet that had lost the will to move forward, to take her far from him. The ache inside her called to her, begged her to go to him as he asked. Yzabeau was his. The throbbing of her body was sweet music. She closed her eyes and drank it in.

"No," she forced out, her body trembling. "This is wrong." A sick certainty that Jörg was not as right as he seemed lodged firmly in her mind. The feeling of abandonment had been strong and vivid. How long would it be until he left her again? Yzabeau shuffled into the alley.

"Yzabeau." His voice was embodied now.

She shook her head and took another step. She couldn't go to him now.

"Come to me. Let me hold you," he pleaded.

Yzabeau wanted to look back, to gauge his mood. No. If she looked back, she'd go to him again. She'd allow Jörg to take her again. Yzabeau sobbed. She'd beg him to take her again.

"No." She took three more steps, each successive one easier than the one before.

"Yzabeau," he shouted in warning. "Do not make me track you again. You are mine. I can find you anywhere you go."

She ran full out, shivering at the inhuman scream of rage she left behind. Yzabeau couldn't see which direction she took through her tears. She made turns blindly, aware only of the driving need to put as much distance between herself and Jörg as she could.

At last, she stopped, gulping in air between wracking sobs. Where could she go? Jörg meant to track her. If she went home—

No! He would harm anyone who stood between them. A vision of Colette harmed in her defense made Yzabeau ill in worry. No. She could not go home, but who else would have her?

Bells sounded close by. Yzabeau raised her eyes, sobbing in relief. Church bells. If God was truly kind and forgiving, perhaps Yzabeau had a chance.

Chapter Twenty-Six

"If you have not arranged—" Father Antoñio's voice raised an octave, seeking to drown out a woman's protests.

Jonrie furrowed his brow, pushing to his feet and striding to the heavy wooden doors engraved with a rather morbid depiction of Christ's sacrifice for mankind. He peeked out at the disheveled young woman in the corridor in curiosity.

"Please," she begged. "This cannot wait."

"This is a matter for the constabulary," Antoñio commented coolly. "If this man is as dangerous as you say—"

"He is not a man, I tell you," she shouted. "Trained soldiers can do nothing against one such as he."

"Mi'lady, I am certain—"

"Can soldiers shackle a black cloud?" she choked out, tears spilling from her green-gold eyes and plastering her deep red-brown curls to her cheeks. "Jörg will own them or kill them before they do him harm."

Her eyes widened. "Or perhaps he owns you," she whispered fearfully. She threw herself at Antoñio and pulled at the collar of his alb, trying to bare him to the shoulder.

Jonrie sucked in his breath in understanding, his fingers going automatically to his own collar. He watched numbly as Antoñio forced the woman's hands away and started dragging her toward the doors, most likely intent on calling a soldier to take her away, believing her mad.

"No," she pleaded. "You do not understand."

"Antoñio," Jonrie called out. "I will see her."

The young priest looked back in surprise. "Monsignor?"

"Release her, and let her come to me," he instructed.

"Your prayers—"

"Will wait until God's work is done," Jonrie answered pointedly.

Antoñio nodded uncertainly and released the woman.

She ran to Jonrie and threw herself at his feet, kissing the hem of his alb reverently, the sign of a desperate penitent. "Thank you," she whispered.

Jonrie nodded and drew her to her feet. He guided her to his office and closed the doors, then seated her in a chair.

She sat tenderly and grimaced, as if she was in pain. Jonrie nodded. That was to be expected. Beasts did not take their pleasures kindly. He sank to his own chair slowly, noting that she didn't meet his eyes. The woman trembled. That was also to be expected.

"What is your name, girl?" he asked gently.

She glanced at him, then averted her gaze again. "Yzabeau," she managed. "Yzabeau de Cambion."

He nodded. De Cambion was a name he knew. There were rumors of the head of the family, Michel, but the man's two sisters were said to be kind and gentle souls.

"Tell me about this creature you encountered." Jonrie didn't make the mistake of calling the beast a man. Unlike Antoñio, Jonrie knew what she'd faced, but he would be certain of the fact before he called for Joseph.

Yzabeau darkened. "I thought at first that he was a man. He—he defended me against men who would have—" She swallowed hard, no doubt unwilling to voice that she'd not found herself spared that indignity.

Jonrie furrowed his brow. A beast had saved her? That seemed unlikely. "How did he save you?" he questioned, no longer sure of his original determination.

"He twisted their heads upon their necks as if they were no more substantial than those of chickens." Her eyes were haunted.

He shuddered at that image, worse at the idea of her seeing such a horror. "How many men did this beast kill?"

"Three."

Jonrie rubbed a hand over his mouth, forcing back a wave of sour acid, trying to work past his stunned dismay. It matched the scene Joseph and William investigated...The Mad Deceiver's kills.

Yzabeau shifted, no doubt uncomfortable with the long silence that stretched between them. "I tried to flee, but he moved so fast that I did not see him move." She shook her head. "Perhaps I should have known him for something horrible then."

"Go on," he urged her. It did sound like a beast. "Why did you not scream?"

She winced. "I cannot say," she whispered. "He frightened me, and yet—"

"Yet?"

Yzabeau blushed. "I knew him. I know him. Every side I see of him is familiar, and yet I do not know him at all. I know nothing of his life and past, only of the manner of man he is." She paled, her eyes darting about. "And now I have angered him. He can be most cruel when he is angry. I cannot explain how I know this, but I do."

Jonrie nodded, taking a calming breath. Yzabeau was a most unusual woman. He'd heard of sensitives, human women who could see or feel the ghosted beasts and Warriors. Her knowledge of Veriel could indicate that she was blessed with the power to see the combatants, but something was not right.

"Tell me about these feelings, this knowledge of him."

She opened her mouth as if to speak, then shut it again, biting her lip. "The things he does— It is a feeling of familiarity, as if I have lived them before. He says...he says that I *have* lived them before." A high twitter of nervous laughter that verged on truly mad escaped her. Yzabeau covered her mouth with a trembling hand, tears filling her eyes. "But that is not possible." Her eyes pleaded with him for confirmation that she could not have encountered the beast in another lifetime.

He couldn't tell her if it was possible or not. Jonrie had seen many things the Mother Church would call heresy. "What else did he say?"

Yzabeau paled further. "He said that I belong to him. He warned— He will hunt me down for leaving him. He calls me—" She forced her gasping breaths to slow.

"What does he call you?" Jonrie asked, his curiosity peaking. What would she be afraid to tell him?

"His bride," she whispered, her trembling more severe.

Jonrie stared at her in dismay. What a horror to live! To be called the bride of one of the most damned, the most vicious and mad of the beasts?

"There is a woman. She will need my help."

He nodded. If any woman needed Joseph's protection, this one did. "I know the one you seek," he assured her. "There is a man who is capable of shielding you from this beast."

Yzabeau sobbed. "He cannot. No mere man can. That is why I came to you."

Jonrie opened his collar slowly, peeling it back to reveal his scars to her. "He can. If Joseph can protect me from the beasts, he can protect anyone. You have my word."

She nodded, fresh tears coursing down her cheeks. Yzabeau straightened her spine. "What must I do?"

"I will send for him, but to protect you, I must know everything."

Yzabeau took a shuddering breath and then nodded. "You have my vow."

* * * *

Joseph looked at the women gathered in the corner in sick resignation. The head of the household was a minion. She reeked of the beast's continued use, of her foul service to her chosen master.

Of the ten women in her employ, seven of them had been used for the beast's pleasures. Joseph found himself caught between disgust that they'd allowed it and pity that they knew no better life than selling themselves, body and soul, for the price of a few moments of comfort.

"I offer my protection," he growled. It was his duty to offer it to all but the minion. It was a matter of honor that Joseph would view the others as coerced into the beast's taking.

They looked at each other nervously, no doubt unsure of what answer to give him.

"You know what he is capable of," he reminded them coolly. "It is day. The beast cannot have gone far. If he felt the need to use his powers at his weakest, most vulnerable moments, knowing they would draw me to him, he is furious. His wrath will be formidable."

The minion sneered at him. "The Master harms only those who displease him," she stated confidently. "It was not we who displeased him. We did as we were ordered."

Joseph ground his teeth, reining in the urge to slaughter the woman. Minion or not, he could not kill her without provocation, though he could easily disregard the fact that she was a woman. The minion wasn't protecting her house and children like most combatant females did. She was as mercenary as any man. Her purpose was completely self-serving.

He laughed harshly. "You believe that beast possesses true honor? Foolish beliefs like that will be your end." *And I pray I see it come to you.* Joseph moved his gaze from one frightened face to another. "None of you fear the beast? None of you wish to be safe from his kind?"

His eyes stopped on a petite blonde with hope shining in her blue eyes. Joseph nodded. This one wanted his protection, but she was afraid to ask for it.

He met her eyes steadily. "He's fed from you. Without my protection, he will track you wherever you go," he cautioned.

The blonde paled, her hand going to the ribbon at her throat.

Joseph watched the movement, as if in disinterest. Oh, yes. This one was afraid of the beast. "Once he has taken your blood, there is only one way to be free of him while you live."

The minion looked to the blonde in a mixture of shock and fury. "Marguerite," she snapped. "Do not believe his lies. You know the Master would—"

"Silence," Joseph ordered.

The blonde was trembling. Her eyes darted about, as if seeking confirmation from the women around her, women who looked away in shame or glared at her in condemnation for her weakness.

"You can leave with me now," he offered. "Under my protection."

Marguerite took an unsteady step toward him, nodding.

The minion made a sound of disgust. "The Master would have forgiven you doubting him. He will not forgive this."

Joseph put out his hand silently. Either the girl believed in the *beast's* honor, or in Joseph's. The choice was hers.

"Let her go, if she wishes," the minion decided coldly. "The Master does not expect us to stop those who turn from him, but you will see what he does to traitors."

Marguerite shot her a wide-eyed look, taking two more steps and grasping Joseph's hand. She looked to his eyes, suddenly looking years younger than moments before. "You would really protect me?" she whispered.

"You have only to ask," he promised.

"Then I ask it," she replied urgently.

Joseph smiled and led her toward the door. "A wise choice," he assured her. "You have requested my protection, and you shall have it. I am under no dictates to protect the others. You may well be the only woman of this house who survives to see the sun rise again."

Chapter Twenty-Seven

Jonrie shook his head at Antoñio. "I need Joseph," he repeated hopelessly, as if the young priest would understand the urgency of this situation. How could he? How could any man who had not faced it understand?

"The man was not in residence, Monsignor. One of the others is coming as we speak."

Jonrie nodded, pinching the bridge of his nose. "Thank you, Antoñio. Please, go about your duties."

He took a calming breath as the doors closed, moving his gaze over the exhausted woman asleep in the chair across from him. Yzabeau had shown courage in coming to him. Many priests would have killed her for her ramblings about lying with a demon.

Jonrie knew better, but her story still bothered him. Yzabeau was undeniably enthralled in some way, though the beast used no coercion on her. If he had, the Warriors would have converged on him. Even now, she feared that she would go to the beast when he called for her, that she would glory in his touch. That certainty terrified her.

Her memories of her night with The Mad Deceiver were muddled, snips of sexual exploits and half-remembered words. Jonrie was grateful that her memories were not clear even as he cursed all the important facts she'd doubtless forgotten.

He looked up at a quiet knock. "Come in," Jonrie called.

William eased into the office, nodding to Jonrie, his stealth announcing that he had used his powers to make sure that he came unobserved, in the way of his kind. Jonrie had argued with himself sternly about the risks of sending Antoñio to Joseph with his message, but Yzabeau's protection had won out. Of the two tasks, he had to entrust one to Antoñio, and Jonrie could not risk entrusting the woman's safety to the young man.

"You called for me, Jonrie?"

"I called for your lord. Joseph told me last night to watch for a woman who would need him. I have found her." Jonrie nodded his head toward Yzabeau.

William went to her, crouching to her eye level. He recoiled. "By the Stone lord, Syth," he cursed. "What beast did this to her?"

Jonrie nodded. The Warriors had a sense for such things. They could smell a beast's touch, their foul uses of a human.

"The Mad Deceiver," he replied quietly.

The Warrior paled. "There was no feeding," he protested. "No coercion. Did he take her in rape?"

"Little better, I am afraid." Jonrie sighed. "Do your texts speak of people being reborn? Of souls living again?"

William's brow furrowed. "I have not heard of it, but Warriors continue to learn until they die. There are hundreds of texts and histories to sift through. Why do you ask?"

"The beast assures Yzabeau that she has lived before, that he holds a claim on her, that he will hunt her down wherever she goes under that claim."

"Beasts do not typically—"

"I know," Jonrie answered miserably, "but there is no denying that the one who had her was The Mad Deceiver, and I believe she has repeated his words in truth."

William nodded. "There is no reason to what he does," he agreed solemnly. "I cannot do this alone. I must find Joseph."

"In case you do not return until after sunset—"

"Yes. Of course. If The Mad Deceiver is intent, I will give her an amulet and my blessing now. You know what to tell her when she wakes."

"You must hurry, William. If the beast comes for her before your lord returns..."

William stilled, the amulet dangling from his hand. "What is it?"

"The Mad Deceiver holds some power over her. I fear your blessing and amulet may not be enough to shield her from that power. If he calls for her, she may take it off."

"Willingly?" he asked, aghast.

"No. If he comes for her, Yzabeau has no choice but to go to him. I do not doubt that what she says is true, William, though I cannot reason it. The beast claims she is one who was once his wife. Perhaps that is why she cannot escape him."

"Then how can I protect her?"

Jonrie shrugged hopelessly. "Joseph said the woman would need him. Perhaps he is the only one who can help her."

William nodded. "Then I will give her the blessing and be on my way. There are only so many places that Joseph would go."

* * * *

Joseph closed the door to the small cottage behind them, drinking in the sight of Marguerite. When the Stone said a woman would need his help, this was the last thing Joseph had envisioned, but Marguerite was no less deserving than any other human, and she was the only one who'd asked for his protection. Who else could the Stone have meant?

Marguerite turned to him. "What does this protection consist of?" she asked nervously.

He produced an amulet from his pouch. Marguerite watched it settle over her shoulders.

"Never take this off," Joseph instructed. "The beasts cannot track you while you wear it, and they cannot touch you."

She nodded. "Then he cannot feed?"

"No. He cannot feed from you." Joseph paused. "Why did he leave your memory of the feeding?"

Marguerite blushed. "The Mas— *He* did not. Some of the others—Blanche and Isabelle—enjoy what he does. They allow him to feed without stealing the memory of it and revel in his mastery of them. Isabelle delights in telling the others how much we enjoyed it, how we screamed in delight when he took from us."

Joseph shivered. "There is more. I must give you my blessing."

Marguerite furrowed her brow. "I am not religious," she apologized.

"You do not need to be. Trust the amulet. Wear it always. You need not even offer thanks for it."

She didn't question that, though she seemed genuinely confused by the concept.

Joseph cupped a hand behind her head and recited the ancient words for the *Zeremonie des Schutzes*. *"Bei den Göttern, die uns alle geschaffen habe, stelle ich dich unter den Schutz des HausSchwertträger. Ein jeder unserer Art und Sippe wird sein Leben geben um deines vor dem Bösen, das unter uns weilt, zu bewahren. Wandele nun gesegnet in unserer Mitte."*

He closed his eyes and sealed the blessing with a gentle kiss on her forehead. "It is done," he whispered.

Marguerite's fingers traced the black tunic he wore. "And now?" she asked.

His mind reeled at her touch. As a Cursed Warrior, his drive was marked. Joseph, like all Warriors, required *Blutjagd*—the blood hunt—and sexual release to remain stable. The smell of Marguerite's arousal, the feel of her in his arms, the sound of her voice, breathy and low—

Joseph pushed his mind back to duty. "If I offered you an honest wage, would you serve my household?" he asked. The idea of turning her out to sell her body again made him ill.

Her fingers trailed down his chest toward the buttons on his breeches. Joseph forced his breathing to a smooth rhythm as he hardened.

"What would my duties be? I should warn you that I am inept in the kitchen." She tickled at his length, her fingers making a silent offer.

"Children," he groaned.

Marguerite shot him a look that spoke of confusion. "What?"

"Do you like children? Would you prefer to care for children, or would you prefer cleaning duties?"

"You have a wife?" Her voice spoke more of interest than concern.

"No," he admitted. "My elder brothers' sons have little ones due soon."

Marguerite traced the head of his cock, the touch of a woman who knew she was driving him mad. "I like children. My mother had six younger than I was." She pulled at his buttons, releasing the first three.

Joseph clenched his hand in the curls at the back of her head, as Marguerite wrapped her fist around his length. He watched breathlessly, as she teased at him, his mouth going dry and his control slipping.

"You do not have to do this," he panted. Honor demanded that he tell her that, that he not allow her to do this out of a sense of owing him something for his protection. "You do not owe me—"

She rose on tiptoe and sealed her mouth to his, her tongue sliding between his still-parted lips. Joseph pulled her head to his, meeting her advance without reservation. Marguerite's nimble fingers teased at his aching length, freeing him fully from his breeches.

He scooped her up and strode for the bedroom, his body protesting the weeks he'd gone without release. By the time Joseph set her beside the bed, Marguerite had unfastened her bodice and offered her breasts to him. He took them hungrily, suckling and stroking at her as he pushed her dress from her body.

Marguerite pushed back, casting him a playful smile. "Shall I show you my finest talent?"

"Please do," he invited her.

She sank to her knees, taking Joseph's full length deep in a single stroke of her hot mouth. He peeled off his cloak and shirt quickly, fisting his hand in her hair, and Marguerite repeated the deep stroke over and over.

"A very fine talent," Joseph complimented her.

Marguerite teased the ridge on the underside of his cock with her soft tongue, groaning as his climax approached. Joseph panted in restraint, sensing her body's cycle and smiling that she had passed high cycle days ago. He could take her with no fear of pregnancy.

"Let me put my cock in you properly," he requested.

She took him more fiercely, as if determined to shatter his resolve.

"It is not your time," he assured her. "A Warrior can tell."

Marguerite groaned into his length. Her movements became more fevered.

Joseph cried out harshly as his seed poured down her tight throat. Marguerite swallowed him slowly, her muscles teasing at his length and her hands caressing his trembling thighs. She stood, guiding him back to the bed and onto his back.

"Is this your way of telling me you want nothing more of me?" he asked, dreading her answer.

She chuckled. "Will it be very difficult to entice you to readiness again?"

Joseph hardened at the invitation in her voice and eyes.

Marguerite arched an eyebrow in appreciation. "I thought not."

Chapter Twenty-Eight

Yzabeau raised her head at the sound of arguing outside the heavy doors.

"I tell you there is no need, Jean," Jonrie protested.

"I will determine that, *Monsignor*. I have dealt with cases such as this before."

"As have I. The girl was taken in rape and fears her attacker. 'Tis nothing more. A guard comes for her even now."

Yzabeau shook her head. The Monsignor lied for her? It made no sense.

"A guard dressed in black with his pagan symbols?" the strange man taunted.

She gasped, fingering the amulet. A sense of familiar foreboding stole over her. Yzabeau searched for a means of escape, but there was none. She took to her feet as the door opened.

The man who stepped through was a bishop. He was tall and lean, almost to starvation. His piercing black eyes scanned over her body, and Yzabeau pulled her cloak shut self-consciously.

"This is no simple rape," Jean growled. "I can smell the beast's foul stench from here."

Jonrie paled, shaking his head. "You cannot make that assumption. The Warriors felt nothing of coercion or feeding."

The bishop snorted. "Then she took the beast willingly and flees her master."

Yzabeau felt her cheeks flush at that. She could not deny what she was to a man of God.

Jean circled her slowly. "But why did the beast not feed? Illness or taint of drink or drug would not dissuade a beast." He stared down into her face. "Why are you special? Why are you different?"

Jonrie shook his head in warning behind the bishop's back.

"I—" Yzabeau faltered. "I do not know, your eminence."

His jaw tightened in fury. "You do not know?" he challenged. "Or you will not say?"

"I do not know." It wasn't a lie. Yzabeau had no idea why Jörg favored her or why this connection existed between them.

"Leave us, Monsignor," he barked.

Jonrie's eyes widened. "Jean—"

"Leave us. I would question the woman alone."

Yzabeau made as if to leave, certain that she was safer alone on the streets than with this man. The bishop grasped her hard, his hands like the talons of a great bird of prey.

"Please," she whispered.

"This is my duty," he assured her with a sad look that struck Yzabeau as false. This was a man who enjoyed his duty a little too much.

The door closed, and her hopes evaporated. The Monsignor had left her alone with a madman.

"Remove your dress," he ordered.

Yzabeau shook her head mutely, suddenly terrified of what Jean was capable of.

"Now." He released one of her arms and motioned sternly.

"No. Please."

He pulled up at her skirts with a growl of warning. "I will examine you."

"No."

She fought, but her skirts ended up around her hips in only slightly longer than it took Henri to pin her to the wall. Yzabeau whimpered, as his hands traced lines over her bruised buttocks.

"Interesting," Jean noted. "Had the beast fed, I would surmise he wanted to taste your pain...or your pleasure. Did you enjoy it?" His smooth voice sent chills up her spine.

"No," she denied, asking forgiveness silently for lying to one of God's servants.

"Ahhh. But I know you did," he accused. "It is possible to enjoy many heinous things in the grasp of a beast. Shall I tell you?"

Yzabeau shook her head frantically. The last thing she wanted was a rendition of the things she should not have enjoyed.

Jean hoisted her across the desk with her bottom up and her cheek crushed to the hard surface. His cold fingers probed at her raw, swollen core, and Yzabeau cried out in pain.

"Sorely used," he decided in a dispassionate voice.

She sagged to the desk in relief as his hands retreated, then stiffened as they played at her last remaining virgin hole. "Do not," she begged.

He didn't linger long, retreating again when his fingertip had scarcely spread her clenched muscles. His hands left her body completely. "The beast left you that. You are luckier than some. Cover yourself."

Yzabeau nodded shakily, pushing off the desk and yanking her skirts down.

"Sit," he commanded.

She ducked around him, praying Jean would not touch her again. Yzabeau dropped into the chair, wincing at the pain of her beaten backside even as she thanked God that her bottom was momentarily protected.

The bishop stared at her as if in deep consideration of some scientific puzzle. "Why are you special?" he repeated.

Yzabeau swallowed hard, remembering the Monsignor's silent warning. "I do not know," she insisted.

"What did the beast say to you?"

"I...do not remember. I do not remember much of the night."

"Were you drugged?" he accused.

She shook her head. "No, your eminence. I do not believe so."

"Drunk? Lost in the sin of indulgence in spirits?"

"No. I did not drink."

"Then what?" he growled, crossing his arms over his chest.

"I do not know. I simply do not remember." How could he dispute that?

He did. The bishop stormed to her, slapping Yzabeau hard across the face. "Liar," he thundered. "Had the beast controlled your mind even that much, the cursed ones who gave you that amulet would have felt it and come to you."

Yzabeau fought back tears, holding a shaking hand to her cheek. She shied as he leaned his gaunt face to her level.

"Tell me the truth of yourself," he demanded.

Her head spun. Yzabeau didn't know the truth of herself. Wasn't that what her whole problem had been the night before? How could she possibly tell Jean what she didn't know?

His face contorted in rage. "Monsignor de Brae," he bellowed.

The door opened, but the young priest came in instead of Jonrie.

"Where is de Brae?" the bishop fumed.

"Gone," Antoñio reported. "I know not where."

The bishop's face twisted into a look of extreme delight. "I know where. He has gone to get those devils in black. That will take time. I will know the truth of you before they arrive."

Yzabeau shivered, her heart hammering in fear at the possibilities. She looked to the door, longing for escape, but something told her that Jean wouldn't permit that.

She jumped at a touch on her arm, then recoiled in the realization that Jean held a crop in his hand, running it down the side of her ribs. He intended to whip her like an animal?

Yzabeau looked to Father Antoñio, praying the young Spaniard would protect her, that he wasn't as mad as the bishop was. He slid his gaze from hers, unwilling to meet her eyes. Her hopes plummeted. Antoñio would be no help.

Jean unclasped her cloak, pulling it from her body. Yzabeau fisted her hands in her lap, steeling herself for the first lash. It didn't come. She barely breathed.

"Unclothe her," the bishop commanded.

Warm hands traced her backbone to the lacing on her stomacher and fumbled with the loose knots she'd drawn in it hours ago. Yzabeau sat, frozen in shock and fear, her entire body numb.

"You have never known when to turn from a fight." She closed her eyes. Was this a fight to concede or one to engage in?

"You will not risk yourself again." But she was already at risk. Yzabeau couldn't seem to act in either direction. Tears streamed down her face.

The lacing loosened, and she turned on Father Antoñio with a cry of fury, clawing at him, her fingernails drawing blood from the soft tissue of his throat. She would not concede to this. She could not accept this without a fight.

The crop bit into her shoulder, and she faltered, shocked to silence by the fire searing through her flesh down to the marrow of her bones. *The fires of hell. Damnation.*

Father Antoñio winced as the crop seared her again. Yzabeau whimpered, a trickle of blood winding down her back. She fisted her hands in his robes, meeting his sky-blue eyes. He swallowed hard and looked away.

"The truth, woman," Jean demanded.

She shook her head, stammering out a plea for mercy, her knees threatening to buckle beneath her. The crop came again, and Yzabeau swallowed a sob. She closed her eyes.

"Why did the beast take you as he did?"

The crop cut deep. Again. And again. Yzabeau staggered, sliding down Antoñio's chest and landing heavily on her knees. She trembled, praying for unconsciousness that refused to take her. The crop crashed down. She lost track of the number of times it tore at her.

Jean grasped her chin, drawing Yzabeau's eyes up to his. "Tell me what the beast wants with you," he crooned.

Yzabeau sobbed. "I do not know," she breathed.

He growled in disbelief. "Stubborn woman." The bishop stepped away. "Antoñio, remove her clothing. We shall see how long she holds to her secrets when all of her bleeds."

She met Antoñio's eyes again, pleading with him. He moved away from her only to return at her back.

"Take that damned amulet as well."

Yzabeau gasped, fisting the amulet in her hand. Jonrie's warning spun in her muddled mind.

"Never remove the amulet. With it, the beasts cannot touch you, cannot track you."

"No," she asserted.

Jean raised an eyebrow, a cruel smile pulling up at his lips. "Why should I let you keep it?"

"He will—" She took a deep breath. "The beast will follow me. Nothing will stop him."

"You were not fed on. The beast cannot track you." He screwed up his face. "Except by your smell."

"He can."

"How?" he demanded. "Why are you different? I know that you are. It hangs about you like a pall."

The words stuck in her throat.

"Take the amulet."

"No," she shouted.

The crop crashed down on the hand she held locked around the amulet. "Release it."

Yzabeau sobbed. The amulet was her only hope of keeping Jörg from tracking her. "I cannot," she pleaded. "He will come for me."

"The beast cannot," Jean insisted, grasping her hand and trying to pry her fingers open.

Panic burned in her. Yzabeau could not lose the amulet—at any cost. "Jörg will come for me, whether you take this amulet or not. Eventually, he will come for me, and he will kill you for this. If I keep this amulet, you may escape him."

For a heartbeat, no one moved. The bishop's eyes narrowed. "Why would your pain mean anything to this beast?"

Yzabeau felt her cheeks heat.

"What manner of demon are you?"

"I... He sees the soul of one who was his wife in me," she admitted, searching his face for some reaction to that, hoping the truth would end her suffering.

"This beast will protect you?" he asked dubiously.

She nodded, somehow certain that Jörg would gut anyone who touched her. A feeling of him as fiercely territorial settled in her deepest heart.

He considered that carefully. Yzabeau took a shaky breath, waiting for Jean's determination.

"He— This beast will come for you?"

"Yes."

"Your pain will infuriate *him*?" That final word was said in distaste, as if Jean detested the idea of the beast being assigned a sex, personified in any way.

"Yes." Yzabeau felt a strange sort of satisfaction in that. *You will feel each lash a thousand times before Jörg kills you.*

The bishop ripped the amulet from her hand and threw it far from her. Yzabeau cried out in shock and scrambled toward it. He dragged her back to him.

"You do not understand," Yzabeau pleaded.

"I understand. I want you to draw this husband-beast to me. I want to kill it."

"He will kill you and anyone else in his path," she protested, straining toward the amulet.

Yzabeau stiffened as a searing pain cut through her abdomen. She sought out the flat, black eyes so close to her own, then looked to the blood spreading from the stab wound, staining her green dress crimson.

The bishop pushed her away, rising with his fouled blade in hand. She crumpled to the stone floor, pressing a hand to the source of the pain ripping through her.

His face seemed to swim before her. "Bring him to me. Atone for your sins."

Chapter Twenty-Nine

Jörg rested uneasily, the rich soil bringing no comfort. It wouldn't restore his powers completely to rest this way, but Yzabeau's upset was preventing a deeper rejuvenation.

He cringed at the depth of her scattered emotions. She bounced from fear and frustration to faint glimmers of hope. The fact that her fear wasn't entirely of Jörg raised a blinding fury in him. The one who'd made Yzabeau fear would pay with his life.

She slept, but even in her sleep, Yzabeau was troubled, as Jörg was himself. His heart ached for her. He was weary, not just from a lack of rest but in the torture of having failed her. In bringing her to this place, in leaving her when he knew Regana's souls suffered in his absence, he had failed her again. As soon as he fed, Jörg would set things right for her.

Her emotions all but left him, a jarring weakening of the connection between them. Jörg cursed inwardly. His adversary had found her in the sunlight Jörg could not travel. Pauwel's amulet graced her neck.

Jörg expected the Stone to taunt him that Yzabeau was with the better man, to suggest that he leave her there to give peace to Pauwel's soul, but for once it was strangely silent.

He searched for Yzabeau, gratified that he still had the faintest sense of her. When her emotions were fierce and disturbing, Jörg always felt her distress and found himself drawn to Regana's souls, amulet or no. Yzabeau was safe. She was well, and that damned

Warrior would keep her that way until Jörg could reclaim her.

Jörg settled to sleep. He would need as much power as he could muster to take Yzabeau back into his keeping. Her current calm and the muting properties of the amulet would—ironically—grant him the rest he would need to take her back from the one who protected her.

The stillness of his rest was interrupted again. Yzabeau's emotions were no longer calm. Apprehension was rising to a fever in her. Outright fear took its place. Her soul cried out for his protection. Where was that insolent pup who should be protecting her? Why did her heart not cry out for Pauwel?

Yzabeau's disquiet didn't recede as one might expect. She became more and more upset, fury rising and falling, desperation taking hold, emotions so startling that even the amulet couldn't block them.

Her heart was grasping for him, calling to Jörg in a way he'd not felt since Regana's first soul had walked the Earth. Jörg believed he could feel physical pain from her and prayed that he was mistaken, that his overwrought mind was torturing him with phantoms. He growled at the hours until sunset, frustrated by his helplessness until then.

The veil of the amulet fell away, and Jörg burst up into the dim sunlight filtering into the cellar, a roar of pain and fury mixed issuing from his lips. His beast forced him into the darkest corner of the space, away from the sunlight that burned his eyes and seared his skin, but Jörg felt that pain not at all.

The pain that coursed through him was Yzabeau's. He arched his back, feeling every ragged wound along her tender shoulders. Jörg ran a hand over his cheek, knowing they'd marked her face as well...and her blade hand.

He cried out in the knowledge that she would be scarred for life by this treatment. Even his ability to heal could not make this right.

Jörg howled in impotent rage, as her foe took a blade to her. His breath caught. There was only one way to save her now—if Yzabeau lived that long, if she accepted what he offered. It was unlikely. Caitrina had loved him when she'd allowed Jörg to turn her. Jörg sobbed in the realization that he would lose her before the sun rose again. He would lose her as he always had.

"Blanche," he bellowed. He had to feed. There would be no rest for him now.

His bought human came down the stairs, her face ashen. Blanche stepped into the stream of sunlight, hesitating, truly fearing him for the first time since the night he came to her and bargained for her services.

He allowed himself to view the situation from her mind. Jörg was about during the day, huddled naked in a dark corner, his eyes glowing in bloodlust and his fangs extended. Coupled with his warning as the sun rose and his earlier outbursts, Blanche was understandably uncertain.

"Come to me," he managed gruffly.

Blanche stepped out of the light and walked to him, her chin high. She met his eyes, offering her throat without further hesitation.

"My vow," he breathed. "Only for Yzabeau."

Jörg sank his teeth deep, shivering in the shared pleasure of his feeding. Blanche caressed his bare chest as he hardened, inviting him to sate his other need, the need for the physical release his beast howled for. She stroked him, but in her memories, Jörg saw Yzabeau's pain as she'd compared herself to the whores of the house.

It was a curse of feeding, this inability to block memories, his only respite the possibility of ordering certain memories to him to drown out others.

He removed Blanche's hand from his body, sick in the realization that it might be centuries before he found Regana's soul again. Jörg bit back a sob in the knowledge that he'd seek solace in Blanche's body within a week, that he couldn't hold off his beast longer than that, even in his grief.

He'd take Blanche first. Then he'd take his women as he always had when Regana was gone from him; by his usual standards but uncaring of who she was, even as he thrust his body into hers to sate the beast.

Blanche reached for him again, the pleasure he was feeding her making her nearly as mad for him as he was in grief. Jörg grasped her wrists in his hand, careful not to snap her bones.

Do not touch me, he commanded her. Jörg ordered a pulse of pleasure that would send her to climax and drew back, sealing his feeding site.

She met his eyes, weaving in a combination of her continuing release and blood-weakness.

He nodded. "It is two hours until sunset. Send me another woman to feed from twice an hour until then."

Blanche gasped at the unusual request. "Jörg?"

"I will have to battle at sunset," he informed her, turning Blanche toward the stairs and urging her to them. *If I feed slowly and glut my system on blood and* emotion, *I will be prepared for the one who has stolen her from me.*

* * * *

"Again?" Marguerite laughed, as Joseph pulled her around his length.

He smiled. "You have no idea what a Cursed Warrior is capable of," he warned her.

She bit her lower lip, as he pounded deep inside her. Gods, but this woman was a lovely diversion.

Joseph stared at her curiously as his body reached for another climax. Where had that thought come from? When had he started thinking of her as an interlude? A strange certainty that something was amiss assaulted him.

Joseph pushed that thought away, capturing Marguerite's mouth as he followed her into bliss. An afternoon of hard release or more, the woman was worth his vow of protection more than any woman he'd ever met was.

Marguerite sank to his chest, laying kisses over a long scar a beast had gifted him with on first night. "Do you think the children will accept me?" she asked.

He groaned at the thought that the trainees would more than accept her. Joseph closed his eyes, trying to decipher when Marguerite became just another woman to take release with, a blade chaser to be passed around from Warrior to Warrior, warming beds as long as she was willing to fill the position.

Hadn't he argued that he wanted to give her an honest wage? To free her from selling herself? What had changed in the last hour? There was something he was missing here, something that was not right.

Her lips traced a training scar his father had left. "Thank you, Joseph."

"For protecting you? That much is duty," he dismissed her.

"There is no duty worth that much risk. Jörg will gladly kill me and anyone who stands in his way."

Joseph opened his eyes a slit, considering her look of near terror. He tangled his fingers in her blond curls. "What did you do to anger him so?"

"I insulted his woman. Blanche all but promised he would gut me for it. I had nowhere to run, nowhere he could not follow. You are my salvation."

Joseph's heart pounded, as her words sank in. "*His* woman?" A beast didn't keep a woman. He sated himself where he wished, when he wished. He was not possessive.

Marguerite nodded. "A fine lady."

He looked to his breeches, to the handle of the ladies' knife protruding from his pouch. *A fine lady.* "The beast brought her last night?" Joseph asked breathlessly, certain that he knew his error.

"Yes. Jörg rode her hard and left her in Madame's care with instructions for her comfort—calling her his bride."

Joseph set Marguerite aside and began dressing hurriedly. *Jörg— Veriel's human name had been Jörg. I have been focused on the wrong woman, protecting the wrong woman.* He chided himself. Marguerite was as worthy of protection as any other, but as he mused earlier, she was a diversion from his true task.

"Joseph?" she asked. "What is it?"

"Which of the women is the one he claims? Which of those I saw?" he asked urgently, pulling his boots over his breeches.

"None of them. She was gone by the time you arrived."

He faltered, nearly dropping his weapons belt in surprise. "Gone? Gone where?"

"She ran from him, from what he is. Jörg was furious. He tried to force her back to him, but he failed—somehow." Her brow furrowed. "I do not understand how he failed."

Joseph said a prayer that the Stone had protected her somehow. "His outlay of power was exerted over her? Or did he threaten you as well?"

"For her alone. Jörg cares for nothing but his lady. I imagine my punishment was to come when she was his again."

He nodded, dragging his tunic over his head. "What does she look like?" He would have to track her, and even with the smell of the beast, that would not be an easy task.

"Deep red curls, and eyes that change from green to golden brown. She wore a green dress with what few underthings Jörg did not tear from her body."

Joseph grimaced at the image that came unbidden to his mind. "And her name? Do you know her name?"

"Lady Yzabeau."

"Stay here. You will be safe until my brothers and nephews come for you." *If I face The Destroyer of Lives, they may be the only ones left to come to you.* He walked quickly, swinging his cloak around him as he went.

"Joseph," William shouted, bolting through the door when Joseph was halfway to it. His nephew took a calming breath. "Thank the Stone," he gasped. "Jonrie needs you."

Hope swelled in Joseph's chest. "Jonrie has found her? He knows where Lady Yzabeau is? Have you seen her?"

William stared at him in open-mouthed shock.

"William," he barked, needing the reassurance that it wasn't a race between his tracking and The Mad Elder's abilities once the sun went down.

"Yes," the pup stammered. "The Stone was kind. She found Jonrie, but she needs you. There is—Jonrie believes—"

Joseph strode past him and through the door. "Slow down. The Mad Elder calls her his bride."

"Yes. He believes or...or says that she is the soul of another he desired, that the lady was born to be his. The beast used her harshly, yet..." William sighed.

Joseph swung up onto his horse. "Yet," he prodded.

"The Mad Deceiver holds her in some sort of thrall. She knows him, and she cannot refuse him when he comes for her."

Joseph took up his reins. "Cannot?"

"It terrifies her, but she has no control where the Deceiver is concerned. Her mind is not her own when he touches her. Jonrie fears the amulet will not be enough. He believes only you can save the lady."

"Then we must get to her before sunset and be well away." He urged his mount to a moderate speed that would pass the leagues without tiring the animal too drastically.

"We have time enough," William noted, matching his pace. "We will have an hour to spare."

The sick twisting in Joseph's gut stole his breath, as it always did. *Feeding.* A beast was feeding, and the sun was still high. There was only one beast that would feel the need to feed now.

"The Mad Deceiver," William verbalized for him in a weak voice. "He is feeding. He anticipates a war."

Joseph nodded. "We will give him that war."

Chapter Thirty

Joseph reined in his horse as Jonrie waved him down.

"Thank my God and all of yours," the Monsignor exclaimed.

Joseph looked around the church grounds fearfully. "Where is Lady Yzabeau? Why is she not with you?"

Jonrie blanched, turning through the gates to the back entrance he knew Joseph would use to reach his office. "A bishop has taken her from me. His name is Jean le Breton. The man is mad, Joseph. I fear for the lady's safety."

His heart stuttered. "She told him about the beast?" If she had, there was a very real possibility that the bishop would kill her in fear or ignorance. Joseph dismounted and tethered his horse to the gate ring.

"We denied it, but this man is dangerous."

Joseph turned to the church. "How so?" It was always best to know one's enemy.

"Jean knows too much. He recognizes the signs of a beast—and an amulet. Jean does not approve of Warriors, Joseph."

Joseph nodded grimly. Such a man in a position of power was a dangerous adversary. "Leave here, Jonrie. Go to the manor where you will be safe."

Jonrie left without question. No protected human ignored an order given by a Warrior, especially a house lord.

He led William into the church and to Jonrie's office. The scene that met his eyes confused Joseph at first. Bishop Jean le Breton sat, sprawled out in a chair with an Armen amulet dangling from one bloodstained hand. His eyes were cold and dark, the eyes of a man who had ceased to live long ago.

The dark bishop stared in apparent disinterest at a bundle on the floor. Joseph examined the gray-covered form in disbelief; a woman half-curled and facing away from him. He moved his gaze from the red of her hair to the edge of a green dress peeking from beneath the cloak to red again.

Her blood!

Joseph vaulted to her side with a series of muttered curses, pushing the young priest kneeling beside her away. The blond man grimaced and retreated, turning his face away. Joseph drew the cloak off slowly, his fury rising at the sight of the lashes laid across her shoulders and back. Still, it wasn't damage enough to cause the pool of blood that lay around her.

He hesitated for a moment. Turning her to her back would be agony for her, but Joseph couldn't assess her injuries without doing just that. He cradled her head in his hand and eased her back.

Joseph cursed loudly at the sight of the wound in her abdomen, at the blood that soaked her clothing. It was too late. Nothing could save her now. Joseph touched the spot in grief. He'd failed her. His life and death puzzle had gone awry, as he'd always feared it might.

Yzabeau winced. Her eyes opened; pale green eyes with gold flecks that stole his breath. Joseph touched her cool cheek. Her skin was so pale that even her lips barely had color.

"I am sorry," he whispered. "I should have been here sooner."

Her eyes widened, and she shook her head. "No," she pleaded weakly. "It is you."

Joseph furrowed his brow in confusion. "Who? What do you mean?" He'd never met the lady before. Joseph was sure of it. Had he met her, he would never have left her side again.

Yzabeau touched his chin, tears streaming down her face. She mumbled something that sounded like "Pauwel," but it couldn't be that. What would Lady Yzabeau know of early Warrior history? What would Pauwel Elder Killer mean to her?

He shook his head. He must have misheard her. "What can I do to ease your pain?" he offered.

She looked to le Breton and back again. "Kill me. Please." Her eyes begged this boon of him, stilling Joseph's protest before it left his lips.

Joseph nodded. Leaving her in suffering would be cruel. "You have my vow."

"No," the bishop ordered. "She must live for the beast to come to her. I will kill it when it does."

William laughed harshly at that. "You cannot even kill a newly turned. What comes for you will not hesitate to destroy you."

Le Breton's eyes burned in a fierce emotion that spoke of madness. "Then I will die as a man, but I will do my best to kill the one who comes for her, and you will not kill her."

Joseph looked to Yzabeau. "William," he ordered. There was no need to say more than that. The boy knew his orders.

His nephew stepped between the clerics and Joseph silently, a deadly look on his young face. At sixteen, William had barely first nighted, but he was a man in size and curse. He knew his duty.

Joseph pulled Yzabeau's blade from his pouch, willing his hand not to shake. It wasn't a Warrior's way to end innocent human life. He couldn't do it with his own blade. That would be a sacrilege.

As if sensing his reluctance, Yzabeau placed her hand over his. "Please. Do not let him touch me again."

He didn't ask if she meant Veriel or le Breton. She would never feel the touch of either beast again.

Joseph eased a lord's amulet around her neck and began the blessing again, though he knew William gave it with his amulet. It wasn't necessary to give it again, but he would. Joseph ached, a feeling of loss settling in his soul, agony as deep as one would feel for the loss of a child or a sister.

The words held no comfort for him. His tongue was thick and heavy, as if he were performing the last rites of Jonrie's faith for her. The end of the ceremony would be her end. That was hard to face, and he was in no hurry to get there.

Joseph paused. He could seal the blessing with a kiss anywhere about the face, but kissing Yzabeau on the forehead or cheek felt wrong to him. He closed his eyes, brushing his lips over hers, half-expecting Yzabeau to recoil from him, to protest his familiarity.

She didn't. Yzabeau lingered, her cool lips warming beneath his. Joseph pulled back slowly, reluctant to lose her, to be the one to end her, though he admitted to himself that he had no way to save her.

Yzabeau's eyes opened again. "I am yours," she whispered. "I have always been yours."

"It will be nearly painless," Joseph promised, unwilling to dwell on the lost possibilities Yzabeau represented to him.

She nodded, her eyes strangely devoid of fear.

Joseph eased her to his chest, ignoring the sudden uproar around him. He shivered as she nestled her face to his neck. He did what he had to do quickly, severing the column through the soft bone in her neck. She stiffened for an instant, then eased into his arms, her pain forgotten.

He counted the seconds, mentally calculating the moment when her lungs would cease to draw breath, when her heart would beat its last. Her lips pressed to his throat in unspoken thanks, and her mouth cooled against him as her breath no longer warmed him. He laid his thumb over her wrist; feeling the pulse weaken...then disappear. Joseph held her to himself for long after he knew she was gone, slowly becoming aware of his surroundings again.

The room was in chaos. William had done his duty, stopping both le Breton and his young acolyte. For all that William was an insolent pup at times, he knew the rules of sanction and performed well. The bishop had been disarmed and restrained without doing the cruel man any lasting harm. Joseph bit back the thought that he would have forgiven William any harm he had done the man far too easily.

Joseph feathered a kiss over Yzabeau's forehead and eased her to the stone floor, crossing her hands over her chest. A wild urge to bury her in the manner of their kind—tearing up the soil with his blade and hands as if she were his mate—settled in him. Joseph shook it off, swallowing the cry of desperation that wanted to burst free from him, the cry that marked a printed man losing his bride.

Yzabeau wasn't Joseph's to grieve, and yet he felt the mounting madness as if she were his in every way, his soul tied to hers in *Ende Spiel,* his printing sealed. Her final words taunted him.

"I am yours. I have always been yours."

He vented the cry, ignoring the sudden stillness around him, the ashen look on William's face. Joseph drew his blade and sliced a cut along his left palm.

"Joseph," William gasped, "what are you doing?"

"Quiet, Warrior." Joseph painted the blood symbol, the same mark of Syth he was born with, on her forehead and breast. "My vow," he croaked, invoking a blood oath for her. "Vengeance."

He kissed Yzabeau's lips one last time and tucked her cloak around her body, turning away, resisting the urge to strike out at the gaunt murderer behind him, the one who'd stolen Yzabeau from him. Were she truly his bride, Joseph would be excused by his brother lords for killing the bishop where he stood for this travesty.

But she was not, and taking direct vengeance would mean his life at their hands. The rules of sanction were clear on that point.

"Leave them," Joseph ordered. "Our work here is finished."

"But The Mad Deceiver," William protested.

"Is welcome to these dogs," he growled.

"The rules of sanction—"

Joseph turned on his nephew, offering a wry smile. "Say we have a duty to protect innocent human life. As pitiful as it is, I have done that duty. I have no duty to protect the likes of that human beast from his folly. He killed an innocent under our protection to draw a beast to him. The beast will come soon. Let him find what he desires."

William nodded mutely and reached for the amulet in le Breton's hand.

The dour man pushed it at the young Warrior with a grimace of distaste. "Your pagan charms mean nothing to me," he assured them. "I have survived without them this long, and I will continue to do so."

Joseph ground his teeth in understanding. This was a twisted form of vengeance for the bishop. "May you find what you seek," he cursed his foe. *And, may Yzabeau have her justice in it.*

* * * *

Jörg lifted his head from Isabelle's throat, heedless of the blood coursing down her chest from the punctures. She slid from his boneless fingers.

Dead. The certainty that Yzabeau had breathed her last seared him. Jörg threw his head back and roared out his loss to the darkening sky. He had never lost Regana's soul so quickly. Jörg had lost her without the benefit of tasting her passion, but never so soon.

He sank to his knees, feeling every day of his twelve hundred and thirty-one years. *Gone.* Jörg cried out again, clawing at the rich soil floor, cursing the gods who'd punished him this way, cursing the damned Stone that had started it all.

The madness dragged him down. Jörg fought it. He could indulge in madness later. For now, he had vengeance to seek.

Jörg met Isabelle's wild eyes, wincing at the sight of her bloodstained bodice. He'd never caused his bought humans pain like this before, never been so wasteful. He calmed her via the blood link. "Come to me," he crooned.

Isabelle crawled to him, her eyes hungry. Jörg traced his tongue up her chest, gathering the spilled blood not yet soaked into her clothing. She laid her head back, inviting his possession, as she always had.

He forced back his beast, as his other needs settled firmly in his groin. Isabelle had always soothed his beast well, but the beast did not control Jörg, and Jörg would not sate himself, even in the most familiar and willing woman, while his duty to care for his mate lay unfulfilled. Jörg closed his feeding site and sent Isabelle from him before he could forsake his duty.

He'd played this night over and over, burying each of Regana's incarnations from Marie to Caitrina and burning the home they'd shared together to ashes, her grave lying in the shadow of what once was.

He sobered at that. Yzabeau had never known a home with him, and his vow prevented Jörg from burning Blanche's establishment.

"I will take everything from the one who wronged her," he vowed. There would be fires. There would be death, but those things would not soothe his madness. Only Regana could do that, and it would be centuries before he would find her again. Jörg was alone—again. *Always.*

Chapter Thirty-One

Jörg rose from his dark corner, clothing himself in the illusion of his leather breeches and tunic. It was a battle he traveled to, and his Warrior-wear was the epitome of the image he wished to convey, the predator he had been trained to be before he'd accepted damnation.

He hesitated for just a moment, aching at the approaching confrontation, the moment when he would hold Regana's lifeless form in his arms again. Jörg chided himself, branding himself the coward he was. He'd survived this moment six times before, and Jörg would survive it as many times as the gods demanded it of him.

It was his punishment, the damnation he'd unwittingly accepted: living centuries without Regana, a few hours or years basking in her light and love, and dying again with her. His printing drove him to her side, unable to live without her while she lived. His printing nearly killed him, driving Jörg further into his madness every time he lost her again. Yet, his damnation did not allow him the solace of death. Not until one Warrior born of *Haus* Jäger would come for him in battle.

Every time he lost her, his honor became more tattered, the man in him more a beast and less human. Every time he lost her, Jörg became more desperate not to lose her again. He wondered, not for the first time, how many times he could lose Regana and not become truly and completely a beast...The Mad Deceiver the Warriors called him. Regana was proof enough that he'd earned his title as The Destroyer of Lives.

Jörg mounted the stairs slowly, tired in body and soul despite his deep feeding. He nodded to Blanche on his way through the kitchen, noting how sorely he'd used the women to feed.

He stopped, his hand on the doorframe. Jörg had taken an oath. He had a duty to these women.

"You will not do business for three days," he ordered. "I will pay you for your time. Rest."

Blanche's voice was choked with emotion. "As you wish, but I do not want your money, Jörg. Just find your bride."

"She is—" Jörg stumbled over the words. "Yzabeau is dead." He left without giving Blanche a chance to recover from her shock. Jörg wanted no one's pity, no empty platitudes—or even heartfelt ones.

He could have dematerialized and hurried to her side, riding the wind to his bride. Had Yzabeau lived this long, he would have, but she was dead. Only pain and battle awaited him. Jörg was in no hurry to reach either one.

His sense of her was strong, perhaps the Stone's idea of a joke. Jörg sighed raggedly as he took in the church. Yzabeau had trusted the priests. She would have felt safe here. She should have been safe here.

He walked the halls, his feet making no sound, not bothering to ghost himself from view. The doors to the room he sought were thrown wide. Jörg swallowed a bitter laugh. The fool wanted to trap him? So be it.

Jörg strode into the room, sliding his gaze over the two men; vaguely noting a weak feed string from the elder one, an ancient feed string, at least a decade old.

He knelt to Yzabeau, taking in the care and respect with which she was laid out in surprise.

He reached out a hand to touch her cheek—and found himself blown away from her. Jörg growled in frustration, his hand stinging from the force of the amulet that kept him from touching her. He turned on his enemies, his fury rising like a red wave, bloodlust nearly crippling him.

"Remove it," he demanded. "Take that damned amulet off of her."

The lean one smiled a cruel smile, waving a hand that—by the smell of it—was lightly coated in Yzabeau's blood. "She said you would come. Does it hurt you not to be able to touch her?" he taunted.

That was the one. He was the one who'd tortured Yzabeau, the one who'd killed her. Jörg was sure of it. He rose slowly, giving the beast rein.

The younger man stepped closer to his master, holding up the heavy cross around his neck with shaking hands. Jörg stepped toward him on his way to the dark one and struck him hard across the mouth. The youth flew half the length of the office, landing in a stunned heap.

Jörg met his would-be tormentor's eyes and licked the younger man's blood from his knuckles. "What other tricks have you, old man?" he taunted in return.

"Did she tell you she was yours? She told the Warrior the same. Your precious bride. Your whore." His words were designed to hurt.

They did their duty well. Jörg swallowed his pain at that. Even Caitrina, sure in her love for Jörg, had been confused by Pauwel's soul. He nodded. "Her other husband," he noted as if in disinterest. "She should have known him. Had she lived, Yzabeau would have given him sons."

The human gaped at him, his black eyes wide and his hands white-knuckling the arms of his chair. "She...what?"

"He didn't offer you protection from me, though you have been fed on before."

He winced, his hand rising toward his throat before he forced it back down.

"The Warrior left you to me. Do you know why he did?"

The man took to his feet, grasping a goblet full of his blessed water and a holy wafer from the desk beside him.

Jörg laughed harshly. "You think that will stop me? You think your God has any power over me? Why? He did not create my kind."

Jörg expected a protestation that the Christian God was all-powerful. The man didn't waste his breath. Jörg stood calmly as the fool threw the water in his face, affecting a long-suffering sigh as he dried himself with his cleansing power and smoothed his hair.

"What is your name, human beast?" Jörg asked the question all Warriors asked of a beast when they battled. In this case, Jörg was the Warrior taking vengeance for a dead mate, a mate he took originally while he was still simply a Cursed Warrior. The human was the true beast in this encounter.

The human beast lunged for him, and Jörg caught his wrist in his hand. He smiled at the old man's frustration, taking the wafer on his tongue and letting it dissolve. He swallowed the tasteless bit of bread with a sneer.

"Your name?" Jörg reminded him.

"Le Breton," he growled, trying to free himself. "Jean le Breton."

Jörg crushed the bones in Jean's wrist with a single squeeze and released him as Jean screamed in agony. "Do you know why he left you for me?" Jörg repeated.

"Demon," the old man cursed, cradling his broken arm. If Jörg let him live, a surgeon would have to amputate that arm above the wrist.

He smiled at that idea, striding to Jean and ripping the crucifix from his throat. Jörg dangled the piece of jewelry in front of him. "Listen to me, old man. Do you know why he left you for me?"

Jean lunged for him with a cry of pure rage, a dagger appearing as if by magic in his hand. Jörg grasped his outstretched arm at the elbow and crushed the bones as if they were no more substantial than splinters of dry wood. The dagger clattered to the stones. Jörg drank in his screams like fine wine, savoring them.

"He left you for me, because he has honor, and I have none. He lives by laws that protect you for no better reason than the race you were born to. I do not. The Warrior left you to me, because he loves her as much as I do. The harshest vengeance he could take on you was to allow me free rein with you. I have all the time I wish to kill you, and I will kill you...slowly, painfully, bit by bit. I will enjoy killing you, and no Warrior will come to save you."

Jean fell back, shaking his head in disbelief. "You cannot—"

Jörg dematerialized and took shape again next to his foe. "You cannot run from me. You cannot hide from me."

He tugged at Jean's collar, tearing it away, his fangs lengthening at the sight of the scarred feeding site.

"You cannot hide from any beast. You belong to us."

Jean tried to run. Jörg grasped him by the scruff of his neck, his beast's interest piqued by the rising smell of fear. Yes. The beast would like that, tasting fear and pain.

Jörg rarely indulged his beast that way. *Only for Regana. Only when she is threatened or taken—or killed. Only for vengeance hunts.* Those were the moments when Jörg sated his beast, when he became more feral and lost the man inside. The man who felt too much.

"You fear that," Jörg growled. He let his fangs extend fully.

The old man stilled, his face slack in horror, his eyes locked on Jörg's, on eyes that would be hot red in the beast's hunger.

Jörg moved slowly, though he could have taken Jean's blood in the blink of an eye. The anticipation increased the man's fear. The emotion would be sublime. He teased the skin at the old bite, drinking in the strangled cry of protest. Jean tried to jerk away, but Jörg tightened his grip, dragging his throat back and sinking his fangs deep.

The human screamed. Jörg closed his eyes in pleasure, drunk more on the emotions coursing through him than the blood his system didn't need.

Unlike his brethren, who were cursed with no kind emotions, Jörg was damned with retaining all of his. Still, the beast feasted on the pain and loathing, fear and horror of the human beast in his arms.

What do you fear? Jörg demanded the information from his prey, but not only so he would have the information to destroy the man. Seeing the twisted vision of Yzabeau this man harbored was more than Jörg could bear. He had to move Jean's mind to other subjects or lose the last of his tenuous control.

A long-ago feeding filtered into his mind. Jörg growled. The one who had Jean was one of Carstol's turned, a clumsy oaf who had lasted only three years before a Warrior took his heart. Clumsy and weak, the turned wasn't capable of taming his beast, and Carstol would have done better to kill the fool himself for his appalling lack of control.

That was one lesson of his Warrior days that Jörg had never forgotten—control. He winced. Except with Regana. Why was it that he never possessed control with Regana?

Jörg hated feeding from a human such as this, experiencing memories of the beast's victory over the man that had once ruled in the body the beast occupied. In twelve hundred years, Jörg had never resorted to taking a man sexually to sate his beast.

His cock rose, as it always did when he fed. His beast whispered to him.

{He fears it most. Use him.}

Jörg pushed away the temptation. He'd never violated a man, and even this human beast wasn't worth giving his beast that much hold on his soul.

His beast was not so easily denied. *{Make him kneel to you. He will service you well even as he hates it—or as you make him love it.}*

Jörg's cock ached at that thought. It would be easy—so easy to order Jean to do whatever he wished, whatever would make the human recoil in horror from his own actions.

The memory of Yzabeau kneeling between his thighs seared him. Jörg glanced to her body. No. He could never disgrace her memory that way.

Jörg owed Jean pain and anguish. Degradation would add to that, but there were much more effective ways of breaking a man—more inventive ways at his disposal than resorting to something he himself despised.

Jörg recoiled, as pain intruded on his feeding, the searing pain of a blade sliding between two ribs and into his lung. It was a danger of feeding that one tended to lose oneself in the course of emotion, in the rush of power blood brought.

It was a fortuitous circumstance that had allowed the foul human to slip past Jörg's usually faultless defenses and land the blow. It was unfortunate for them both that nothing short of a sacred weapon wielded by that blessed Warrior of Jäger could do what the young priest sought to do.

He closed the feeding site almost completely, keeping the link open to control his prey, unwilling to let his victim escape to death while he dealt with his attacker.

Jörg pushed the bishop away, turning to his adversary. He pulled the blade from his ribs, wincing in the realization that it was Yzabeau's blade the young priest had used. It had been more than a millennium since Regana had planted a blade in him, and it still hurt to remember it, her face set in lines of fury and desperation. Jörg tucked the blade into his palm, the only memento he'd have of his fiery bride.

"You," Jörg spat, ignoring the young man's gagging. The blood of a beast was foul and dark, a smell that would make a weak man swoon like a corseted dame. "You," he repeated, grasping the man's arm, "will remove the amulet."

"If I do not?" he managed, his eyes watering.

Jörg sent an agonizing spike of pain through Jean via the blood link, smiling a fang-heavy smile as the old man screamed.

The young priest paled, his dark skin going nearly pure white under the blood staining his face. He shook his head. "I cannot. She has been used sorely—by you and by others. If you truly care for her, give her peace."

It was a bold challenge. Jörg met his light blue eyes, took in his earnest expression. It shook him. This man cared for her? The thought irritated Jörg. Regana's souls drew too many admirers—those who would protect her and those who would destroy her.

"Remove the amulet, and I will let you live," Jörg growled.

The priest stared at him, swallowing hard. "No," he whispered. "I cannot."

"You will not deny me." Jörg didn't linger, piercing his throat and drinking in the memories circling in his mind.

Jörg demanded his name, the mad wish to know his enemy nearly overpowering. The name came at his bidding, couched in with much more disturbing information—Antoñio Pablo Polero.

The other information would not be denied. Jörg sobbed at the sound of Yzabeau's pleading and her screams, the sight of her tears as Jean le Breton whipped her, her horror when he stabbed her.

Polero fought him, trying to escape the feeding, but Jörg held him still, allowing Polero to feel the pain as Yzabeau had felt pain.

Jörg jerked his head, tearing the feeding site at the realization that Yzabeau had held to Polero as she took her lashes, perhaps seeking his comfort. The young priest had allowed her to take those lashes, though he'd loathed the sight of it—for a misguided sense of power.

Polero stiffened in response to the increased pain, whimpering in his breaking resistance.

Still, Jörg fed, giving in to desperation, needing to see every moment he'd missed of her: her anger, her fear, and even her end.

He did sob at that, at watching Joseph Lord Armen's grief, screaming his madness at losing her much as Jörg had himself. If Jörg were a kinder man, he'd kill Joseph to save him his pain, but Jörg could not be kind. Though Joseph had given Yzabeau peace, he'd done it by taking her life. Worse, Joseph had those precious memories that should have been Jörg's, the words of love when she spoke her last and the taste of her cooling lips. Jörg would let Joseph live in the same madness he suffered himself, the worst vengeance he could take on his Warrior adversary.

Remove the amulet. Jörg issued the order, drawing back from his feeding but leaving the link open to keep control.

Polero went to her, kneeling beside Yzabeau, pulling the amulet from her body. His eyes filled with tears. "You will kill me now," Polero slurred.

Jörg examined the man's thoughts, stunned that his tears were not for himself but for whatever fate he'd delivered Yzabeau to.

"The choice is yours," Jörg offered without a real understanding of his motives. Was it that this man hurt at the loss of Yzabeau? That he was more of a kindred spirit than Jörg had known since his life as a Warrior? That he was the first man Jörg had used to know Regana by virtue of feeding since Pauwel himself?

"My choice?" Polero asked weakly.

"Yours. You know true power now. I seek vengeance this night, but I do not always cause such havoc. Your life is mine. I have taken of you, tasted your soul. You will serve me faithfully as long as you live—or seek death. The choice is yours."

"Serve?"

"The rewards are great," Jörg tempted him. "Even feeding can be pleasurable." He advanced on Polero, cleansing himself, clothing himself in the finery of a nobleman. "I can show you things you have only dreamed of, the wonders you wished for when you agreed to serve the Christian God."

Jörg bent his head to Polero's throat, feeding as he normally would, sending pleasure across the link, ruthlessly driving the young priest to release in his arms. Jörg closed his feeding site, allowing Polero a clear mind to make his choice.

"You do want to know the secrets of life and death, the true power in the universe."

Jörg knew he was lying. It wasn't that the Christian God had no power. The deity simply had no power to interfere in the workings of another religion, in that which other gods owned. Polero could choose to end his association with the god he knew, to embrace another, to be owned by another. Jörg wanted him to agree to that, and so he played on the weak link in Polero, his thirst for power.

"How do I agree? What must I do?"

"Anything I command," Jörg admitted.

Polero nodded slowly. "It will not always be easy to do as you command," he guessed.

"No. It will not."

"And if I fail you?"

"I will kill you. I will make you suffer as I kill you." Jörg said it simply, without embellishment, smoothing the illusion of his shirt in distaste and exchanging it for a replica of the outfit Pauwel had worn for the public joining ceremony that celebrated Regana becoming his bride. "I truly detest the styles of the current century," he apologized.

Polero nodded, his eyes wide.

"Your answer?" Jörg asked, as if in disinterest.

"You will kill me either way," he noted.

"And?" Jörg prodded.

"I want to know," Polero whispered.

Jörg smiled his victory, baring his fangs. "Your first duty," he commanded coldly, motioning to the crop on the desk, the crop Jean had used on Yzabeau. "Beat the dog you once served, but do not kill him. I want him to burn with his church."

Chapter Thirty-Two

Jörg touched Yzabeau's cheek tenderly, letting his tears fall on her lifeless face. He pulled piles of dirt into the grave, tucking it over her with hands battered and torn from digging the hole in the garden behind the church.

Polero reached for one of the mounds of dirt. "Let me, Master," he offered.

Jörg grasped him by the throat, growling his displeasure. "It is not your place," he warned. This was something Jörg had never shared with anyone—save the first of her souls he lost, when Gawen had buried his sister and Jörg had suffered his failure in the soil of the place they'd once loved.

The young man nodded frantically, drawing his hands from the soil. Jörg released him, waving him away.

Polero withdrew. "The preparations are made, Master. The night is nearly over."

He nodded. The smell of lamp oil was heavy in the air and about Polero's clothing. The man had followed his orders well: beating their mutual enemy until even Jörg could barely hear his pleas, binding him in the sacristy of his beloved church, and spreading the oil.

Jörg pressed the last of the soil over Yzabeau. "You know what you must do."

Polero scanned his eyes gaze the church. "Burn it," he noted. "Then retire to the place you have instructed me go."

"Do it now and be gone before the sun rises."

"And you?"

"I will take my rest here," Jörg smiled weakly, "where I can hear his suffering as he dies."

Polero shivered, though whether the idea of burning Jean le Breton alive or the idea that Jörg could rest in blessed soil bothered him more would remain a mystery. He nodded quietly.

"Go. Leave me."

He stood as Polero fled the grounds, the first tendrils of smoke teasing at Jörg's nose, the first of le Breton's cries of fear making him smile. Jörg ghosted himself, watching in dark amusement as the humans tried to control the fire, listening to the weak screams the humans couldn't hear over the roar of the flames.

In the end, the foul creature he destroyed had cared for no one but himself, nothing but his faith and vengeance. With a minimum of destruction, Jörg had taken everything from the human beast.

It was a given that his life had been forfeit, but in his death, Jean pleaded with a god who would not intervene for him, even as he was beaten by a former underling and one of that god's holy places crumbled around him.

Jörg sighed, sidestepping a human rushing to wet down surrounding buildings to stop the spread of the fire. Jean should have known that his god would forsake him, but as it had with Jörg, the realization of how completely he had been abandoned came too late.

* * * *

Polero knocked lightly at the door, his heart hammering. Would his Master keep his vow, or was Jörg sending his hapless servant to his death? It would be no more than Polero deserved for his silent tongue as the lady suffered.

He scanned his eyes over his alb and stole, noting the blood and dirt ground into the tan and green vestments with distaste. He had been dressed for inside work and for ceremony—the ceremony of destroying a beast that had proven more than a match for the God he had served.

Polero pushed away the thought that his flight to the place his Master had sent him would have been easier had he been wearing a cassock when Jörg came for him. The black would have shown his misdeeds less clearly, especially in the blackness of pre-dawn.

Why should his Master make this easy for him? Wasn't atonement supposed to be difficult? Or did Jörg believe in atonement?

Perhaps he only believed in vengeance. His Master had carefully explained how each blow they'd dealt Bishop Jean le Breton would crush the man and take away what he believed in. If Jörg was sending Polero to his death, there was no question how it would end. If Polero died now, with sacrilege and murder on his tarnished soul, he would burn for eternity in the fires of hell.

It was his weakness that had damned him. Polero knew that. He'd wanted the power le Breton offered, the power in using their God to kill a foul, soulless creature, even when le Breton's power lay in unholy acts of suffering rained on an already tortured innocent body.

When Jörg had offered Polero the knowledge of true power, in those moments after he'd seen that power crush what he'd always believed was the ultimate and all-powerful, he'd been weak. Polero craved the power as he always had. He'd simply never known that the most powerful force was the dark soul.

He knocked again, placing his trust in the darkness that he served. If his Master turned on him and sent Polero to death, he'd at least die having tasted power, having basked in the glory of its glow for that shattering moment when Jörg had owned him, body and soul.

A woman's voice came to him, muffled by the thick door. "We are not doing business this night," she informed him.

"The Master sent me," he pleaded. "You must let me in." She could not send him away. What would the Master want of him then? Where else could Polero go?

"Tell me his name—this master you serve."

Polero took a calming breath, praying to his Master for mercy. "Jörg," he said calmly, though fear pricked at him at the familiarity he presumed in speaking the name aloud.

The door opened, and a pale face seemed to glow in the light of her lamp. The woman raised her light to see him better, and Polero relaxed as he spied her mark. He raised his hand and uncovered his own. The woman nodded and let him pass.

She led him down a corridor to a sitting room full of women. All conversation stopped as he looked from face to face.

"Blanche?" a blond woman asked in confusion.

The woman at his side smiled in comfort. "Jörg sent him to us. He is welcome here."

The blonde's eyes lit in some emotion Polero could not name. He'd tasted a passionate woman intent on him once, but this wasn't passion. It was a hungry look, almost feral.

"Did he? Should I see to his comforts then?" the blonde asked.

Blanche raked an appraising look over him. "Jörg's men usually are well cared for when he sends them here."

A dark-haired woman rose with the blonde, both of them sauntering to him, as if they intended—

His heart stuttered, and his cock rose. The remembered pleasure of Jörg's second feeding made him ache. If these women were of Jörg's kind, they could drink him to a husk with his thanks.

The blonde reached him first, pulling Polero's mouth down on hers. She kissed him slowly, deeply, drawing him to a fierce need.

Hands traced his body...four hands. Then six. Then eight. Polero groaned in his loss as the mouth moved away. The hands pulled at his clothing: unknotting the cincture and letting it fall to the floor, easing the stole from his shoulders, dragging the alb off. Hands caressed the skin they uncovered while they divested him of the last of his coverings.

He let his hands wander over the mass of bodies surrounding him: soft flesh, nipping mouths, beaded nipples, hot, wet centers that pulsed at his questing fingers. Another mouth pressed to his, this one more urgent. Polero vaguely noted a cloud of dark hair as he closed his eyes.

"Jörg has never sent us a priest before," a voice whispered next to his ear.

Polero stiffened as a tongue lapped at the engorged head of his member.

"Jörg sent him over." The voice came from below him, laced with amusement. She licked him again. "I can taste him."

"Let me."

The mouth kissing his was abruptly gone. Polero jerked in surprise, as heat and moisture surrounded his length, his breathing ragged.

The hands continued their tireless exploration: cupping his sac, smoothing over the planes of his chest and abdomen, teasing his thighs, and testing the movements of his buttocks as Polero met the rhythm of the mouth encasing him in ecstasy.

His body was not his own. Polero gave himself up to sensation. The hands became rougher. Mouths joined in: nipping at him, licking at his skin, one after another tasting his kisses. The sex seemed to take on a life of its own, a throbbing beat that pulsed in his soul.

Climax crashed over him. The mouth surrounding Polero suddenly swallowed him whole, muscles working around him as she took his essence in. Polero's knees buckled as he cried out harshly. The hands held him up, allowing the mouth to continue pleasuring him until the last of his tremors died down.

The room spun around him. Polero fought for coherent thought as he stumbled, guided by those faceless hands, to a lounge. The hands began their magic again, stroking him to readiness.

A red-haired woman rose up over him, the globes of her breasts capped by beaded nipples. Polero raised his head, suckling at her, ravenous for whatever she offered. Her silken sheath surrounded him, gripping Polero tight.

"Yes," he groaned. "My thanks for this, Master."

The woman smiled, levering her body up and down his length. "With Jörg, the rewards are always great."

* * * *

Jörg sank into the waiting soil as the sun was but a gray line on the horizon.

{And does your vengeance warm your heart?}

Jörg ignored the Stone, trying to hold to his feeling of accomplishment.

{Accomplishment?} Disbelief coursed through his mind, the Stone's emotions. *{Allow me to congratulate you, Jörg. You have set a good man on the road to becoming a monster, destroyed your chosen mate again in your selfishness, and you now revel in your most brutal murder in twelve hundred years. A mother should be so proud.}*

The Stone's sarcasm rankled him. *She is my mate,* Jörg fumed. *A Warrior will avenge his mate when she is murdered.*

{Not this way. You know no self-control. Will you never relinquish Regana's soul to her true course?}

She is mine. If you did not wish that, you should have prevented my printing. I have suffered for twelve centuries, because you allowed—

{You would have suffered only one,} the Stone roared, *{had you learned the lesson you should have learned with her first death. How many times will you choose to see her die?}*

And what lesson is that? Jörg knew he was being petulant, but the Stone had never been an ally.

{No. I am not your ally. I am your mother, as I am mother to all my sons. You leave me no choice but to still your hand personally.}

Terror coursed through him. The Stone had never threatened Jörg with its power. It had always remained neutral, contenting itself with offering unwanted advice. What could the Stone do if it wished to intervene? *What lesson?*

{She is not yours—not in this lifetime of yours. Every time you touch Regana's soul, you destroy her. You may not hold her. Until you learn to leave her to her true mate without destroying their lives together, this cannot end. I will not permit you to crush my plans again. I cannot allow it again.}

Permit?

The Stone was silent.

She is my mate. I cannot leave her.

{She has always been his.}

I will not lose her. The madness spoke for him, out of turn at a moment that Jörg knew it was unwise to balk the Stone.

The Stone was silent.

You have never taken sides in our battle, Jörg noted, pleading for some proof that the Stone was bluffing, that it could not choose this course.

{And that is why you continue to fail. I have not taught you your limits.} The Stone paused, as if calming itself. *{Next time, she will not know you. Next time, the advantage will not be yours.}*

Epilogue: Freedom

June 27th, 2002

Jörg smiled in understanding. *Freedom.* He said the word, tasting the sweet flavor of it on his tongue. He had given up hope of tasting death long ago. Jörg embraced it happily, as it stole the pain from him.

His gaze settled on his angel, his royal pardon from the new König line, his salvation. *My murderer.* As always, she was the woman he loved, Regana.

For once, Jörg had bought his own redemption with his misdeeds. By separating Erin Jayde from her family, he had created the one Warrior who could bring him peace.

His list of sins was formidable. Usually, they caused Jörg nothing but more pain. Who would have guessed that the most concerted effort he ever made to be selfish would bring the opposite result of what he had come to expect?

True to Gawen's word, any mention of the fact that Jörg was anything but a beast elder like any other—except in his cunning and brutality, which was reported to far surpass that of his peers—Destroyer of Lives, Mad Deceiver, murderer, and traitor was omitted from the written records and oral stories passed down by the houses. His former brother had painted him as a fiend who, unprovoked, had sentenced Pauwel to his glorious half-life as a beast killing beast.

He couldn't begrudge Pauwel the notoriety that Gawen had granted him, and he understood why the old goat had refused to share the tale with the younger

Warriors until after Andris's death at Lorian's hands. Jörg winced in the memory of his son's loss.

Andris had left behind two sons and a daughter, his oldest barely trained. Jörg had repaid Lorian's misdeed with a battle that had sent the other beast to ground for five days, with no explanation forthcoming as to why he'd chosen to strike out at his old adversary after so many years of ignoring his actions. Lorian had given Jörg a wide berth for centuries after that, almost enough time for Jörg's fury at the loss to dim.

The knowledge that Andris had killed his 'father' was blessedly absent from the tale, even after his death. Only those who'd buried Pauwel the night he died would ever know that fact. So, Pauwel had become the hero all aspired to be, elder killer in life and great beast killer, if any elder ever again dared turn a Warrior.

Meanwhile, Veriel had been the most hated and feared, the most hunted of all beasts. Being hunted was tedious, but it had given him ample chance to test each Warrior of Jäger he encountered with the hopes of finding that one Warrior who would set him free. As time went on, Jörg had given up hope in frustration.

It had been well over a century before he'd found himself drawn to Marie. At first, he had been confused by what he saw. Then, Jörg had thought himself mad. One touch had told him all he needed to know. She was—Regana.

The young woman had borne no resemblance to his lost love. Her dark blond curls and shining blue eyes had almost hidden whatever resemblance there was to his chosen wife and mate. The true connection had been in her soul, a soul that had glowed with Regana's essence, her fire.

He'd lost Marie before he'd even learned his purpose, to protect and cherish her as he should have protected and cherished Regana. Jörg had failed her again and had been left with nothing but those damnable dreams of holding her in the midday sun to sustain him through time.

Six more times, he'd felt himself called to a woman who shared Regana's soul, a woman who needed his protection and love. He'd had limited success, but in the end, he'd lost them all: Andaswintha, Syrith, Ilona, Caitrina, Yzabeau, and Anna.

The women seemed cursed to draw possessive human men, beasts, and Warriors alike to them, and the outcome had always been explosive. Every one had as fiery a spirit as her soul mothers before her had. Every one was unique in her looks, despite it.

After Jörg lost Marie to a brutal human attack, he'd fallen into a deep apathy, while the Warriors had scattered to follow the beasts spreading like a plague over Europe. The village had been overrun, the pact broken, as he'd known it would someday be.

Jörg knew the pact with the village had long since crumbled, and whatever lord had been destined as Stone lord at the time had carried the precious rock with him until he'd built a stone room in a home worthy to hold it. The destruction of the village had gone largely unmourned.

Jörg's only quest at that time had been tracing Marie's past. He'd discovered that she had indeed been a descendent of Andris, of his freed daughter who had married a human and moved on to produce her children far from the doomed village. He'd been too late in his discovery. The many descendents were too numerous, too scattered, and intermarried to search for another like her.

Andaswintha had drawn him west as far as the islands in the sea off the mainland. Determined not to lose her, Jörg had recruited humans in need of protection to guard her during the day and sold himself into their service for her sake. In the end, he'd lost her when a sizable force of turned beasts kept him busy while another took her from him.

In his fury, Jörg had refined his approach in preparation for the next of Regana's souls to reach for him. There would be another. He'd been sure of the fact, even then.

By the time Syrith drew him east to what later became known as the Ukraine, Jörg had hand-chosen men that he'd turned and trained for this task.

Unlike the other elders, he hadn't horded his power from his turned brothers or turned those who did not wish to be turned. Jörg didn't fear his turned, and he didn't strand them as a distraction for the Warriors with no defenses, living or dying by their intelligence, speed, and cunning alone.

His loyal turned had kept the beasts at bay while Jörg had given his protection to those he had pledged in trade. Until a Warrior had taken her life when a turned dematerialized, leaving her in the path of his blade, Jörg had believed that he would succeed with this woman. The Warrior and the turned that cost him Syrith dead by his own hand, he'd sunk into despair again.

Ilona had called him to the far northeast next. Jörg had decided that only his personal protection would do for her. His turned beasts had handled other beasts and protected the bought humans while he'd stayed by her side, leaving only to feed in the moments just before sunrise or just after nightfall.

His undoing had been his close proximity to her. Jörg had reasoned to himself that it had been six hundred years since Regana. The woman, even if she was of the same line, could not be of blood close enough to consider her a distant relative anymore. So, when Ilona approached him eagerly, Jörg had responded to her with all the passion he'd wished that he could have given Regana in those years after he'd lost her love.

He'd been so intent on her that the fact that one of his bought humans saw the exchange had escaped him. She'd been dead by the next nightfall, his small force overwhelmed by larger numbers and undone by the traitor who'd spied them together.

The swift, bloody retribution Jörg and his turned beasts had taken on the traitor, his family, and the attacking force was the stuff of legends and nightmares, even his own. Finding his beloved taken from him so brutally, when he had only just discovered peace in her arms, had sent Jörg into a dark rage that lasted centuries.

Caitrina had dragged him to France after a suitable time of mourning. She had accepted him utterly, and she'd remembered her soul's past. Of all of them, perhaps even including Regana, losing Caitrina had hurt the worst.

That time, he had been betrayed by one of his turned. The beast, knowing him distracted by his new love, had made a deal with that incarnation of the Lord Kaufmann. By the time Jörg killed the beast and the lord, Caitrina had been at the brink of death, and he had been desperate not to allow another of Regana's souls to die in his arms.

When he turned her, Jörg had thought he'd found peace at last.

The other elders had tried the same, with the thought of having true mates, though not ones that could bear them children. They'd waited a year before they'd attempted it, but when Caitrina was still the same woman Jörg loved after that time, they'd attempted it for themselves.

Theirs had turned feral first, almost immediately. The other elders had killed them in a fury, believing Jörg was hiding another secret from them that brought him happiness and them disaster. He had prayed it was his printing saving her, one of the few prayers he'd uttered since he went to the Stone, but it had been the hunt.

Jörg had always hunted for Caitrina to keep her from harm. After five years, she'd snuck away to prove she could protect and provide for herself. She'd gone feral immediately, and a Warrior had killed her before Jörg could find a way to repair the damage done.

For two centuries after that night, he had been alone and miserably glad of it. When Yzabeau appeared in his life, Jörg had almost abandoned her rather than face losing her again. He'd gone grudgingly, cursing the printing that drove him to her. Jörg had gone to her angry and frustrated, and he'd been brutal in his first kiss.

To his surprise, Yzabeau had responded passionately, as if she had been the one waiting the long centuries for him to come love her. The firestorm that came at her touch had seared them both even as it had consumed them utterly, over and over. He'd taken her endlessly that night, with her always ready and responsive to his every touch. Jörg hadn't been able to deny her any pleasure, and he'd left her for the day, sure that he had found peace at last.

But his power over her had frightened Yzabeau, and when he left her to go to ground, she'd sought aid from a priest who'd taken her life, believing her damned for her sins with such a beast. The retribution Jörg took on the priest and his church was the most vicious he had ever taken.

He'd argued with himself for centuries. As much as Jörg knew he couldn't ignore the pull when it came again, he'd wished he could do exactly that.

Instead, he'd made a plan that should have been foolproof. Jörg had planned to use all his power to shield the next one, to make her invisible to his enemies. His turned beasts would keep their distance, only acting when it was absolutely necessary. There would be no bought humans. His shield would do their job for him. That and the coercion that he could still manage if he felt her in distress during his resting hours.

He had perfected a way of linking himself to a certain few with only a touch and no feeding. Jörg could recognize their minds and read strong emotion, even from a distance.

Any Warrior who troubled her would be executed for his trouble as Jörg ghosted away back to his lady. Every ounce of his power would be spent on her. Every kill and feed would be undertaken for the sole purpose of protecting her.

As for the physical relationship, Jörg could not make the mistake of using any force or pushing her too far too fast. The woman, whoever she was, had to come to him willingly and accept his advances passionately without fear of what was happening between them.

But each time he touched Regana's soul, the fire burned hotter and letting her go was more painful. How could Jörg take her slowly?

Of course, if he fed, he could print whatever memories of the encounters suited him, but the memory of feeding on Regana herself made him reject the idea in shame and distaste. No, she had to be in a firestorm for him before he laid hands on her or he'd not lay hands on her at all.

The answer had come to him slowly as he'd experimented with his power to read human minds. Over time, Jörg had found that he could place a portion of his disembodied mind into a dream, if the dreamer was amenable and he had sensed them actively—touched them beforehand. A happy dream was all he needed to slip in unnoticed and lead the dreaming. But how would he explain it?

Jörg had wrestled with that idea for more than a decade, until the resurgence of mysticism in the 1960s and 1970s. Suddenly, his problem had been solved—if the woman was born while the craze for such things lasted. He could formulate any number of reasons for her dreams, ranging from precognition or telepathy to past life insurgence and reincarnation to soulmates, any one of which was close to a portion of the truth.

When Anna pulled him all the way to America in the mid-1970s, Jörg had been bubbling over in anticipation. He'd touched her on a crowded street, scanning her quickly and ghosting away, as she'd turned to investigate the instant connection that simple touch had foretold.

She'd been Regana. She'd been closer to Regana than any other woman Jörg had met since his beloved wife. Save her red hair and leaf green eyes, she could have been Regana in the flesh.

He'd started his long, slow seduction of her that very night. Accepting that it was all a dream, Anna had given herself up fully to him each night, and Jörg had learned how to excite her most readily. While his experimentation had left him painfully aroused and in desperate need of release before almost every dawn, the lack of physical contact meant his control hadn't slipped while he'd patiently worked her into a frenzy for him.

Jörg would have taken her when she visited Texas. She had been more than ready for him, and away from home would be the perfect place to start a torrid love affair.

Jonas Lord Jäger had plagued him until he'd sent the man to his gods in frustration. Worse, the damage Calvin and Kord of Maher had done had kept Jörg from doing more than sustaining Anna's heat for him over the next few days while he healed, but the wait had been too much. Anna had tried to turn to another man for the release that was Jörg's.

Dealing with Matt Collins had been a simple affair, though he'd taken a little too much pleasure in hurting the human before he bled the man dry. His feeding had been brutal. Jörg couldn't seem to help himself when he'd read the other man's plans for Anna in his mind. Sated on his blood hunt and secure in his protection of his mate, he had returned to her to quench the other fire in his blood.

There'd been no choice but to take Anna then. Her heat had been uncontrolled, and the short interaction with her in the dance club had left Jörg walking the edges of madness again.

He'd cringed later at the choices he'd made that night. He had been the beast again. Jörg had to have her, and despite his careful planning, no strategy was out of the question as long as he took her. When Corwyn Lord Jäger stole her from his arms, Jörg could have easily skinned the young man alive for his interference, and the months he'd kept her hidden had been pure torture.

Finding her carrying Jäger's child had been a shock, but not for long. If Pauwel could play father to Jörg's son while setting aside his prior claim, Jörg could play father to Corwyn's while taking back what was rightfully his. In fact, had he not earned as much, watching his son raised by another man and trained to hate his true father, denied the knowledge of his true parentage and the father who would have done anything to hold him just once?

But, to his surprise, Anna's baby had not been a boy. It had been a girl, and she was Regana. Not like the others had been *like* Regana... There was some indefinable quality that was uniquely Regana, some quality that the baby growing inside Anna had shared with Regana that none of the others had possessed, even her mother. Having two souls calling to him that way had been confusing but exciting.

Some mad part of Jörg had seen the babe as his salvation. She was Regana and she was Warrior born; without being freed, she could be the mate none of the others could have. She could carry his children as none of the previous reincarnations could have. Jörg could have the experience of running his hands over the pregnant belly of a woman who carried his child and actually raise it with her, as he should have with Regana.

Their children would be the rest of his salvation, atonement for his many sins incarnate. The perfect meld of beast powers and immortality—matched with the ability to use the sacred weapons, walk in the daylight, eat human food, and have emotion—would make them the ultimate beast killers. They would be the supreme beings on the Earth. Raised correctly, with the proper training and respect for life instilled in them, the Warriors would accept them as they had Pauwel...the slayers and their parents both.

The problem had been in keeping Anna and her baby secure. If the babe wasn't freed, elder and Warrior alike would be determined to take her from him. That was not something Jörg had been prepared to undertake at the time, but Jäger was.

He'd cursed himself for allowing the other man to retain custody of Anna in the meantime, but Corwyn's skill was far superior to that of his brothers. Simply put, Colin and Stephen had not been strong enough to be trusted to protect his mate and his wife, and so Jörg could not kill his rival.

Long before he came for Anna again, he had prepared everything they needed.

Corwyn's attempts to keep them hidden from Jörg had been laughable at best. Once Jörg had connected with the babe, he'd been able to trace her as long as she was within a certain range of him. Even with Anna's amulet, he had touched and could continue to touch the child in her womb independently.

Babes in the womb sleep for much of their lives, which allowed Jörg to form a true bond with Erin over the long months of waiting. She would know him and accept him from the first breath she took.

Jörg would have taken them sooner if it wasn't for two problems. First, he could not guarantee Anna medical care that was as skilled, dependable, and trustworthy as Jäger's would be. And second, he could not risk feeding on Anna once her pregnancy became advanced.

Without that step, she would live in constant terror of him, and Jörg could not bear that—or ask her to bear it. It had been better to let Anna stay where she felt secure and happy until it was safe to take them, no matter that it meant her sharing that damned Warrior's bed.

The plan had been simple. Jörg used cues from the babe to discover when she would be born.

There had been variations to the plan. If the birth looked to be a daytime event, his bought humans would make sure the Jäger men were out of the house until well after nightfall, so that there would be no chance to free Anna's child before he took them both. If her birth seemed slated for the night, Jörg would have to take them quickly, as soon after birth as he could manage.

The twist would come if Anna required extra medical care. Jörg would have to decide whether to take only the babe and come back for Anna when she was recovered...or take their doctor and both women. That would be a tricky situation. Jörg could lose Anna either way, and losing Anna would be painful, even with his mate still in his custody.

He'd prepared for it, regardless. Jörg had harbored no fears of losing the babe. Unfreed, she would be as hardy as any male Warrior child was. Erin would not be lost to miscarriage, at birth, or to illness. Warrior babes did not suffer such things.

But nothing had gone right somehow. Corwyn had returned to his home and had started the ceremony to free the child before night fell fully.

Jörg would have taken her still. She was Regana, but he would have reaped down much punishment for the loss of his children. As if that was not enough, Anna had escaped to death before he could learn where Erin was hidden or calm her to his true intentions.

He grimaced at that. He'd not done a good job of calming her. Jörg had been furious at her for hiding the child. What had Anna been thinking to do such a thing? In the dead of winter, it would have been far too easy for Erin to freeze to death. There had been no time for games, and so Anna had seen the beast in him for the second time.

In a moment of crystal clarity, Jörg had known that Anna would never be his, and it hurt him as nothing in his life had save the loss of Regana...or Caitrina. Erin had been the only one who mattered then. Jörg would have left Anna to her chosen Warrior mate, despite his threats—if only he'd had Erin by his side. But Anna had not been easily threatened, and so she'd escaped him to death.

Worse, her amulet had hidden Erin from him and his turned beasts until she was far outside his range. By the time the search took him to Kreuzträger range, her mind had changed sufficiently that he could no longer recognize her, unless her being called to him without that damned amulet as a shield or he touched her.

Over the years, Jörg had watched for unusually high concentrations of beasts, and he had noted the congregation of beasts in and around Salem, New Hampshire several times. Even with that knowledge, he'd been no closer to finding her.

The run-ins Jayde had with Grelden and Shorig—coupled with losing her maidenhead—had been a major source of frustration for Jörg. Always, he was too late to keep her from slipping through his fingers. Always, she was in danger, and he couldn't protect her. Again, his prior claim had been cast aside as another laid claim to the soul he had printed to.

It didn't surprise Jörg to find Jayde pregnant to Kreuzträger. After all these centuries, he had come to expect it of the damned Stone and the gods who'd punished him. So, when he sensed her, when her arm touched his chest early in their battle, Jörg had smiled to himself. If the Warriors were good for one thing, it was sowing their seed.

Despite what he'd said to anger Talon, he would have let Jayde keep the Warrior's son, Jörg's so many times removed grandson through both of them, though eighty generations or so removed from him either way. Jörg would even have raised the child as his own, as long as Jayde gave him children of his own as well.

The only one of his promises that had been a lie was letting Talon live. Jörg had learned from experience that he could not risk it any more than he could inflict that suffering on another printed man. He would have returned to kill Corwyn later, but Jörg had been in a hurry to find Anna and Erin at the time.

It had been a mistake to let Corwyn live, but not one that had cost him dearly. Jörg would not make the mistake again. All else that he'd promised Jayde had been a solemn vow, but nothing he promised or threatened had swayed her from her chosen course.

Jörg had been surprised by her fighting skill. No man had ever fought as she did. No single man had ever caused Jörg such damage, not even a Warrior. Not even Pauwel, until he'd been made beast, had lasted so long against him. Still, he'd thought—foolishly, Jörg realized now—that he was the victor in the end.

He'd known that he would have to feed briefly to make her accept the pleasure he would give her and to reorder her memories to his cause, but Jayde was still early in her pregnancy, so the risk to her child would be minimal. Jörg's body had screamed for release with one who was truly Regana. He would have loved her endlessly, and when Jayde knew herself his in body and soul, he would have taken her to his home as it should have been.

What Jayde had gifted him with was vastly different though no less precious. She'd granted him death. The blow to his heart had shocked him, and Jörg had backed away instinctively. When she'd wrapped her legs around him and taken his throat, his body had tightened in response to the move.

Jörg remembered Pauwel's words to Regana when the Warrior had been educating her in pleasure. *"Hold me to you," Pauwel asked her as he wrapped her legs about him in just such a way.*

Jörg hadn't even felt her blade slice through him in his ecstasy.

His smile widened as he lay dying. The only better thing would be dying in her arms, as Regana had died in his, his lifeblood flowing from his neck as hers had so many centuries before. Still, Jayde had granted him death, and that was more than he had dared hope for in so very long.

"Free," he assured her.

As the light left his eyes, Regana was the last vision he saw. If only he could understand why she seemed so concerned, so upset. Only in death was he freed. Didn't she know that? Didn't she remember?

The light came at him suddenly, the starfire that had seared his soul so many centuries before. Jörg welcomed it, praying it would burn away the rest of him to ash, to the oblivion of nothingness he had prayed for so many times.

The light took form, the rising sun over a wooded hillside. Jörg shied from it, the habit of centuries, then straightened to meet his death when his beast didn't balk at the move. There was no burning, no pain in the warmth on his skin.

Tears ran freely down his cheeks. Jörg could walk in the sun. There was no beast calling to him, no Stone taunting him. He'd found peace, freedom in a way he'd never dreamed of.

"Jörg!"

He startled at the voice, turning to meet Regana, but it wasn't Regana. It was Caitrina as he first saw her, her color high and dressed in the dark blue brocade she'd worn to greet him. Her blue eyes sparkled, and she laughed, a joyous sound that made his heart ache, sure that she would be stolen away the moment he touched her.

Jörg reached for her with a shaking hand, unable to stop himself. "Caitrina," he rasped. She was the only one of Regana's souls who'd fully accepted him, the only one he'd married, the one he'd held longest in his arms. Jörg gasped as he touched her, but she didn't melt away.

Caitrina threw herself into his arms. "You have been gone so long," she whispered. "I was worried. I don't like it when you leave me."

He buried his face in her hair, holding her to his chest. "I will never leave you again," he promised.

The End

Bonus Read:

Becoming a God

The Chronicles of Carstol
A Night Warriors Story

The beast elders—
Jörg, the beast Veriel
Tilbrand, the beast Resten
Dado, the beast Lorian
Bertolf, the beast Draden
Redulf, the beast Carstol
Geldric, the beast Cerran

August 25th, 2000

Carstol lounged on the rooftop of an abandoned church in South Boston, watching the people below in a mixture of boredom and dismissal. He'd been watching humans in one form or another for the last fifteen hundred years, hunting them, tricking them, and making them his own. "Humans..." He laughed in a bitter, dark humor that marked one of his kind, devoid of any true mirth, a completely cynical sound that no human he'd yet encountered could match exactly.

Humans were pitiful creatures. He remembered that well enough from his own life as a human.

His brow furrowed at that. Had he ever really been human? Before he'd been damned as a beast, he'd been cursed as a Warrior. True, the curse had changed his body and mind at ten and five years of age, culminating in the *Krankheit* that sealed the curse at ten and six. Before then, he'd been *called* human, though all added that he was stone chosen for more.

But had he been human? *Not really*, he decided. *Not in the many little ways that a human was shaped and defined by life.*

He'd bled. He could have been killed, if anyone had dared kill a Son of the Stone. Otherwise, he'd never suffered. Warrior children were a hearty bunch. They were never lost to miscarriage or died in childbirth. They didn't get ill—not even the most common rashes and viruses.

Have I ever been human?

"Yes," he noted miserably. He'd been human...of a course. He'd been frail in his own way, a coward so afraid to die that he was desperate to live in any manner that presented itself. Thus, he'd become host to a demon beast and given up the parts of himself that made him most human.

When he'd been Redulf, he'd been capable of kind emotion. He'd been able to walk in the sun. Food had sustained him fully. He'd been powerful as a Cursed Warrior, more powerful than five human men yet not nearly powerful enough.

All of his cursed brothers had been better than Redulf was in battle. If they hadn't been, he probably wouldn't have agreed to this damned half-life.

The women's eyes had followed the others and not him. Why would Redulf be noticed? He hadn't fought dual. He hadn't been destined to be stone lord. He didn't have Wil's blue eyes or Jörg's silver. He hadn't possessed Pauwel's wit and humor, Ditrich's prowess with words, or Tilbrand and Cunczel's pure size.

The only notice he'd been worth had been scorn and laughter. More often than not, he'd ended training sessions covered in dirt and blood—his own, and blade scrapes—usually Jörg's, Gawen's, or Pauwel's, though any of the other twelve might have left a few for good measure. Not even Riberta had found him worthy of her seduction attempts, and she'd tried at least half of the others.

In short, Redulf had been plain, unimpressive, the cruel joke of a sentient stone entity desperate to fill Her quota of thirteen sons. She had to have been desperate to mark Redulf as Her own.

Or perhaps She simply needed six worthy traitors to start the second beast war. In that one respect, Redulf had been stellar—nearly the best of the lot.

Tilbrand had bested him even in that, of course. Someone had always wrested Redulf from top billing.

The eldest brother save Gawen, Tilbrand had been vicious, bloodthirsty, a demon in the flesh before going to the stone. Tilbrand had dreamed of being a god. He'd done all he could to become the esteemed leader of the most powerful beings that walked the Earth.

Carstol snorted at that, took to his feet, then dematerialized to mist. He raced along on the chill night wind, doing what Tilbrand—Resten had always feared doing. *Well, he feared it until Jörg and Pauwel killed him.* The "god-beast" Resten hadn't even figured out how to be a god before he was one damned dead deity.

Had he been embodied, Carstol would have laughed aloud at his play on words. Better, he would have laughed until his sides ached at the memory of big brother's surprise at being taken so easily. *Most powerful, indeed! Resten had been a fool, not a god.*

Still, who wouldn't want to be a god? The perks were too appealing to pass up. Who wouldn't crave respect, servitude, whatever you desired being given happily to you, even fear...in the right circumstances? Wasn't it better than being the least as Redulf had usually been in his Warrior life?

By virtue of their physical attributes as Cursed Warriors alone, they'd been akin to gods. Ranging from six feet two to six feet eight in height, they'd dwarfed other men. Their looks were striking: broad shoulders, thick dark hair, and dark eyes. They were strong, fast, possessing of great stamina, and virile men. Even Redulf would have been impressive had he not been seen in conjunction with a dozen more impressive than he.

But, as damned beasts, they surpassed even the ideal Warrior. The beasts that inhabited them gave the elders powers that astounded, enthralled, and kept the faithful coming back for more. Forever young, the beast elders could only be killed by a Warrior, and in the last millennium and a half, only Resten had fallen to the leagues of Cursed Warriors hunting them.

It was good to be a god!

Only Resten and Carstol had fully embraced the damnation of the stone. The others had been threatened, bought, or blackmailed into their choice.

Some had been easy to convince. Dado had known that Wil would kill him if Dado's relationship with Wil's sister, Riberta, became common knowledge. Others had folded to promises of riches and power. But Jörg...

Even dematerialized, the thought of what they'd done to Jörg brought the sensation of his skin crawling over Carstol.

Their youngest brother had been the most moral of the traitors, amazing when one considered how corrupt Jörg had been then and what a terror he'd become in the long centuries since that night. Of course, saying he was the most moral of their group was no compliment. Between those willing to kill or die to steal the power of the stone, mundane wealth, and continued existence and the many rules of sanction they'd broken between them, they were hardly celibate priests. Then again, considering the priests of this age and his own, they hadn't been much worse.

At least, Jörg had truly loved Regana in his own mad fashion, unlike Dado with Riberta.

And we stole it from him. Carstol fully admitted that he should loathe what he did to Jörg. Self-loathing wasn't a kind emotion; as such, he was more than capable of feeling it. He'd helped steal a man's love from his arms, to take the one thing that made another's life worth living from him and hand it off to his mortal enemy. Jörg would never have released the stone to them without the threats they made to Regana's life. Their youngest brother had vowed to die rather than do it, until his lady's continued existence depended on his actions.

But Jörg's selfless act had been the only way to release the stone. Since the damned chunk of sentient rock spelled Carstol's salvation, he couldn't regret his crimes against Jörg to obtain it. After all, had Jörg not broken the rules of sanction, he wouldn't have left himself open to attack.

Becoming a god is a painful venture. The starfire in the stone burns away all that might hamper the demon beast's possession of the flesh. In short, the best, most human portions of the man are emptied from the shell to make room for the beast.

The burning is no trite analogy for what happens; it is a tangible part of the process. As the last to turn, Carstol had heard the screams of all the others before he took the stone from Dado's—Lorian's—hand. Coward that he'd been at the time, he'd almost refused to touch it to escape such a horror. Then the truth that his damned brothers breathed still, something he might not do if he faced the coming army as a Cursed Warrior instead of a damned beast, drove him to motion, half fearing his beast would refuse such a man as host and leave him to die in battle...or on Sibold's weapon for his deceit.

It hadn't refused him, of course, a lowly host being infinitely preferable to continued imprisonment within the stone. Thus, he'd sealed his fate.

At first, they'd hardly seemed like gods. Aside from Jörg, they were clumsy, dirty creatures, consumed by hungers for sex and blood they couldn't control. Their clothing had been ragged or—when they stole something new—ill fitting. Since their own possessions had been burned by the enraged villagers and they were half again as large as most human men, it wasn't easy to replace what was ruined by continued wear. Not even Resten had been foolish enough to steal from the only men of a size, their remaining cursed brothers.

Only Jörg had been reborn with innate knowledge of their gifts and the ability to use them from the moment of starfire, most likely a reward from the beast elders he'd freed to their lives in new hosts. Predictably, their young protégé had refused to teach them all he knew. They had stolen all from Jörg, leaving him without even the kind emotions necessary to use his chosen mate against him a second time.

Carstol had fared better than most, mainly because he listened to his beast, bargained with it for scraps of knowledge that might make his time easier, learned from it on those rare occasions that he could, no matter how distasteful the lesson. The ancient ones were stubborn demons, selfish with their knowledge, even if it would help their hosts to know something.

Of course. We were damned. Why would the sadistic creatures help us? We were their first, closest, and most amusing pets...at least until we learned enough not to find ourselves cowering in the soil, our bloodstained and torn clothing hidden nearby, slaking our hungers violently more often than not.

Just thinking about those hungers would have brought a smile to his face had he not been disembodied and flying north toward Wilmington. It was time to make his grand entrance. The moon was high, and the humans were waiting to serve him.

Carstol materialized in their midst, causing the closest few to startle with gasps of delight. The crowd was a good one, about five dozen; he'd seen less, and he'd seen many more at a gathering. Most were people he'd seen before, but there were always new faces in the crowd. Perhaps he would choose a new one to serve him tonight. Though the "regulars" knew how to please him well enough, the new ones always gave the purest responses, whether the response was fear or ecstasy.

He strode through their parting ranks, clothed in the illusion of tight black leather breeches without fasteners of any type and soft buckskin boots, his bare chest inviting their hands and mouths to play. He allowed his fangs to peek past his upper lip just enough to draw the eyes of the curious. The pulse of sensual music and the haze of drugged smoke added atmosphere to the blank warehouse walls surrounding yards of cushions, velvet, and silk draped and tossed here and there.

Where they held the gathering was immaterial. These humans didn't come for decoration or a popular setting. Few of them came for the drugs that flowed freely; a few more came for the promise of unencumbered sex. They didn't even come for his pedantic magic tricks, simple powers he'd learned soon after accepting his demon half.

Still, they came, prepared for him, more than half of them already nude in anticipation of the night to come. At the full moon and new, these humans came to whatever hovel or palace his most trusted appropriated in whatever city Carstol indicated he wanted to grace next with his presence, never the same state two gatherings in a row. It didn't matter how far off the beaten path the gathering was held or how long Carstol had stayed away. When he passed this way again, a majority of the men and women in this room would come to him and bring eager new blood with them as an offering.

They came for one reason only; Carstol gave them what they sought. If they wanted sex, they could find it with Carstol or one of the humans he didn't choose to share with that night. If they sought pain in their sex...or blood, they would never find his equal, for his beast enjoyed the pain in sex nearly more than anything else in life. Those who were led in by the whispers of "the vampire" and wished to play the old scene with him were obliged near to sunrise so as not to give Cursed Warriors the chance to disrupt his games. Nothing Carstol did on these nights save the teasing at night's end would draw Warriors. He enjoyed his "nights of worship" too much to allow such a thing.

The bids for his attention started almost immediately. A young blond man stood, his head thrown back and eyes closed, his hand fisted in the woman's hair. The redhead kneeling at his feet had started the usual sexual antics early, his cock sliding in and out of her parted lips. She tilted her head, scanning Carstol's body slowly, making her offer without a single sound.

Carstol wasn't impressed. After fifteen hundred years, such shows did little to stir him; he'd gotten more of a rise out of spying on Dado and Riberta, and her show had been less believable than this one. Admittedly, more than a little of Carstol's enjoyment of that scene came in knowing that another of his "mighty brothers" had fallen, that one not even for a woman who meant something to him but for a single pleasure from a scheming she-beast.

No, this bid did nothing for him. Any of the women in the room would offer him as much as this one was, and more than half of the men would as well. Carstol had decided early in his life that a warm, eager mouth snug around his aching length need not have a single gender to it. What use had a god for such mundane moralities?

He moved on, going still, then turning toward the sharp tang in the air. "Little minx," he growled at the smiling woman with the ribbon of blood winding down her chest.

She lowered the small blade and tossed her short blonde hair about her elfin face. This one had followed his gatherings for several years, enough time to note that he only took his blood in direct feeding near sunrise, but imbibed indirectly earlier in the night.

Carstol made it to her in two long strides, wrapping his hands around her waist and lifting her without effort. He captured the blood on his tongue, bathing her skin in quick, efficient strokes, smiling darkly at her moan of delight. He sealed the cut, then deposited her none too gently on the floor, licking the last traces of her blood from his lips.

He took the knife from her hand, throwing it so that it imbedded deep in one of the wooden posts holding up the roof. If he didn't do that, one after another would cut themselves to gain his attention, and Carstol had every intention of indulging in other pursuits tonight.

Her eyes pleaded for more, but there were many lessons he'd learned when it came to dealing with his worshippers. The first was that you should never reward an action you didn't want to repeat.

Carstol set her away from him. "Tonight is not your night," he informed her.

She gasped as he traced the slight discoloration that marked her wound.

"Next time, I will let you bleed...to death, if necessary." He turned and strode away.

And felt it.

Her mind was open, her thoughts and desires as crystal to him. She saw him as all powerful, untouchable, terrible; she had to have him. It was precisely what he wanted them to think.

He turned back with a scowl. "And you will have my attentions when you learn your place," he answered her unspoken comment. "For tonight, take another." Carstol turned and continued his circuit, paying just enough attention to her loud, highly-detailed inner plans to please him by obeying absolutely that he wagered some man in this room would be happy tonight by her body and the god's command.

There were more attempts to curry his favor. He passed by many without comment; they would learn his tastes soon enough, and their shows would become more worthy of notice—and reward. Many of them lived for his rewards.

Others were more inventive. Those, he favored with fleeting attention, a kiss, a touch, or a few words of encouragement. He allowed more than one to taste his skin, to cup his lengthening cock, to prepare him for what he would soon take from some prized chosen.

When he saw her, Carstol knew that she showed the most promise of any at the gathering. The woman was new to his fold, nervous yet hopeful. She looked around in disbelief as he headed toward her, taking a step back without seeming to realize that she had. The cushions tripped her up and then broke her fall.

Carstol took the direct route, dematerializing then taking shape between her ankles, on his knees, nude and more than ready. Her eyes widened in surprise, but she didn't ask the dozens of questions circling in her mind.

"How convenient," he noted in wry humor. "How well you anticipate me. You are just where I wanted you."

She looked around, self-conscious, scooping a lock of dark, shoulder-length hair behind her ear, her hazel eyes wide.

Carstol sent the others to their own amusements with a snap of his fingers and a sharp hand movement. In moments, all but the most stubborn were breaking off in pairs or groups for intimate encounters, their eyes straying occasionally to what he was doing. The remaining were hopeful he'd take more than one lover tonight. If this one left him wanting, he might, so he didn't order them away. If they left here unfulfilled, it was their own choice to do so.

The one who'd brought this morsel to him was among them, knowing Carstol would reward him one way or another for his service in recruiting. From past experience, he knew the young man would enjoy a sexual encounter almost more than a feeding. His reward, of course, was Carstol's to choose when he felt the time was right to reward his servant.

He searched his partner's mind, picking out the surface information he wanted with ease. Her tastes were simple: hetero, no notable kink, just a thirst for hot sex. It was vanilla for Carstol's tastes, but she was an eager concubine. Convincing her to exotic practices—perhaps to a tangle of pleasuring bodies—should not be overly difficult, and he dearly enjoyed being covered in adoring sexual partners intent on experiencing both him and each other, just as he liked it.

"Your name?" he rumbled, cursing the fact that he would need to feed or use other powers a Warrior could track to find information not floating at the surface of her thoughts.

"Rachel," she breathed. Her cheeks darkened, and she added a hasty "My Lord." Her sponsor had taught her well.

"I am your dreams personified," he promised.

"Yes. I believe you are." Rachel sank back onto the cushions as he leaned over her. She offered herself silently, offered him anything he wanted.

Carstol stroked the column of her neck. "For tonight, you are mine. You will serve me in every way, bend to my every command. In exchange, you will feel pleasure you never dreamed possible."

Rachel stared at him, at the fangs he'd let extend fully, giving his beast free rein to play along with him. It was the moment of truth. She'd agree to follow the needs screaming at her, making her wet for him, or he'd choose another and banish her from his gatherings. Those who refused the attentions of the god were left wanting his touch. The chance did not come again.

"Oh, god."

"Yes?" he asked, dark amusement coloring his tone. She didn't mean it yet, but she would very soon. When she was writhing to his touch, repeating those words over and over, she would know her master well.

"Yes," she assured him, a small voice that was very close to begging. "I'll serve you..." She stared at his fangs again and licked her lips slowly. "...in every way."

Carstol waved a few of the others closer, his aching cock giving his fertile imagination a wealth of ideas for the ways Rachel could best serve him. And serve him she would. *It is good to be a god!*

The End

Warrior Poetry

Two Hearts Beat as One
Pauwel of Regana
(Third Place for Poetry in the P&E Polling 2004)

The dark earth enfolds me in healing sleep
While my love lays apart in daily rest.
My heartbeat with hers steady pace shall keep.
Her absence, as always, leaves me bereft
And fear for her safety my patience tests,
'Til darkness comes and she lay in my arms,
Bringing peace to my soul and far from harm.

Veriel of Regana's Soul

Time and time again, I find you my love.
I rush to your side when I hear your call.
Your need flies to me on wings of a dove,
And at your feet to serve, I gladly fall.
To protect you, I always join the brawl,
But, ne'er are you mine to hold in the end,
Though to every whim of yours I would bend.

Corwyn of Anna

My love, before I leave, grant me your kiss.
I go to hunt the beasts that stalk the night.
Your body next to mine in sleep I'll miss
'Til the morning brings peace again and light.
Protecting you drives me forth to the fight.
A single moment in your loving arms,
And I'd welcome death to keep you from harm.

Regana

As the mother of all, proudly she stands.
The Stone knows her secrets as no man can.
Happiness and love she holds in her hands.
Heedless of laws that control every man,
The flames of passion her loveliness fans,
Drawing her lovers to deepest desire.
Silken hair dark as night and heart of pure fire.

Talon of Jayde

Your guardian, I have chosen to be
As the Stone asks, though I hear not its voice.
I have my orders. I know my duty,
But my heart screams to make its lifelong choice.
Call me your own, and my heart will rejoice.
Until that day, in torment I will live...
Until yourself to me you ever give.

Pauwel of Regana

My soul cries out as the earth holds me tight
Far from my love and the peace of her hand,
'Til freed am I to walk one more dark night
To meet with my lady as we had planned...
Her first touch a salve on this burning brand.
Every moment apart, she fills my dreams
And cold earth muffles my tortured screams.

Regana of Pauwel

Foul sun, may the clouds hide thy face from me.
No longer your visage sweet comfort brings.
My love lays trapped 'til darkness sets him free

Then flies to my side on the night mist's wings,
And my sun-hardened heart relearns to sing.
My heart hides as I scurry 'neath your eye,
'Til my love's moon rises to draw him nigh.

Excerpt from Early Histories

Section One

By Gawen first Lord Schwertträger, Stone lord and master trainer

Know you now that I set ink to paper in the year 535. The Stone, as always, amuses itself at our expense. When I took my place as Stone lord, I believed this war would be short as the last beast war was short. I thought that stories could be held as knowledge only to those few first cursed and taken to our graves with us. With the passage of time, I find that I will soon pass from this realm into the Warrior's rest, and there are things I would tell before the gods take me.

Some are those tales known only to those first cursed, but with the deaths of many of the first lords and more importantly of my beloved nephew Andris, they are truths I would have future generations know for the protection of all. Those most affected, my dear sister and her family, no longer live to be harmed by these truths.

The Warriors are strong, but the end hinges not on the strength of men but rather on the strength of a woman.

Born to my household and given to me as my own in the Stone's trust, Regana was strong and bold as any Warrior ever was. Known for her importance only to Sibold, she was raised in battle play with the young Warriors and educated as a lady by Kethe, sister of Pauwel.

Though her coloring was that of the Stone-Chosen, the gods hid her blood mark well. Not even I saw it as I cared for her as she grew. Not even Pauwel saw it as he took her to his bed as wife. Beneath her hair lay the symbol of Ani, and Regana was granted protection of the Stone as befits a mother. It was not until long after Sibold's death and my succession as Stone lord that this was made clear to me.

In retrospect, such a thing should have been clear even to the blind! Her coloring aside, Regana could have been naught but the Stone-Chosen mother. From her earliest days, she was never one to follow commands, as much to my dismay as Sibold's. A Warrior's heart beat in her chest, but untamed as any woman's soul.

Raised with the young Warriors, she knew them all well; but she knew myself, Pauwel and Jörg best of all. Jörg was as her brother. Only half a year separated them in age, and to my great shame, the young pup was raised by me in place of his dead father. Many a year, I have been tortured by how I might have done different by him, but in the end, 'twas his curse that undid him.

When Jörg began his training, our number was complete. Sibold partnered us for battle: Wilhelmus with Olbrecht, Cunczel with Dado, Ditrich with Geldric, Gerhardus with Bertolf, Tilbrand with Redulf, and Pauwel with Jörg. I, as leader, partnered no one.

Sibold matched the Warriors to complement each other in battle. Pauwel and Jörg were our strongest, named by the Stone as such and proven in trial with the others. Marked by the symbols of *Ori* and *Reg*, they burned bright as their symbols foretold. Pauwel with his cool grace and Jörg as a fiery berzerker complemented each other well, as if born to fight side by side instead of head to head. Closer than brothers in many ways, they knew each other's fighting styles like no other could.

But the stronger the Warrior, the stronger the curse. While the other elders went to the Stone in greed or fear, spurred on by Marclef's promises, Jörg was lost to madness. It was the only likely way for him to circumnavigate the Stone's protection and deliver up the ancient beasts, earning his title of The Mad Deceiver.

NOTE: In the original text, there is a section here scratched into unreadability, presumably by Gawen's own hand.

Pauwel succumbed to his own form of madness, reaching *Endspiel* and pursuing Regana for his own. Whether he fell because of his stronger curse or because the object of his printing was Regana was never clear. Either way, Raga went to the lord elder slayer as was right.

That transgression might have cost Pauwel his life, not by Sibold's hand but by my own and the hands of our cursed brothers. Safe from my hand by virtue of Regana's love for him, his need and love for her, and the fact that Andris slept in her womb; it fell to me to keep peace as master trainer.

Pauwel was the lord elder slayer. While none of our brethren had any more knowledge of what Pauwel and Regana represented together than I did, still none matched him in battle and this they knew well. It was better to have him fallen but fighting than dead by a blade, whether that blade be my own or Sibold's.

Those Warriors who remained after the beasts were released chose their mates as the Stone intended for them, none interfering with another. The elders, now beast, knew only one drive. Drawn to Regana by some unnamed force, they sought to possess or to destroy her, each in his own way. Veriel came for her the first time the night after he went beast, but he was driven off by her amulet and my blades.

I thought at the time that it was strange that the beasts were granted this knowledge denied the Warriors themselves. Or perhaps, they knew not why they pursued, as Pauwel knew not why he burned for her so. Still, they pursued.

The beasts fought the battle on the basis of Marclef's lies, lies that ultimately cost the leader his life for his treachery. Veriel turned the leader and left him to me to kill. Thus, I became the first beast killer of the new war. The fact that Marclef faced the same fate he enticed others to embrace seemed to amuse The Mad Deceiver. In this case, I could almost agree that The Destroyer of Lives had only obliged one who sought to destroy his own life with his underhanded ways. Veriel and Resten left immediately from the battlefield to accomplish this task once they learned they had been lied to—and to try for Regana as their prize.

Resten tried for her first, killing Sibold in his bid to gain access to her within the Stone's keep. Veriel sent him to ground and returned to claim Regana for himself.

But, Regana was never one to accept a man's rule. While the elders had been gone in their battle, she had left the protection of the Stone to save Sibold. Veriel came for her before she had the master trainer inside the stronghold, but Regana did not accept his claim on her lightly. Taking Sibold's blades from his dying hands, she threatened to plant them in the beast if he remained in her sight.

The idea seemed laughable. Regana played at battle with wooden weapons and even found herself in her share of barehanded matches with the older and much larger boys, but she was not a trained Warrior. She was half the size of the beast she faced and human with only my amulet and blessing to protect her from his wrath. Moreover, unknown to any of us but herself, Regana was with child. Still, she refused to yield Sibold to the beast. She placed herself between Veriel and his prey, oblivious to the fact that she was the beast's true prey.

In truth, Veriel laughed at her attempt, but he left her regardless. Whether he left to play another night—admitting some time later that she amused him with her threats and her stubborn spirit—or something about her unnerved him was unclear even to the end. He left her without incident, and she brought Sibold into the safety of the Stone to wait for daybreak.

In the end, her valiant efforts could only delay Sibold's death long enough for me to reach them and take my place as Stone lord properly. In the intervening hours, the master trainer gifted Regana with his blades for her own protection and the protection of the innocents in their midst.

The fact that she nearly took Pauwel's head as he entered the stronghold in the weak pre-dawn light was simply the final blow for us all in a very trying night. Perhaps, the fact that Regana was to be trained should have been apparent to us, then, but without Sibold's word or the Stone's comment, we could not know such a thing was in store for her.

Still, I had no idea of the secret vows that lay between Pauwel and Regana. As the choosing night approached, Regana became withdrawn and unsettled—volatile on a scale that disturbed me, but I had no clue of the origin of this strange upset save the beasts' interest in her.

In reality, she became afraid, realizing that Pauwel could face death when her baby's arrival proved their crimes. In a panic, Regana refused her place in the choosing, hoping to take dishonor alone and spare his life.

Pauwel was a printed man and could not choose another. In desperation, he confided his indiscretions to me and begged my mercy in judgment of Regana, begged for the one woman who eased his pain.

My shock was overcome by my anger, but I was calmed by my choosing of Bavin and that she would have me as her own. In truth, had his confession—or my discovery by other means—come at any other time, I might have taken a deathblow without letting my mind rule my curse.

Reserving my judgment until they could face me together, we returned to my lands to find Resten and Veriel vying for Regana yet again.

NOTE: Again, there is a section destroyed by Gawen, as he wrote.

Pauwel killed Resten in her defense, and Veriel fled our combined strength. That in itself nearly sealed my decision to take my single blow and give Regana to him. Surely, I could not kill the first lord elder slayer nor lose him to the madness of losing one he was printed to.

The announcement of Regana's gravid state shocked me, but it was even more of a shock to Pauwel. Regana had not told him of her condition out of concern of his reaction to their inattention to the details of checking her cycle of late, fear that Pauwel would come to me with a confession at a time when I would not be capable of showing mercy to either of them.

Still, Pauwel held his ground, waiting patiently for my judgment before accepting his blow gracefully and scooping his wife to him in joy for his son in her womb. Thorald joined them formally the very next day, though my stone-duty to protect her meant she retained my personal protection even in her married life. Pauwel did not question why he could not give her his amulet. It was a small boon to ask of him in return for Regana, his son, and his life.

Even with this new information about her, there was a puzzle about Regana that the Stone intended us to solve. In the end, Regana solved it herself.

Rumors abounded about Regana—dangerous rumors because of her coloring and unladylike actions in the face of Veriel. Complicating matters were the jealous streak Riberta bore Regana for capturing the love of the Warrior she wanted for herself and the half-mad stories Eberhard told which proclaimed Regana an evil omen.

With Sibold dead and Eberhard a madman, Regana went to the last remaining person with memories of her birth, Emecin, the midwife. Breaking her oath to Sibold at last, Emecin confirmed for Regana that she was Raga, the mother.

That fact was not enough to sway the villagers. Bermer, the oldest son in the family of blacksmiths, tried to kill her in the belief that her death would send the beasts away. Regana felled him, though Bermer was almost the size of a Warrior and she large with Pauwel's son. She ran from him, but he gained on her quickly and attacked her bodily and with intent to slit her throat. Bermer would have killed her were it not for the boy healer, Landric, who took the man's life in her defense and brought her back to her lord for comfort and care.

Finding his game with Regana threatened and never one to blithely accept an interruption to his play even before he went mad, Veriel used and killed the fair Riberta, Wil's sister, for spreading the dangerous rumors that almost cost him his prey. Then, Veriel orchestrated a full beast war on the village. Spanning days, the battle sought to destroy every villager who harbored thoughts of injuring Regana before Veriel played out his game. The people were executed in the most gruesome manners imaginable.

Intent on his game, Veriel came for Regana again. His threats to her and to Pauwel stated clearly, he left her presence, amused by Kethe's threat to use blades on him in defense of Pauwel's wife and son. To protect her from villager and beast alike, Pauwel and I undertook formal training for Regana as a Stone-Chosen would.

Desperate now to minimize the effects of the sons of Raga, Veriel sought to use Pauwel in his plan. He defeated the strong young lord in battle and fed from him deeply until he controlled his will. His will not his own, Pauwel was forced to drink of Veriel's foul blood, turning him to a beast.

Veriel brought Pauwel to Regana, believing that she would choose to let him kill her husband when posed the choice of accepting him as he was or death for him. To Pauwel's dismay as much as my own, Regana tore off her amulet to cradle her husband to the babe growing within her. Undone by his own game, Veriel learned that turning Pauwel was a mistake he would live to regret.

As a printed Warrior, Pauwel was not the puppet the elder had hoped for. Rather, Pauwel retained his love and all things that made him husband and Warrior even as he was turned beast. Veriel lived to regret that night, forced to ground again and again and thwarted at almost every turn. By turning Pauwel, he did naught but create a more powerful barrier between himself and his prey. He could not hope to touch Regana while Pauwel lived as beast, and Veriel lacked the ability—perhaps because Pauwel was a Warrior beast—to kill his adversary.

Still, the elder was determined enough to plague Regana at her son's birth with threats of ending the only son of Raga. With Pauwel as beast, there could be no more sons from him, and so he protected his son fiercely, if anonymously.

Only the first cursed, Kethe and Bavin shared Regana's secret of her beast husband. To the rest of the world, he was dead and Regana a widow. So it came to pass that at his birth, I granted Andris the amulet of his father's personal protection and my own blessing, one of the many things Pauwel could no longer give his son as beast. Still, never a more doting father had I ever seen—in the early days before Andris was old enough to repeat what he saw, and Pauwel was still able to hold him and care for him as a father would.

In the meantime, Pauwel became the ultimate Warrior, killing turned whenever he encountered them and sending elders to ground for up to a week at a time. The reservations the other first lords had with this strange arrangement were set aside quickly as the irony of the beasts' folly became ever clearer.

Veriel tried to take Andris three times before he was a man and finally—on the young man's first night.

NOTE: Yet again, Gawen destroys a portion of what he has written and begins again.

Driven to ground by one of his many turned, one of the many who did not wish damned by him, Veriel lost his opportunity to kill Andris before he claimed the seal of Lord Kreuzträger. The young Warrior freed the injured high-level and won his seal, a most noble bit of generosity and caring that he showed the beast who had no wish for his damned life.

Knowing his son was lord and Regana safely in the care of myself and her son, Pauwel came to me when next he was seriously injured and begged me to free him. With a heavy heart, I did as he bid me. Regana wept for him, as the other first lords and I gave her husband a Warrior's burial.

It was our only chance to free Pauwel, the only chance we would likely ever have to defeat him and give him peace while Regana still lived to stabilize him and keep the Warrior in him alive and in control of the beast in himself. Pauwel knew this sad truth, and so he sought death before the time when Regana could die and leave him a danger to all.

Had I known the results his death would have on Regana, I might have chanced the beast in Pauwel and denied him his respite still. My beautiful sister fell into a deep melancholy without Pauwel's love. Andris claiming Ger's daughter, Berna, as his bride cheered her but hours. News of their coming child barely touched her in her grief.

Little more than a year after her husband's death, Regana could stand her isolation no longer. She slipped into the dark night with her weapons, and with nothing left to lose, she searched out Veriel.

She fought him as a Warrior fights, without an amulet to protect her, seeking to find Pauwel in the Warrior's rest at her death. Skilled beyond even my comprehension, Regana sent The Mad Elder to ground for three days, but her own life was forfeit in return. Veriel fed on her and left Regana to bleed to death in the spot where once they played together as children, the ultimate show of disdain for the one he once called sister.

I failed in my stone's duty to Regana. She was gone. I should have been able to stop her—or to save her. Still, I have no concept how that beast could feed on my own lands and not have me know that he was there. Perhaps, the Stone was taking some measure of pity on Regana by letting her join her lord with no interference from me. I can only hope that is the case, though I fear it is not.

Regana was given a Warrior's burial by her lord's side, together in eternity as they could never be in life.

With the wrath of Andris and myself looming, Veriel wisely backed from his assault on Raga's family. After all, his own death would not come at the hands of a Schwertträger or Kreuzträger. Veriel turned his attention to the young Warriors of Jäger. His death was slated at the hands of that house, and so his brutality moved to them.

Excerpt from The First Book of Texts

By Gawen first Lord Schwertträger, Stone lord and master trainer

The Rules of Sanction
Part One (penned in 510 AD)

A Warrior must be mindful always of the humans around him. More than human, less than damned; the cursed have the potential to do great good. Inherent in that potential is the ability to do great harm.

A Warrior will have enemies, and to protect those humans bound by the Stone's sacred trust, the Warrior will kill in honorable battle those enemies.

A child is never truly an enemy. He may be disarmed and even rendered unable to continue the present battle, but though the child of today may grow to be the enemy tomorrow, today he is naught but a boy.

A woman may be slain in battle only as a last resort. If she raises her blade against a Warrior, he will first treat her as he would a child. Remember always that a woman battles most fiercely for child and home. Whenever possible, a Warrior should seek his true enemy elsewhere and leave her to protect what is hers from less honorable men—and less dangerous.

In battle, unforeseen events will occur. In battle, innocents will often die. The Warrior should never carry a battle to innocents that can be fought elsewhere. When there is no choice, the Warrior must be mindful of the innocents in his midst. An innocent life taken in honest error is lamentable. One taken in negligence is unforgivable.

More than human, less than damned. The Warrior must never forget that humans are powerless before him. This is not a reason for pride but rather a warning.

The Stone made a pact in its wisdom. One of the foundations of that pact is the Warrior's promise to do no harm. Those under a Warrior's protection and innocents all, the Warrior must protect to death.

Humans are fragile things in that they are frail and unable to heal as Warriors do as much as in that they fear and attack any perceived threat. Warriors possess the power to be perceived as a threat.

As the chain is only as strong as its weakest link, so the pact is only strong as the trust imparted by its weakest to its strongest. For the safety of Warrior and mate, no Warrior may threaten that trust and live.

Warriors are cursed. Stone-Chosen or passed from father to son, the curse manifests in the same fashion generation after generation. Akin to the damnation of the beasts, never doubt the curse for what it is.

Blutjagd, the blood lust, comes first and foremost. Where the beasts are driven only by darkness, the darkness in a Warrior's soul will be very strong. The urge to kill the beasts is at its heart, for dark knows dark, as the Warriors and beasts each sense the other and seek each to destroy the opposing dark.

Blutjagd in its purest sense is naught but good, but that is not only how it will make itself known. The gift of *Blutjagd* is also the ability to protect what a Warrior holds dear to him and what he has a duty to protect, but there is a fierce streak in him that rivals his love and loyalty.

When a wrong is done by a human to him and his, a Warrior must not allow darkness to rule him. Capital offenses require the ultimate price. Of that there is no doubt, but the price must be exacted on the one who has wronged him alone. Revenge is not something a Warrior indulges in. The ones who have not acted against him are innocents. The pain of their loss is more punishment than they deserve.

If the offense is injurious but not capital, retribution should be taken in kind. If no injury is sustained, no blood may be spilled in return unless the guilty attacks in earnest.

A Warrior must ever be mindful of the nature of the crime against him. He cannot allow his pain to rule him. Capital crimes involve grave harm and disregard of innocence. Murder or rape or the attempt of either, an unprovoked attack on a Warrior's mate or child— In such a case, the interloper must pay the ultimate price as the pact demands. The Warrior who exacts the ultimate price for a crime that is not capital or not in defense will face death himself from his true judge, having proven himself lacking in control and respect for the fragile sanctity of life.

Likewise, the Warrior must gauge his punishment of Warriors who wrong him by the rules of sanction. A Warrior has the right to face the Warrior he has most wronged as judge—or his house lord as case may be when the injury is to his own house or to a human not of a Warrior's household. One who acts as judge in another's stead faces sanction by both the true judge and the Warrior he judged out of place—or the Warrior's lord if he is incapable of judging for himself.

The drive to print can lead to madness in *Endspiel*. Printing can make a Warrior the most stable of men unless his mate or children are endangered, but the time of printing is the most dangerous and unstable time of all for a Warrior.

Warriors are not lawless soldiers. A Warrior must rule his curse, lest the curse rule him. The sanctions in taking women are understandably rigid because of the great danger printing poses.

The beasts take women brutally, without care and concern. Until a Warrior finds his mate—or after he loses his mate, he will require release with women aside from his mate. While he has a mate, she will provide the only true release he will find. She is a balm for his soul, calming his *Blutjagd* and appeasing his sexual appetite as no other woman can while she lives. He will have no need and no wish to perform with another as long as he has her.

But, a Warrior who cannot control his curse is no better than a beast. A Warrior may not take an unwilling woman, even if she is the woman of an enemy or an enemy herself. Neither shall a Warrior use his whiles to sway an unwilling woman to some form of willingness to bed her. Such a move is dishonorable in that it exploits her innocence and does her injustice.

A lover must always be treated kindly and with respect. It is the Warrior's duty to repay the peace a lover grants him with pleasure. If she gifts him with her maiden's blood, he must ease it from her and repay her tenfold for her sacrifice.

A Warrior must never take a child to his bed. A woman shy of fifteen years, though she bleeds, is not a woman for the taking. Her body is not adequate to carry a Warrior's child until she matures, and her innocence is still largely intact.

If the woman of a Warrior's desire is the freed daughter of another Warrior, she may not be taken without her father's consent or that of her house lord if her father is dead. The Warrior protecting his child is a dangerous man, and the interloper may be perceived as a threat to that family. For the safety of all, this rule must be adhered to.

The Warrior who takes simple pleasure without permission from her keeper owes a solid blow for every instance to the one who would give his permission. Judgment of whether or not the Warrior is worthy of the woman will, then be rendered by her judge.

If the Warrior takes his satisfaction in her in such a case, he must submit to that same man as judge. It is within his judge's rights to exact one of three punishments. If he deems the Warrior without either honor or control, he may take his life for it. He may take him to trial and forbid his interaction with the woman again. Or, he may take a single blow and give his consent—with any reasonable restrictions he deems fit the situation from the question of when children are appropriate to loyalties in repayment for his trespass.

In any case—satisfaction taken or no—the judge has the right to strike the woman a single open-handed blow if he feels she is without honor in her actions.

A Warrior who cannot control his curse is no better than a beast. A Warrior who returns to a forbidden woman a second time faces the certainty of death.

A Warrior must always submit absolutely to his judge. If he raises a hand in his own defense to any Warrior—judge or no—or does not meet and live by his punishment gracefully—even unto a sentence of death, he will face death, as he has shown himself without control. If the Warrior lies to his judge to hide his misdeeds when asked for the truth, he will face any penalty up to and including death as his judge wishes, for he has shown himself lacking in honor.

If the woman wronged is human not of a Warrior house, the house lord of the Warrior who wronged her will sit as his judge. If the accused is a house lord, the Stone lord will stand as judge. If he is Stone lord, a council of the lords will stand as judge. In the case of the house lord, he will no longer be deemed worthy of his position and shall forfeit his place as house lord to the next in line to hold the seal. The Stone will take care of its own succession as it always has.

Taking any woman—human or of a household—unwilling, automatically warrants a sentence of death, as would attempting her murder or the murder of a child. The body of the Warrior would, then be presented to the woman and her family and personal protection be granted them in repayment by the house lord.

If the Warrior is come upon in the act, the woman's safety is paramount. If he can be restrained and presented to his true judge, it should be done despite the fury driving the Warrior who comes upon the scene. If such a thing cannot be accomplished without the threat of further violence to his victim, he should be executed as he is. She should, then be tended to medically and returned to her family with proof of the attacker's state.

If a human family wishes to exact their own punishment on a Warrior, they will be permitted the right of inflicting their own beating with the protection of the Warrior guard before the judge passes his own sentence. Remember always that when a Warrior breaks the pact, the safety of all depends on restoring the peace with the humans injured.

Only in a challenge of trial is the Warrior to defend himself physically. Only to his true judge, at the appropriate time is the Warrior to defend himself in words—if such is the case that there is any excuse for his actions—or to plead mercy for the woman involved. A Warrior should never plead mercy for himself, as his actions are his own, dishonorable or honorable, and honor demands he take responsibility for them.

The Warrior may demand his right of his true judge and no more of the Warrior who places him in custody. If he raises a hand to that Warrior he will be restrained or killed as the situation unfolds. Should he survive his punishment of his true judge for his first crime, he still faces death at the hands of the Warrior holding custody for his lack of control. If the Warrior taken into custody attempts violence to an innocent— In such a case, no move will be made to restrain him. His life is forfeit.

The Stone Alphabet

Ⱦ Ani (birth/the mother)- Regana first Lady Kreuzträger, Jayde Marie Albright

Ɗ Baroo (thunder)- Olbrecht first Lord Kaufmann

ſ Dobler (twin peace-bringer)- Ditrich first Lord Jäger

Ɋ Fih (twin war)- Geldric/the beast Cerran, Cody König-Armen

Ɉ Geil (iron)- Bryon König-Kaufmann

ⱦ Hir (the cool wood)- Gerhardus first Lord Landwirt

Ȣ Iol (immovable ice)- Redulf/the beast Carstol

Ɏ Jee (justice)- Mikel of Crossbearer-König and all descendants thereof

Ƥ Kor (the bear)- Corwyn of König-Maher

Ⱡ Len (mountain)- Wilhelmus first Lord Maher

Ʋ Mul (flowing water)- Mitchell König-Farmer

Ơ Nul (stealth of the night)- Bertolf/the beast Draden

Ȣ Ori (the sun)- Pauwel first Lord Kreuzträger, Hunter Lord Crossbearer-König

Ɑ Pol (the horse)- Dado/the beast Lorian

Ǝ Reg (intensity of the fire)- Jörg/the beast Veriel

꿎 Syth (the Stone lord)- Master Trainer Sibold, Gawen first Lord Schwertträger, Etienne Lord Kaufmann, Joseph Lord Armen, Carrick Lord Armen, Corwyn Lord Hunter, Lewis of Maher

𝒥 Tes (stars and moon)- Kevin König-Smith

𝒪 Vin (wind)- Cunczel first Lord Schmied

Wul (the wolf)- Tilbrand/the beast Resten

Zel (ending/death)- Erin of Crossbearer-König, Kaitlyn "Katie" of König-Maher, Skye of König-Armen, Victorious Ellen "Vick/Vicky" of König-Smith, Margaret Elizabeth "Maggie" König-Farmer, Colette "Lettie" Kong-Kaufmann

About the Author

Brenna Lyons wears many hats, sometimes all on the same day: former president of EPIC, author of more than 100 published works, owner of Fireborn Publishing, columnist, special needs teacher, wife, mother...and member in good standing of more than 60 writing advocacy groups.

In her first ten years published in novel-length, she's won 3 EPIC e-Book Awards (out of 15 finalists) and finaled for 3 PEARLS (including one Honorable Mention, second to NY Times Bestseller Angela Knight), 2 CAPAS, and a Dream Realm Award. She's also taken Spinetingler's Book of the Year for 2007.

Brenna writes in 26 established worlds plus stand-alones, poetry, articles and essays. She's a bestseller in indie/e fantasy and horror, straight genre and cross-genres thereof. Brenna has been termed "one of the most deviant erotic minds in the publishing world...not for the weak." (Rachelle for Fallen Angels Reviews) Milieu-heavy dark work is practically Brenna's calling card, with or without the erotic content.

She teaches classes in everything from POV studies to advanced editing, networking to marketing. Brenna enjoys hearing from people who read her work and can be reached by e-mail.

Website: http://www.brennalyons.com/

Facebook: http://www.facebook.com/brenna.lyons

Email: brennalyons4168@live.com

Also by this Author

STAR MAGES
The Master's Lover

XXAN WAR
Daahan Rising
Crossbred Son
Raashh Decisions

Enslaved
All I Want for Christmas is You
Fates Magic
All's Fair...
Black Sail
Mama's Tales
Dream Walk
Unexpected Daddy
Phaze in Verse
We Shall Live Again
May the Best Man Win
Nevermore
Marked
And It Was Good

Available from **Mundania Press**

STAR MAGES
Written in the Stars

Fairy Dreams
Monsters of Myth Anthology

Available from **Under the Moon**

RENEGADES SERIES
TYGERS
Renegade's Run
Max Sec

URBAN GRIMM
Catch Me, If You Can
Three Wishes
Temptation of Eve

With Great Power
Undead in Blue
Evil Overlords Union Issue #1 Anthology
Undead Embrace
"Playing Games" in *Forbidden Love: Bad Boys*
"Marked" in *Forbidden Love: Wicked Women*
"The Master's Lover" in *Forbidden Love: Sacred Bands*

Available from *Logical Lust*

"Mine for the Night" in *The Cougar Book* Anthology

Available from *Coming Together Charity Anthologies*

INSTINCT SERIES
"Foundling" in *Coming Together: Into the Light* Anthology

"Claim Mate" (available separately and as part of the *Coming Together: Against the Odds* Anthology)
"The Fire God's Woman" in *Coming Together: Under Fire* Anthology

Available *self-published*

KEGIN SERIES
Earth-Born Lord
Graham: Training the Earth-Born Lord

NIGHT WARRIORS
Claiming a Lady
Stone Lord

Mother's Son

COLOR OF LOVE
A Safe Heart

Snapshots from a Poet's Life

Award-Winning Books

EPPIE/EPIC eBOOK AWARDS WINNERS
Coming Together: Against the Odds- 2010
Time Currents- 2010
Coming Together: Into the Light- 2011

EPPIE/EPIC eBOOK AWARDS FINALISTS
Fion's Daughter- 2004
Collected Poems: Book One- 2005 (now titled *Snapshots of a Poet's Life*)
Renegade's Run- 2005
Rites of Mating- 2006
All I Want for Christmas- 2006
Phaze in Verse- 2008
"The Fire God's Woman" in Coming Together: Under Fire- 2009
Three Wishes- 2010
Matchmaker's Misery- 2010
The Cougar Book- 2011
The Master's Lover- 2011
Bride Ball- 2011

DREAM REALM AWARDS FINALIST
Last Chance for Love- 2003

PEARL HONORABLE MENTION
Night Warriors- 2004

PEARL FINALISTS
Schente Night- 2003 (now included in *The Last of Fion's Daughters*)
König Cursebreakers- 2004 (now titled *Will of the Stone*)

JOYFULLY REVIEWED BEST BOOKS OF 2010
Written in the Stars- 2010

SPINETINGLER'S BOOK OF THE YEAR 2007

NOBODY: An Anthology of Dark Fiction- 2007 (Brenna's pieces of the anthology can be found in *Beyond the Veil*)

TRS's CAPA FINALISTS
Ultimate Warriors- 2004 (Brenna's portion is now available as *With Great Power*)
Written in the Stars

LOVE ROMANCE AND MORE CAFÉ BOOK OF THE YEAR RUNNER UP
Last Chance for Love- 2008

ROAD TO ROMANCE REVIEWERS' CHOICE AWARD
Prophecy: Revelations- 2004

LOVE ROMANCES REVIEWERS' CHOICE AWARD
Black Sail- 2003

ROMANCE JUNKIES BOOK CLUB STAFF PICK
TYGERS- 2003

FALLEN ANGELS ROMANCE RECOMMENDED READ
Devon's Price-2005 (now available in *Bearing Armen*)

JOYFULLY RECOMMENDED READ
Fairy Dreams- 2008
The Last of Fion's Daughters- 2009

TREBLE HEART FINALIST
Prophecy: Revelations- 2003

www.ingramcontent.com/pod-product-compliance
Lightning Source LLC
Chambersburg PA
CBHW050909250626
47155CB00001B/155